Maria Lewis is an author, screenwriter and film curator based in Australia. Getting her start as a police reporter, her writing on pop culture has appeared in publications such as the *New York Post*, *Guardian*, *Penthouse*, *Daily Mail*, *Empire Magazine*, *Gizmodo*, *Huffington Post*, *the Daily* and *Sunday Telegraph*, *i09*, *Junkee* and many more. A journalist for over 16 years, she transitioned into working in television as a segment producer, writer and guest presenter on live nightly news programme *The Feed* on SBS. She has worked as a screenwriter on documentary, film and scripted television projects.

Her best-selling debut novel *Who's Afraid?* was published in 2016, followed by its sequel *Who's Afraid Too?* in 2017, which was nominated for Best Horror Novel at the Aurealis Awards. *Who's Afraid?* is currently being developed for television. Her Young Adult debut, *It Came From The Deep*, was released globally in 2018, followed by her fourth book, *The Witch Who Courted Death*, which won Best Fantasy Novel at the Aurealis Awards in 2019.

Her fifth novel set within the shared supernatural universe – *The Wailing Woman* – was nominated for Best Fantasy Novel at the Aurealis Awards in 2020, followed by the publication of her sixth novel, *Who's Still Afraid?*, and book seven *The Rose Daughter*. She's the host, writer and producer on audio documentaries about popular culture and film history such as *Josie & The Podcats* on the 2001 cult film and *The Phantom Never Dies* about the world's first superhero.

Visit Maria Lewis online:

Twitter: @moviemazz
Instagram: @maria___lewis
www.marialewis.com.au

T0035866

Also by Maria Lewis

Who's Afraid?
Who's Afraid Too?
The Witch Who Courted Death
It Came From The Deep
The Wailing Woman
Who's Still Afraid?
The Rose Daughter

Her Fierce Creatures

Maria Lewis

PIATKUS

PIATKUS

First published in Great Britan in 2022 by Piatkus
This paperback edition published in 2022 by Piatkus

1 3 5 7 9 10 8 6 4 2

A CIP catalogue record for this book
is available from the British Library.

ISBN 978-0-349-42726-3

Typeset in Sabon by Hewer Text UK Ltd, Edinburgh
Printed and bound in Great Britain by Clays Ltd, Elcograf S.p.A.

Papers used by Piatkus are from well-managed forests
and other responsible sources.

MIX
Paper from
responsible sources
FSC® C104740

Piatkus
An imprint of
Little, Brown Book Group
Carmelite House
50 Victoria Embankment
London EC4Y 0DZ

An Hachette UK Company
www.hachette.co.uk

www.littlebrown.co.uk

In loving memory of Ron Cobb
A dear friend, a jolly neighbour, a legend of his craft.

Chapter 1

Sadie

When she cried, someone died.

That was just the weird, new reality of Sadie Burke's life. To be perfectly frank, it wasn't even the weirdest aspect in what was a pick 'n' mix of absolutely weird shit. Sitting on a hill that overlooked a massive, sprawling farm, Sadie snuggled deeper into the puffy coat she was wearing to protect against the cold. It wasn't snowing yet, but even on a warm day it would be unusual if the temperature got above ten degrees.

Spending her entire life stuck in Australia – like every other banshee who had been shipped there in chains by the supernatural government known as the Treize and forced to die out on that continent – Sadie was used to the heat. She was also used to the fleeting cold, but not to days that started freezing and continued so. Yet hidden in Arrowtown, on New Zealand's South Island, in a tiny town few people remembered, it was adapt or die at this point.

Flinching as a tiny foot reminded her exactly why with a swift kick to her bladder, Sadie ran a hand over her swelling belly. Among all the grief and pain of losing their father, Texas

1

Contos, Sadie had promised herself that she would survive for *them*: the three daughters that were apparently playing FIFA in her womb. Her due date wasn't for another few months but – as her very own personal physician Dr Kikuchi had told her – with triplets they needed to be ready for anything.

Weirdly, it wasn't the babies she was worried about. They were *one* of her worries, definitely, but she knew her daughters were safe inside her. It was when they got out that things would get complicated. There were powerful forces that wanted them dead and her along with them.

'Stay in there, my darlings,' she said, barely above a whisper. 'Stay right where you are.'

Even just the murmur of her voice was something Sadie Burke was still trying to get used to. The same supernatural government that had punished her species had punished her as a child as well, slitting her throat and severing her vocal cords when she was nine. It had been to suppress a power she wasn't supposed to have, a power that was the greatest and purest example of what a banshee could do: the wail.

Yet its deadly force was supposed to have died out with her ancestors, just as the Treize had intended. It turned out banshees were a lot harder to kill than their enemies thought. Australian sign language – Auslan – had been her primary form of communication for over ten years, right up until her powers manifested once more. Now not only could she speak, she could wail. And the results were catastrophic.

Sadie hadn't meant to kill the farmhand at the property of the Dawson werewolves where they were staying. He was a nice kid around her age, with a ginger beard that matched a mop of ginger hair and a smile that was maybe a bit too flirty for her liking. The first and only person she'd ever loved, the father of her children, had bled out in an English field while she had cried and begged for Tex to survive. The memory felt like both a lifetime ago and something that was incredibly raw to her, so romance was off the menu for the next . . . while. Yet the farmhand Wallace – everyone called him Wally for short – had been nice to her. He had made Sadie a cup of tea while she watched him load up bales of hay to distribute among the animals.

She hadn't felt it coming, she rarely did. When one of the babies Jackie Chan-ed her internal organs, she had let out a pained cry. The mug had slipped from her hands, falling to the ground as if in slow motion as the child kicked again and her cry increased. Sadie had been so focused on her own pain, clutching her belly, that she hadn't realised what happened at first. She hadn't even been at full volume, but there on his knees, eyes wide and dead, was Wally as he collapsed to the ground.

The blood never stopped flowing from his ears, her many sisters and cousins stepping through the horrific puddle as they rushed to her side. Sorcha, the only sibling who had seen the full extent of Sadie's powers, was prepared: a pair of heavy-duty noise-cancelling headphones always dangled around her neck in case of emergencies. She'd made sure the Burke family members had a pair at all times. Sorcha had witnessed what could happen when Sadie *really* unleashed: human skulls turned into pumpkins exploding like they'd been hit with a sledgehammer. Poor Wally never stood a chance.

After the accident Sorcha made certain all of the werewolves protecting the property started carrying headphones too. Sadie never got a moment to ask what happened to Wally, who took care of the body or where he was buried. She knew he was one of the nephews of the Dawson werewolf pack's leader, yet she couldn't bring herself to find out more. It was one thing for her to use her abilities with intent, to *intentionally* set out to hurt those who deserved it or posed a threat. It was another thing entirely to pose just as much of a lethal risk to those she didn't mean to hurt at all.

All six of her sisters, her mother, auntie and cousins, had been sharing the same sprawling farmhouse since they first reassembled in New Zealand after breaking The Covenant and fleeing Australia. Dr Kikuchi and her wife – along with the elite squadron of female werewolf enforcers known as the Aunties – had been living in the surrounding cottages, close enough to the big house but far enough away that they didn't have to be embroiled in the daily drama of Irish families. Although they were well and truly *in it* now.

Sadie wasn't sure where the Dawson pack lived and she couldn't find out since she wasn't allowed to leave the farm for her own protection. Yet this property spanned acres, with a raging rapid at the base of a ravine on one side and snow-capped mountains surrounding them on all others. They were in the dip of a valley, remote and unseen but still accessible by private road. Tiaki Ihi, her friend, had chosen this location because it was both easy to defend and unlikely when it came to physical places to stash a young woman pregnant with the three children that could flip the fates of their supernatural world.

That young woman was living alone now. Sadie demanded it, in fact, taking a cottage further away from the rest of the property and encased in a thick blanket of dark trees. If she wailed again, she was sufficiently far away for the nearest person to survive without headphones. Or so she hoped. She hadn't put that theory to the test yet, but she was being extra careful by only speaking to her babies and reverting back to sign language with everyone else.

Her family members had fought her on this decision, but the werewolves had welcomed it. It was an easier outpost to monitor and defend: even if they were discovered, she was tucked away out of sight. It meant they could continue doing their job – protecting her until the birth of the triplets – without killing off members of the pack they might need for any upcoming conflict. Yet it was Dr Kikuchi who had been the biggest supporter of Sadie's urgings. She insisted that wherever Sadie felt most comfortable, wherever she felt safest and the least stressed, then that was where she *had* to be for her final trimester. Regardless of what anyone else thought.

And there were thoughts to be had. There was never any lack of them in her family, to the point it could be suffocating at times, each of her siblings as loud and pushy as the next. She watched as the consequence of one of those thoughts barrelled down the farm's main road, driving past the house and continuing towards her one-woman cottage. She had been told to expect him, but that didn't mean she had to like it.

Sadie stayed exactly where she was, perched on the hill in her favourite spot like she could oversee an imaginary kingdom as she watched Simon Tianne get out of a battered four-wheel drive. It was testament to his size that he looked formidable alongside it, not just his height but the significant bulk of his muscles. She also wondered if the temperature felt different to him here, given New Zealand – Aotearoa – was his home and his people were as much a part of it as the trees, the rivers, the mountains and the animals that brought it to life. The loose football shorts and oversized hoodie made her think that was the case, but then he gave an involuntary shudder and hopped on the spot for a moment.

'Fucking cold as South Island,' he muttered, the words almost lost on the icy breeze that picked up and ruffled Sadie's hair. Up until that point, he hadn't seen her. He'd come to this part of the farm knowing she'd be around there somewhere. Probably inside, curled up and reading *What To Expect When You're Expecting To Either End Or Ignite The Apocalypse with the Fruit of Your Womb*. She was downwind and the gust must have blown her scent his way as he stiffened. He turned in her direction, his werewolf senses telling him exactly where she would be without him needing to have laid eyes on her.

Sadie didn't smile at him. Didn't wave. She liked his auntie, Tiaki, more than most people she'd encountered. She was not only Simon's literal auntie but also the head of the Aunties and the whole pack that he was a part of, the Ihi clan. It was partly because of Tiaki and Simon's own mother, Keisha, that the werewolves had given up valuable resources to transport Sadie safely from the North to the South Island during a time when there were considerable threats lurking around every corner. It was strange watching one of those threats climb up the slope towards her, brown calf muscles flexing against the mix of grass and rock and just the slightest dampness after a morning rain. He wasn't a threat to her, however. The exact opposite.

Over a video call, Tiaki had told Sadie that she was sending her most trusted werewolf to Arrowtown to act as Sadie's personal bodyguard. She'd been momentarily excited, thinking it would be the blue-haired woman who had guarded her and Sorcha in Galway. But it wasn't Tommi Grayson, she learned with disappointment. It was a relative of hers, Simon. With the exception of the video calls – which were encrypted and ran through the Ihi pack's private server – no one was using digital communications any more. They couldn't risk an accidental digital footprint leading the Treize or – just as bad – their soldiers, the Praetorian Guard, to their location, especially not after everything they had done to create a sanctuary here. So Sadie couldn't know what was happening in the outside world, but the dark circles under Tiaki's eyes and the sending of Simon told her it was bad.

Usually by the time she reached this point of the hill, she was puffing and straining, not just because she was unfit but because she was carrying a cart of watermelons inside her body. This man didn't look put out at all, his breath barely irregular as he stood before her, noise-cancelling headphones firmly on his ears. These weren't the ones Sorcha dispensed like candy. These were fancy, cool, black and masculine, if such a thing was possible for an inanimate appliance.

'Hi,' he said, first verbally then in sign. He must have registered the shock on her face, as he continued uninterrupted. 'I'm Simon Tianne, Tiaki's nephew, Tommi's cousin, and hopefully soon . . . your friend.'

Her surprise turned to scepticism as she signed her response back, face solemn.

'I'm not here to make friends.'

'That's fine,' he replied, mouthing the words as well as signing them to make it easier for her to read as she processed both the movement of his lips and the hand gestures. 'We don't have to be friends if you don't want to be. I find that usually makes things easier but . . . I get it. You've been through a lot. And I've been sent here to make sure you don't go through anything else.'

She laughed out loud, literally, but there was little joy in it.

'If only signing it would make it so,' she communicated to him.

His smile held little joy either, yet it made her pause. There was something she hadn't expected there: understanding. Sympathy, even. She didn't know this wolf, didn't know what he'd been through or what he'd had to leave behind to be here and guard *her*. There were few places more dangerous to be. Maybe that's what made her soften towards him, just in the slightest and most imperceptible way.

'Come on,' Sadie signed. 'I'll show you round, although there's not much to show.'

She braced her gloved hands on the ground to get up, hesitating when Simon offered his own to help. After a beat, she took it. Sadie wasn't light to start with and her curves had manifested to almost spherical portions as her pregnancy had progressed. Simon's strength was evident as he firmly but gently pulled her to her feet, no strain on his face as he did so. He didn't let go of her hand as they descended the hill either, offering her his arm in a way that felt gentlemanly rather than like she was being pandered to.

'I'm sorry,' she signed, when they reached the pathway that led up to the cottage. 'I'm not very good at accepting help from other people, even when I need it.'

'These past few months must have been hard, then,' he replied, Sadie responding with little more than a nod. Besides, her gaze was too focused on his hand movements and the way they varied on words in ways she didn't expect.

'Where did you learn to sign?' she asked.

'My father was deaf,' he replied.

That was not the answer she was expecting and from her reaction, it was clear he knew it.

'Yes, there are deaf werewolves,' he smirked.

'I didn't mean to be rude,' she signed. 'I just thought all your senses were . . .'

She gave a double thumbs-up to indicate what she was trying to say, cautious of offending him with another careless comment the way people often did with her.

'Werewolf healing is definitely' – he mimicked her double thumbs-up – 'but he was born deaf, it wasn't something acquired in battle or for a fight over dominance.'

'Is he Māori too?'

'Yes, he was. He's dead.'

Sadie stopped mid-step, turning to face him. She went to say something, anything, yet it felt insincere. She didn't know Simon Tianne outside of his name and association to people who had done a great many things for her, people who had put their lives on the line for her.

'If there are words . . .' he started.

'You don't seem out of practice.'

'No no, it's not that. I'm using New Zealand Sign Language, which is mostly the same as Auslan except there are Māori words – *te reo* – in there, so if you don't recognise something, you have to let me know.'

She gave him the 'okay' symbol, before guiding him to the entrance of the cottage. It was beautiful, with a stone path and resilient flowers leading to the thick wooden door and the warmth that awaited inside courtesy of a roaring fireplace. It didn't have centralised heating; it was small enough it didn't need it as long as there were a few logs burning. She'd thought it looked like someplace hobbits might live the first time she set eyes on it while walking the grounds with Sorcha. She still thought that, except *she* was that hobbit and now she insisted on walking alone.

The door was unlocked and she held it open for Simon, noting his frown at the lack of deadbolts and reinforced steel or whatever. Locked doors wouldn't stop the kind of enemies Sadie had. Plus, if they could get past all the guards and security measures on the farm to make it as far as the cottage, nothing else would stop them.

She followed Simon as he prowled through each of the three rooms inside, inspecting the latches in the bathroom and any potential hiding places, then the final space. It was the kitchen/lounge combo, with the centrepiece being the beloved fireplace she all but worshipped at this point. There was a television and DVD player, a couch, but in terms of recreation that was the last normal item one would see. The rest was set up as a birthing suite of sorts, with Dr Kikuchi coming by at least once every day to perform check-ups and tinker with all the machines and devices she'd wrangled for the forthcoming ordeal.

Sadie had been there at the birth of her nieces and nephews, so she had no romanticised view of this being a beautiful, empowering experience. It would be hell and hellish. That's what they were preparing for and that's what she was preparing her body for, working through tedious stretches and breathing exercises that bored her senseless but could mean the difference between a seven-hour early labour before her caesarean or an eight-hour one. That single hour could make all the difference.

Simon touched the pile of thick, grey foam that was stacked on the kitchen counter. Sadie had been cutting it into squares the night before while listening to a podcast and trying her darnedest not to think. He held a square up for her to see, a question in his eyes.

'Soundproofing,' she signed.

'In case you wail again?'

'Oh, I'll definitely wail again, whether I want to or not.'

The werewolf looked surprised to hear her admit that and Sadie realised she needed to add a further explanation. *Men,* she thought.

'How many silent births have you heard of, Simon?'

'Ah.' He nodded, finally understanding. 'Smart.'

He asked for a list of everyone who came to visit her at the cabin and she gave it to him, written down so it was easier. It was too many people, he said, too many scents for him to keep track of. He made her trim the list to two people, including Dr Kikuchi and excluding him.

'This is bullshit!' she exclaimed, her temper rising exponentially with every additional moment he was in her presence. 'I've been doing fine without you! You can't just sweep in—'

'Actually, that's exactly what I can and *have* to do!' he yelled, forgetting momentarily to sign, and she waved him away when he attempted.

'I can read your lips,' she gestured.

'Good, then read them now: I have to keep you alive and safe. I have to do that by any means necessary and right now, that means limiting your visitor list. That means securing this place better. That means me getting intimately acquainted with every inch of this farm. And yes, that means pissing you off as well if that's what it takes.'

'All I have left are the women in that house,' she rebutted. 'The only thing that separates us right now is a God-damn sheep paddock, yet it may as well be an ocean. You can't make me pick. I need them.'

'You isolated yourself in this cottage to protect them, right? Them not coming here is protecting you, a choice I know any brother or sister would make for their sibling.'

She growled in frustration, which was ironic given the conversation was with a creature who was probably the DMX of growling. Yet she did it anyway. She needed her oldest sister, Shannon, because she had kids of her own and her gentle, quite musings on childbirth were endlessly soothing. She also needed Sorcha, the sister she had once thought dead and the sibling she was closest to ... even though the likelihood of them tearing each other's hair out was always high. Shannon had just left for Australia to attend a secret supernatural summit, so she didn't have to make that tough choice yet.

'Sorcha,' she answered, Simon making a note next to her name. 'And Barastin.'

'I said only two, with Dr Kikuchi that's—'

'Barastin has no scent, he's a ghost.'

She had him there, but Sadie resisted the urge to smirk as she smoothed her hand over the mound of her stomach, much like Blofeld would his hairless cat.

'Fine,' Simon relented.

'Fine.'

For a moment, she felt triumphant. Right up until he asked if she had a preference to which room he took. Because of course he'd be staying there, *of course*. She felt like a dickhead for not horrifying over this sooner. She couldn't think of anything worse than the cottage being occupied by some random man she barely knew when she had a crying spree at three in the morning. Or *him* being present for the inevitable peanut butter binge that followed at three fifteen in the morning.

The truth was it had been a long time since Sadie felt like she had any power over where her life was headed. She had never expected to be powerful in the way she was now, one of the few – maybe only – surviving banshees who could wail. Yet there was a difference between power and being powerful. She felt powerless in that moment and she hated it. Worst of all, she knew there was no other way.

As Simon excused himself to get his toolkit and start making the adjustments needed to the cottage, she fought back the urge to cry. It was the hormones, she knew it, and even the smallest things could make her bawl hysterically as she was mainlining pickles straight from the jar. He paused in the doorway, looking back at her.

'Older,' he said.

'What?'

'I thought the woman who had the fate of our worlds in her hands would be older.'

Sadie hesitated before she signed her response. 'Me too.'

Chapter 2

Tommi

Tommi Grayson couldn't believe what she was hearing.

She couldn't believe what she was seeing either, for that matter, but it was weirdly easier to push past an enormous collective of supernatural beings meeting in secret to overthrow the government than it was to fully process the words of this sprite. Firstly, she thought sprites were kind of made up (wrong) and every image of one she could muster in her mind's eye looked less like the woman standing in front of her and more like a spiky insect thing (also wrong). With wings. And mischievous teeth, if that was possible.

Secondly, if she had to guess what they could look like, it wouldn't be Dreckly Jones: a beautiful Asian woman who didn't present much older than forty. She had a world-weariness to her that resonated with Tommi and indicated she was a lot older than she looked. That last point made the most sense, actually, as no one gathered under the star-spangled sky of the Nullarbor Plain presented as they appeared. Goblins, selkies, witches, mediums, sprites, immortals, demons, shifters, elementals, werewolves, banshees, ghosts and spirits. They were all there, those last two keenly seen by Tommi and few others thanks to her just slightly dying for a brief period of time during the werewolf coming-of-age ritual. It left her with one whitish-grey eye, which aesthetically looked creepy next to her usual dark brown, but practically looked *through* worlds, meaning she could see ghosts and spirits that had previously been invisible to her.

There were *so many* of them there that night, surrounding the gathering like an army that couldn't be seen but could certainly be felt by those keenly attuned to it. The coven of witches that had dominion over this old, old country had been there for as long as it had existed. The well of power and history and knowledge they could tap into was so great, the Treize didn't dare come near their territory. It's why this place had been chosen, with the Nullarbor coven welcoming strangers and supernatural dissidents to the safety of their lands.

'We knew this was coming,' an elderly witch with white hair and the blackest skin she'd ever seen had said to Tommi when she first arrived. She'd embraced her like she was a sister she had always known. 'Just thought you'd all have hurried up and done it bloody sooner.'

She had seemed harmless as she'd barked a laugh, wandering over to welcome the next person, but from the stiff posture her boyfriend Heath had held next to her Tommi knew the woman was dangerous. And powerful. And much, much more than she seemed.

That recollection felt relevant to the present as Tommi watched the glistening, acrylic nails of Dreckly slicing through the air as she gestured through her story. Even after her very first night of transforming into a werewolf, she had learned that appearances were deceiving. So much had changed since then. Friends had died. Lovers had become foes. Foes had become lovers. And she had somehow endured it all. That's what they all had in common, she realised, while listening to this sprite explain how she was over a century old and had been born in the very supernatural prison they wanted to break into.

Looking around at all the different faces, some presenting young, some presenting old, some presenting horned, some she loved, some she had only met that day, they had *all* endured. They would have to endure a little bit more if they were going to make it through this. And if there was anything Tommi was certain of, it was that they wouldn't all make it through this alive.

* * *

'Well, that went about as well as expected,' she said, hours later, as she flopped down on to the mattress Heath's enormous body was already sprawled across. Technically, it had gone well if your barometer for success was 'did anybody get disembowelled mid-summit?' The answer to that – thankfully – was no. Tommi had considered disembowelling a preferable solution at one point when the opinions and the arguments and the theories and the suggestions started compounding on top of each other. The people in attendance were a select group, yet the supernatural world was a diverse one and with even just a few representatives from each species, it was *so* many voices.

What felt like an entire city of caravans just outside their window – some modern, most retro – was testament to their sheer numbers. It was the witches' convoy and practical housing for their situation, of course. She knew Heath liked the mobility of it all because if danger came and they had to push further and faster into the desert, they could do so at a moment's notice.

'Aye,' he replied, reaching out for her as she wiggled closer to him. He looked as exhausted as she was, but he didn't look hopeless, she noted. He looked thoughtful as he played with the long, black strands of her hair with four fingers rather than the five he'd been born with. The Treize had cut off his pinkie while torturing him for information, but she and her cousin Simon Tianne had managed to swoop in before they cut off much more.

Their caravan wasn't tiny; it was the ideal size for a wee family of four. Yet while Tommi was just a regular-sized person, Heath was a towering six-foot-six and a hulking mass of a man. He barely passed for human in the regular world, that's how big he was. If you had the benefit of viewing him shirtless – as she did now – the size would quickly fade to the back of your mind as the intricate, swirling blue patterns of his tattoos consumed you instead. They were the traditional markings of his people, the Scottish warrior tribes known as the Picts, because that's what Heath had been once . . . a Pict. It made Tommi's brain strain every time she tried to do the maths, but he was *old*. Hella old.

Her last boyfriend before him had been old too – Heath's ex-best friend Lorcan – but that was only an odd 412 years or so compared to, what, a thousand? A thousand and one? She imagined numerical formulas floating in front of her face as she squinted, going full John Nash about it before she inevitably gave up, as she always did. The important thing was Heath –

after spending a few centuries working as an immortal soldier in the Praetorian Guard for the Treize – had flipped and turned spy. In his eyes, he'd realised the malicious motives of the organisation he'd dedicated his immortal life to way too late. He'd spent years slowly trying to course correct, working behind the scenes and risking his life to save when he could, spy when he couldn't.

Yet every turncoat has an expiration date and his had come right in the middle of Tommi and her half-sister Aruhe Ihi completing the werewolf coming-of-age ritual known as *ahi hikoi*. Aruhe had crushed it, rejoining her blood pack the Ihi clan, whereas Tommi had barely survived. She came out changed, but with unlikely allies in the family she once thought of as enemies. That was only a few months ago, but if you'd told her it was a few years ago she would have believed it. She and Heath had been Bonnie and Clyding it ever since, Tommi even ditching her signature blue locks for black and a rotating roster of wigs that made it easier for her to blend in. Heath was now the most wanted man on the Treize's hit list and there was a bounty out for his capture, dead preferably. There was a bounty out for Tommi, too – alive, though – along with bounties for basically every banshee in Australia . . . many who had broken the sacred orders known as The Covenant and attempted to flee the continent they were supposed to be imprisoned on.

The banshees weren't the only beings finding their voices and learning how to use them – quite literally – as shifters and selkies had broken out in open rebellion against the Treize and destroyed a prominent strategic asset in Sydney. That's what had led Dreckly and those that clearly cared about her to

Western Australia, to the Nullarbor coven, and right into playing an integral role in their merry band of rebels.

Heath's thumb brushed along Tommi's lip, pulling her out of her thoughts and into the present. There. With him.

'Where did you go?' he whispered.

'Where else?' Tommi replied, playfully nibbling the digit before she rested her head on his bicep with a sigh. 'I can't stop thinking about . . . everything.'

'I know,' he murmured, pulling the blanket over her shoulders to keep her warm. She'd snuck into the country in secret, but even if she wasn't a fugitive she wasn't sure whether she would like the place much because of the weather. She'd gone from her native Scotland to Berlin, then on to New Zealand, and she had expected Australia to be warm even in winter. Instead, she had come to the conclusion that she was not built for the dry, oppressive heat of the day and the mood-swinging temperature drop of the night.

It was also dangerous for them to be there. They were in the safest place in maybe the second most dangerous spot they could have been in the whole world. The ruckus in Sydney and Heath's breakout in New Zealand had drawn the gaze of all kinds of beings Down Under. That focus needed to be elsewhere, so their plan was to create a huge distraction *and* do something extremely useful: break in to the supernatural prison Vankila and break out anyone imprisoned there or worse. The 'worse' was the experiment part, where the Treize had been slicing and dicing abducted supernaturals to try to find a cure that would save The Three.

A trio of mystical women who had otherworldly insight into matters of past, present and future, Tommi had crossed paths with The Three just once as she lingered in the in-between space between life and death. They had shown her a glimpse of Vankila, encouraged her to do exactly what she and Heath were planning. They'd been bloody persistent about it, actually. So Tommi had to believe this was important. She wasn't foolish enough to think she'd survive, not after everything she'd seen. She knew the odds and Heath knew them better than anyone. Yet if they carked it, their carking would mean something, damn it.

'You know,' Heath pressed, 'I was thinking about The Three.'

She lifted her head, surprised, as if he'd managed to pluck the very words from her cranium. 'Go on.'

'They assign you this mission of breaking into Vankila, right? Liberating the imprisoned, and all that?'

'Boy, way to cram meaty themes into Lemarchand's Box. And your involvement was implicit in all this, just FYI.'

'Fine, they want *us* to do it.'

'Better.'

'Or at least attempt it, which seems impossible because no one has ever attempted it before.'

'Less better, but not wrong.'

'And then who should fall into our laps,' he smirked, 'but a sprite who was *born* inside the prison and the first – maybe only – person to escape it.'

'Huh,' was the only response Tommi could muster at first. 'Is that why you looked like the cat who ate the canary when I came in here?'

'It's not a coincidence, love. You know what The Three can see, what they can perceive . . . Those old ducks may be dying, but they're still shuffling the last cards they can get their hands on.'

Tommi was thoughtful for a moment, but just a moment. If she puzzled over the stakes too long, she would feel like she was drowning. So she tried to avoid that pesky habit, concentrating on the next thing in front of her and then the next thing after that and the next. She had started thinking of her survival as problem solving and that made her feel slightly more in control. Solve one problem, pivot to the next.

'What kind of cards do you think they play?' she asked. 'Like, they don't strike me as Uno ladies, but I'm not sure if their poker face would be any—'

'Bridge.'

'What?'

'They're mad for it.'

'You've played *bridge* with *The Three*?'

He was beaming at her reaction.

'Holy shite,' Tommi breathed. 'Sometimes you just drop stuff like that into the conversation and I have no concept of time or space any more.'

'I've got the time to have you in my space,' he growled, rolling on top of her and kissing away the laugh that she barked out in response.

Sex with him was hot, always, but it was fun too in a way she hadn't necessarily thought it could be. She cackled as Heath grunted out a 'fuck' as he hit his elbow trying to wildly throw off his pants in the limited space. Tommi had managed much better with her werewolf dexterity and considerably smaller frame so that she had the time to lay there naked, appreciating the view, as the Pict battled with the laws of physics.

'Oh for God's sake, ya bampot,' she hissed, pulling him towards her and rolling him on to his back in one smooth gesture. She pinned his wrists above his head, watching the evil glint in his eye as her breasts came in range of his mouth. His lips and tongue could start wars, or end them, she wasn't sure as she lost her composure and let out a low groan as he sucked and softly bit.

'Moan for me,' he ordered, Tommi about to snap a reply when he spread her legs apart and used his hands to illicit the response he wanted. She could feel him hard beneath her, but it was clear he wasn't keen to rush it as he curled an expert finger towards her centre. The expression on Heath's face as he looked up at her, like she was a marvel to be worshipped, told her that he was entirely focused on making her fall apart for him and on him.

'*Heath*,' she moaned, the words sounding slurred and drunk to her as she clenched around his fingers. Tommi's eyes couldn't stay open as the internal sherbet at her very core fizzed and exploded through her nerve endings. Collapsing down on him, sweaty and elated, she felt like air as he reached for the foil wrapper of a condom nearby. They had done this so many times, yet her body was still always asking him questions. His response wasn't verbal, but physical, as he made love to Tommi like their lives depended on it, no matter how much of that life was left.

Closing her eyes, Tommi took a long, deep drag of the cigarette she held between her fingers. She watched as the tendrils of smoke from the vice she had vowed to give up eventually spun into the glittering night sky. Technically, it was the morning sky as it had crept past midnight some time ago, but the deep, majestic blue black of the abyss seemed just as hypnotic.

Sitting on the steps outside their trailer while Heath showered inside, there was something deeply soothing about the sensation of the red dirt against Tommi's bare feet. She wiggled her toes, observing as the fine granules were swept up with the gesture and dusted her foot like sugar. She had sensed the presence of the ghost several seconds earlier, but didn't react because she knew how much he loved to shock people with his arrivals.

'Boo!' he cried, leaping forward and even throwing out his tongue for emphasis. Tommi didn't leap back in horror, scream or drop her lit cigarette so that she had to frantically put it out with her hands as it tried to set her sweater on fire. She just smirked with satisfaction, because as much as Barastin 'Creeper' von Klitzing loved to scare people when they least expected it, Tommi loved to take the wind out of his sails.

'Creeper,' she murmured, taking another drag.

'Damn it,' he huffed. 'My sister and you are the only ones who never give me the reaction I want.'

'Well, Casper's a medium like you were once,' she said, thinking it through. 'I guess she has super medium senses or something, right?'

'And you have the ghost eye, so that's basically cheating.'

'Don't call it a ghost eye!'

'What would you prefer? The Eye Formerly Known As Normal?'

She laughed because he wasn't wrong. Before the 'ghost eye', as it were, the ghosts that had popped up to say howdy *had* scared the shite out of her. They never appeared when you expected them to (or disappeared, for that matter). With her flashy new iris, however, she could sense their presence before they materialised. Sometimes they visited her in her dreams, which was annoying because she didn't get much sleep lately. And at other times, spirits – the more powerful and dangerous of the undead beasties – were drawn to her just like they were to Creeper's twin sister, the notorious Corvossier 'Casper' von Klitzing.

Casper and Creeper had once been the two most powerful mediums in the world, working together as a team . . . up until he was murdered and she lost her right arm trying to save him. Technically they still worked as a team, except one had a physical body and the other could go 'fully transparent, bro' when he wanted to. As if conjured from her very thoughts, Casper appeared around the corner and smiled as she walked towards the scene of Tommi and her brother.

Floated was perhaps a better word, as like Heath it was hard for Casper to pass as anything but otherworldly. Over six foot, with pale white skin and long hair to her waist in the same shade, she didn't try to tone down the power that oozed from her pores. The excess of fabric that fell at different lengths from her long, patterned skirt fluttered in the breeze for added impact.

'My God, you look like a vision,' Tommi grumbled. 'It's sickening.'

'The night is the only time I look good here,' Casper replied, in a thick German accent. 'If I step outside during daylight hours, I combust.'

'It's true.' Barastin sighed. 'Our beautiful, pearly –'

Casper rolled her eyes. 'Here we go.'

'– alabaster, ivory –'

Tommi scoffed. 'Pick a descriptor, will you, man?'

'– effervescent skin is not meant for Australian desert climates such as these.'

'Sonnet aside,' Casper smirked, 'he's not wrong. I look like a beekeeper when I venture out.'

'Aye, well, I look like I'm bloody thriving externally,' Tommi began, holding out her bare arm for inspection and the olive skin that glistened there from her mixed-Māori ancestry. 'But internally I'm sweating my tits off. At least at night the temp drops to bearable, but otherwise how do people just get used to being, like, always moist here?'

'Ew, keep it in ya pants,' Barastin gagged.

'Speaking of pants,' Casper pressed, making a wrapping-up gesture with the bionic arm she so often wore now, 'has your more-annoying-half got his on?'

'I'll check,' Tommi said, putting out the cigarette with one hand and banging on the door of the trailer with the other. 'Oy, Heath! Put your willy away, we're needed.'

The werewolf didn't miss the way the siblings' eyes met before Casper half-laughed, half-murmured 'the straights'.

'Oh, honey,' Barastin replied, 'I've met some ghosts and our boy Heath Darkiro here is quite curvy.'

Ever the shit-stirrer, he cast Tommi an indulgent look like that was some big revelation.

'*Oh, honey,*' she responded, blinking at him like the dainty Venus flytrap she was, 'if you think I don't know all the dirty details, then you've really underestimated my allure.'

Barastin's shocked expression lasted for only a second before the trailer door was swung open and right through him.

'My willy is sheathed!' Heath declared triumphantly. 'What are we up to?'

'Babushka doll,' Casper responded, jerking her head for them to follow her.

'Oooooh,' Heath beamed, grabbing Tommi's hand and yanking her up off her feet, 'I love a meeting *within* a meeting.'

Strings of solar-powered fairy lights illuminated the sprawl of land their combined parties operated on, lighting the way for those unlike Tommi who didn't have the benefit of werewolf vision in the evening. Heath was in jeans and she hung back just enough to watch that fine ass do what it did as their quartet proceeded to their destination: a campfire with a small group of familiar faces clustered around it.

'All right, first person who starts playing "Wonderwall" gets eaten,' she whispered to Heath, who always found her funny no matter how shit the joke.

Casper moved around to the other side of the fire, where she joined the witch Kala Tully, who Tommi was delighted to learn had been the reason she'd up and left her home in Berlin and transplanted to Australia. She was a sucker for a love story like that. She was unsurprised to find Dreckly Jones there, accompanied by a man she'd clocked as a werewolf the second she got a sniff of him *despite* the fact he looked like a drummer in a punk band. His name was Ben Kapoor, Heath had told her, the leader of one of Australia's most powerful werewolf packs and with a surname that rang through her core. His family had worked closely with her deceased father, Jonah Ihi, as they had attempted to lead a werewolf rebellion against the Treize in the nineties.

They had been unsuccessful, and the cost of the Outskirt

Wars had been brutal for every pack involved, from Singapore to Samoa. Her father's identity had been a tightly guarded secret in her own family, a toxic one that was fed with lies and horror to try to protect her from the truth: that she was a werewolf and descended from the most significant werewolf family to ever live. Jonah was dead by the time she knew his name, but Tommi's journey to accepting that truth about herself had been bloody and brutal.

She had refused to join the Ihi pack and the Aunties, yet she was irrevocably linked to them because of her DNA. Now, she was irrevocably linked to them because she *chose* to be, building a relationship with not just Aruhe, her brother James and her cousin Simon, but with the true power in the pack: matriarchs Tiaki Ihi and Keisha Tianne. They currently had a very important task; in fact, it was a task so important the very fate of their world relied on them pulling it off. So while they were somewhere that was else, Tommi had been tasked with representing the Ihi pack here.

'Welcome,' one of the Nullarbor coven witches said as they joined them. She addressed the group like a schoolteacher used to wrangling unruly children. 'My name is Yolindi, head of this here coven as my mother was before me, my grandmother before her, and all of my ancestors that fill this place with their spirit. This meeting was called to come up with a plan of action among a tighter body of people following tonight's revelations. Perhaps it might be easier if we all go around and introduce ourselves, one after the other, and state why we're here.'

Definitely a schoolteacher, Tommi thought. Casper was first, then Creeper, Kala, Dreckly and Ben. It was when it got to the others that it started to get interesting.

'Sharon Petersham,' a tough-looking woman barked. She had Linda-Hamilton-in-her-fifties energy that Tommi found captivating. 'People just call me Shazza and this here is Bazza. We represent not just the wombat shifters, but the lot of 'em: ibis, brown snakes, dingoes, quokkas, roos, basically everything except the devils.'

'Fuck the devils,' Bazza nodded in agreement.

Tommi's mouth was already open and poised with the question of 'hello, are there literal fucking devils in this world and why did nobody mention that until now?' when Heath leaned in.

'Tasmanian devils,' he whispered.

'Like Taz?'

Heath snorted. 'Weirdly, kind of yes. Like Looney Tunes with a body count.'

She didn't mention that she always thought the Looney Tunes had a body count regardless as goblins Ruken and Katya introduced themselves. Then there was the selkie representative Avary, Sadie's banshee older sister Shannon, and finally demons Fairuza and Mildred, who couldn't look more different from each other if they tried. The former had a Pam Grier meets earth mother aesthetic and the latter looked like Lauren Bacall trying to go incognito. There were others, just two more, elementals whose names Tommi didn't catch because she was trying to see if flippers were hidden beneath Avary's long, flowing skirt.

'Heath Darkiro,' her lover said, although she could tell that everyone there knew who he was and had probably encountered him at some point. Such was his reputation. 'Former PG turned spy turned resistance fighter turned most wanted man on the planet right now, yada yada yada. You could say I'm the George Smiley of this outfit *if* you wanted but, oh stop it . . . it's too much.'

She smirked, his confidence and cockiness simultaneously maddening and addictive.

'Tommi Grayson,' she said, when her turn came at last. 'Werewolf. Here representing the Ihi pack and the interests of those affiliated. Uh, guess it should be noted that I too have a bounty on my head courtesy of the Treize so . . . you know, no selfies for the gram.'

Her joke landed about as heavily as the wooden log that was thrown on to the fire, sparking a rise in flames as they licked the air. Even then, the warmth generated wasn't enough to stop her snuggling deeper into her Ivy Park hoodie.

'So,' Heath boomed, clapping his hands together, 'there's too much heat out this way and from meeting A we have established that we need to divert that to something big and bombastic: breaking into Vankila. As a bonus, every super-natural prison is packed full of unlucky buggers who have been poked, prodded and live lobotomised to save The Three who – straight from the old crones' mouths – don't wanna be saved. Vankila is no exception and up until a few hours ago, we didn't think it was gonna be possible to get in and outta there.'

'Enter stage left, Dreckly Jones,' Shazza chuckled. 'Who would've thunk?'

Tommi hadn't imagined the tension that rippled between Dreckly and Ben, who had been sitting tightly together during their first, larger assembly and were now positioned quite far apart. She flagged that rift in her mind as something to examine later. The sprite, coincidentally, didn't look too comfortable with all the attention that soon focused on her.

'Listen, it's not as easy as just breaking folks out,' she started. 'As I said before, there are creatures in there – real monsters – that aren't just going to be our allies because we provide an open door. Then there are the things made not born, the abominations the Treize have fucked around with, like what we saw in the Sydney laboratory. There are *a lot* of things to consider here, really carefully.'

Heath shrugged. 'Hey, that's what meeting B for babushka is all about. And if you can think of a bigger distraction further away from here then I'm all ears.'

'What are we trying to distract them from?' she countered.

The group grew quiet, with Tommi not the only one who was tight-lipped. The sprite didn't miss much, however, as her eyes swept over those assembled.

'Okay, so you know,' she said, pointing at Heath before pivoting to Tommi. 'And you, the werewolf. Casper, Kala, the banshee and . . . that's it.'

'Believe me,' Shannon implored, 'soon you'll all know, but until then we can't risk it.'

Tommi nodded, backing her up. 'All we can do in the meantime is some fookin' good deeds that have some fookin' good side effects.'

'That still doesn't answer the question of how we do what we need to do,' Avary said as she spoke up for the first time in a voice that felt as if it wasn't meant for human ears.

Everyone was hushed, as she had an exceptional point. It wasn't one that could be solved easily . . . yet maybe it was one that could be solved stupidly? And when it came to dumb-ass ideas, that was Tommi's speciality. As the silence pressed down upon everyone, she felt the beginning of an absolutely foolish and brilliant notion forming. It would be one that could take her home, back to the place she grew up in and the people she grew up alongside. It might also be something that could work. She cleared her throat, drawing the focus.

'Maybe to break in,' she started, 'we need to first . . . break out?'

Chapter 3

Dreckly

Dreckly Jones had known this werewolf for all of six hours and already she knew Tommi Grayson was absolutely cooked.

'No one who has been inside Vankila before would suggest that,' she replied carefully.

'Oh, I'm not intending on staying there long,' Tommi countered with a nonchalant shrug. 'But think about it: we need to get in to get out. Half the supernatural community in Australia is on the run.'

'More,' Shazza noted.

'Right. And that's not even factoring in New Zealand, the rest of the Pacific Islands and all the other countries in the Southern Hemisphere that have read the signs and gone underground.'

The big, blond Scottish monster next to the werewolf woman pinched the space between his eyebrows with frustration, letting out a groan like whatever she was about to say next would cause him physical pain.

'No one inside Vankila currently has the tools needed to get out so we need to take them in. But even if we had a plant or a spy on the inside, how far are they getting?' Tommi pressed.

'Not very far,' Heath admitted. 'Administration level at most, but not close to the cells for anyone above a minimum-security rating. You're basically just one escalator down from the war room shoved with musty mannequins.'

Dreckly tilted her head with interest at that comment.

'There's a tourist attraction built above Vankila now,' Mildred, her long-time demon friend explained. 'A Cold War bunker.'

'Of course,' Dreckly scoffed. 'A front. Everything's a front.'

'Those medium- and maximum-security prisoners, who's down there with them?' Tommi questioned.

'Just the guards,' Dreckly answered, thinking of the early childhood years she had spent in that hellhole. 'But those guards might be the biggest obstacle besides getting in, because they're highly trained. The one who tracked me down over a century later, Lorcan, was—'

'Lorcan?' Tommi interjected.

Dreckly paused, examining the strange expression on the werewolf's face. She heard the medium mutter something that sounded close to 'uh oh'.

'Yes, Irish,' she continued. 'Praetorian Guard. Or was, he's a Custodian now, apparently, but he was the prick who threw me into the Sydney laboratory with the others so we could be broken down for parts.'

Tommi and Heath exchanged a loaded look before the older Scot spoke up.

'Dearest Barry,' he asked of the ghost, 'think you could locate our unfortunate friend, find out what continent he's on?'

'With the utmost discretion,' the undead ally answered, before disappearing in a flash.

'Why does it matter where this Legolas guy is?' Ben huffed, speaking up for first time in what felt like hours to her. 'Think we can flip him?'

'No,' Tommi and Dreckly said together, eyes darting towards each other with mutual surprise.

'He's the kind of person who's good at his job,' the werewolf said, evidently cautious with her words. 'There might have been a time when ... If he was the one who locked Dreckly up again, I think that time has passed.'

'We don't want him within a one-hundred-kilometre radius,' Heath added. 'He's a threat and wherever he is, it's likely more Treize will follow.'

There was a significant pause between everyone in the group, the height of the stakes suddenly dizzying once again. For Dreckly, she was doing her best to confront her mixed emotions. Whenever she thought about the man she'd once called the Kind Guard, something that can only be described as a deadly wrath started to curl up inside her. Her skin – in contrast – broke out in goosebumps as she was transported to the tiny cell she had once existed entirely within before she got to learn anything about the enormous world outside of it. She thought of the father she had been forced to leave behind, who had died there, and the terrifying demon Yixin, who had become her friend and sacrificed his own freedom for hers.

Dreckly had killed before, many, many times. She was over a century old and it was inevitable she had a bloody ledger. She had fought in human wars and she had fought in what she now realised was the beginning of a supernatural one. Yet the deaths that stayed with her were the ones that weren't caused directly by her, but indirectly: her great love, Harvey Schwartz, and her father. She had killed the men responsible for the former, but revenge for the latter relied on Dreckly being the one to end Lorcan's long, immortal life. She'd accomplish that task and close that loop, whatever it cost her.

'What we need is someone to be arrested,' Tommi was saying, 'and someone to be taken in to Vankila, preferably someone dangerous and preferably someone they wouldn't be, like, "Oy, innit weird that this Australian witch was just conveniently nearby singing 'You're the Voice'?"'

Kala Tully, the Australian witch in question, looked amused. 'Thank you for the inclusion, but that is not the song of our people.'

'Whatevs.' The werewolf shrugged. 'Now, Dreckly is out of the question cos they'd never put someone who had already escaped from there once back in. The perfect person for this job is Heath, but he has a "kill not capture" order on his head right now. I, on the other hand, happen to be a highly sought-after werewolf from Dundee, Scotland, just a mere howl, skip and a jump across the River Tay.'

'This is good,' Casper mused. 'They put you on that squad of assassins who had to exterminate the Laignach Faelad so they consider you dangerous. Dangerous enough for maximum security, at least.'

'They've always considered her dangerous,' Heath muttered, throwing the werewolf a look that was so mushy it was as if her ability to threaten murder was a declaration of love itself.

'I haven't been home in *years*,' Tommi added. 'If I'm alone, it could seem as if I'm believably trying to slip in, see my people, and slip out again without being noticed.'

'You will not be bloody alone!' Heath growled.

'Aye, of course not,' the werewolf huffed. 'If we're busting open Vankila, all of you cunts will need to be somewhere nearby . . . waiting.'

Dreckly leaned forward, warming her hands near the flames as she thought deeply for a moment.

'It could work,' she mused.

'It very well could,' Mildred agreed. 'No one has ever directly attacked Vankila from the outside before, let alone while there's a simultaneous attack happening from the inside.'

Getting to her feet, Dreckly slowly began pacing around the fire. It helped her think.

'Who is going to do the breaking *in* of it all?' she asked. 'I know you lot all clearly have resources, but moving this many of us will be noticed.'

'We use a team on the ground,' Heath supplied. 'There's no shortage of disgruntled supernaturals in the UK waiting for a chance to tear off one of the Treize's limbs. No offence, Casper.'

The medium sneered. 'Fuck yoooou.'

'But some of us here need to go, obviously,' he continued. 'And I know that seems like a death sentence, so let us draw straws if we have to. I doubt there'll be vol—'

'I volunteer,' Ben Kapoor barked, Dreckly closing her eyes with dread because of course he would.

'Fuck yeah, Katniss,' Tommi beamed, clearly delighted to have another werewolf willing to be as stupidly reckless as her on the team.

'Ben, you could die,' Dreckly said quietly. This was a conversation better had in private, but from the second she had been forced to reveal her unfortunate origin story she knew Ben had felt betrayed. His sister Sushmita – the former leader of the Kapoor werewolf pack – had been locked up in Vankila for over a decade for her involvement in the Outskirt Wars. She wasn't sure what he expected of her, but as her newly acquired lover Ben didn't know Dreckly well enough to understand how close she kept her cards to her chest. He *said* he understood, yet he had only just started to unravel the enormous burden of her many secrets and many lives when they'd been forced to come here.

'And Sushmita could die in Vankila. I'm going.'

Ben turned his eyes back to Tommi in a way that made Dreckly furious, as if that was that settled, and he was looking to her for his next set of orders.

'Dope,' the werewolf responded, offering him a fist, which he bumped. Dreckly had heard Tommi say that a half-brother of hers was locked up there too, so she knew the woman's skin was just as firmly in the game.

'You'll need to go too,' Heath said, pointing at her. 'We need your expertise; we need your direction in and out of there if all other senses are lost to us.'

As the offspring of air and water elements, Dreckly's abilities as a sprite were various but mostly pertained to controlling and manipulating air. The Scot had clearly listened intently to her story of escape, of how she had crawled her way to freedom through the dark by following the threads of fresh oxygen.

'Of course,' Dreckly said, her voice deadly. 'Why shouldn't I happily foxtrot back into the one place I fear most in the world? The one place that took everything from me: my mother, my father, my friends, my freedom?'

'Well, I didn't say *foxtrot*,' Heath scoffed, rolling his eyes.

She felt skin brush against her own and she looked down, surprised to see the fingers of Mildred's hand interlinking with her own. Even without noting the unusual air current that seemed to follow the demon everywhere, Dreckly would know it was her based on cuticles alone. She had the same red, heart-shaped manicure that she had been wearing when they first crossed paths during Hollywood's Golden Age in the nineteen twenties. That was Mildred in a nutshell: classic and everlasting.

'You're forgetting one major difference,' Mildred said, practically purring.

'What's that?' Dreckly exhaled.

'You won't be alone this time. You won't be alone plunging into that dark, terrible place, Dreckly. And you will not be left behind: you have my word on that.'

She couldn't formulate a response as she stood there, mouth opening and closing, as she attempted and failed to say something as significant as what Mildred had just said to her. Instead, her mind did what it often did and interwove the past and present simultaneously. She saw Mildred touring the old production design workshop in Burbank, listing the people she should avoid and those who were 'okay enough for humans'. She felt rather than saw Mildred physically holding her up on Santa Monica Pier when the news of her father's death was confirmed. She saw Mildred leading her through German-occupied France as they hunted Harvey's killers. She saw the last time they had seen each other properly, sweat glistening on Mildred's dark skin as they drank and danced in a Los Angeles bar during the eighties. Mildred had said she'd see her 'at the next war'.

All of these memories poured through Dreckly's mind as this demon – who had never wasted *a second* of her enduring life – stood beside her, held her, and told her she'd be by her side as she plunged into her literal trauma. She knew her eyes were welling up with moisture and she knew everyone saw it, but she cared little. In that moment, she was just completely and utterly floored by whatever she had done to earn friends like this when for so long she had worked hard to make herself an island. Mildred wasn't looking at her, though, she had turned towards Heath and Tommi, her lips pressed into a resolute line.

'I'm coming too,' she said. 'Many of my people are there also and I know others who would help.'

'Yixin,' Dreckly muttered, recalling some vital information. 'You were able to get a message into Vankila and get one out when you communicated with Yixin. Is he still alive? Could you do it again?'

'When was this?' Heath asked, clearly impressed.

'The twenties, I think?' Mildred replied, looking to Dreckly for confirmation.

'Thirties,' she corrected, noting the ripple that ran through the mortal supernaturals in the group at such a casual mention of what was nearly a century ago.

'And yes, Yixin is still alive. I could get a message to him again, tell him to prepare, although ... since Dreckly escaped, things tightened up for a lot of the survivors down there.'

'Can he be trusted?' Tommi asked. 'We can't risk giving the Treize any kind of heads—'

'He's the reason I escaped,' Dreckly cut in.

She and the werewolf locked eyes, the younger woman clearly aware that there was more story there but satisfied with the answer. Her nod communicated to the sprite that if Dreckly vouched for him, then Tommi trusted that.

'Right,' the werewolf said, pivoting to the next tactical step. 'Heath, we're going to need a breakdown of how many staff are at Vankila at any one time, and I need you to put that into threat tiers. Askari, for instance: not much of a threat and easy to dispatch. But how many Praetorian Guard soldiers? How many good ones? What species are they and what kind of mystical threat can we expect?'

This werewolf was young, but Dreckly had been around enough soldiers to recognise a strong strategic mind. Her body was also laced with scars of varying sizes and significance, which told her she'd seen her fair share of battles too.

'They have alchemists on site, but that's it,' Dreckly said. 'Most of the prison population tends to lean towards the mystical, so they want as few bodies that can sympathise with that as possible. Immortals, mostly.'

'And goblins,' Katya, one of two resident goblins, said. She was also Dreckly's manicurist, but somehow she felt like the woman's gift with glitter acrylics would be of less interest to their present company. 'Vankila was built and designed by goblins.'

'Of course,' she sighed, annoyed that she hadn't realised this sooner. Goblins had incredible minds for intricate, complicated work like architecture, engineering – anything meticulous and micro.

'What happened to them?' Heath asked. 'Can we—'

'They were slaughtered afterwards,' Katya interjected. 'Taking their designs and every Vankila secret with them to the grave.'

Yolindi, the old witch who leaned on a custom timber walker imbued with power, tsked from her position at the unofficial head of the fire. 'So many untold atrocities. So much pain at the hands of the Treize. We have no shortage of emotional and intellectual allies, but we need to make sure they're willing to be physical ones as well.'

'Vankila being busted open like an egg on Easter will help with that,' Dreckly mused.

'Which is why we have to be successful,' Tommi responded.

Dreckly agreed and said so, their party beginning to dive into the specifics of what they needed to do, how they were going to do it, and when. It was agreed that Mildred, Tommi and Ben would travel legally: Dreckly would be making their various ID documents so they could be certain those wouldn't fail. If there was a better forger alive, she was yet to see their work. Each of their routes would be different and roundabout, while Heath and herself would travel via means known as 'Duo'. She was concerned about what that was for a moment before she was informed that Duo was actually a person.

In fact, they got so far into the detail of the details that they were able to let the fire burn out as dawn broke instead. A few beautiful, handwoven blankets had appeared at some point and despite the yawns and blurry eyes of those not nocturnal, everyone pushed through. Because they had to. They had broken up into smaller, separate groups to work on specific problems when Barastin appeared with news about Lorcan's whereabouts. London, he said, along with 'the ginger', who Tommi seemed to know as she nodded enthusiastically.

Her eyes couldn't help but land on Ben, or rather, the absence of him. He had separated from Mildred and Ruken to quietly make himself a cup of tea at a trailer nearby. She could see him through the open door, his lanky frame hunched over as he dunked the teabag. He was alone and it felt like the right moment to try to speak to him as she let herself be drawn to the werewolf. He knew she was there, of course. The combined hearing and scent abilities of his kind too good to give Dreckly the element of surprise. He didn't turn around and fling the tea in her face, so she took that as a good sign and stepped into the trailer behind him. Wordlessly, he turned to face her as she pulled the blanket around her shoulders tighter.

'God, you're so beautiful,' he murmured, shocking the hell out of her. 'It kills me.'

'That . . . is not what I expected you to say.'

He let out a long, shaky breath as he rubbed his face with hands, fighting the fatigue. 'I don't know what to say to you, honestly. To think you had the answers to my sister's freedom this whole time—'

'And what great answers they are,' she scoffed. 'We're all probably going to die attempting what we're about to do and that's with a mystical menagerie by our sides. Even if you had known, you could have done *nothing*.'

'I would have had hope, Dreckly, that it could be done, that you could escape from that place and be a person again.'

She frowned, intrigued by the comment. 'Is that what you're afraid of? That you won't recognise the sister who comes out from the one that went in?'

'Yes, of course I'm terrified of that. She won't be the same, how could she be? I'm not.'

'You had to take over a werewolf pack at nineteen, Ben. I guarantee you her life in there has been hard, but yours has not been easy either. You will not be the teenage little brother she remembers. And that has to be okay, because that's the only reality we've got.'

He hesitated, just a beat, before grabbing the fabric of her blanket and yanking her towards him. He enveloped Dreckly in a hug, his greater height like an umbrella as he bore down on her and held her to him. She realised he was crying just a few seconds after she inhaled the scent of him with relief. She would never admit it, but she hadn't wanted whatever they had to be over so soon and so easily, like she feared it would be. It was a delicate thing, this. Especially in the early stages, and she'd forgotten what the anxiety of it fracturing beyond repair felt like. So she hugged him back, clinging to his waist as he cried on her shoulder. When he stiffened suddenly, she thought it was because he had come to his senses and he was back to being irrationally mad at her.

'Tommi's coming,' he muttered, turning away from her as he wiped his face. The werewolf appeared in the doorway barely a second later, Dreckly turning to see her eyes dart between the pair and register that *something* important was happening.

'Ah, sorry.' She grimaced. 'Just came to get a cup of you and me, I can—'

'No no,' Ben cut in. 'All good, I'm out of here. Brew away.'

'Oh, alrighty then . . .'

Ben offered a weak smile as he headed out that told her a) he was okay and b) they were okay. Those two revelations back-to-back had been too much to move Dreckly from the spot she had been standing in. On the contrary, she felt like she was cemented there as she sat with the feeling for a moment. Eventually her eyes flicked over to the werewolf that had taken the other werewolf's place, watching as Tommi silently and awkwardly made a cup of tea as quickly as she could. It was evident she wanted to be out of there as soon as possible.

'You know, you're the only other person I've heard call it that,' Dreckly said, breaking the silence.

'Call it what?' Tommi asked, glancing over her shoulder.

'Tea. A cup of you and me. That person was a soldier too.'

'Ah, well, that person must've been a legend then. But I'm no soldier.'

Dreckly chuckled. 'You can't even say that with conviction, please.'

The werewolf paused, before rephrasing. 'Aye, all right then. Let's just say I've always been good at killing and that's not a skill one slaps on their résumé along with "proficient in Excel". I've never liked that about myself, but I've come to accept it. There's a rage within me and so long as it's pointed in the right direction, I can be useful as a weapon.'

Pulling on the air particles around them, Dreckly tugged the air towards Tommi's steaming mug that was decorated in glaring characters from the television series *Wentworth*. It was obviously harder with a full vessel, especially one with scalding liquid, but like the werewolf Dreckly also knew a lot about her own particular talents.

'Better,' she mused, smiling as the werewolf stared at the mug that floated towards her.

'That is fucking *dope*!' Tommi exclaimed, cautiously taking the object. 'Do me, do me!'

Dreckly laughed, the reaction so genuine it reached right down into her centre.

'Another time,' she wheezed.

'You know,' Tommi started, sipping her tea, 'he's exactly the kind of trouble I used to get myself in to.'

She grinned. 'Ben?'

'Oh yeah,' the werewolf scoffed. 'Tatts, piercings, green hair, ethnic, reckless . . . I had a type.'

'I know we seem like an unlikely co—'

She snorted. 'It makes perfect sense. You're both smoke shows. It's just science two people as hot as y'all would have to smash flesh at some point.'

Dreckly wasn't quite sure how to handle this woman, who was deadly and direct in equal measure. Her own discomfort seemed to delight Tommi no end.

'Smash flesh,' she repeated, shaking her head. 'Actually, on a more serious topic . . .'

The smile fell from Tommi's face and Dreckly felt bad. Yet like the conversation with Ben, this was something that had to be done.

'Lorcan,' the werewolf whispered.

Dreckly nodded. 'You two have history.'

The woman looked uncomfortable as she tugged at the hood of her jumper.

'Aye, but you two have *actual* history – as in, have been through and survived history – so my past romantic indiscretions seem quite wee, really. Teeny.'

'He started out as a friend, almost,' Dreckly offered. 'One of the few people who was kind to me in a truly unkind place.'

'Girl, that sounds familiar.'

'My father never trusted him, warned me about him.'

'That was Heath in my case.'

'And he was right. A nice Nazi is still a Nazi. And I should know, I've fought and killed literal Nazis.'

'Jesus, fuck, okay.' Tommi flinched. 'The discussion's over as soon as someone brings up Nazis.'

Dreckly smiled. 'I need you to promise me something.'

She knew Tommi was clever by the way the woman hesitated, assessing Dreckly warily as she took a slow sip from her mug.

'How about you tell me what it is first and I decide whether that's something I can promise?' Tommi offered. She felt like it was as good a compromise as she was likely to get.

'I need you to promise me that if it comes down to it, you won't kill Lorcan,' Dreckly asked.

The werewolf's surprise and maybe something else – grief? – was clear.

'Why?' Tommi asked.

'Because I had a chance to make things right once and I blew it. That won't happen again. I need you to leave Lorcan alive so he can die by my hand.'

The two women stared at each other, neither blinking nor breaking as the request was received and registered as serious.

'I promise,' Tommi responded after a long moment. Dreckly gave her a stiff, solemn jerk of her head and, just like that, the conversation was over. It was testament to Dreckly's recent involvement in the supernatural antics she used to work so hard to avoid that she felt comfortable with the werewolf at her back as they stepped out of the trailer. They didn't speak again; there was nothing left to be said. Instead, they both just stood there, watching as the reddest dawn Dreckly had ever seen broke over the horizon.

Chapter 4

Casper

'You little witch!'

The fact Casper was hissing at a literal *little witch* was beside the point, yet there wasn't much else to say as she watched her settlements get absolutely annihilated by an eleven year old.

'Mine mine mine,' Sprinkle hummed happily, collecting the pieces off their Settlers of Catan gameboard. 'Mine mine mine, mine mine . . . mine!'

Sprinkle – real name Mayra North – was the daughter of Kala Tully's twin sister, Willa, who along with her husband had been murdered by the same people that killed Casper's twin, Barastin. That was all water under the bridge in the truest sense of the word as once Casper, Kala and Barry had teamed up with Heath, they had slaughtered those responsible and washed their ashes out to sea.

For all intents and purposes, Kala was Sprinkle's mum now and Casper something of her . . . other mother, she guessed? She'd fallen in love with the witch and moved to Australia to be with her and the kid, something she considered one of the best decisions of her damn life. They'd had fake names when she met them, fake ages too, but from something false they'd managed to build something real. Unfortunately, the peace she had found was only temporary. They'd had to leave their cottage in the Blue Mountains and join the rest of their kind, both women unwavering in their decision because they knew it was the right thing to do.

Never before had there been this many beings united against the Treize and that meant something. She and Kala were powerful, Sprinkle too, and staying on the sidelines didn't guarantee there would be any peace left anyway. With her partner laying down enough protections and charms to make sure not even a mosquito with malicious intent could step foot on their property, some members of Kala's coven had set up camp there while others had split to every corner of the country.

The gathering of supernatural rebels in the Nullarbor was not the only one. It was the largest, to be sure. But it had been decided it was smart to make sure they were all moving targets if possible and that Treize resources would be divided when trying to track them down. Watching Sprinkle clear the board, Casper frowned as she realised the little witch had deployed the exact same strategy here.

'I'm nearly three times your age, how did you beat me exactly?' she harrumphed, her heart only half in it as she tried to follow the feeling that was awakening in her gut. When it came to dealing with the dead or the living, Casper made it a point to always trust her instincts.

'Easy peasy lemon squeezy.' Sprinkle grinned. 'Divide and conquer!'

And there it was: the answer to the problem that had been niggling at the back of her mind for a week as they planned and replanned the forthcoming Vankila break-in. Sprinkle carried on explaining her strategy, outlining in detail how she had slowly built up enough resources so that she could deploy them against Casper all at once. And that was *exactly* what they needed to do.

'Sprinkle, you're a fucking genius!' she exclaimed, reaching forward and pressing a kiss to her temple with a big, over-the-top smacking sound.

'Ew, grooooooss.'

'Language!' Kala called from the kitchen, which was really also the dining room, which was really also the bedroom, which was really also the living room in the caravan they'd been occupying. 'And dinner is served.'

'Kangaroo bolognaise yeeeeew!' Sprinkle cheered, leaping up from the now finished game and towards the steaming bowl that had been placed on the table.

Kala was about to chastise her manners when she paused, glancing and then doing a double-take as she caught sight of Casper's expression. With her long, rope braids now with colourful strands tied in among her natural hair and a flower tucked behind her ear, the witch looked like a Disney princess in Casper's eyes. A sexy, deadly Disney princess with tattoos of Australian flora running across her chest and arms and a mouth that co—

'Casper?' Kala asked, cutting in to her thoughts. 'What is it?'

'I . . . I need to . . . ' She glanced at Sprinkle, who wouldn't have noticed a bunyip tap-dancing in to the room so long as there was food in front of her. Yet she and Kala had made a choice to be pointed in what they told her about everything that was going on. The kid was too smart, that was the problem, so she could never be outright lied to and she had an amazing bullshit radar. So they told her as much of the truth as they could, keeping the full scale of the danger to themselves. The conversation she needed to have was not one that could happen inside this caravan.

Casper jerked her head towards the door, mouthing the word 'Barry'. Kala's eyes widened just slightly, but knew that if she was interrupting their dinner with a chat to her undead brother then it must be important. Moving with purpose towards the Holy Grail – her iPad – Kala snatched the device from where she hid it from Sprinkle and tapped the screen quickly.

'All right, coming to a mini movie theatre near you ... *ParaNorman*!' she proclaimed.

Sprinkle paused mid bite – which was notable – looking up at her aunt's declaration like it was some kind of ruse.

'I ... can watch a movie? While I eat? Dinner?'

'That's right,' Kala responded, setting it down in front of her.

'But you said I'd already met my screen-time quota.'

'You also managed to ignite and put out an entire burning tree today with your eyes closed,' the older witch countered, clearly proud of her niece's pyrotechnic abilities. 'So as a special treat, you can watch *ParaNorman* over dinner. Casper and I are going to be just outside, okay?'

'Omigooooodyou'rethebestthankyooooou!'

Grabbing the two glasses of red wine she had already poured them, Kala stepped through the trailer door as Casper held it open for her. When it clanged shut behind them, Casper downed the entire contents of her glass in one smooth gulp. She could see the sharp eyes of Kala through the base of the stem, her partner rarely missing much as Casper wiped the corner of her mouth.

'Damn Sam Neill,' she said, examining the empty glass. 'That's a lovely drop.'

It didn't take much for her to reach out to her brother, Casper calling his name in her head and sending her urgent desire for his presence down the line that kept them both tethered to each other. It had been there when Barastin was alive, yet in death their bond had become stronger than ever. Wherever he was – on this plane or the next – doing whatever he was doing, she felt rather than heard his response.

'This must be bad,' Kala murmured, watching Casper over the rim of her own wine glass as she sipped slowly. Like a lady.

'It's not bad per se—'

'All right, all right,' her brother interrupted, appearing between the two of them and making their duo a trio. 'Stop pulling ya hair, Barry's here.'

'I had an idea,' Casper began, not wasting any time. 'Uh, technically, Sprinkle had the idea.'

'Let me stop you there,' Barastin said, holding up a hand to do just that. 'I'm not sure we should be taking advice from someone in a training bra. No offence.'

That last comment was directed at Kala and she shrugged in agreement. 'No argument here. Kid named herself *Sprinkle*.'

Her brother laughed at the witch's joke and Casper did her best not to get annoyed. 'You guys, this is serious. We were playing Settlers of Catan and—'

'Certainly sounds serious.'

'Barry!' she yelled, putting a stop to his interruptive quips.

The greyish blue of his body brightened just a little bit as he reacted to the force of her power when she directed it at him. Kala – the smarter of the pair – was perfectly quiet, and Casper was relieved to see her brother follow suit.

'I've been going over and over the plan,' she pressed. 'I've looked at this from every angle over the past week to make sure this is as foolproof as possible. Heath and Tommi are right: Vankila is the target that will make the biggest impression. It will really *show* the rest of the supernatural world rather than *tell* them that this fight is on and we're fucking serious about it.'

Kala and Barry were listening intently to her as she held court in the quaint little area between trailers, the tinkle of a wind chime caught in the breeze the only other sound.

'Vankila *is* the biggest facility, but we know for a fact there are others,' Casper continued. 'Sydney is gone and destroyed, great. Yet how hard would it be to gather intelligence on the rest?'

'Not very,' Barastin said, considering for a moment. 'They're rebuilding the Sydney one on the Gold Coast. Less supernatural presence there, much easier to defend. We know the Bierpinsel is back up and running in Berlin for much the same purpose and there's at least half a dozen others across Europe. Other countries . . . I don't know, but we have contacts there. Local packs and covens who would know the locations where the most of their kind have gone missing.'

'Like a black hole,' Kala murmured.

'So we take them all.' Casper grinned, no warmth to the gesture. 'We attack them all simultaneously and make sure it coincides with the main assault on Vankila.'

The air seemed to hang between them as she let the seed of the idea grow into something fully formed just by saying it out loud.

'The Treize won't know where to look and we'll be continuing to divide their resources,' she continued. 'Not to mention freeing as many of the abducted and imprisoned supernaturals *globally* as we can. Whoever survives, that's potentially more allies for us.'

'And what about those who die?' her brother countered. 'Sydney they took down with *dozens* of selkies and shifters and werewolves and fucking humans in that Ravens motorcycle club working together to form an unprecedented united front. That was a stroke of luck, no disrespect, because a) they had Dreckly, who was there to unite them, *and* b) the geography of that facility being on the harbour meant they could flood it. Who's going to lead merry bands of rebels all over the map, huh? The idea is solid and the cause too, but it can't be Dreckly again. Not enough people know her and she has made a point of that. Not enough people trust her. Heath, Tommi, Ben and Mildred are out because they'll be in Scotland. Shazza and the shifters are needed here with the witches because we can't leave whatever sanctuary we have left unguarded. Who are we left with?'

This is exactly why Casper had needed to talk it through with Barastin and Kala. Ideas were only as good as the holes that could be poked in them. It was easy to be blinded by the pros and not see the cons, which is why these two were her infallible sounding boards. Her brother had raised significant points and she was about to tell him that when Kala spoke up.

'You,' the witch said, as if it was the most obvious and simple answer in the world. Like she knew Casper would counter that statement with a 'you who?', she gestured with her wine glass for emphasis. 'They'll rally around Casper.'

Eyes wild, she turned to her brother in order to scoff at the suggestion but he was nodding in agreement with Kala.

'You've been famous among our kind since you were a child,' the witch continued. 'Everybody knows you, knows the two of you, and knows what you can do. You're trusted and respected and your connection to the dead is singular. No one else can do what you do and because of that, folks believe you're connected to a higher power.'

'It's not untrue.' Barastin shrugged. 'And Europe was our base for years. Say we start there and span out, recruiting and planning, if we don't know at least one monster per city then we can know their deceased easily enough. The ol' "I just spoke to your dead grandma and she said your favourite food was her homemade gnocchi so join the cause already" trick works like a charm for any reluctant non-believers.'

Casper scoffed. 'Slow down, both of you. No one is going to agree to potentially risking their life because I asked them to.'

'Why not?' Kala pushed. 'I did.'

She blinked. *Damn it,* she thought. *The witch was right.* That was exactly what she had done, converting a resistant and downright murderous witch to risk it all against The Oct in Boscastle.

'Shit,' Casper whispered, drawing out a laugh from her brother and a knowing smirk from Kala.

'It's all fun and games throwing paint on the canvas until you've gotta sell the fucker, isn't it?' Barastin chuckled.

'When I suggested this, I didn't mean me,' she mumbled, recognising the fear in the pit of her stomach that started to creep up and consume her vital organs as she thought about how dangerous this would be.

Kala was intuitive as all heck, placing down her wine glass as she surged forward and wrapped around Casper like wisteria did an old, country cottage. Almost a full foot shorter, the witch's body enveloped her own as their hips pressed together and Kala's skilled fingers skimmed the skin of Casper's arms, creating goosebumps she couldn't control. Looking up at her, Kala must have seen the doubt and the dread that Casper was sure were flashing like a neon sign from within her own irises.

The witch smiled, nails gently tracing Casper's jawline as she soothed what was inside. Kala's scent was intoxicating to her, even all this time later, and especially in this proximity, as she wondered whether the lavender was some kind of charm to make sure Casper was forever in her thrall. If that was the case, she didn't care. It was worth it.

'My love,' the witch purred, 'I've never met someone so afraid of their own greatness. That's why you're perfect: the person best suited for power like yours is the one that fears it.'

'Will Sprinkle and you come with me?'

Kala's eyes crinkled with a smile that seemed to spread from the inside out. She had an internal glow that Casper had been drawn to like a moth ever since they first met.

'No,' the witch replied. 'You know covens are strongest on their own land and we're going to need every bit of strength and protection we can get Down Under. This is a task meant for you and only you.'

'All right, Gandalf,' Barry chuckled behind them, and Casper suddenly remembered her brother was there. He always complained about third-wheel moments like this, but it was unavoidable in her opinion. She leaned down, brushing Kala's lips with her own just briefly before she stepped back. Her long, white hair was twisted and clasped up behind her in a crocodile clip yet that didn't stop the same three strands escaping at the front *every time*. They fluttered across her vision as she steeled herself for the mental strain of the task.

'Okay, I go,' she confirmed.

'We go,' her brother corrected. 'If you're Simon Cowelling a whole continent, you're going to need help.'

'I'm more concerned about her doing this in the Treize's backyard,' Kala noted. 'Their Transylvanian headquarters are much too close for my liking. Recruit if you have to, Barry, but watching Casper's back should be the top priority.'

'Agreed.' The ghost nodded.

'What about Scotland?' Kala asked. 'They were going to use you.'

'They'll have to do without,' Barry murmured. 'This is a better division of resources.'

She didn't disagree as she tucked hair behind her ear and began working through the machinations. 'I start in Berlin. With the Rogues. I know the most people there, but they'd know even more. Yu and Dolly will be all in, but Sanjay, Clay, Zillia and Gus can be just as useful.'

'Good.' Kala nodded. 'That's also where you'll be most protected to start.'

Casper glanced at her brother. 'Go tell the big guy. He'll have as many contacts there as we do. Also, I think we gave him Collette's address book after she died.'

'We did,' Barry agreed.

'Get that off him too. People looked at us like Collette's children and that still carries weight. Her people will be ours.'

'Absolutely.' He beamed. 'Where are you going?'

'The lobby,' she said with a sigh.

'I'll see you there,' he saluted, before vanishing.

It took a beat before Casper turned to Kala, not needing to say a word before the witch took her hand.

'This way,' she said. 'I know somewhere quiet.'

At first Casper thought it was the hidden billabong where Kala had taken her and Sprinkle swimming on their first few days here. She had been reluctant to go near the water, knowing too many stories about too many creatures that could eat you in too many ways in Australia. Once they snapped their jaws and dragged you under the surface, you were done.

'There are no crocs here,' Kala had laughed. 'It's basically just a big pond, honey.'

She'd observed from a safe distance under the shade of a tree anyway, refusing to get in the water while Sprinkle and Kala splashed and swam about. This place was not that, the visage shifting as they got closer and the landmarks that Casper thought she recognised were distorted in the dark. It was the entrance to an underwater cave system, with clusters of rocks and steep arches surrounding it like an ancient, red fence. This place had weight to it and Casper could feel it tingling under her skin as she approached.

'Yolindi brought me here,' Kala said. 'Told me if there was ever a place the "dead girl needed to commune with the spirits" then this was it.'

'Where are we?' Casper whispered, the reverence audible in her voice.

'It's a sacred place of her people,' the witch replied, gently running her fingertips over the surface of the black water. The reflection of the crescent moon shimmered with the motion. 'The word is not one I have any right to say, but it means *gateway*. If you're not from Yolindi's coven or country, you can only visit here with permission. And before you ask, there are no crocodiles in that water.'

'Aussies always say that,' Casper grumbled. 'And yet ... crocodiles remain.'

Kala smiled, leaning against her as she planted a kiss on the medium's shoulder. 'Your body is safe here. I'll leave you to it.'

Casper squeezed her hand, gently releasing it as the witch receded into the night. She didn't watch her leave, she couldn't: she was too enthralled and captivated by the place she had been taken to. It was thrumming with life, not just that which could be seen but, more importantly, that which was unseen. Sitting down, she moulded herself into the cold ground and crossed her legs. Externally it would have appeared as if she was about to perform some night-time meditation, which wasn't entirely wrong but not entirely right either. One's pupils didn't usually become uniform like Casper's did during this process, the grey spreading like an infectious storm. Her body remained in that special, sacred place yet she let herself get pulled somewhere else.

When they were kids, she and Barastin had called it the lobby. It had a thousand different names in a thousand different cultures who expressed it through a thousand different religions. As her consciousness shifted from the human plane to this new one, Casper thought the lobby was the best damn name one could bestow upon it. If you were unlucky you ended up here after death, waiting for a pull that would either take you up or take you down. Of course there was no gravity in this place, yet it was easiest for the mind to process the unlogic of the many phases of death using things one already understood.

It was endless, impenetrable darkness stretching in every direction. Yet she wasn't afraid. This black was like a blanket to her and Casper could always find her way through here, often with Barastin by her side. Yet her twin had more important things to do tonight and there were any number of ghosts she could call upon to help her: ghosts who dipped and weaved in and out of the human realm as well as she did. The being she was meeting there tonight wasn't dead, however. In fact, she saw them more often on the physical plane than on this one. Yet during sleep, it was just as easy to pull the living here when she needed them. It was the safest space one could possibly find, with the conversations unable to be monitored or spied upon.

'God, I hate this joint.'

Casper smiled at the disgruntled tone as her friend came into view, wearing what she had been dressed in as she'd fallen asleep, which was an oversized N.W.A. T-shirt.

'What would you prefer, an underground car park? A trench coat and a lit cigarette?'

'If anyone could materialise an underground car park in the desert, it would be you.'

The medium laughed, unable to help herself as long-time friend and werewolf Tommi Grayson joined her. Although Casper could drag anyone to the lobby if they were asleep or unconscious, Tommi could move around here freely and choose to join her if she wanted.

It was sadistic to think of the woman's brush with death as a gift, but truly that's what it was. She couldn't control and manipulate the dead like Barastin and Casper could. What Tommi could do was receive and perceive, which made her an invaluable asset. Casper hated to think about it, but the reality was that if she or her brother were occupied or incapacitated they now had a back-up option. Their ghost network had someone else they could communicate with besides the twins.

That's what they had been doing together over the past few months during these sessions. After Tommi had reached out following the acquisition of her 'ghost eye', as Barry called it, Casper had promised to help her given she was the only medium the werewolf knew and the only living medium powerful enough. And she *needed* help. This had all happened on the lands that belonged to her ancestral pack, so the ghosts she'd first been exposed to had been her relatives, her blood, her allies. They had been friendly. They had been familiar.

Ghosts by their very nature weren't always this way, as Tommi soon found out. You can't control who you see, how many you see or where you see them. They had always been there for Casper, but she'd also had Barastin, so it never quite felt as terrifying as it probably would have been for a normal kid. What was scary had become her reality, her normal, and she had never known any other way.

She was conditioned to it and she couldn't imagine the reverse: suddenly being hit with it all as an adult. So Casper was introducing Tommi to some of the new friends she'd hunted down, ones that would help her navigate the concrete labyrinth of Vankila, which was even more vital now that Casper wouldn't be there to do it herself. And okay yes, they were undead friends but there had been so many years when undead friends were all she had.

'You ready?' she asked, as Tommi fell in step beside her.

'No,' the werewolf replied. 'I'm always worried I'm gonna sneeze in here and accidentally send myself to hell.'

'Don't think of it in such linear terms. I—'

'I know, I know, it's not really hell. But raised in a lapsed Catholic household, how else am I supposed to make this work in my mind?'

There was a light up ahead, not that light-at-the-end-of-the-tunnel bullshit but one that meant something. It contained a person, an essence of what had once been and still was in some small, incremental way. She could sense the tension from beside her as they neared.

'Don't be afraid,' Casper urged.

'I'm trying, but I'm used to being able to physically dismember the things that scare me. This is . . . different. Harder.'

'I understand. Just remember, how Broom looks isn't reflective of who they are on the inside.'

Tommi dropped her voice to a whisper. 'Yes, but the last time I met him his insides were on the outside.'

Casper bit her lip to hide a smirk. It was true, Broom O'Neary had made sure all of his entrails dragged behind him like a gory tail for Tommi on their debut meeting. It had taken time to find him, to use all of her ghost contacts to locate those that had died in Vankila. There were *so* many of them and *so* many that had moved on. Yet like the sprite Dreckly Jones, there were still some who harboured rage over the injustice of it. Those feelings were useful and those beings even more so, as it meant they lingered.

And they had been waiting a long time for someone to give them a purpose. Broom had been a werewolf in life and at the time of his death, imprisoned on the same level of Vankila as Dreckly and her father. He had died in the prison riot the sprite had started as a child, and although he could make himself more presentable to Tommi if he wanted to, this was a ghost that didn't like to make things easier. Tommi was a shiny new plaything after so long with just Casper and Barry.

'I've tucked away my small intestines,' a voice croaked out. 'Don't worry.'

Casper felt relief for just a moment before she heard Tommi's rasp beside her as she realised the small intestines might be gone, but the large ones were draped around his neck like a scarf.

She rolled her eyes. 'Motherfucking ghosts.'

Chapter 5

Sadie

'YOU'RE A GOOD-FOR-NOTHING WEREWOLF AND IF YOU DON'T LET US IN THE HOUSE, YOU WILL RUE THE FUCKING DAY, MATE!'

Sadie smirked at the exasperated expression on Simon's face as he returned to the main room, the sound of her sisters banging on the front door still echoing through the cottage.

'You're not gonna help me with this?' he huffed.

Sadie gestured to her exposed belly, where Dr Kikuchi was using a paddle to smooth ultrasound gel across the swollen mound. A series of wires and notches and nozzles extended from several different parts of her as she lay there on the enormous monstrosity of a bed they used for daily check-ups.

'Sorry.' She smiled sweetly, although there was nothing sweet in the gesture. 'I'm otherwise occupied.'

He looked like he was about to pull his hair out as he gripped the thick, black tuffs at the top of his head in frustration.

'It has been two weeks; they can't keep doing this every day!' he cried, before a look of horror crossed his face. 'Can they?'

His dark brown eyes bore into hers, as if urging Sadie to tell him something comforting as eight or so banshees continued to berate him from the other side of the front door. Since they'd first arrived in New Zealand, her sister Sorcha hadn't missed a single daily check-up and she was stretched out next to Sadie, delighting in all of the chaos their siblings were causing.

'What did you think?' Sorcha quipped. 'You saw how everyone took the news when you "gently" broke it to them. You can't keep our sisters away for ever, especially when they already fought Sadie so hard to stop her moving out here.'

'I'm actually impressed he has been able to hold them off this long,' Dr Kikuchi murmured.

'Listen,' he growled, 'I don't want to set up bear traps around the perimeter, but if I have to, I will. I have strict instructions to protect Sadie at all costs.'

'You have strict instructions to protect my babies at all costs,' Sadie replied. 'I'm just the incubator.'

He glared at her, and Sadie was surprised to see the first flash of what she thought was genuine anger cross his face.

'That's not true and you know it,' he signed.

She felt Sorcha stiffen beside her as she recognised the rage too. In most instances, werewolves could be pretty volatile. Yet the Ihi pack – of which Simon was a prominent member – was different. Their control and their power and their abilities were unrivalled, meaning he and the Aunties made the perfect bodyguards. It also meant that while being confined to a cottage with a werewolf under usual circumstances would be ill advised, in their case it was the ideal scenario to guarantee her safety from outside forces. The inside forces, however . . .

Letting out a grunt of annoyance, Simon stormed from the room and right out of the cottage to face the assembled Burke women. The pitch of their collective voices rose just slightly at his appearance, bubbling and frothing over the top of each other as they hassled him. Their volume was cut significantly as she heard the front door slam behind him and the boom of Simon's own voice as he yelled in response. She couldn't make out the words, but the tone was terrifying. The Burkes, however, didn't scare easily and she wondered if the silence on their end was a gesture of respect as they tried to let the man say what he needed to say. More likely, it was to create a false sense of security before they verbally castrated him.

'What night is it?' Sorcha asked quietly.

'Full moon is tomorrow,' Dr Kikuchi replied, answering the question her sister had *really* been asking. 'If they keep riding him this hard, someone is going to end up dog food. My money is on Catriona.'

'She and Keavy are basically twins,' Sorcha smirked. 'It would have to be double or nothing.'

There was a pause as her brow furrowed and she ran a cloth of over Sadie's belly, wiping it clean of the ultrasound goo.

'I'll speak to them,' Sorcha said. 'This close to the full moon, we shouldn't push him.'

'Or any of the wolves, for that matter,' Dr Kikuchi countered, beginning to pack up her equipment. 'It's all good in there. The babies are happy and healthy. Now, before you ask me how much longer they need to bake, I don't know. And no, I don't care if you're uncomfortable. I mean, I do care but the longer they're in there the better chance all three of them have out *here*.'

This was a speech Dr Kikuchi gave her almost every day, and even though she was a Paranormal Practitioner, she assured her that the speech would have been exactly the same even if her triplets weren't unborn physic banshee beings meant to fill the void The Three's death would inevitably create.

'Excellent, well, send someone if you need me,' Dr Kikuchi said. 'I'll see you tomorrow.'

She went to leave the way she had come in, before pausing and reconsidering.

'I'll go out the back,' she murmured, taking a hard left and slipping out through the only other entry or exit to the house.

With a groan, Sadie started to sit up slowly, inch by inch, as Sorcha helped support her back. In just a pair of sweats and her bra, she couldn't have felt less attractive if she'd tried. She looked down at the mountain currently blocking the view of her feet as they dangled over the bed.

'Jesus, your tits are huge.' Sorcha gawked while fiddling with her noise-cancelling headphones to make sure they were still working. The little blue light indicated that they were. 'I mean, they've always been the biggest in the family but now—'

'They're sore,' Sadie signed, before touching them self-consciously through the pale blue lace of her maternity bra. She used to wear several necklaces at all times in varying lengths, in part to hide the silver scar that ran across her throat. The old wound where the Treize had once tried to quash her abilities remained, yet she cared less about covering it up now. The chains and the threads and the stones and the crystals that had once adorned her neck and the bracelets on her wrists and the rings on her fingers were gone now, each one having slowly annoyed her more and more as her body swelled with the pregnancy.

Just one necklace remained, a sturdy silver chain that dipped between her bosoms and rested at the start of the linea alba line on her belly. The line ran down the length of her abdomen and to her pubic area, cutting her in half and making Sadie feel like a giant Kinder Surprise. There were only two objects on the necklace: rings, cheap ones that could be acquired from any mall jewellery store. Hers had been sterling silver initially, but it was now bronzing around the edges as she had refused to take her necklace off when getting in the shower – or ever, really. It was a twisted series of roses all interlocking and inter-linking together like a pretty, Celtic chain, with a pink stone set in the middle. It had been a cubic zirconia initially, but was now just a cavity where the fake jewel had once been before dislodging and falling loose somewhere along her journey. The other ring had belonged to Texas Contos, her dead love and the father of her unborn children. They'd never been married; hell, they'd barely had a chance to be together with the exception of a few months when their romance had been tied up amongst their escape from the Treize and the pursuit of a hidden truth.

Yet Tex had chosen these rings from the sprite Dreckly Jones as she had made them fake identities and fake documents to get them out of the country. The metal had once been warm from the heat of his skin. When she had slid it off his dead, bloodied body it had felt as cold as his corpse. Sadie had kept it anyway, it being one of only three things left that she had of him. There was this ring, there were these babies, and there were her memories. Soon the ring would disintegrate and she guessed that eventually, over time, her recollections would too. With his father and his uncles dead, their daughters would be the last piece of proof that Tex had ever been alive.

'I'll talk to them,' Sadie signed, thinking of a different man and a different set of problems.

'Talk to who?' Sorcha asked.

'Our sisters,' she replied. 'They'll listen to me. They won't listen to Simon. And if they think it's what I want and what I need, then they'll obey.'

'You don't need to do that.'

His voice came from the darkened hallway, where he had been leaning against the doorway and watching her as she played with the trinkets on her necklace. She hadn't heard him come back inside; she rarely did, such was his ability to move so quietly unless he wanted to be heard with a door slam or a stiff yell at one of her siblings. She rushed to reach for the oversized shirt she had been wearing, conscious of her belly and her boobs being on full display. Sorcha was right: her tits were huge and the spillage on either side of each cup was just as scandalous as what was actually inside of them. *Damn it*, she hissed inside her head. The shirt was just out of reach and she strained to grab it, but Simon was quicker. In two strides, he had it in his hands and held above her head as he waited for her to put her arms inside it.

'I've watched you go through this same routine for fourteen days straight,' he said slowly. 'I've seen every bra you own, Sadie. Now do you want in this shirt or not?'

She looked up at him, blinking. After a few seconds longer, she raised her hands above her head and Simon pulled the material down, tugging it over her belly, before he retreated to the position he'd previously been occupying.

'I thought *I* was the stripper,' Sorcha smirked, sipping from the hot chocolate she had made for herself like the Cheshire Cat. 'And you don't need to speak to 'em, Sades, I will. After I finish speaking to you.'

There was something in her sister's tone that made her consider Sorcha more closely. That and the fact a ghost was slowly, gradually appearing behind her like an old-school PowerPoint transition. It was Barastin, their undead friend, and much as he usually loved to make a dramatic entrance he had taken to slow and obvious ones now so as not to frighten Sadie into a wail.

'Uh oh,' Simon remarked. 'This can't be good.'

'We-he-ell, it's nice to see you too, my Polynesian prince,' Barastin purred, and Sadie noted how red the werewolf's checks went.

'Don't call me that,' Simon mumbled, crossing his arms tightly across his chest in a way that made his muscles flex. It was unintentional, she knew it, but she could see the mischievous glow in Barastin's eyes as he opened his mouth to say something.

'It's the night before the full moon, Barry,' she said, cutting in. 'Leave him alone.'

She felt the werewolf's gaze on her but ignored it, keeping her stare focused and intent on the ghost. He would bow to her if she urged and, eventually, he did.

'Fine.' He pouted. 'How can I disobey a pregnant angel like you, dear Sadie Burke?'

She laughed, letting him butter her up regardless of what was coming. 'Oh, it must be bad if you're trying to be this smooth. What's going on?'

'Big things,' Barastin began. 'Big break-in things that we need some additional bodies for.'

She didn't like the sound of that, even though she knew her body wouldn't be moving anywhere. For a moment, she thought he was there to take Simon and she felt a pang. She was just getting used to him, she told herself.

'They need me, Sades,' her sister said, cutting into her thoughts.

'What?' This was worse than Simon, way worse. *I take it back, take him,* she thought. *Take him instead.*

'Need you where?' She could see the hesitation on both their faces, the stakes so high at this point secrecy was vital. 'Tell me! I literally can't go anywhere so—'

'Vankila,' Barastin answered.

'*WHAT?!*' Sadie and Simon said in unison. She was just as shocked by his shock.

'Why would you ever want to go there?' she asked.

'We're not moving in,' the ghost scoffed. 'We're breaking in, then breaking out.'

Realisation washed over her, as now she understood why Sorcha was needed. Each of her sisters had a different, watered-down version of the abilities their banshee ancestors had once had. Except they weren't so watered down any more, with every banshee who had broken The Covenant and fled Australia – which was a lot of them at this point – growing stronger by the day. Their resistance had brought redemption first and, now, power. Sorcha had been the first to successfully escape, so her gift of being able to manipulate others with her speech and movement was significant.

If you were planning a break-in of the world's toughest supernatural prison, Sorcha's skills would be an invaluable asset to whatever team you were assembling. Yet Sadie could also do the maths. It wasn't impossible, but it was unlikely they would be successful. It could be months before she found out the result, meaning her sister could be either killed or imprisoned. Either way, she wouldn't be by her side when the time came.

'Don't cry,' Sorcha pleaded, dropping down to her knees and resting her head on Sadie's lap.

'I can't help it,' she whispered, knowing fat tears were dribbling down her cheeks. 'It's the hormones.'

'It's not and you know it.'

Sadie sniffed, brushing a hand through her sister's bleached-blonde pixie cut, which highlighted her incredible bone structure.

'Shannon's coming back from Oz in the next few days,' Sorcha continued. 'She's going to take my place at the birth and, Sades, she's going to be way more useful than I would be. She's had kids, she actually knows what she's talking about! And she's going to take over my daily visits, too, so you'll have a lot more guidance in the weeks leading up to it. In fact, I know Dr Kikuchi wanted her here as your one visitor instead of me anyway so she'll get that wish.'

Sadie wanted to tell her not to go, wanted to beg her, yet she knew Sorcha would never leave her unless there was no other way. It was likely their world and whatever might be left of it depended on this.

'It's just so dangerous,' she signed. 'There has to be something else you can do that utilises your abilities and doesn't put you at risk.'

'Sweet, swollen Sadie,' Barastin beamed, quite literally, as he moved closer to her. 'Your dear ancestors The Three expended some of their last vestiges of strength so Tommi and I could understand how essential it was to take Vankila down. On paper, I know it seems like a suicide mission. Outside of the friends we can liberate, the innocents we can get out of there, we have to believe it will serve a greater purpose overall, even if that purpose is just drawing their attention away from this side of the world.'

'I know,' she responded, wiping a tear as she steeled herself. 'I'm okay, I know.'

'Who else are you taking?' Simon asked. 'Cos I know you didn't just come here for Sorcha.'

'Clever wolfie,' Barastin teased. 'And no, I didn't. We need Atlanta, too, and Aruhe.'

The first name Sadie had expected, as wherever Sorcha went the selkie named Atlanta tended to go as well. They'd both escaped a sinking ship run by Tasmanian devil shifters and ever since then, they'd made the choice to keep their lives entangled. When Sadie had first tracked down her sister – who she'd been told was dead – at the supernatural strip club Hue in London, Atlanta had been there too. And when they'd fled to Galway, Atlanta came with them. Even when she wasn't physically there on the farm, she was there in sight as her visage was inked on the tattoo portrait that decorated Sorcha's arm.

It was love, Sorcha had told her eventually. Her sister was such an open person in so many ways and such a private person when it came to matters of the heart. Sadie had long suspected this was the case, yet she knew it was better not to push her. If she'd thought her relationship with Tex had been doomed, her sister's was just as consistent as the pair of them making it work when one lived in water and the other on land seemed impossible. It had been years since they first met, however, and somehow they functioned. The second name she didn't recognise, yet from the pronunciation alone she could tell it was someone near and dear to Simon. His reaction confirmed just as much. A girlfriend, perhaps?

'No,' he growled. 'You can't take her. We *just* got her back!'

'Hey, don't maul the messenger,' the ghost responded. 'We needed someone from the Ihi pack.'

'You have Tommi!'

'She's like a mascot at best.'

'Not her.'

'She volunteered, Simon. So take it up with your cousin, because *I know* that *you know* she's just as stubborn as you are and won't back down from this.'

Simon looked heartbroken, the odds of survival playing out on his face. 'My mother,' he muttered. 'My mother would go in her place in a heartbeat.'

'Keisha and Tiaki both would, but they know it's not the smartest strategy. With odds like this, we need to make sure we're only doing smart things. Those two women are the power core of this pack and this country in a way. They need to stay here in case things get ugly.'

'*When* they get ugly,' Simon countered, acknowledging what everyone knew. He sighed, the heavy gesture indicating that he understood he had lost a battle that had never really started. 'This is because of Quaid Ihi. She thinks that it's her fault he got locked up in Vankila.'

'So does Tommi.' Barastin nodded. 'So they can guilt each other to death over that one, but the reality is they're going,

Simon. She is, Atlanta is, Sorcha is, Tommi is, and if we're lucky they'll be coming back too. Speaking of . . .'

'She's in Arrow River,' Sorcha said. 'Near Edgar Bridge, before it meets Kawarau. You should go and see her soon. Atlanta likes to stay close so it will take her a little bit of time to get back to the ocean.'

'I'll take care of that,' Barry said. 'You need to take care of how you're getting there. What's the nearest rendezvous point?'

'Piopiotahi,' Simon said, the word sounding beautiful on his tongue. 'Milford Sound. It's a three-hour drive usually, but it will take every bit of four hours this time of year with the ice.'

'Won't you freeze?' Sadie signed to her sister, worried about how she was going to survive with Atlanta.

'Don't worry about me.' Sorcha smiled, rubbing her knee. 'Atlanta and I have done this plenty of times; she knows how to find the warm currents and use the fast channels.'

'What about Aruhe?' Simon questioned.

'We're picking her up in the Bay of Plenty,' Sorcha remarked. 'And don't sweat, big guy, travelling by sea is the safest way. She might never have done it before, but she'll never wanna go back after she meets some of Atlanta's friends. We're gonna rendezvous with the others in Australia and go from there.'

Simon looked the way Sadie felt, but neither of them had a lot of choice about what their loved ones were doing in that moment.

'When will you leave?' Sadie signed. The expression on her sister's face immediately made her wish she hadn't asked that question. 'No, Sorcha—'

'It has to be today, honey. I'm sorry, I'm so sorry, but there's no time to waste on this. We need to make sure there's a buffer in case anything goes wrong and we've got business to attend to on the way.'

'What business? Sorcha, not today please.'

Getting to her feet, her sister embraced her. Then she bent down and, lifting the hem of her shirt, Sorcha planted three quick kisses on the skin of her belly.

'I will see you and my three nieces before you know it,' she whispered, her touch lingering for just a moment before she dashed from the cottage. If it felt abrupt, it's because it was. Yet Sadie understood Sorcha's hasty exit was because if she didn't force herself away now and *right* in that moment, she never would. She hated other people seeing her vulnerable so Sorcha had sprinted towards a dangerous future and a dangerous mission leaving just Sadie, Simon and the ghost.

'Welp, this has been bleak,' Barastin said. 'I've got a mermaid to visit. See you all soon!'

Correction: leaving just Sadie and Simon. Suddenly the cottage felt very quiet and very empty, even though it had often been just the two of them.

'I should drive her,' the werewolf said, breaking the stretch of a silent few minutes.

Sadie liked that idea, liked the idea of any one of the very capable werewolves doing just that, but she tossed it out immediately.

'You can't,' she signed, pointing up at the roof. 'Full moon.'

'It's just past ten; I know these roads better than she does. I can make it there and back before the moon rises.'

'And if you can't?' Sadie countered.

'Then I'll shift in the mountains. It's just as remote out there, I won't run into anyone, and I'll be back by morning.'

He stepped out of the hallway, moving closer towards her so that she had to arch her neck up to look at him from her position sitting.

'That's if you would be okay with it,' he continued. 'You'd be here by yourself, with just the Aunties to guard you.'

'I was here by myself with just the Aunties to guard me long before you arrived.'

She didn't intend to sound so mean, but she couldn't help it. She was hurting.

'I'm sorry,' she said.

'I'm sorry,' Simon matched.

'What are you sorry for?' Sadie questioned.

'That Sorcha's leaving. I know how close you two are, I know ... I don't know, actually, how hard this must be for you. And she made it a little bit bearable, so I'm sorry about that.'

'We don't all get what we want.' She shrugged. She gestured down at her belly for emphasis, attempting a smile that didn't hold on her face before she felt tears forming again.

'Oh no,' she grimaced, furious that she was crying *yet* again. These fucking hormones. But instead of running away like most men when heterosexual kryptonite was displayed – *female tears* – Simon moved closer to her, bumping her legs apart with his own as he cradled her in a hug. His frame folded around hers seamlessly, like a protective shield, as he let her cry against the comfort of his weight. His hands ran down her back in a soothing gesture as the werewolf held Sadie tightly, eventually letting her sob herself out. He didn't retreat, and she found herself profoundly comforted by that as she listened to his heartbeat.

'I am sorry,' she said, risking the words she expended so rarely. 'I'm sorry about your cousin.'

'You were right,' he replied. 'This is war. We don't all get what we want and when those we love make sacrifices, we have to be brave enough to support them.'

She tried to commit those words to memory, to sear them into her heart for whenever she felt a weak moment and needed to be reminded of the strength of those around her. She felt a profound loss as the werewolf pulled back, gently wiping the remaining tears from her face as he did so.

'I'll see you soon,' he said, grabbing his keys and jacket as he stepped away. 'And Sadie, I mean it. I'll be back.'

She watched him leave, believing that *he* believed that but once again knowing fate often had other plans.

Chapter 6

Tommi

'If anyone gets eaten by a shark, this is gonna be so embarrassing.'

Tommi was staring at the surface of the ocean, eyes narrowed as she scanned for any indication of what was to come. Her body was tense, even though thick hands were kneading the knots in her shoulders as she waited.

'No one is going to get eaten by a shark,' Heath replied, making about his fiftieth comment that was some variation of this mantra of support.

'I looked it up,' Tommi huffed, her toes digging into the cold sand like it was snow. 'West Australia is famous for great white shark attacks and it's night-time. They're *night* hunters.'

She felt the rumble of amusement from behind her. 'That's from *Jaws*, sweetie.'

Heath stopped massaging her shoulders, his hands pulling her to him from behind as he held her in place against his broad chest. They were standing there on a remote, isolated beach with a coastline that seemed to stretch endlessly in every direction. Avary the selkie had been with them, but several minutes ago she had left to walk into the sea. Tommi had watched with fascination as the woman just stripped, one item at a time, and slowly stepped into the ocean, her arms extended like she was Jesus. For all she knew, she might be: *mermaid* Jesus.

'Great white sharks hunt at dusk and dawn,' Heath was saying, trying to soothe the nerves she felt. 'It's the middle of the night, firstly. And sharks aren't the top of the food chain when selkies are around, secondly.'

He was trying to reassure her, she knew it, yet the idea of her half-sister and several others being *swum* over from New Zealand to Australia wasn't one that sat well with her. She knew nothing about that world, and as much as Dreckly had tried to explain how it would work, Tommi couldn't shake the image of Aruhe ending up as the entrée for a hammerhead shark or something.

'Sharks love dogs, right?' she continued. 'What is a were-wolf if not a big dog? And we're just supposed to believe the little mermaid is gonna be strong enough t—'

She didn't finish her sentence, the words replaced with a small gasp as a figure broke the surface. Not just one either, dozens, with selkies and their passengers popping up like a game of aquatic Whac-A-Mole. It was just a few nights outs from the full moon, so there was enough light for Heath to see as well as Tommi did in the evening as the silhouettes began moving closer to the shore. She was silent for once, not a word on her lips as she stared at the glorious sight before her and the beings emerging from the depths.

Avary didn't look like the Avary she'd known the past few weeks on land. Even though Tommi had understood she had to disappear for long periods of time to be able to return to the water and reacquaint herself with her preferred habitat, this was like seeing who someone *truly* was. Her long hair was out and floating around her body like it was alive in the water as she beamed, her sharp teeth flashing with a smile and her eyes practically illuminated.

She realised the woman she had seen was like a photocopy of an oil painting that should be hanging in The Louvre. The version she'd viewed was accurate visually, but it paled in comparison to the original, which *shone*. Suddenly Tommi didn't feel quite so in the dark about Avary and the rest of the selkies. She felt a synergy instead, an understanding, as these creatures so rarely ever presented a face to the world that wasn't authentically theirs. That's why they were hardly ever seen. It was pure what she was looking at and Tommi understood that she was blessed to witness it.

She slipped free when she recognised a face among the selkies, her sibling Aruhe laughing as she unlinked her arms from the back of a male selkie and continued the swim to shore on her own. They'd all ditched electronics long again, so Tommi had no phone to worry about as she waded into the sea, tossing off her jumper so it was just her jeans and a singlet that were getting soaked. Aruhe was swimming breaststroke, her slicked-back hair glistening with the wet as she kept her head above the water and swam to shore. Her eyes lit up when she spotted Tommi, her smile growing even wider.

'Sis!' she shouted, her feet making ground as she waded forward. She wasn't upright for long, however, as Tommi dived and tackled her into the depths. Aruhe let out a surprised laugh as they both disappeared under the water for a moment, splashing and shrieking as they came back up.

'Hug me like you're happy to see me next time!' Aruhe laughed.

Tommi splashed her in response. 'You're fucking glowing! I thought you'd come out covered in barnacles or something.'

'Just my clam-shell bra,' her sibling joked. In fact, what she was wearing was nothing so elaborate: it was a simple but effective full-body wetsuit. With the slickness of the water, it made her look like a cool assassin in Tommi's eyes as they both stumbled into the shallows. She understood why that attire was necessary, as after just a few seconds in the depths Tommi's teeth were chattering. It was bloody freezing.

'Hold up, wait one second,' Aruhe said, tugging on her arm. 'There's someone I want you to meet. Amos!'

The selkie her sister called swam forward, the kid looking not much older than Aruhe with greying skin like all of his people and piercing blue eyes.

'Hi!' He grinned, offering Tommi a webbed hand to shake. Just as their skin was about to touch, the webs disappeared with a *thwick* so it looked like a regular, land-dwelling human hand.

'You're Dreckly's friend,' Tommi remarked – the sprite had told her she was going to assign someone she trusted implicitly to transport Aruhe. 'Thank you for taking such great care of my sister.'

'Ah, you're welcome. She's welcome. It's just so great to be out there swimming again, amongst the *open* ocean.'

Dreckly had told her a little of this creature's story, that he had grown up with a scientist away from his people only to accidentally come across some kind-hearted humans who'd helped him return to the ocean. That victory had been short-lived, however, with Amos ending up captured and in the clutches of the Treize when Dreckly had come across him. They'd escaped and together they'd managed to work on liberating as many of the Sydney survivors as they could.

'Tommi, it was so cool,' Aruhe was saying. 'You would love it; it's unbelievable how fast they can move! And we swam alongside the maki! They gave us a guard, following us for hours as Atlanta spoke with them.'

'Maki?'

'Orcas, killer whales.'

'And they didn't eat you? What about sharks?'

Amos and Aruhe laughed like she'd just said some hilarious joke.

'I don't know why people think the shark stuff is so funny,' she grumbled, pausing as she saw not one but two familiar faces. 'Sorcha!'

The banshee was dangling over the shoulders of a selkie that was talking to Heath, the woman's dark seaweed hair bringing back a memory that felt like a decade ago. A river in Galway at night, Heath diving in while Tommi watched as he exchanged words with this same creature. It had been the day she'd first met Sadie, the pregnant banshee, and her protective older sister.

'You're not blue any more!' Sorcha exclaimed, making her way over amongst the crowd.

'And you're not on land.' Tommi smiled.

'Eh, I prefer to travel like this. It's safer and I can stay with Atlanta, which is always my preference.'

'How's Sadie?'

'Being guarded by your cousin, actually.'

'Simon? Well, that's brilliant.'

Sorcha raised her chin. 'You say that like you mean it, not a shred of sarcasm in your voice.'

'Look, among werewolves, among *most* creatures, you'd be hard pressed to find someone more capable of protecting her.'

Tommi and Simon hadn't always seen eye to eye, yet she meant what she said. Sadie's babies being brought safely into this world was vitally important, and Simon would be a formidable force in making sure that happened.

'And there's, like, six Aunties on site,' Aruhe said, splashing over. 'Tiaki and the other packs will reassemble there if they have to, but they're worried too much presence will draw too attention.'

'Totally,' Tommi agreed. 'The rest of the world's ignorance is one of the biggest things we have going for us. The longer no one knows about Sadie, the longer no one knows that The Three are dying because she's about to give birth to their heirs.'

'And the safer she is.' Sorcha nodded, her short hair spiky from all of the salt as she readjusted the goggles on top of her head. 'The safer we all are.'

'I'm glad you're coming with us to Vankila,' Tommi said, meaning it.

'I can't say that I am.' The banshee sighed. 'Leaving Sadie right now is the last thing in the world I wanna do, but there's also no one else in the world who can do what *I* do so . . . can't deny I won't be useful.'

'What can you do?' Aruhe asked, intrigued. 'I never really had a chance to ask in-between the whole selkie-carpool-between-countries thing. Like, I know you're one of the banshee sisters but that's about it.'

Tommi barked a laugh. 'Sorcha can put men under her *thrall*.'

Aruhe's eyes widened with interest. 'Really?'

'Not just men, anyone really, but it's a temperamental skill,' Sorcha smirked. 'Depends on the person and their attachments. Yet given what youse are trying to pull off, you're gonna need every bit of help you can get.'

'Fucking oath,' Tommi snorted.

'It's all resting on you, werewolf, and that sprite,' Sorcha noted. 'Think you can handle it?'

Tommi swept the wet hair back from her face, considering the combined gazes of Amos, Aruhe and Sorcha.

'Live free or die hard,' she snorted, Aruhe taking her hand as they started to walk from the water. She paused when Sorcha didn't come with them, turning back to watch her observing them from the sea as Atlanta swam over to embrace Amos.

'You're not coming?' Tommi questioned.

'I'll see you over there.' Sorcha nodded, reaching back as her hands interlinked with the dark-haired selkie.

'*Sea* you soon,' Tommi smirked, earning a laugh from the banshee before she slid on to Atlanta's back. She was the only non-selkie left among the pondant now as they began to swim off, their heads bobbing along the surface of the ocean until – with a splash – suddenly they were gone.

'How do you breathe under there?' Tommi asked her sister, but the question was answered by Amos, who was wrapping himself up with a towel.

'There are air pockets we use,' he said, 'just like the warm currents and channels for speed. When transporting folks like you all, however, we stay a little closer to the surface or on it entirely. It takes longer, means we have to be more careful about being spotted, but it's just as effective.'

'Hey there, big guy!' Aruhe shouted, grinning as Heath tossed her a towel. 'Look at you, all Fabio by the sea and everything.'

Tommi warmed as she watched them. 'Oy, remember when you two wanted to kill each other?'

'It's called growth, Tommi,' Heath replied, rolling his eyes as he spun the towel he had for her in the air, turning it into a deadly whip.

'Don't you dare,' she warned him, dashing out of the line of fire as he attempted to lash her with the cloth. She was too fast for him, sand flying up as she pounced away and *ooft*, right into his barrel of a body. They fell to the sand, Tommi straddling him as they landed.

'You made some terrible mistakes to end up here,' she told him, her wet body pressed into his own.

'Oh, did I?' He shifted his hips just slightly, so she could feel just how intentional this whole thing had been.

'Gross!' Aruhe exclaimed. 'I can see neither of you has eased up on the public displays of humping.'

Tommi laughed, ignoring her as she gave Heath a salty, searing kiss. His fingers sunk into her wet hair, holding her to him for longer than was strictly appropriate before they broke apart. Springing up, Tommi helped pull him to his feet and quickly gave up on the prospect of washing herself free of sand until they were back at the caravan city. Or what was left of it anyway, as those who weren't actively preparing to do battle in Vankila had started moving on to other sites. The shifters – led by Shazza – and the goblins had all hit the road again to link up with a motorcycle club Dreckly knew. Together, they were going to find local targets they could hit when Vankila's assault got underway. This was Casper's idea and Tommi couldn't deny it was brilliant: hitting multiple sites at the same time, globally, to disorient the Treize. Without the predictive abilities of The Three on their side, there was never a better time to attempt this. It also undermined the strength of any retaliatory attack, which was a massive plus.

'Hold up,' Tommi said, pausing as they began to pick their way up the sand dunes towards the waiting car. 'Where's Avary?'

'We swapped,' Amos remarked, pulling on a jumper that had been left for him neatly folded on top of a pile of fresh clothes.

'Swapped?'

'She needs time at sea,' the selkie said, looking somewhat unsteady on his feet as he continued to get dressed. 'We can't shift and stay on land for prolonged periods of time before it starts to get to us. Heck, I couldn't shift at all until Avary and Atlanta practised with me.'

'Atlanta is Sorcha's girlfriend,' Aruhe supplied. *And the selkie Heath knew*, Tommi mentally added.

'And my older sister,' Amos beamed. 'She'll meet you over there with everyone else, but until then you have me while Avary takes a break.'

'Aight.' Tommi nodded, grabbing his arm so he had a body to steady himself against. 'Come on, then. You ever ridden in a car?'

'What's a car?'

Tommi looked at him in horror. He cackled with laughter.

'Just kidding,' he said, patting her arm. 'I've been in the tray of a ute, but that was quite a dramatic situation. Hopefully this will be different.'

'It's a jeep,' Heath shouted, reaching the top of their sandy summit first. 'So *extremely* different.'

Helping him into the back seat, Tommi pivoted to assisting Aruhe as she wiggled out of the difficult-to-disrobe wetsuit. Offering her a sweater dress in return, her sister undid the top of her bikini and tossed both it and the bottoms into a nearby bush. Freeballing it like a fucking legend, she climbed into the jeep after Amos and slammed the door shut. A selkie, an immortal and two werewolves embark on a road trip . . . There was one hell of a joke to be made in there somewhere, Tommi thought as Heath threw the vehicle into gear and sped along the darkened dirt road.

Glancing in the back seat, Tommi hesitated as she observed her sister and the selkie fast asleep, heads resting on each other in an adorable fashion.

'Should I . . . ?'

'Nah,' Heath whispered. 'Leave the wee bairns. They've had a long journey.'

That they had. Gently and quietly, she pressed the door of the jeep shut as they disembarked.

'I threw a blanket in there,' Heath said, tossing an arm over Tommi's shoulder as they walked back to their caravan. 'They'll be fine.'

'You don't think they're—'

'No,' he scoffed. 'Just new mates. He's got a human lassie on the opposite coast. And I think Aruhe's fucking Joss.'

'Ha, *as if*!'

'I wouldn't discount my dick-stincts so quickly. There was such a brief window of time for that to be a possibility, but there's for sure something going on.'

She stepped in front of him, forcing him to come to a dead halt. 'How? When? Oh my God, *why*?! You're so full of shite!'

'So,' Heath leaned in, conspirator's glint in his eye, 'I'm pretty sure they boned for the first time after he was caught tracking her in New Zealand.'

'When I was deadish and you were imprisoned?'

'Aye, of course! Emotions were heightened! Space was cramped! Ideal conditions for a heated encounter.'

'Stop,' she laughed, waving her hand at him like she could magically make the thoughts go away. 'Stop stop stop.'

'The added danger of trying to keep it going now only makes it hotter.'

'Ah, Heath! I said stop! There's no way in hell.'

He was booming with laughter now, dragging her with him into the caravan and dragging her thoughts away from the horrendous theory that her sister and her best friend were, indeed, hooking up. He did this by joining her for a long, hot shower that had her screaming his name and not in frustration. A significant amount of time later, he asked if she'd meet him up on the roof.

'Course,' she said, drying her hair. 'But we've got that strategy meeting—'

'In thirty-five minutes,' he interjected. 'I know, there's no way we'll miss it. Just give me time with you alone first.'

'You just had time alone with me,' she purred, rubbing against him. 'You just had four times alone with me.'

She smiled as she looked up at him, watching the way his determination faltered whenever she touched him just right, just like this, just—

'Tommi,' he begged. 'Stop making this so difficult and get up there.'

She grinned an evil grin. 'Fine, but you better be following me.'

'Oh, I am.'

She chuckled as she hopped out of the caravan, practically swinging from the front steps to the small ladder that led up the side of the mobile home. She climbed, pausing as she reached the top and the scene that was waiting for her. Heath had a point, they rarely had much time alone together and when they did, they didn't waste it by keeping their clothes on. The roof of the caravan had become one of the few places they actually did both, taking brief reprieves up there under the stars as they sat, often wrapped in blankets and sharing a bottle of whiskey as they talked through their fears about what was to come. It was usually kind of crappy up there, a little milk crate used for their empty bottles and another flipped over as somewhat of a mini coffee table where they burned citronella candles to keep the mozzies away.

Tonight, however, it looked *beautiful*. Tommi climbed the last two rungs on the ladder slowly, taking in the scene. Several strings of those solar-powered fairy lights she loved had been repurposed, roping off the space so that it looked like someone's pretty balcony. There was a chilled bottle of Dom Perignon, her favourite, waiting patiently along with several small, wrapped boxes around it. She heard the strain of metal as she spun around to see Heath joining her, one hand balancing a cake that was illuminated with a small forest fire worth of candles.

'Heath . . .' she started, before the words fell away completely. She was about to cry, she could feel it, and she didn't want to do that so she slapped two hands over her mouth to stop herself. She watched him approach her, cursing the tears she felt brimming at the corners of her eyes as Heath held the cake up to her face. It was chocolate, also her favourite, with thick chocolate icing smeared all over the damn place like a Francis Bacon painting.

'Happy twenty-fifth birthday, Tommi,' he said, eyes beaming as the glow of the candles reflected in them.

'It's not till tomorrow,' she replied, like an asshole.

'As of ten minutes ago, it *is* tomorrow, so just blow out yer damn candles, will ya?'

She laughed, hesitating for a second as she thought about her wish. There was only one logical wish her heart wanted to make and she poured all of her hope into it as she blew out the candles with a series of puffs.

'There, ya bawbag,' she sniffed, wiping away a tear. 'Happy?'

He set down the baked goods, popping back just as quickly as he lifted her off her feet and into a tight embrace. Feet dangling off the roof, she threaded her hands around his neck as he kissed her, slow and deep and good. Every bristle of his blond beard against her cheek felt like home as she inhaled his scent, her werewolf senses practically making it a tattoo.

'Aye,' he whispered, pulling back. 'Now I'm happy.'

He kissed away several of her tears as he set her down, pulling a knife from his pocket as he sliced the cork off the bottle of champagne with the kind of expertise you expected from a professional killer.

'I couldn't wrangle bloody champagne glasses in time,' he said, as it made the triumphant popping sound and bubbles erupted from the top. 'But I figured we're more "straight from the bottle" people anyway.'

'Damn right,' she chuckled, grabbing the vessel as he handed it to her and taking a massive swig. 'Holy shit, that's *so good*.'

She downed another huge sip, closing her eyes as she enjoyed the stars bubbling away in her mouth and the stars sparkling in the sky above her. Heath pulled her into his lap on the beanbag, the two trading the bottle between them in contented silence for a while.

'How did you know?' she finally asked, turning to him.

'How did I know when my fookin girlfriend's birthday was?'

'Yeah, but—'

'Because other people forgot in the past? I'm not other people.'

He wasn't being cute in leaving out Lorcan's name. It wasn't just him, but Joss and all her nearest and dearest who had managed to forget the past few years as life had gotten justifiably complicated. It couldn't have been more complicated right now, yet somehow Heath had not only remembered but managed to organise this intimate celebration for the two of them. Her fingernails combed through his facial hair as she stared down at him, watching as he took another hearty swig of champagne. They were two Scots after all; it wasn't going to take much for them to get through the bottle.

'Hey,' she whispered.

'Hey,' he replied.

'I love you, you know?'

'Aye, I know. But I also know you'd say that to anyone who baked you chocolate cake.'

She threw her head back, laughing. 'Wait, *you* baked this? Oh my God, fuck the champagne, I need to try it.'

Straining, she pulled the plate towards them and began eagerly cutting into it with the same knife Heath had used on the Dom Perignon. The inside was soft, gooey even, and she groaned as the crunch from the outside and the icing and the beautiful thought of it all came together in her mouth.

'No one told me you could bake as well,' she said, cutting another piece to feed him. 'That just seems like an additional skill you shouldn't be allowed to have.'

He looked smug as he ate the cake, licking the chocolate icing from her fingers in a way that would have made Aruhe dry gag if she'd been around.

'I haven't baked for a woman in nearly forty years,' he said.

'Who is she?' Tommi joked, holding up the knife. 'I'll kill her.'

He smiled, but there was sadness there. 'Someone already beat you to it, love. It was Collette Blight.'

'Oh,' she said, grin immediately dropping at the mention of the woman who had died at the hands of the same people as Barastin. 'I'm sorry.'

'Nothing to be sorry about,' he said, rubbing her back as she rested her head on his chest. 'It was a good joke otherwise.'

'Meh,' was her only response.

They stayed there, tightly entwined, bellies full of champagne and chocolate cake as they stared up at the cloudless night. This wasn't her home, but Tommi was starting to love it here. There was a knock against the metal of their caravan and a swift 'oy' shouted up to them. Tommi squeezed her eyes shut with frustration, not wanting this moment to be over. Yet it had to be.

'Be right down,' Heath shouted so Tommi didn't have to. She sat back up, tucking his hair behind his ears as she sighed at the thought of the coming meeting.

'*Tha gaol agam ort*,' he said, not for the first time. It meant I love you in his native language, Gaelic, and every time he said it she could feel that he meant it deep in his bones.

'*Aroha ahau ki a koe*,' she replied, her own *te reo* pronunciation still a work in progress but this sentence probably her strongest. Keisha had taught her, Tommi knowing she could never have safely asked Aruhe the Māori language way to say that without relentless mocking. He kissed her, and she him, before they broke apart again.

'Open your presents when you get back,' he said, helping her to the ladder.

'Ooooh, presents,' she beamed, skipping the ladder altogether as she launched herself from the caravan roof like the werewolf she was. Arms wide at first, she pulled them close and tight as she spun twice, fast, and landed in a perfect crouched position on the ground. 'Something to look forward to,' Tommi said, grinning up at him as he shook his head.

'Show off.'

By the time Heath joined her on the ground, there was another couple waiting for them: Casper and Kala. Tommi had felt like she was positively cheesing as she and Heath fell in step beside them, but the two women seemed to be emitting actual beams of light from the centre of their being. That might have sounded like an exaggeration, but that's how it felt as she glanced between the pair.

'What's going on with you two?' she asked, sensing something was up given they could have just met them at the strategy meeting like everyone else. They were walking hand in hand and looked like poster babes for lesbian mysticism if Tommi had ever seen it. She was particularly a fan of the witch, who she knew less well than Casper but had an immediate connection with in the same way she'd had with the tall medium when they first crossed paths years ago. Whether it was chemistry or vibe, she couldn't be certain, but there were just some people you clicked with instantly.

'I've got a favour to ask,' Casper started.

'*We've* got a favour to ask,' Kala corrected. 'And it's kind of a big one.'

'If you're looking for a third, the werewolf's otherwise occupied,' Heath said, earning a dirty laugh from the witch and an elbow from Tommi.

'No.' Casper blushed, pushing a strand of long hair over to one shoulder. 'We need both of you.'

'A third *and* a fourth?' Heath pushed. 'You dirty birds, I'm so proud.'

'Can you be less of a mess for two seconds?' Kala said, half laughing. 'We're trying to ask you something important!'

Heath came to a stop, gesturing wildly. 'Spit it out then!'

Casper and Kala exchanged looks, their hands interlinked as they stood before Tommi and Heath. Several beats passed before the medium eventually spoke up.

'We were hoping you'd be our best man,' she said to Heath, who was mercifully quiet for once. 'With an amendment noting that there really aren't that many options out in the desert.'

Kala giggled, before adding her own two cents. 'You've known Casper since she was a child and Barry since he was, well, alive. And you were there right at the beginning of our relationship, as annoying as that was. You fought by our sides when we were fuelled by hate. Now, fuelled by love, we'd like you to be there again.'

Tommi was shocked, but not as shocked as Heath, who was speechless for once as she pivoted to stare up at him.

'I-I . . . I'd be honoured,' Heath stammered, looking like he truly meant it.

'Ugh, don't be over the top about it,' Casper deadpanned.

'Tommi?' Kala asked.

'Yeah?'

'If you're not otherwise occupied, we've got another spot we need to fill. Will you be our best la—'

'OHMYGODYESOFCOURSE!' she screamed, practically pouncing as she embraced the two women. 'OF COURSE I WILL!'

Casper and Kala laughed alongside her, Tommi overcome with emotion as she bounced from hugging the medium to the witch with just as much enthusiasm. It was joy, she realised, this intoxicating feeling spreading slowly through her limbs like molasses. It was weird, because she hadn't felt it this purely in so long. Yet as their foursome basked in the imminent celebration of love in a little pocket of desert, she knew that's what it was. Maybe it had something to do with rain after years of drought or the calm before a storm, but that moment of *joy* among all the foreboding terror and fear and risk felt all the more special. And she cherished every second of it, even if it was just that: seconds.

Chapter 7

Dreckly

'Wake up, swimming beauty.'

Dreckly smiled as she watched the twitching face of her friend Amos. She splashed water on him and he stirred in the back seat of the jeep where he'd been sleeping, his long body taking up more of the space than she thought possible.

'I told you, it was a hard swim,' Aruhe said as she sat on the hood of the vehicle, downing a bag of chips. 'He is *out*.'

'He was imprisoned for a long time.' Dreckly frowned. 'He's still building up his fitness but . . .'

'What?'

Dreckly looked at the girl, whose face mirrored the relatives she knew better, whose voice reminded her of her father Jonah Ihi, now dead, and whose demeanour was a reflection of her mother, Tiaki Ihi, now guarding an entire country with a dozen or so werewolf packs at her back.

'But he's always pushing himself too hard,' she said, answering the young werewolf's question.

Aruhe smirked. 'Uh, now that I can relate to.'

'Thought you might.'

'Stop talking about me,' a voice groaned, Dreckly and Aruhe leaning into the vehicle's open window to greet the person it belonged to.

'Fishman!' Aruhe beamed.

'Hello, friend.' Dreckly smiled. Amos reached out, squeezing her fingers as they dangled over the door. 'Ready to join the living?'

'If I have to,' he murmured, slowly climbing out of the back of the car and accepting Dreckly's assistance. She stared down at him, impressed at the legs contained within a pair of loose, muslin pants that screamed of Avary's own personal aesthetic. He had come so far from the first time she'd seen him shift and utilise one of the many gifts of his people, selkies being some of the truest shape shifters there were. She embraced Amos, his hair longer at the back than the last time she'd seen him at the entrance to the cave system that ran under the Nullarbor Plain. Dreckly inhaled deeply, breathing in the salt on his skin so that it felt like the ocean ran through her veins once more.

'How was it?' she asked, leaning back and examining his face. He did look tired, yet she had a feast of seafood prepped and ready for his imminent arrival that would help ease a little of that fatigue.

'Wonderful,' he replied, sighing wistfully. 'I'd never been that far, never been that close to Antarctica really. It gets cold, but the other selkies knew the route and it was just . . . so *wonderful*.'

She smiled, the gesture feeling like it lifted up her whole body. Amos had volunteered for the mission to retrieve Aruhe from New Zealand, Sorcha and Atlanta meeting them at a rendezvous point. The other selkies – Avary included – had been cautious because he'd never done a swim that large before, but Dreckly was one of his biggest champions. She encouraged him and pushed for him to be included on the team, knowing that it would test the limits of his rapidly evolving abilities. It was necessary, however. If he couldn't make it and couldn't keep up, they needed to know that now. Given what was coming, there would be no capacity for coddling.

'Here,' she said, handing him a burner phone that would need to be tossed as soon as he had finished using it. 'Call Kaia as we walk, the meeting's at the main house.'

He took the device like she'd given him Holy communion and she threw him a wink, knowing how much it meant for him to be able to speak to the woman he loved, even if it was just for five minutes. Every second of that was invaluable and she knew it. Amos knew it. What wouldn't she give just to hear the voices of those she'd loved and lost? That was an impossibility for her, so instead she could give that possibility to someone else. She politely ignored the parts of the conversation she heard as Amos fell behind and she led Aruhe towards their destination.

'When Tommi said there was a rebel hideout in the desert, I thought she'd been watching too much *Star Wars* again,' the werewolf said, eyes scanning the spread of structures they navigated their way through.

'This is nothing,' Dreckly replied. 'You should have seen it when we first got here. The Nullarbor coven are always in this general vicinity, but there were nearly fifty caravans full of people from all over.'

'Banshees?'

'Lotta banshees, yes. Sorcha's older sister, Shannon. I think your mum and Shazza have their hands full smuggling as many banshees out of the country as they can, but there were still some. Oh, and arachnia.'

'Shut up!'

'Yeah, just two. I think they're on the fence about whether to join the coup or not, but I was still surprised to see them.'

'You don't think they'll snitch?' the werewolf asked.

Dreckly shook her head. 'No. I've been around a lot of them in my time and they're not narcs. Sit back, observe, and opt out entirely? Much more likely. They keep to themselves.'

'Sure, whatever. Just feel like some giant fucking spider people would help throw things in our favour, but what do I know?'

Dreckly smirked; she hadn't seen any physical similarities between Aruhe and Tommi at first. Now she recognised the spirit the two sisters shared. Turning around the last caravan, they appeared in front of one of the few permanent structures: a weathered but beautiful Old Queenslander. The house had a balcony that wrapped around the entire building like a wooden moat. It was now occupied with witches and other beings conferring in rocking chairs and comfy outdoor furniture sets.

Dreckly waved to them and they murmured replies as she headed up the main staircase of the property. She heard Amos say his farewells behind her and rush to catch up as they weaved through the interior of the house, coming to a stop in what would have been a massive dining room if this was a normal scenario. The 'normal' word didn't apply here, however, and instead the space had been turned into one of several war rooms. Yolindi, Fairuza, Shazza and Kala had their own base of operations one room over where they'd planned the upcoming Australian defence and offence, while this one had inadvertently become spearheaded by Dreckly.

Given how hard Ben and Shazza had pushed her to step up and join their stupid movement when she was determined to keep her head down and stay living on her boat, she thought they must be positively delirious about how deeply she was *in it* now. Aruhe immediately split off to join the werewolves where Ben was laughing heartily at a comment from Heath. Tommi was wedged between Casper and Kala, the trio chatting excitedly about *something* that she suspected had nothing to do with the upcoming Vankila bust because of how happy they looked. Yolindi wouldn't be participating but she was there, observing as she sucked on the tip of an antique pipe and sat with Mildred. Amos lingered tightly by her side as he surveyed the room. The second Barastin materialised from wherever in the world his ghostly form had been moseying, it meant there was no time to waste.

'All right,' she said, drawing all the eyes in the space towards her. 'Thank you to those who have joined us, we can't tell you how much we appreciate it and how invaluable you are. I guess the best way for us to get started is to revise the plan as it stands and make sure everyone is up to speed.'

It was a simple process first, those fresh off the metaphorical boat listening intently as they drank and ate their way through the next stages of planning. What was tricky, of course, was the layout of Vankila.

'Usually it would just be a matter of me ducking in, having a poke about,' Barastin explained. 'Yet the alchemists they have on site have protections in place to make sure it's impossible for outside ghosts to enter the perimeter of Vankila in any capacity.'

'We're blind?' Dreckly asked, not liking that thought one bit.

'Not exactly,' the ghost's sister Casper countered, nodding at her partner.

'Alchemy is a mix of science and magic, right?' the witch Kala Tully began. 'So in order to understand and – in our case – break it apart, we just need to know the properties. Thanks to Tommi's man on the inside, we've been able to get a copy of the ritual used to put up those protections. It's all about finding a loophole. Now we can't break what they've put in place, it's too strong, but we can circumnavigate it.'

'The protections block ghosts from the *outside*,' Casper continued. 'That is to say, ghosts like Barastin who didn't die on the property and have no connection to it. Thankfully, there are a lot of people who have died at Vankila, a few of them mad and angry and not quite ready to make peace with it all.'

Dreckly sat up from where she had been slouched on the couch, intrigued as she turned to face Barastin. 'They're stuck there?'

'In a way, yes, and I'm trying to find more as quickly as I can,' he said. 'They can move around freely and unseen in Vankila and relay information back to us about who's in what cell and where.'

Casper got to her feet, rolling out a sheet of butcher's paper where she had begun making a crude diagram of Vankila with annotated notes about who was on what floor and the security measures in place.

'It's important to note these ghosts aren't strong enough to be physically seen by the occupants of Vankila,' the medium began.

'Well, how's that gonna help us?' Aruhe questioned. 'They need to know we're coming, they need to be ready.'

'Quiet, pup,' Mildred cautioned. 'They know. The demons have taken care of it. The prisoners will be ready.'

Aruhe looked like she was about to rebut that verbal chastising when Dreckly noticed a subtle but stern headshake from Tommi across the room. She was grateful for it. They had to let old histories and species conflicts go, it would get them nowhere.

'So how do the ghosts help us if no one can see or communicate with them?' Dreckly asked, voicing a question that was clearly on the minds of several in the room who nodded in agreement. 'Casper, you're leading the European front so you won't even be there and Barastin can't get inside.'

'But I'll be inside.' Tommi spoke up. 'And I can see the ghosts.'

She tapped at her greying eye for emphasis, Casper smiling smugly behind her like they had both just cracked the Enigma Code.

'Over the past few weeks,' the medium began, 'I've been getting Tommi acquainted with a very useful dead Vankila prisoner that I was able to find.'

'How have you been doing this exactly?' Aruhe asked her sister.

'When I fall asleep at night, Casper – uh, how would you say it? – Freddy Krueger's me to the lobby where we can all safely communicate and practise the run without being observed.'

The younger werewolf shook her head, looking worried. 'Tommi, you need to be careful about how much time you're spending in that world. You're not meant to be there; the lines between the two will just get blurrier and blurrier.'

It looked like Aruhe had voiced a concern Heath had raised, if Dreckly was reading the situation correctly.

'Firstly,' Tommi said, counting off points on her hand, 'look at my fucking face. Those lines are well and truly mush, dear sister. Secondly, how much more careful can I get with the world's most powerful mediums as my guides? Thirdly, what other choice do I have? If you have a better suggestion, there's a room full of ears desperate to hear it.'

All they heard instead was silence. Dreckly didn't miss the discreet high five Barastin gave Tommi – down low and behind her back – as their shared point was made.

'Okay.' Dreckly nodded. 'Inside as a prisoner, Tommi will have the guidance of the ghost. They will take her to the cells of Yixin and those most vital, whom she will release using the charms pre-made by Kala. Once freed, they in turn will release others and create a domino effect as they work their way up.'

It was a copy of her father's plan for a reason: it had been extremely successful. Unfortunately there were no earth elementals currently imprisoned at Vankila, perhaps the guards had learned their lesson, so they didn't have the added environmental assist there. Kala had assured Dreckly that the spells she would have Tommi smuggle in would be sufficient and she had to trust that the witch knew what she was talking about. There had been a suggestion from Ben initially to 'do it like the Sydney job' and flood the prison, given that it too wasn't very far from a massive body of water, the River Tay. Yet that plan had been tossed, because Vankila was much too deep and it was unlikely they would be able to save anyone.

Instead, they'd be dooming potentially hundreds to a watery death.

'As the breakout gets more momentum,' Barastin was saying, 'some ghosts will get stronger. They'll become seen and, in some cases, we hope able to physically manifest.'

'They can release others?' Ben asked.

'No,' Casper countered. 'They've been waiting decades, centuries for some of them. They'll be consumed with vengeance, that's why they're still there. They'll go after the guards, which is just as useful.'

Dreckly nodded. She couldn't agree more. The guards posed a bigger threat and while they were equipped to deal with physical prisoners, they wouldn't know what to do with dead ones. It was the ace card they needed.

'Good, all right, so Tommi will be working upwards,' Dreckly repeated. 'I'll be working from the top down. Sorcha will be monitoring and assisting with what she can. Everyone meets in the middle and . . . fucking hopes for the best?'

Heath spoke up, the old warrior's presence commanding a level of respect that was unparalleled in the room.

'I've been thinking about that,' he mused, 'and I think we need another body on the inside, a back-up to the back-up.'

'Couldn't hurt,' Dreckly agreed. 'But who?'

'Ben,' Heath replied.

She said 'no' immediately while Ben answered with an enthusiastic 'fuck yeah'. She flashed him an angry look and he stared back at her defiantly.

'Let's play this out,' Heath said, holding up his hands like he was mediating a lovers' quarrel. 'Tommi needs to get caught and dragged into Vankila.'

'Can't wait for that part,' she grumbled.

He smiled. 'Our plan to make that happen relies on her getting pipped in Dundee. Now, for that to be believable you have to present as reckless. You don't want to be caught, but you're just so damn *Tommi* you can't help . . . what?'

'Partying,' the werewolf suggested. 'Fucking around, trying to hold on to the threads of my old life. I have to lean into not just things they know about me, but bait that Lorcan will take. I'll need to tweak my appearance, actually make it look like I was trying to hide, yet I'm still unable to stop myself when it comes to giving in to my base instincts and impulses.'

'You've gotta play into the werewolf stereotype.' Ben nodded, picking up what she was putting down. 'We're the dumb blondes of the supernatural world. That's how they view us.'

Tommi laughed. 'Now I'm gonna have to dye my hair blonde, aren't I?'

'You should be there,' Heath said, pointing at Ben. 'The two of you, together and in shitty disguises, partying and going hard on all the worst things they think about your kind.'

Dreckly wanted to audibly groan, knowing this idea would never leave Ben's head now that Heath had put it there. He'd volunteered for this mission, knowing how much he'd be at risk, because he wanted to break his sister out. Becoming an integral part of it would be a dream come true for him.

'Think how great it would look on paper,' Heath continued. 'Two descendants of the Kapoor and Ihi packs, who worked together in the Outskirt Wars. It would make *so much* sense to them and they wouldn't be able to resist that lure.'

'Or the source of the tip,' Tommi added.

'That would put someone in the middle,' Mildred mused. 'They'd take Tommi to maximum security first. Ben, you're a pack leader and they know you were involved in Sydney. They'd want to interrogate you. That all happens at medium security, level three, above the labs.'

Dreckly stood up, extremely frustrated and needing to voice it. 'I don't like the idea of Ben just being tortured – because that's what the interrogation will be – until we can all get in and get the breakout happening. That's an hour, maybe two.'

'And I don't like the idea of Tommi making herself human bait,' Heath countered. 'I'd gladly do it in her place if I thought it could work, but that's not my choice to make.'

Kala nodded. 'You think I want Casper trying to bust open supernatural prisons and labs in the Treize's backyard while I'm on a different continent? Not a chance, yet we can't let our personal lives impact this right now.'

There was a tug on her hand and she looked down to see Amos, staring up at her from the remains of a plate of seafood that he had absolutely demolished as they'd been talking.

'Kaia, Cabby and Storm are all helping to take down the Gold Coast lab with Shazza,' he said. 'She's just a human, they all are, and I couldn't be more terrified for them.'

'We're all putting things on the line,' Ben said, speaking up. 'I had no say when it came to you sticking your neck out to get back in to a place that traumatised you. I'm sorry, but you have no say in me doing this, *especially* when I'm the best person for the job.'

She held his gaze, so mad and so angry and so desperate to chew him out. The worst part was that she knew he was right. Staring up at the ceiling with annoyance because she couldn't look at the faces of those around her any more, Dreckly let out a deep exhale.

'Fuck, I hate this,' she huffed.

'Sweetheart,' Mildred said, getting to her feet and standing by her side, 'if we do this properly, the dream is no one else will have to make the sacrifices we're all making right now.'

Nodding, she locked eyes with the demon she trusted more than most other beings on this planet. She agreed without needing to say she did, it was obvious to everyone around her. Instead, they worked through the ground team specifics, with Heath and Mildred leading that assault with the local supernaturals who had volunteered. The escape team was being headed by Aruhe and Amos, the approach two prong so they had a plan A via land and a plan B via sea. Dreckly, of course, wouldn't be going in alone. Solo operators tended to stand out and she was being joined by someone she had once sold fake identity documents to: Sorcha Burke. The banshee's subtle ability to manipulate those around her with movement and speech would help them navigate their external entry point. When they finished going through everything for a fourth time, Dreckly felt content with their progress. Not over the moon about it – there were still too many holes – but it was the best they could possibly do for now.

There was something else they needed to talk about in depth. She understood why nobody had broached the subject because their hesitancy was hers too. It required each of them to allow something they didn't want to risk entertaining just yet: hope.

'We need to start thinking about what happens after,' Dreckly said, jumping in once there was a significant pause.

'What . . . what do you mean?' Aruhe asked. The question on her face was so pure, so innocent, Dreckly felt envious for a moment.

'We need to ask ourselves what happens if we don't all die? What happens if we're actually . . . successful?'

Tommi made something like a hissing sounding, sucking air between her teeth like she didn't even want to *hear* that word.

'Let's not jinx it,' the werewolf said, waving her hand in the air like it was on fire and she was trying to put it out. 'Let's not even risk saying it and jinxing it.'

'Burying our heads in the sand is not going to make the issue go away,' Dreckly snapped. 'We keep talking about this, planning this, like it only impacts us. We're trying to change our world, but no one is acknowledging that it will change theirs too.'

'Fuck the humans,' Ben spat.

Tommi snorted. 'Okay, so you're off the envoy list.'

'This isn't funny,' Dreckly nearly yelled. 'We've all had humans in our lives: good people who have meant something to us individually and to the world as a whole.'

She stared around at the group, right into their eyes, as she urged everyone non-verbally to think of those people. Lord knows, Dreckly had them. Not just Harvey Schwartz, but Meili and Li Jun and the whole Han family, Wyck and the Ravens M.C. Ben had lashed out and she understood why: all these years of terror and fear and sacrifice in their world while the humans got to go on, unbothered. They had problems too, wars and diseases, but comparatively they didn't suffer like *we* had suffered. Yet for all the big game he spoke just now in a room full of people who were about to put their lives on the line, many of whom wouldn't survive, she knew that wasn't how he really felt.

Ben Kapoor had humans he cared about too, just like she did. Just like they all did. With the exception of Wyck, he was better friends with most members of the Ravens M.C. and had known them just as long. Amongst all the tattoos and the piercings and the boldness and the bluster, there was a sweetness to him as well. That was one of the things she found so attractive about him, those conflicting elements, and she saw them struggling to the surface now as he rubbed his face with frustration.

'Fuck,' he sighed, 'you're right. I didn't . . . What are we going to do? How the hell are we supposed to handle this with everything else going on?'

Dreckly smiled at him. 'We handle it like a film set, right, Mildred?'

She didn't even need to glance at the demon to know her mind was already whirring.

'Right,' Mildred agreed. 'We delegate. We can't do it, we're too busy, we find a team of *smart* people who can come up with a strategy for—'

'Instantaneously exposing the world to the fact monsters exist?' Tommi scoffed. 'In a matter of *nine days*? Even Olivia Pope could never.'

'They know,' Heath murmured. 'They have always known we've been here, even if some have chosen to forget.'

'Cool, let's just use that for our branding then,' Tommi pressed. 'We've been here all along, sorry y'all forgot!'

Heath grinned manically and one shared glance between Mildred and her told Dreckly they were thinking the same thing. If it was left to these two, that really would be the motto of their revolution.

'Nine days is very tight,' Mildred mused. 'I don't know what good assigning people to this now, stretching ourselves even thinner, will do. And I'm not sure that it's wise to make our circle any wider.'

Dreckly didn't disagree, yet there weren't any easy solutions to this one. 'So we just keep chugging, hope we make it through this battle and the next and the next and then come up with a solution once the dust has settled?'

'Basically.' Ben shrugged. 'At most I think all we can do is come up with a list of names who would be perfect to present a public face to the humans and liaise for the rest of us. And one name that should be on top of that list is Dreckly Jones.'

She had chosen that precise moment to take a sip of water, which was promptly spat through the air and on to Mildred.

'Sorry,' she murmured, wiping the woman down as gently as she could. 'I'm so sorry, but also – fucking what?'

'You're perfect,' Ben said, getting to his feet and going over to her. There was more than just that surface meaning to her as his fingers brushed against Dreckly's and it felt extremely private . . . albeit in a room full of people.

'How exactly am I perfect for it?' she questioned, wishing this conversation was in a different setting.

'For starters, you don't have horns,' he smirked. 'You're beautiful and you look harmless, that's what they'll see. And you look like the rest of the world. Can't have no delicate blonde flower rolling up to represent us like they would.'

Dreckly grinned in earnest at his description.

'I'm not joking,' Ben said, reading her amusement.

'He's right,' Mildred agreed. 'We need to pick human-facing supernaturals. We need to pick diverse faces that can appeal to a majority of the human world. And, importantly, we need to pick young: people who are going to be around for a while so the human population can get used to dealing with them in the same way they would a politician or a celebrity.' As a sprite, Dreckly could understand why she was a smart choice: on paper she was forty-four so that would add some weight to any kind of youthful ensemble. Yet her actual age was much older, throwing on an additional hundred years to that so she aged slowly. She had seen a lot of humankind and done her best to blend among them. To a degree, she could understand them.

'Fine,' she began. 'If I survive, I'll be your public face. But we'll need someone visibly old too: someone sweet and disarming and just like the neighbour you wave to across the street every day.'

'What about Casper and Tommi?' Amos offered, earning a hearty chuckle from both of them.

'I'm not sweet or disarming,' Tommi began. 'Look at my body: it's covered in scars. Plus, the eye thing. I look a little too close to the reality of what and who we are. I look battle worn and also, I don't have . . . restraint, shall we say? If someone asks me a question in a press conference that pisses me off, they're gonna know about it.'

'Tommi is a very bad idea,' Heath agreed. 'And Casper is even worse. She'll look too weird to them, no disrespect.'

'None taken.' Casper smiled. 'Tommi looks battle worn because she is and I look like I can speak to the dead because I can. You should consider one of the Burke sisters.'

'Why?' Sorcha questioned. 'Because we're white?'

'Yes,' Casper replied. 'And soft and exactly like the kind of girl you would grow up alongside. My other choice would be Aruhe.'

'Uh uh, no way,' the younger werewolf cautioned. 'If Tommi's too rough then—'

'You're not me,' Tommi countered. 'And I mean that in the best possible way. If people started digging into my past, I have bodies on me. More than a few. You can't have a spokesperson who has committed murder en masse. You have cultural ties and prominent family ones. I think Aruhe is a great choice, Casper.'

The medium and Tommi exchanged nods of agreement, as if that settled it.

'This is all only theoretical,' Dreckly said. 'If we die, it's moot but it's worth considering. It's important to start thinking about those names now, as big of a list as you can entertain. And if we make it through this, then we have to hope there's people left willing to take those places.'

It was a harsh sentiment to wrap on, Dreckly realised that. Yet the pressure of what was coming could suck the oxygen out of the room and she needed to at least raise the idea that maybe, just *maybe*, they might all be able to breathe again one day.

'On that depressing note,' Barastin laughed, 'I should be off, ghosts to wrangle and spirits to negotiate with.'

'Wait,' Casper said, grasping the hand of the witch next to her. 'I need you to stay for just a second longer. I need everyone to stay, actually. Only a quick yes or no is needed to see who can make it.'

'Make it where? To what?' Dreckly asked. She glanced at a few of the faces nearby and no one seemed to have any clue what was going on. Except for Tommi and Heath, she noted.

'If everyone's free tomorrow night, we're hoping you can come to Kala's and my wedding,' the medium said. If her ghost brother could have died again, Dreckly thought he might very well manage it.

Chapter 8

Casper

They'd been lying in bed when it happened, Kala's head resting above Casper's left breast as she ran her fingers down the witch's back absentmindedly. They were both deep in their own thoughts, neither having slept well since they'd come to the decision that Casper would take charge in Europe. She and the witch knew it was the right thing to do, knew it deep in their bones, yet it terrified them both in equal measure. It would be the first time they'd been properly apart since they got together, when Casper had left behind her life in Berlin and shown up at Kala's door.

She'd never looked back, the two of them just clicking together so perfectly it was funny to think about how hard they'd tried to fight it initially. They fit, like two halves of a whole and all that other clichéd nonsense the poets wrote about. Casper wasn't a poet. She'd met a few good dead ones, though, but that was about it. When Kala lifted her head, a serious question in her eyes, Casper wondered what the witch was about to say. She could rarely predict it.

'Hey,' Kala said, voice low and seductive, 'I've got an idea.'

'What's that?' Casper smiled, lifting a braid away from her girlfriend's face.

'How about you marry me?'

Her hand had been reaching out when she paused. Froze, in fact. She would've thought Kala was joking except she didn't have that playful glint in her eye. There was warmth there still, from the sex they'd just had, and love. Deep, powerful, magical love that told Casper this beautiful woman she'd somehow conned into caring about her was for real. Still, she had to be sure.

'Are you serious?'

'Deadly serious,' Kala said, flipping over so that she was propped on her elbows and nose to nose with Casper. 'I love you. You love me. We've put our lives on the line for it before and we've survived to create this family with you, me, Sprinkle and Barry.'

'I don't disagree,' Casper replied. 'I just . . . I'll be honest with you, I've never thought about it.'

'You never thought about marriage?'

'No,' she laughed. 'I don't even know a real-life person who's married, Kala. It just seems so human.'

'Then be human with me,' the witch urged, sitting up so that her posture was perfect and her legs were crossed neatly in front of her. She was a woman who wore a lot of rings, but as Casper watched her pull one from her finger she gasped. It had an opal at the centre of it, a stone that was mined from the same earth here in Australia that was so important to Kala. It also held extra significance to Casper, Opal being the name Kala had first used when they met each other. She took Casper's only hand, her bionic arm currently charging via a

USB port beside the bed so her limb difference was on full display.

'Corvossier von Klitzing,' she asked, 'will you marry me?'

She blinked, needing a moment to comprehend the situation, even though she knew what the answer was.

'Kala, how can I say no when you're sitting there, staring at me with that perfect set of tits?'

The witch laughed, the nerves Casper had sensed dissipating with the comment just as she'd intended. She sat up, pulling the woman to her and kissing the answer into her with the movement of her lips. The witch was breathless as Casper pulled back, their noses brushing against each other as she stayed dangerously close.

'Yes,' she whispered. 'Of course I'll marry you.'

Kala pushed her backwards, giggling with delight as she slid the ring on to Casper's finger. It sparkled there, stunning and unique. Just like the pair of them. When they'd told Sprinkle the next day, the high-pitched shriek of delight would have put a banshee to shame as the kid practically levitated on the spot.

'My second big wedding!' she beamed, clasping her hands together like a minute event planner.

'Second?' Casper asked, leaning over to Kala once the kid was distracted with 'arrangements'.

'She was in Willa's belly when she and Alistair got married,' the witch replied, speaking of her dead twin sister and brother-in-law.

'Scandalous,' Casper winked, earning a chuckle from Kala. Their wedding would be anything but. For the most part, it would be in secret given there was a murderous supernatural government who would have loved to crash the ceremony. Yet it wouldn't have mattered if it was in a Vegas chapel or an Italian cliff side, to Casper all that was important was the person. So there she was, trawling an op shop in a small, West Australian country town with Tommi Grayson and Dreckly Jones as she desperately looked for something to wear to her own wedding. That night.

'What about this?' the sprite suggested, holding up a hideous number.

'Personally, never been a fan of mustard taffeta,' Casper murmured. 'I'm weird like that.'

Tommi snorted a laugh as she passed the both of them, the werewolf having torn through the enormous warehouse of pre-loved clothing like a tornado with intent. She had six or so items already hung up in a change room for Casper, none of which she'd been allowed to see and all of which she'd been told to 'just trust my judgement on this one'. Kala, on the other hand, had been ordered away for the day by Barastin while everyone else 'prepared' for that evening.

Kala and she had only discussed their engagement briefly with Tommi and Heath, yet on the night of their technical meeting it had become clear those gathered needed joy. They needed a distraction. Breaking the news to the room had been Kala's idea, and she'd been right as usual. Everyone was desperate to think about something other than what each of their improbable missions were. Heath was on ring duty, that's all she'd been told. Aruhe and Ben were apparently the best cooks of the bunch so were all over the cuisine and refreshments for the evening. Yolindi and the Nullarbor coven had insisted on handling the music, while Mildred was working with the militant devotion of Sprinkle on decorations. The only task Casper and Kala had to concern themselves with was finding something to wear, with her wife-to-be deciding to 'whip something up' because apparently that was an additional talent she had.

Casper, on the other hand, was thrift shopping. Tommi had offered her services for hair and make-up, while Dreckly had been up early in the morning – or maybe she'd never been to bed to begin with – working on the florals. She'd joined them for the thrift shopping sojourn because she needed the break, and although Casper didn't know the sprite all that well, they were all deeply and madly embedded now. She was gently but forcefully dragged away from the racks of clothes to the change room by Tommi, who seemed relatively confident in her ability to find something Casper would like more than mustard taffeta.

'Now there's no one else in here,' the wolf was saying. 'It's just us, so I put a dress in every change room. Stick your head in, take a look without any other frock to cloud your judgement, then jump back out. If it doesn't grab you instantly then it's not worth trying on.'

'Tommi, I don't know if we can be that pic—'

'I used to work in an art gallery, remember? I have an eye besides the ghost one.'

Casper was just about to make a snappy remark when she was shoved into the first change room, the curtain drawn behind her as Tommi and Dreckly retreated. She couldn't remember what she had been about to say, because the gown before her took the words right out of her mouth.

'It's stunning,' she whispered, mostly to herself. It was old, certainly, but as her hand ran over the silver fabric she couldn't find a single other fault with it.

'You said no white,' Tommi called from behind the curtain. 'And it's really more metallic grey than silver if I want to get nit-picky about it. I thought it would look beautiful against your skin.'

Casper had said no white because she was white, both her hair and complexion close to pearl. Usually she stuck to darker jewel tones, but your wedding wasn't a usual occasion and this was ... *perfect*. There was no other word for it. Five minutes later, she had Tommi zip her up at the back as the delicate lace covering kept getting caught in the zipper. Stepping out of the change room, she did a slow spin for the sprite to digest the full effect.

'I'm desperate to know what six-foot-three supermodel donated this to charity,' Dreckly smirked.

'Right?' Casper laughed. It was ethereal and just a little bit sinister, like her, with the shimmering fabric falling down her body like a spiderweb as she stared at it.

The sprite spun around, eyes narrowed as they all examined Casper's reflection in the mirror.

'It needs something ...'

While Tommi had been gathering gowns, Dreckly had been gathering accessories and her hands skimmed over a series of costume jewellery pieces that she had assembled. She settled on what was less of a tiara and more like a cosplay crown, woven from wire and silver beads into elaborate shapes. She wasn't much taller than Tommi and she'd never reach the top of Casper's head, but she didn't need to. They really were the only people there and with a subtle motion of her hands, she gently floated the jewellery on to the top of Casper's head.

'It's stunning,' Casper said again.

'I don't disagree,' Dreckly murmured. 'Mildred would insist on a strong lip to make everything pop.'

'Keep in mind where that lipstick is gonna end up when deciding on strength,' Tommi countered. 'And are you sure you don't wanna try anything else on?'

'I don't even want to look at the others,' Casper remarked, watching the way the long sleeves draped around and over her wrists. That used to be the way she preferred it, when she was trying to hide her limb difference from view. Yet that wasn't who she'd been for a long time now. 'I'll lose the sleeves, cut them shorter so my arms are bare.'

'That will make it easier to do the Macarena,' Tommi nodded, solemn.

'What are you going to wear?' Dreckly asked her. 'And Heath?'

The werewolf smirked. 'He's not as opposed to mustard taffeta as Casper here is.'

'Kala is making her and Sprinkle's outfits so I don't care.' She shrugged. 'Whatever you and Heath would prefer, honestly. If you find him a suit we can make it a double wedding.'

'Bleurgh.' Tommi gagged, sticking out her tongue. 'What are we, the Bennet sisters? No fucking way. I'll find something; you two stay put.'

The werewolf reset her tornadic trajectory for the other side of the warehouse while Casper examined her reflection once again.

'It really is beautiful,' Dreckly whispered. Casper couldn't agree more.

* * *

The wedding was to take place at midnight, which may have seemed weird for a civilian celebration, but this was a supernatural festivity. Nothing about this would be by the numbers and Casper could tell that as Tommi affixed the last strand of her hair into an elaborate braid she'd recruited Aruhe to help her with. The crown was in place, with a few tweaks so it was slightly less gaudy, and Casper nearly gasped as she glanced at her finished face in the mirror.

She was never someone who wore a whole lot of make-up and the werewolf had respected that, adding little more than a light dusting of foundation, brow powder, a slight hint of blush and a few quick strokes of mascara. In fact, it was her eyes that really drew focus with a silver shimmer that matched her dress starting at the corner of her inner eye and moving to a darker, smokier shade on her outer eye. Casper had decided against anything more than a light lip gloss, so Tommi had been given freedom with the eyeshadow situation.

'If I was paying you, I'd give you a tip right about now,' Casper said.

Resting a chin on her shoulder, the werewolf beamed. 'Give me an extra slice of the wedding cake and we'll call it even.'

'Deal.'

'Anyway, I should leave you to it. There's someone else who wants to see you before you step out there.'

Tommi planted a swift kiss on Casper's cheek, her red lipstick somehow not leaving a single mark.

'The magic of matte, baby!' the werewolf exclaimed, before leaving her in the trailer all alone. Not for long, mind you. She could feel Barastin's presence lurking nearby and sure enough, he flashed inside to join her.

'Galadriel eat ya damn heart out,' her brother grinned, taking in the full sight of her as she stood up.

'Lord of the Wedding Rings?' Casper offered, the question in her voice confirming her weak attempt.

It was testament to how emotional Barastin was feeling that he didn't even tease her. Instead, he looked like he was about to cry, which made Casper want to cry, which would ruin her make-up.

'Don't you dare,' she sniffed, dabbing her eyes. 'Tommi will kill me.'

'And I'll kill Tommi if she didn't use a proper setting spray,' he scoffed. 'It's a vicious cycle, babe.'

She pulled him towards her, utilising the power they held over each other as she physically hugged him. Casper had never imagined this day, yet as they grasped to each other and two plains simultaneously, she realised she could have never envisioned it without him. They had been born together, they had lived together, and they had nearly died together. It was vital to her being that Barastin von Klitzing was there with her that night. Separating from each other, it was clear he felt the same way.

'Look,' he started, 'this isn't the big ol' gay wedding I would have planned for myself, but I'm so happy for you, dear sister. I'm so happy for Kala, who gets to keep you always. And for Sprinkle, who'll get you as a mum, which is a thousand times better than we ever had.'

'Don't you dare say any of that during the ceremony,' Casper warned. 'Or I'll lose it, you know I will.'

His ghostly hand ran down her cheek, Casper feeling the charge there as energy flowed between their otherworldly bond.

'Just remember,' he whispered, 'your first wedding is only your starter marriage.'

She laughed, needing the relief of tension it offered her.

'And if you split, she takes all the living friends and you keep all the dead ones, all right? Now come on, we can't keep everyone waiting.'

There wasn't an aisle per se, yet Barastin led her from the trailer like life was his own personal aisle as they headed towards the festivities. She could hear music playing, not lyrical at first but deep and thrumming as she caught sight of the Nullarbor coven. Casper had no musical ability so she was only able to recognise the most basic of instruments like two acoustic guitars and what she thought were a form of wind chimes at first. There was a man playing a didgeridoo, the bass sound mixing with the more angelic chorus of the witches in a way that shouldn't have worked on paper but sounded perfect to her ears. Yolindi smiled at Casper as she came into view, opening her mouth and adding a majestic human voice to the proceedings. She didn't know the song they were singing, but she would remember it for the rest of her life as she turned the corner and her eyes settled on the breathtaking scene in front of her.

The rustic, wooden furniture from the house had been brought outside and used as seating for the fifty odd people gathered. Beautifully arranged bundles of eucalyptus leaves had been hung on the back of every chair, with small glass jars of native plants marking the entrance to each row as she passed. Sprinkle was up ahead, wearing a crown made with the same flora that was decorating so much of the setting and which adorned Kala's body in the tattoos she had inked along her skin. The witch had taught her the difference and because of that she was able to identify the red banksias, wattle, kangaroo paw and bottlebrushes all woven on top of the little girl's head as she tossed more flowers from a basket. There were eucalyptus leaves too, mixed with dried flowers, and the smell was intoxicating.

The whole scene looked like an indoor barn that had been turned outdoors somehow, with the guests standing and smiling as she moved past them. Tommi and Heath waited for her at the end of the aisle and she laughed when she saw what they were wearing, unable to help it. She had said tuxedos would be ideal but likely impossible. Tommi had gotten close, with both wearing T-shirts that had a cartoon tuxedo drawn on them complete with black and white bow-ties and ruffles all illustrated on to the fabric. The classic novelty shirts had been given a bit of spin, however, with real red flowers – bottlebrushes, of course – pinned on the outside so they matched perfectly. Heath's hair had been pulled back in a tight braid and his beard looked more manicured and sculpted than usual as he beamed down at her. Tommi's own long, dark hair was curled and running down her back. There were even numbers for both brides, three on Kala's side, and Tommi and Heath were both positioned on Casper's side with . . .

She stopped dead in her tracks as she stared at the woman there. The figure alone immediately ignited feelings of comfort and love and *home* in her before she even met the eyes of Collette Blight. She and Barastin had never known their parents, with the Treize's appointed Custodian becoming all that and more for them when she first came into their lives as children. She had protected them and pushed them in equal measure, with the warmth of her personality drawing all those around them to her. That's how she and Heath had met, the immortal soldier being a former long-time flame of Collette's, who she had maintained a friendship with as she moved into her fifties. When she had been murdered on the same night as Barastin, it had left a hole in Casper's life that she knew would never be filled. It had become one she had grown used to living with. She felt tears stinging her eyes as the ghost of the short, portly, neon-haired woman smiled back at her. Casper was staggered by the power of her brother, who had somehow managed to get her there when Collette had never been the type of dead to linger.

It was just for tonight, Casper knew. She knew it in her bones like she knew the ghost glowing next to Sprinkle and holding her hand as they waited for Casper was Willa North, Kala's twin sister. Which brought her, of course, to the sight of the woman who would soon be her wife. Her brown skin seemed to glow under the illumination of what felt like thousands of warm, yellow light bulbs that were strung above her head to create the altar. While Sprinkle had been wearing a crocheted dress made of different shades of brown with the red crown of native flowers, Kala was red personified. The hem of her own crocheted frock mixed with the red dirt beneath their feet so it looked like she was an extension of the very land itself.

It was entirely unsurprising to Casper that she made a sexy bride, flashes of her skin visible through the strategic holes of the red fabric as it knitted and weaved and twisted together along her body. Her braids were piled on top of her head in an elaborate up-do, with red ribbons and flowers nestled amongst it. Her beauty sucked all the breath out of Casper's lungs as she came to a stop across form her. Kala reached out to take her hand, as if she couldn't bear a second longer without touching Casper, and she clung to the witch's warm flesh. Casper wasn't wearing a prosthetic or bionic limb that evening, she was appearing just as and who she was. It was clear by the fire in the witch's eyes that this was exactly the woman Kala wanted to marry.

'Well then.' A throat cleared next to them, her brother positioning himself between the pair as their celebrant. 'We're gathered here tonight to witness the union between medium Corvossier von Klitzing and witch Kala Tully. I'd say this is the weirdest wedding I've ever been to – something so magical dangling on the edge of an Apocalypse – yet it has always felt like the most natural progression of fate that you two should meet and fall in love as hard as you have.'

'Gross,' Sprinkle whispered, causing a ripple of laughter to run through the crowd.

'I'm getting outshined by a tween,' Barastin sighed dramatically, before sticking his tongue out at Sprinkle to show that he was joking. 'I believe you have both prepared your own vows.'

They had, yet they had also promised to keep it tight. They were getting *married* so it was clear to everyone there how much they loved each other, but the exact specifics they had wanted to keep between themselves. So short and sweet is what she and Kala had agreed and short and sweet it was.

'Casper,' Kala began, 'since you first walked into that witchcraft museum in Boscastle, I knew I was in trouble.'

She beamed at the witch's admission, Kala herself grinning so wide it looked like her face might crack open.

'I knew that if you asked me to jump, my only question would be how high,' she continued. 'But you've never asked me to jump. It has always been a willing leap, together, with our hands clasped around each other. And I'm more than willing to leap with you again, now, into forever.'

Kala was crying, something she rarely did as she looked down and repositioned the opal ring on Casper's finger. She hadn't wanted another, a wedding ring unable to replace how special the engagement one was to her, so she had insisted they stay the same.

'Kala,' Casper started, 'it's no secret I always preferred to spend more time with the dead than the living. Meeting you and Sprinkle changed that for the better. Instead of being a woman who walked between two worlds, you made me want to be someone who walked solely in yours.'

With a subtle nod to Sprinkle, the little witch dashed forward and held up a ring. Heath had made it. Casper was unsure exactly how he'd managed it, but the ring was somehow a merging of the two Willa and Alistair had once worn. Their conflicting shapes and metals were now twisted together in unison, their lives having ended but their love getting to continue on with Kala. Casper slid the ring on to the witch's finger, only half listening to what Barastin was reading out before she answered.

'I do,' she said.

Kala's turn came quickly after, the witch looking impatient as she finally blurted her own response: 'I do.'

Barastin pronounced them something she supposed. She thought it sounded eerily like 'wives for lives' and it might have been for all she knew, the crowd certainly laughed. Yet she wasn't listening any more, instead she was tugging Kala towards her by the fabric of her dress as she leaned down and kissed her. The witch fit against her like she was meant to be there, the shapes of their bodies so familiar to each other now as Kala's hand reached up and held Casper's face to hers. The gathering erupted in cheers around them, with whoops and yells and the music starting back up again in earnest. There was a Xena cry amongst it all and Casper didn't need to pull her lips away to know it had come from Tommi.

It was the tugging on their dresses that did eventually pull them apart, Sprinkle springing up into Casper's arm as her height always presented a better vantage point. With her limb difference holding the witch in place, her other arm reached for Kala as they linked hands and threw them up in the air. They were pelted with rice and as it rained down on them, she realised there was confetti and glitter and flowers and heaven knows what else mixed up amongst the celebratory shower. Party poppers were let off and paper streamers fell down around them, a flash firing before Casper spotted Mildred ducking and weaving out of the crowd with a Polaroid camera.

It felt clichéd to say the rest of the night was a blur, yet it truly was. A folding table had been turned into a buffet of the best local seafood and meats, along with a whole portion that was dedicated just to elaborately prepared and seasoned vegetables done a thousand different ways for Dreckly and the other veggos. Those in the coven who had been playing a stripped-back wedding procession pivoted hard and fast into party music, Casper laughing as Barastin coaxed the selkie Amos into dancing with him: a request that was clearly more than the merman had bargained for.

Wooden barrels were turned into tables, small lamps and the flower arrangements in jars positioned on top like rustic place settings. There was cake and drinking and raucous singing and love, *so much* love that it felt as if the entire sky would be elevated by it like a hot air balloon. That's how buoyant it felt to Casper. She looked around to find Collette, to speak to her for a moment, before realising the woman was gone. Willa was too, she noticed, but Collette's absence was the first and only drop of disappointment in her stomach that evening.

'She couldn't stay,' a voice said next to her. Casper turned to find Heath leaning against a barrel as he watched her. 'It's a miracle Barry was able to pull it off for this long.'

He was alternating between a huge slice of wedding cake and an even huger tumbler of whiskey, Casper squeezing his shoulder with understanding.

'It meant the world to me,' she said. 'I just wish I had a chance to tell her that.'

'She knew,' he smiled.

'Heath, you've gotta stop Aruhe! She's trying to get them to play Dave Dobbyn's "Slice"—'

Tommi's words fell away as she stumbled to a stop next to them, assessing the mood.

'Shite, sorry.' She grimaced. 'I've interrupted.'

She looked ready to yeet herself back into the fray of dancing bodies when Heath's hand snaked out and grabbed her wrist, slowly pulling her back to them. He raised his shoulder, letting her slip through so that she was trapped comfortably against his body.

'Have some cake,' he said, kissing the side of her neck.

'I've had, like, four pieces. I can't possibly—'

Her sentence was abruptly cut short as he shoved a fork in her mouth, causing icing to smear all over her face. Casper laughed as the werewolf reacted, half chuckling, half swearing at him as he tried to kiss the mess away.

'When are you two going to do all this?' Casper asked, gesturing between the pair and their ridiculous matching tuxedo shirts. Their love had been a slow burn, yet it was well and truly ignited now. Heath didn't look horrified by the question and neither did Tommi, who simply shrugged.

'This is a weird thing to say to someone who just got hitched, but marriage has never been my thing,' she said. 'Plus, I'm twenty-fookin-five. Maybe when I'm your age I can have a whole ghost ceremony. Shite knows I've got enough dead to attend.'

'Third time's a charm,' Heath smirked. 'You'd be marriage number three for me.'

Tommi laughed as she looked up at him. 'We know, that's enough. Besides, what if you royally start to piss me off in a decade? I saw how keen Collette was to get outta here.'

'She's dead!' Heath exclaimed.

'And they're busy, are they?' Tommi replied, smugly licking icing off the fork as she baited him. 'There's usually so many dead broads hanging around you, this one defo didn't want to stay.'

Heath looked like he was about to argue with her, but the comment made him pause and he looked to Casper. She nodded with confirmation.

'Always has been,' she agreed. 'Men too, but the redhead resurfaces the most.'

'My first wife.' He nodded.

'No, no,' Tommi countered, 'not her. This broad has a scar right here.'

The werewolf ran a finger across his forehead and over the bridge of his nose as he simmered at her.

'Scáthach,' he smirked.

'You lie!' Tommi practically shrieked.

'Who's Scáthach?' Casper asked, sipping from her glass of champagne. She recognised the woman on sight, but not her name.

'She was a legendary Scottish warrior woman thought to be myth,' the werewolf said, eyes alight with excitement. 'She and her sister had big biffo for years, but Scáthach became a teacher in the art of war. Only the best would be sent to Dunscaith Castle on the Isle of Skye to train with her.'

Tommi leaned back in Heath's arms, eyes narrowed as she scrutinised his expression. 'She trained *you*, didn't she?'

'Aye.' Heath grinned, draining the remaining whiskey from his glass. 'How else did you think I learned to throw a spear?'

'Shut ya puss!'

Casper didn't pay attention to the rest of their conversation, Tommi's chastising of Heath for keeping 'this treasured Scottish information' to himself registering in the back of her mind as she watched Kala return to the wedding party. She had slipped away with a sleepy Sprinkle drowsy at her side, putting the girl to bed and now rejoining the group as she scanned the crowd for her wife. *Wife,* Casper thought to herself. She was someone's *wife* now and Kala was hers. The witch's gaze finally settled on her, eyes warming as she stared across the space.

Casper didn't bother to excuse herself as she left Tommi and Heath, weaving her way through the throng of dancing super-naturals until her arm was wrapped around Kala's waist and her hand was linked tightly in hers. They moved together, slowly stepping and spinning through the dancing crowd that seemed to part for them. There would be no honeymoon for them. Casper had to leave the day after next for Berlin. The werewolves had to brace their bodies for the first night of the full moon tomorrow. Kala and Sprinkle were going to Melbourne to defend against whatever attack was imminent.

They just had tonight, really, and she was aware of that. Yet as she pulled the witch closer to her, resting her cheek against hers, Casper told herself that was enough. It had to be.

Chapter 9

Sadie

Simon hadn't made it back yet.

A snowstorm had blocked the route home to the Dawson farm and Arrowtown. It was almost as if Sadie knew something would happen, so she wasn't surprised when Barastin appeared not long after the full moon rose to tell her Simon was stuck and had to shift in the mountains. Sorcha had made it safely, however, which was something. Now she and Atlanta were with Aruhe and then swimming onwards towards danger. Unfathomable danger, the kind of danger that made her want to throw up when she thought it about even though she was well and truly past her first trimester. That was the most vomity stage.

'He'll be back tomorrow,' the ghost told her. 'And he said to make sure you lock the doors and stay inside tonight. No evening walks.'

She wasn't stupid. The three nights of the full moon were not a time to take a leisurely stroll outdoors, even if you weren't isolated on a farm largely occupied by werewolves. So she had curled up with the book written by a woman Barastin and his sister Corvossier had once known, and listened to the wind and howls that mixed together outside the safety of her cottage.

She almost knew *The Collected Banshee Histories* by heart, having consumed these tales so many times since the sacred text had first come into her possession through mysterious means. Yet she thought it was important, thought there was some way her babies might be able to absorb the knowledge and the weight of their history when she'd never had the fortune to. Sadie read it for them, mostly, because they would never be cursed with the same things her sisters, her mother and her grandmother had been cursed with. They would have knowledge and power and freedom, which is all any parent could hope for.

She had fallen asleep repeating that mantra to herself like she did most nights, stirring only a few hours later for the first of many toilet runs given her limited bladder capacity.

Dr Kikuchi's morning visit had the bonus addition of her eldest sister Shannon, which she was delighted about but also stung just slightly because it reminded her of Sorcha's absence. The two couldn't be more different, with Sorcha a steady presence as they ran through the daily medical checks while Shannon was all up in Sadie's business as she checked the amount of food in the house, the steady supply of snacks, the type of pregnancy reading material, and the baby clothes that had been showing up all while maintaining consistent chatter about everything she'd seen and heard in Australia during the supernatural summit.

'Have you been taking your vitamins?' Shannon asked as Dr Kikuchi checked her blood pressure.

'Yes, of course,' Sadie signed.

'Everyday?'

'Everyday.'

'And have you been using the heat pack on your lower back?'

Sadie lied with a thumbs-up, Shannon nodding with satisfaction at the gesture. In truth, she could never get the damn thing in the perfect spot and would end up with one ass cheek burning and zero heat on her lumbar.

'Have you got enough batteries for your vibrator?'

'Jesus!' Sadie remarked, embarrassed and verbal about it.

Dr Kikuchi paused her movements, looking up. 'It's a serious question, Sadie.'

'I've had two kids, hun, I know how horny you get during pregnancy,' Shannon continued. 'It's nothing to be ashamed about. The hormones are off the charts!'

Sadie buried her head in her hands, mortified.

'It's less about the hormones and more about the blood,' Dr Kikuchi countered. 'You get extra pounds of it throughout the pregnancy and it's gotta flow somewhere, which is usually the lower half of the— Shannon, can you come here for a sec. I need you to tell me what she's signing, I can't read that quick.'

Her sister did as ordered. 'She's asking you – no, both of us – to stop talking about her sex drive when you literally look at her vagina every day and no one has vibrators with batteries any more, Shannon, they charge via USB.'

Dr Kikuchi smirked. 'Yeah, I was never gonna get all that. All right, off with your knickers, then. Let's double check the plumbing.'

All up, it was a *terrible* fucking morning in Sadie's opinion and by the time she was done being poked, prodded and personally invaded, she was craving her own company.

'What about a walk?' Shannon asked. 'Sorch said you usually like to go for at least two, sometimes three, especially after second breakfast.'

'Not today,' Sadie lied, again, it being incredibly easy to do so via sign. 'It's too miserable out.'

It was true, it had been raining most of the morning but a pair of gumboots and a raincoat hadn't stopped her in the past.

'Well, if you're sure—'

'I'm sure, thank you. And thank Nora for the caramel.'

'Look, long as you keep asking for it she'll keep making it.'

They hugged and Sadie walked Shannon to the door, waving her sister off as she trampled through the mud after Dr Kikuchi, who waited for no one. With a sigh of relief, she locked the cottage door behind her and made for the fresh jar of home-made caramel in the kitchen. Toasting an entire packet of crumpets and smearing them in butter and her sister Nora's liquid gold, Sadie made a contented murmur as she munched. Dr Kikuchi had warned her that gestational diabetes was a thing and even though there was no family history, they had to keep an eye out for it. Thankfully that scrutiny had been fruitless so far. She didn't want to be dramatic, but if she learned she had to give up sugar during this pregnancy she would perform a C-section on herself with whatever utensils were in the top drawer.

Every woman had their limits. Sadie had been chased, shot at, nearly eaten by ghouls. She *could not* and *would not* remove sugar from her diet, so help her God. Brewing a pot of fresh tea after she demolished the last of the crumpets, she leaned against the counter as she sipped slowly and warmed her fingers against the mug. As she watched the world outside, the rain slowly began to ease until it was nothing more than a soft pitter-patter. *Good,* she thought, rinsing her dishes in the sink. Sadie had made a massive vegetable pie last night for dinner and sent Shannon off with two others for the main farmhouse along with a bag full of rabbit carcasses. She was out of fresh meat and a hungry, full-moon-depleted werewolf would be returning at some point today. And werewolves loved nothing more than raw meat on the days between the lunar cycle.

Sliding on her gumboots, raincoat, beanie and gloves, Sadie grabbed the handle of the trolley-like structure she would drag behind her when checking the snares. It had little wheels with tyre treads so it could navigate the outdoor terrain and it saved her from having to carry back anything she'd been lucky enough to catch. All of her sisters thought it was weird that her isolation hobby had been learning to catch and kill her own meat, but Sadie had found it empowering. On their road trip down to the South Island, she'd watched with curiosity as one of the Aunties, Meri, would emerge from the forest each morning carrying everything from birds to deer. The more she caught, the less they had to stop at shops or any major town centres that could make their security vulnerable. And Meri was bloody good, so that rarely happened.

'My sisters are weavers and carvers,' she said. 'They all have different gifts, like yours.'

Meri's gift was a different kind of intricate art and the woman had been kind enough to share her knowledge with Sadie over the past several months. The process of learning how to make her own traps and snares, how to disguise them and how to rebuild them once she'd caught something, had kept her mind busy. It had given her something to do on the many, many walks which she knew could be taken away from her at any moment if bed rest was ordered during the final trimester. Yet Dr Kikuchi had approved Sadie's consistent routine, not only because it kept her body fit and her mind fresh, but because it kept her circulation flowing. Sorcha and she would usually check the traps on the morning walk, with Meri joining them as their bodyguard and helping Sadie reset them. Surprisingly, she had a knack for it and it had made her feel capable of something outside of her body.

'Shooting them is easier,' Meri had said, as they carried a catch of three enormous rabbits back to the cottage one day, 'and quicker, but you can get better meat this way.'

Sorcha hadn't understood her fascination with the whole procedure, yet Sadie knew that even when the triplets were born she was going to be in danger for some time. She couldn't always rely on the kindness and generosity of others. After she learned that she was going to be a mother, Sadie had a slight existential panic about having no practical life skills. So learning to snare rabbits had been first, skinning them second, and preparing the meat third.

Like Australia, rabbits were pests in New Zealand, so getting them off the land was encouraged. The meat, too, was particularly good for pregnant and nursing women, Meri had told her. Once she had started incorporating it into her diet regularly, she began to crave it. That and Mi Goreng noodles, for some reason: the spicier the better. On the days after the full moon, many of the Aunties weren't about. Or members of the Dawson werewolf pack, for that matter. Those days were physically and mentally hard on the werewolves, so her walks would usually be with just one of her sisters. In lieu of Sorcha and desperate to be free of Shannon, Sadie was blissfully alone.

She smiled as she picked her way through the forest, her first two snares being empty but the remaining six extremely fruitful. She sent a prayer to the werewolves, whose presence on the property had no doubt chased these critters free of their burrows. Meri had taught her to send another prayer, one to the *mana whenua* she had said, thanking the power of the land for giving them its gifts. She did that as well, placing the carcasses in her trolley and picking her way back to the cottage as the rain started to pick up again. The forest floor was carpeted in leaves and fallen sticks, their usual crunch under her feet muted by the dampness. Yet there was something else about the quiet that made Sadie pause, something that dipped past the serenity she had found earlier and into . . . eeriness. The birds were silent, the usual chatter of the kererūs and pūkekos non-existent as she stopped, examining the trees around her. She felt watched.

Suddenly she had a flash of a scene and stumbling back, she scrunched her eyes shut as the vision intensified. Besides her wail, Sadie's other prominent banshee ability was seeing the last few moments before someone died. Previously that had meant she and her sisters were able to run the most lucrative forensic cleaning business in Sydney. Yet Sadie hadn't had proper visions in months, not since she learned that she was pregnant. Sorcha's theory was that it had something to do with the babies, who were perhaps feeding off her visions the same way they were feeding off her body. The very thought of her foetuses experiencing that kind of trauma so early – even if they couldn't understand it – pained her, but Sadie also knew it was out of her control. Her sister Ina had been three the first time she sensed a terminal illness in someone, Shannon even younger when she'd seen her first death scene play out in a body of water, and Nora sketching mortality murals from the first time she was able to grip a crayon. This was just the banshee way and death to them meant something different than it did to everyone else.

This death, however, was hers. She saw how she looked in the killer's eyes, short and fat in the forest, drowning in an enormous coat as she squinted through the trees. Her cheeks were rosy and her lips were pink, the colours standing out against her pale skin and the wisps of ginger hair peeking out from under the wool of her beanie. Her visions were usually ahead of time, but this scene was barely in the future, maybe a few seconds at most. It kept distorting, kept blurring as trees rushed by, branches snapping and snow flying as something raced towards her.

A *wolf*, she realised. Sadie stumbled as she fell out of the vision, her mind snapping back to the present. She was still disorientated as she looked around, processing the scene she was actively in rather than the sizzle reel she'd viewed in her head. It was still deathly silent in the forest, no sound of snapping branches or growling like she'd seen in the vision, and certainly no snow. It was wet around her, the rain having picked up now to something slightly heavier but still bearable enough that she didn't need to wear more than her raincoat to stay dry.

Her clothes! Looking down at herself, she examined her ensemble and everything she was wearing to make sure it was the same as in the vision. She could have seen another day, after all, her vision being truly in the future even if it was in an identical geographical space. Of course, she wasn't that lucky. She had on the same raincoat, the same gumboots, she was just as pregnant, and her cart had been just as full. Sadie was used to picking up on the minuscule details after years of viewing other people's deaths. A clock hand, a background photo, a street sign, a smell: all of it could be a context clue when it came to working out where this person was going to die and when. She spun around to count the number of rabbits to make sure they matched up to her vision as well when she froze. There really was someone else there, watching her.

'Wally?' she whispered, dropping the handle of the cart with a *thunk*. It was impossible to forget that face, given she had been staring at it as the life drained out of his eyes. Yet as soon as Sadie said the name out loud, she realised she was wrong. This wasn't Wally, the farmhand she had accidentally killed when she had cried out in agony and unleashed her wail on him. This person looked very much like him, but he didn't have that same easy smile. There was a hardness to this man, both in their jaw and the way they pushed themselves off the tree they were leaning against. A brother, perhaps, or a cousin, who looked just like him. This wasn't Wally, but it was definitely someone who had been close to him.

That was confirmed when they revealed the gun inside their coat, a flash of vengeance and satisfaction in their eyes as they aimed it squarely at Sadie's chest. They were shaking, so much so they had to steady their weapon by using both hands to secure the grip. There were dark circles around their eyes, their whole face haunted as they stared at Sadie like she was the only thing they had been seeing in their mind for weeks.

'I can't hear you,' they said, a thick New Zealand accent on their lips, which told her, yes, this person was indeed a relative of Wally's. 'But I understood what you said. *Wally.* Only his friends called him that. The stupid slut who killed him shouldn't be able to call him that!'

Spit flew from his lips as he yelled, the gun shaking even harder, and Sadie held up her hands in surrender. She was just as terrified of the weapon going off by accident as she was of it going off on purpose.

'I'm sorry,' she said. 'I'm so, so sorry. I never mean to kill h—'

'SHUT UP! Shut the *fuck* up! I can't hear a word you're saying and if you try to use that banshee witchcraft, you won't kill me like you did him. I'm wearing multiple headphones, all noise cancelling, and I won't suffer like he did.'

It wasn't hard to see he was telling the truth: both in-ear and outer devices, she guessed. It looked like he had a pair of industrial earmuffs on top as well and duct-taped to the side of his head for good measure.

'He was my little brother, you know? I always thought he was mad, working here with werewolves and all you other weirdos. But noooo, Wally couldn't be told. Thought he was getting to see something special, thought he was someone special by hanging around all of you *freaks*!'

Sadie had been slowly backing away as the man continued to rant, inching closer and closer towards a thicker density of trees. The unhinged nature of Wally's brother was obviously extremely dangerous – albeit understandable – yet it might also be her salvation. If he kept talking while distracted in his own pain, she might be able to make a run for it. It would be impossible to get a clear shot of her if she was weaving and ducking through those trees.

'I've been waiting months for this, months!'

He wouldn't need a clear shot, however. All he'd need to do is clip her and it would all be over. Plus, Sadie wasn't a runner at the best of times and these were the three-babies-full worst of times. She wouldn't get very far or fast. And if this man had been able to get on to the grounds, watch her and wait for her undetected, it was clear he knew the Dawson farm better than she did.

'I tried on the last full moon, tried waiting until the days when the werewolves were at their weakest and you'd be alone.'

She heard the growls before he did. In fact, he couldn't hear them at all as something *big* and *fast* and *vicious* smashed through the trees of the forest and raced towards them. Whatever, whoever it was, they were still too far away. Sadie was still in range and this man was much, much too close to miss. So instead, she tried to stay calm as she stood there, terrified and shaking and willing his twitching fingers not to pull that trigger and urging her face to stay neutral so as not to give away the fact they soon wouldn't be alone. *Keep him talking*, she thought. *Let him rant. Stall.*

'Now it's finally t—'

Those last seconds felt like some of the longest of her life as she tried not to scream, tried not to wail or react or panic as the forest roared around them. He didn't have to hear it to know something was coming, the ground shaking beneath their feet with the arrival of the unexpected visitor. Sadie bit her bottom lip and slapped a hand over her mouth to stop the scream she so desperately wanted to let erupt from her body as an enormous, black werewolf burst through the trees.

She dropped to the ground, desperate to be out of the firing line as she watched the whole scene unfold like it was it was a flip-book animation, second by painful second twitching by. She fixated on the huge, drooling teeth of the werewolf as it opened its jaws and bit the gun *right* out of the man's hands. He bit off the man's hands too, dropping to the ground and severing contact to both limbs with a stiff shake of the head from side to side. It forced him to pull back, screaming, as he stared at the bloody mounds where his hands had once been.

The werewolf shuffled in front of her, growling with bloodstained teeth as it spat out both the hands and the weapon like they tasted disgusting. They probably did. She felt its eyes sweep over her as it pivoted around, back hunched as it refocused its attention on the perpetrator. Its positioning blocked Sadie from view, protecting her from not just the man's vision but his body as well. Not that it would have mattered, he was in so much agony. The only thing he posed a threat to were the ears of anyone within a hundred-metre radius as he screamed and screamed and *screamed*.

On the forest floor, wet and cold and scared, Sadie was shaking uncontrollably as she watched the back of the wolf in between them. The man cried out for his brother, calling Wally's name over and over again in a way that broke her heart. Sadie could hear other people coming now, further commotion and growls, but she wasn't sure they would make it there before the man was dispatched entirely.

'Don't k-kill him,' she said, her words coming out uneven. She knew the wolf heard as they'd been taking a step closer to their prospective prey. '*Please.*'

The wolf turned back to face her and she knew she should have been terrified, should have felt fear deep in her bones as this apex predator assessed her with the blood of another man on its lips. Yet she wasn't afraid. Instead, she repeated her request.

'Please don't kill him,' she whispered.

There was human intelligence set deep within those animal eyes as they narrowed, a growl never ceasing to rumble from its mouth the entire time. With what sounded like a bark of frustration, the wolf threw its head back and howled. The cry was met with responses from all around the forest, the trees seemingly brimming with werewolves as several howled replies and others growled in recognition. They burst through the trees, forming a tight cluster around the man, who was still in so much pain he hadn't seemed to realise how much worse his predicament had gotten.

Sadie had never seen a werewolf in the wild before and now she was suddenly staring at ten of them. The black one that had saved her was the biggest by a large margin. She could see that the other wolves deferred to this one as they half growled, half barked out orders. She glanced at the long claws extended from paws that looked as big as her face, noting the clumps of ice and snow that remained there.

The wolves began dragging the man off, carefully using their teeth and claws to pull him away from Sadie and through the forest. She'd asked for him not to be killed and someone had listened to her, yet the wolves weren't exactly being gentle about it either. She felt a warm, wet thing make contact with her cheek and she jumped. There was a whining sound and she twisted her head to see the black werewolf was the only one that remained. They were gently nudging her, licking her face, checking that she was all right.

'I'm okay,' she said, running a hand down her belly to check that was actually true. As if sensing her concern, there was a series of swift kicks to her abdomen from the babies inside telling her 'yeah, Ma, we're okay too'.

'Ow.' She winced, trying to calm the ruckus in there with several pats to her flesh. 'Chill out, you little bitches, I get it.'

Sliding a hand through the silky tuffs of fur, Sadie slowly and carefully got to her knees while balancing against the werewolf. Waiting a few more seconds, she got to her feet properly, the beast helping her all the while with nudges and pushes until she was standing steadily. Looking over her moon of a stomach, Sadie glimpsed the severed and half-chewed hands on the forest floor below. Closing her eyes, she thought for one moment she might be sick before she forced herself to gulp away that notion. It was like the werewolf knew, pulling her away from the scene by gripping the edge of her raincoat between its teeth. She obeyed, taking slow and careful steps as she started to regain her composure. The werewolf barked at her when she paused at her cart to grab the handle, as if telling her to leave it and she snapped back.

'There's good meat in here,' she hissed. 'I caught this for you; I'm not letting it go to waste!'

The werewolf's big, brown eyes blinked back at her and she realised that she'd known subconsciously from the second it had burst through the trees that this creature was Simon.

'Go on then,' Sadie urged. 'Lead the way back to the cottage. I'm borderline delirious and you're the werewolf.'

She didn't suppose he could laugh while in monster form, but the half sneeze, half bark he made in response certainly sounded close. He did as she asked, guiding her back through the trees on a walk that seemed to take forever because it did. Sadie wasn't steady on her feet, she realised, and the werewolf knew it because he was moving just as slowly alongside her. When the roof of the cottage swam into view, she immediately felt like she was about to pass out with exhaustion. It was the relief, she told herself, pausing to rest her shoulder against a tree for just one moment. The wolf beside her barked, but she waved him away with an errant hand. Instead, he cried and twisted and contorted, his form shaking in what looked like an excruciating display as the beautiful fur she'd held on to fell away to reveal the man underneath. Suddenly it was Simon hunched over the forest floor, panting with the exertion of the forced change. And naked.

That last part was impossible to miss, with his muscles rippling as he shuddered and let out a low groan of pain. It woke Sadie up, that's for sure, as her eyes focused on the patterns of tattoos she'd only glimpsed peeking out from under the sleeve of his shirt but which were now exposed in full glory, wrapped over his shoulder and down his back like a protective plate. His vertebrae seemed incredibly exposed to her as she followed the path of those notches down his back and towards the ass and legs that were now moving as he struggled to get up. She went to help him; it was clear Simon was in pain as she extended a hand. Yet in one smooth gesture, he moved hers out of the way as he dragged her to and around him.

'I've got you,' he said, pulling them both towards the cottage. Sadie realised with surprise that he did indeed have her. One hand was gripping his bare hip, while the other was still clutching the handle of the cart that carried her prized bounty, it clanging along behind them. Simon turned around to inspect the noise like he was annoyed by it, realisation crossing his face as he saw what was there.

'For God's sake, woman, leave the meat,' he chuckled, hand on the back door as she handed him the keys.

'But I've got to skin it first,' Sadie responded, the words slurred as they came out of her mouth. She sounded drunk.

'Don't,' he replied, dragging her inside. 'I like it better that way.'

'Ew,' was the only response she could manage. He shrugged, unapologetic, as he stormed through the cottage and checked every safety measure he had in place.

'He never came in here,' he told her. 'You're safe.'

'You're naked.' Sadie heard the words leave her mouth, but she was too tired to stop them. 'Why did I say that?'

'You're in shock,' Simon answered, like her weirdness was perfectly normal. 'The adrenalin is leaving your body and you're losing your inhibitions.'

'Trauma is truth serum?'

He laughed at that. 'If you want to look at it that way, sure. Now come on, we need to get you in a warm shower.'

While he had been chatting to her, trying to keep a steady stream of nonsense going, Simon had been taking off the layers of her clothing one by one. First the gumboots, then the raincoat, then her gloves, then her beanie, then her sweater, and with each layer he inspected her for injuries. She was fine, she knew she was. Physically there wasn't a scratch on her, but mentally she was rattled.

'With you?' she asked. 'I have to shower with you naked? I shouldn't do that.'

'No, no, keep your clothes on if you want and I'll wait outside. Or I can get dressed and come in with you if you don't think you can stay standing. However you're most comfortable, Sadie, you just need to get warm.'

'Oh good,' she nodded, pulling the T-shirt over her head as she waddled in the direction of the one bathroom they shared, 'cos I shouldn't shower with naked men in my state.'

'I think it's a little late for that,' he muttered, earning a slap on the shoulder as she spun around. 'Ow!'

'I hope that hurt.' She smiled, half wriggling out of the maternity tights she was wearing. 'And it has nothing to do with you; any naked man would get a girl randy at this point.'

'Randy?'

'You're super horny when you're pregnant, Simon. Ask Shannon and Dr Kikuchi, they won't shut up about it.'

She thought she saw him trying to suppress a laugh out of the corner of her eyes as he adjusted the temperature to the shower nozzles. In her undies and bra, Sadie stepped into the stream and let out a moan of satisfaction as the warm water rushed over.

'Please don't pass out,' Simon said. 'I'll be right back.'

He ducked away for barely a few seconds, returning in a pair of jocks and stepping into the shower with her. Plucking several leaves and errant twigs out of her hair, Simon washed the dirt and grime off her body. They were both quiet, just the splash of water and squish of soap the only noises as he washed himself clean as well.

'Sadie?'

His words startled her and she realised with some surprise that she was leaning against him, heavily, with her eyes closed.

'S-sorry,' she murmured. 'I—'

'Out,' he ordered. 'You're about to drop any moment.'

'Drop it like it's hot,' she mumbled, as he turned off the shower and wrapped her like a burrito in towels. It was a dumb joke and she laughed softly at it as Simon steered her towards his bedroom. He'd acquired her favourite nightie at some point, the tartan pattern bright in his hands as he handed it to her.

'Slip this on, get under the covers, and go to sleep,' he said.

'Where will you be?' Sadie questioned as she followed his orders. He spun around to let her change in private. Somewhere in the back of her mind, a part of her was saying she was going to be mortified about showering in front of Simon in her intimates. Yet coherent thought was fighting under a fog now.

'I'll be just outside the door. Dr Kikuchi is coming to check on your condition and I need to let her in when she arrives.'

'You'll wake me when she gets here?' Sadie said, climbing beneath the thick weight of his blankets.

'No,' he said. 'I won't wake you under any circumstances. She can check you unconscious or wait till you're up.'

Peering at Simon over the top of the covers, Sadie could barely see him as her eyelids grew heavy. She said something else to him, she couldn't understand what exactly, but it didn't matter. Soon she was gone and lost to blissful blackness.

Chapter 10

Tommi

'FUCK ME UPPPP!'

Tommi slammed the shot back after she shouted, not even flinching as it burned down her throat and she quickly downed another one. It was years since she'd last stepped foot inside Eggs & Ham, the bar that had been so seminal to her growing up. The people she had once frequented it with were dead, the exception being James Hughes who had a new life in London as a prominent street artist. She was happy for him, he'd really done the best out of all them when you considered she was there pretending to be about eighty per cent drunker than she actually was in the hopes of getting arrested.

'You have to make it believable,' Heath had told her as she and Ben had crouched in the back of a van nearby, waiting for the right moment to join the fray of Dundee night owls. 'They need to *believe* you're reckless and wasted so the tip is *believable* too.'

Tommi had nodded, smudging her eyeliner to give it a messy effect that was now conveniently trendy. If you knew her, really knew her, you would recognise the woman underneath.

Yet her long, blue-then-dyed-black hair was gone, replaced by a blonde mullet she'd hoped would be more Joan Jett than the Rick James her curls had steered it closer towards. Ben's green hair was now that faded orange only a bad bleach job could give you, Tommi having used what was left from dyeing her hair to run her fingers through his and mess up the identifiable shade.

'That means you too, Ben,' Heath had continued. 'If you have to get handsy to make it believable, do it. Now is not the time for moral absolutes.'

Tommi had flashed him a glance, frowning as she stared at her partner. It had been discussed, of course, that they needed to appear like drunk and messy werewolves in order for the Treize to bite at the carrot they were dangling. She just hadn't expected those words to come from Heath's mouth. She'd heard a whack on the door outside, indicating it was time to go, yet Tommi had been reluctant. She'd wanted to hug him, kiss him goodbye in case this was the last time. Since they'd all left Australia to journey here and pull off this mission, they had banned themselves from each other. His scent couldn't be on her, meaning they'd slept in separate rooms and been apart more than was bearable if she was being honest. She'd had to spray herself in Ben's cologne, making sure that she smelled like him and he smelled like her, just in case the Treize had werewolf trackers try to identify their individual scents.

With a steadying breath, Tommi had got up and yanked her mini-dress down over torn fishnets and combat boots. She'd leapt out of the back of the van, landing closer to Fatties and blocks away from where they needed to be. Yet that too had been intentional. The engine of the vehicle had rumbled to life behind her and she'd looked back, Heath's face visible for just a moment as Ben slammed the door shut. The last thing she'd seen was Heath's smirk as he gave her a knowing wink. Whether he'd seen her smile or not, she couldn't be sure, but she'd hoped he felt it as Ben had thrown his arm around her and they'd begun the walk to Eggs & Ham.

They looked right together, just as scene and rough around the edges as each other, which was entirely the point, of course. Casting a sideways glance up at him, Tommi couldn't deny the Big Black band shirt that was tucked into his torn jeans fitted him like it was designed to be worn by Ben Kapoor and Ben Kapoor alone. The album title – *Songs About Fucking* – was scrawled across his chest and a bit on the nose, but she smirked none the less as she led them through her old stomping ground.

'So this is where you used to live,' Ben said, as Tommi performatively stumbled.

'Aye, how do you like it?'

'Bit bleak, if I'm honest.'

'You mean grey,' she laughed. 'That's just Scotland. Wait until winter.'

'No thanks, I'm no good with the cold.'

Thankfully things had warmed up considerably once they got inside, the bar always crammed way past the legal capacity and a mass of bodies heaving to the Slick Rick track that thudded through the speakers. Ben slid her over another shot, Tommi noticing that his was actually thrown over his shoulder and into a passing patron who looked around with confusion. No true Scot could fathom why any drink would be discarded. The Aussie werewolf had admitted he couldn't drink like her after their first few hours bar hopping, so he had switched to 'straight vodka' – aka water – or just ditching his bevvies altogether when he had the chance.

All he needed was to have alcohol on his breath and that would be enough. She grabbed his hand in hers, pulling him to the centre of the floor she had danced on with Lorcan a lifetime ago. She tried not to think about that as she rolled her body, dragging his hands to her hips as she moved against him in time with the beat. There was little to no fresh air in Eggs & Ham and soon sweat was pouring off them, Ben's shirt sticking to his lanky frame in an appetising manner. Tommi lifted her hands above her head, still not used to the short hair as she instinctively went to lift the usually long strands off her neck only to find nothing there.

It would have killed her under normal circumstances to cut her hair short, Tommi preferring it at Rapunzel lengths if she could manage. Yet a wig would have shown she was only trying to temporarily disguise herself. It needed to look and feel permanent, so she had squinted her eyes shut as Ben had snipped away her locks and Tommi had finished the rest to make it look like it had some semblance of style. She was a big, scary werewolf, who had faced big, scary monsters in her time but she still had a wee bit of a cry when she first caught sight of her reflection. Yet it only made her more determined for the mission ahead. Tommi *would not* die with a mullet.

The hair didn't feel like her, but that was entirely the point. She closed her eyes as Ben ran his hands through it, pulling her closer to him on the dancefloor and she felt the alcohol coursing through her veins. Tommi couldn't be sure if he danced this dirty all the time as his fingers skimmed over the slick skin of her neck, bringing her lips to his. They barely brushed each other, though, his mouth moving to her ear as he whispered.

'Four o'clock.'

Tommi didn't react for another full song. Grinding her ass against him, it gave her a better view of the direction Ben had flagged and sure enough, there they were. Two Praetorian Guard members, she was sure of it. She knew Lorcan wouldn't risk scaring her off by showing his face there and he wouldn't have been dumb enough to use the twins Jakea and Jaira either. So these were faces she didn't know, a man and a woman pretending to swig from beer bottles that she could see were empty. *Amateurs*, she thought.

Tommi clocked another near the balcony, making sure their exit was closed to them, yet they didn't circle closer. Instead, they just watched. And waited. She flagged the other PG member to Ben by deploying his own move against him and giggling as she whispered in his ear, gently biting his earlobe for added effect. She might have been a little too convincing as she felt his body react, but that was even better: if they could witness actual arousal, there would be no question about whether they were faking it. And yet, none of them made a move. They kept Ben and Tommi in their line of sight as discreetly as they could, wasting time that she didn't have. She could sense Ben was annoyed too.

'There's too many people,' she said, smiling up at him like the words meant something else. 'They'll never take us like this; they think it's too public.'

'Too many witnesses,' Ben countered, sweeping her newly acquired fringe to the side, the ends of which were damp with sweat.

She didn't disagree. He was scanning the crowd above her, a flash of something in his eyes when he spotted it.

'We need to be isolated,' he said, looping a finger through the buckle of her studded belt. 'Come on.'

It didn't take her long to realise where he was taking her, Tommi practically growling as Ben passed one of the Praetorian Guard soldiers who was doing a very poor job of subtle surveillance.

'Eyes to the front, bitch,' Tommi hissed, the woman jumping as she diverted her eyes away.

'You trying to win the jealous girlfriend Oscar?' he smirked, once they were out of earshot and heading into the bathroom. There were no gendered loos in this place, the row of cubicles instead being a free-for-all as they marched inside. There were two men necking in the corner and another cluster of people lighting up a joint as Tommi pushed Ben into the cubicle furthest from them all.

'Smart,' she said, locking the door behind her.

'Believable, right?' he puffed. Tommi could hear his heartbeat through his skin as their blood raced with adrenalin. There was so little space in there, barely enough for the two of them, as he was pressed up against her considerable chest and gave Tommi's push-up bra an even greater assist. His hands were running up her thighs, toying dangerously with the hem of her dress as he twisted her fishnets in between his fingers.

'Look, I won't lie to you and say I haven't snuck into this exact bathroom to have a quickie before,' Tommi said, recognising the heat in his eyes because she felt it too. This was dangerous, both of them too wired as werewolves and too close to the other side of the full moon for this to be anything but a lit match ready to consume. They needed to be caught alone, vulnerable and in flagrante, she told herself as she wrapped her fingers around the back of his neck and pulled his face closer to hers.

'I want to know what that feels like,' she whispered, eyes fixated on the many piercings around his lips. It was like she had said the magic word, with Ben's mouth pressing down in a flash. His tongue moved against hers, the metal brushing up and in and around her lips as she kissed him back. There was a tearing sound as he shredded her fishnets with his hands, his fingers kneading into the bare skin around her G-string as he pushed her hard against the wall of the cubicle. Her act to turn him on had worked a little too well, Tommi herself burning as she reached between them and felt the bulge in Ben's pants.

'Fuck,' he panted, lips mumbling against her neck. 'Tommi, I'll—'

She gasped for air as she threw her head back, gripping the edge of the cubicle wall above them for support and wrapping her legs around his waist, giving in to the sensation of the cool metal tickling her neck. This was a dirty and dangerous distraction. Ben's tongue ran along a droplet of sweat that had trickled down from her neck and between her breasts, making her shudder. In the back of her mind, she registered the bathroom doors swinging shut and not opening again. There was the dull scrape of metal as a bin was pulled in front to block the entrance and she clocked the six bodies she heard moving into the space. She didn't know if he realised they had company, the thud of the music still insanely loud but the chatter of the other bathroom occupants now gone as Praetorian Guard soldiers surrounded their cubicle.

Sure enough, the door was kicked forward and the lock went flying. Tommi realised Ben really hadn't known they were about to be jumped as he thrashed forward. She, meanwhile, was yanked backwards and over the cubicle by her neck. She let it happen, not properly attempting to fight until she was on solid footing and could assess the three people in front of her and the one behind. One of the flimsy straps holding her dress together had been severed in the struggle as she fought against the chokehold.

'Off–the-shoulder suits me better anyway,' she gagged. The harder she fought it, the more it would hurt, so she hurled herself forward and got one free kick in before giving up and copping the punch to the face she knew was coming. Ben was fighting harder and she urged him without words to give up, to not get too bloodied or bruised before everything they had left to accomplish. *Just a believable amount*, she told herself before squinting her eyes shut with regret when she thought about what she'd just done. *Not now, not now,* she thought. She needed to focus on the more pressing task at hand. Two figures were let into the bathroom, Tommi glimpsing a flash of badges that were shown to dumb-ass patrons outside who were supposed to believe they were cops.

'That's enough,' the first one said, Tommi doing her best not to snarl at the mere sound of his voice. Instead, she pivoted to the second face.

'You fucking traitor,' she snarled at Joss, who flinched at her words. 'How could you?!'

'I'm sorry, Tommi,' he said, holding up his hands in surrender. 'I had to! You're out of control.'

'What did you think would happen coming back here?' Lorcan asked her, picking through the debris of the brief fight. 'Joss has his own sources, Tommi. People who recognised you. He had to do his job and send up a flare.'

'Weak ass little bint!' she said, spitting at Joss's feet.

'You should be proud of him,' Lorcan countered, looking like he always did in his knee-length duster and all black: a cowboy out of time. 'He put his personal feelings aside to do what was right.'

'What do you know about *right*?' she snapped. There was something missing as she stared at him, something she wasn't sure had even been there the last time she'd seen Lorcan and punched him in the face for turning her dying best friend into an immortal operative just like he was. Just like Heath had been. If he hadn't, Joss would have died and for as long as she'd known him, he had been desperate for a cure. Shackles had been the answer Lorcan provided and she couldn't forgive her ex-boyfriend for that.

'It smells like sex in here,' he said, his flat eyes that had once felt so alive turning to her male companion. He strolled over to examine the man, who had been forced down on his knees by two Praetorian Guard soldiers. Lifting his chin up with a jerk, Lorcan's eyes widened for just a moment.

'Ben Kapoor,' he whispered. 'I thought it couldn't be true when Felg here said that's who you were with, but my God . . . it makes sense. It's only surprising you two didn't cross paths sooner.'

Letting Ben's head drop, Lorcan turned to face her. 'Where's Heath?'

'Fuck Heath,' she said, knowing that a small cut was bleeding into her mouth and dribbling out the side.

'I'm sure you did,' Lorcan answered. 'Ben too, I can tell. I know that look in his eyes well, I felt it.'

'The only thing you ever felt was your own self-importance, Lo.'

He looked hurt for just a moment, her words slashing him the way she had intended. Yet it was for just a moment.

'I'm so sorry things ended up this way,' he murmured. Tommi really believed he meant it. 'I failed you, but I won't fail others.'

She huffed. 'What the hell does that mean?'

'Tommi Grayson, I'm ordering you to containment within a maximum-security facility at Vankila.'

'NO!' she screamed, really laying it on thick as she struggled against her captors. 'For fucking what, having a good time? You're just gonna lock me up for no reason, like you did Quaid?!'

'Like *you* did Quaid,' Lorcan corrected, pointing at her with annoyance. 'Actually, that's where I'm sending you. You can go spend time with your destructive family line, since that's exactly who you've turned into.'

She cried out again, shouting her objections and curses repeatedly in a stream so that eventually she would have to be put under. Her eyes grew heavy as the chloroform rag was pressed over her mouth, taking a big gulp so she could be out and through this faster. Lorcan was resting a hand on Joss's shoulder as her best friend looked ashen at the situation.

'You did the right thing,' he said, or least that's what she thought he said as the words mumbled together. 'You did the only thing left for us to do if we have any hope of things returning to normal.'

'What do we do with him?' someone else asked.

'He's coming too,' Lorcan ordered.

The last thing she saw was Ben's unconscious body being hauled upright by several of the Praetorian Guard soldiers and the toe of Lorcan's boot walking closer and closer towards her.

She came to with a wheezing, rattled scream as she did her best to suck in oxygen as quickly as possible. The air tasted too sweet and Tommi gagged as the residue from the chloroform seemed to stick to her lungs.

'If you don't lean over, you'll choke on your own vomit,' an emotionless voice said. She couldn't see who it belonged to, but they were right and she did as ordered. She vomited anyway, but at least she didn't choke on her own chunder. It was completely dark where she was being held, yet that didn't matter much to werewolves. She could still see everything with her night vision, which she guessed was why they'd eschewed the needless electricity cost in this cell. Closing her eyes, she leaned back and rested her head against the cool concrete.

'*Kia ora*, Quaid,' she croaked.

She hadn't laid eyes on him yet, but she would recognise that scent anywhere. Tommi sensed her half-brother Quaid Ihi stiffen across his side of the cell as she spoke to him. She couldn't be sure what he'd expected when she was brought in here, looking the way she did, but apparently her cognitive comprehension was not it.

'You . . . how do you—'

'They got anything besides cameras monitoring us, my guy?' she asked, cutting him off. 'Any secret recording devices, shit that makes your werewolf ears crackle?'

Stuff that could have been added between now and the last time she'd received intelligence on the exact set-up of this cell.

'N-no,' he replied, shock evident in his voice. 'Just the cameras. There's no audio.'

'Sweet as,' she said, getting to her feet with a groan. Stretching her body and cracking her neck, Tommi jumped up and down on the spot for a few seconds before she reopened her eyes. Clocking the camera, she crouched down low and sprinted right towards the corner Quaid was sitting in directly underneath it. He tensed, thinking she was coming to attack him, but at the last minute she pivoted and launched herself against the wall, springing back and through the air to grab the camera. She dangled from it like she was Michael Jordan post dunk before she tugged and heaved it from the wall with a triumphant cry. She took a good amount of concrete with her, the whole set-up crashing on the other side of the cell with a *poof* of dust and electronic sparks.

'Well, that was pointless,' Quaid said, now on his feet and staring at her like the crazy person she was. 'You have ten minutes before they come right down here and punish you for that, replacing it with another.'

'Seven minutes by my count,' Tommi rebutted. 'Hey, can you come here and help me get this contact lens out?'

He looked hesitant at first, like this was a trick, and she could understand why. Yet after years of not much excitement, she was about to bring it crashing into his world in just a few minutes. He inched forward, slowly inspecting as she pointed at her left eye.

'Yeah, yeah, that's it, done!' she beamed, plucking the barely visible object from his fingers. 'Thanks.'

'Your eye,' he breathed.

'I know.' She nodded, marching over to the glass door of the cell, which had been reinforced with an alchemist's charm. 'I couldn't let them see it, especially Lorcan. If they knew I'd come out the other side of *ahi hikoi* seeing the dead, they would have never brought me in here to kick over their deck of cards.'

Scanning the wall as quickly as she could, she looked for the barely visible markers before she placed the contact lens against the glass. There were faces peering out from the other cells, watching what she was doing as she pushed hard to make sure the tiny sphere was flat. Among them she saw some-one that had been described to her in acute detail: a hulking demon with horns that curled tight to his head like hair. He was staring at her, waiting, and she offered a wave. The camera from his cell was already in a pile of rubble at his feet.

'Sup, Yixin,' she called.

He nodded, face solemn, as she took several steps back from the wall. Quaid had been coming forward and she used an arm to push him back behind her.

'Uh uh, I wouldn't,' she cautioned. 'That baby is about to blow.'

'Blow? You put a *bomb* in your contact lens?'

'Lol, no – as if! How would that even work? I had a witch craft a nifty little unlocking charm on to that eyeball cover and in a few seconds we'll hopefully see how effective it is at breaking an alchemist's magic.'

She'd barely finished the sentence when there was a loud crack, followed by several others, and then eventually the whole transparent side of the cell exploded inwards. It showered them in glass, Tommi and Quaid crouching down as the pieces fell around them. Giving it a second, she glanced up to inspect the damage.

'Ha!' she beamed, leaping into a triumphant pose. 'Bloody love ya work, Kala!'

'Who's Kala? And what are you doing with your boobs? Wait, holy shit . . . Are you breaking me out?'

She grinned as she turned to face him, properly noticing for the first time that he hadn't grown weak and thin while in here. Quaid was full Sing Sing: properly shredded and with the bonus of hitting puberty for the added growth spurt. He had gone in a boy in Tommi's eyes and he would come out looking like a man who more closely resembled his brother James than he did Steven. She felt a morsel of relief spread within her bones at that thought. All the while, she was indeed rummaging deep into her bra and feeling her boobs. She knew they would have searched her properly before going inside, pouring over every inch of her while she was unconscious. The contact lens went unnoticed because it helped her look exactly how she was supposed to. She had no doubt the rest of her would have been checked and she pushed that uncomfortable squirm to the side as she thought about some faceless Praetorian Guard soldier patting her down.

They had checked her bra because the underwire was gone, of course, but the shape of her breasts must have felt normal. So they hadn't checked what was *in* her bra. If spotted, it would have looked like film placed over the areola like a clear nipple pasty or covering. Away from her body and held out in front of her, it appeared like a sheet of zit stickers with dozens of circles pressed into the surface. Thankfully she had a large rack, so one covering for each boob was pretty damn sufficient.

'Come with me if you want to live,' she said, in her best Kyle Reese voice. Quaid was still looking at her like she was an alien, but there was the faintest twitch of a smile at her impression.

He followed her out of the cell and directly to Yixin's, where Tommi held up the sheet for the werewolf to see.

'You peel off one sticker for one cell, got it?' she told him. He nodded as she demonstrated her point. 'You need to place it as close to dead centre as you can and – this is the most important bit – place it with *intent*.'

'Intent?'

'Aye, intent – you got me? You need to *intend* for the glass to blow up but even more, you need to intend for what and who is inside to be released. Then you bolt, pray it works, and sprint on to the next one.'

She moved Quaid back from Yixin's cell and they turned away as the glass exploded, the alchemist's charm broken.

'This feels like déjà vu,' the hulking demon said, stepping out and roaring with triumph. The sound echoed down the dark halls of Vankila, soon answered by other cries and growls and howls as Yixin all but rang the dinner bell for everyone who was confined there.

'I've heard great things about you from our mutual sprite friend,' Tommi beamed, her neck arching up to look at him. 'And a demon who speaks very highly also. You've got all my friends singing your praises.'

'Hopefully I can make their acquaintance again,' Yixin said, nodding down at Quaid by her side.

'Right,' Tommi huffed, handing them each a sheet. 'Free as many as you can, as fast as you can.'

Quaid hesitated. 'There's not enough here for everyone.'

'I know,' she said, slowly jogging backwards as a ghost illuminated her path. 'That's what I'm going to work on.'

'How?' Quaid called after her.

'By finding a living alchemist who can help.' She grinned, turning around and sprinting down the path between the prison cells. 'Howdy, Broom.'

'Lovely to see you again, Tommi. Causing a sufficient amount of trouble already, I see,' the ghost remarked, flying alongside her as she ran.

'It's just nice not to see your bowels, if I'm honest.'

'Take a hard left here.'

She almost had to skid to a stop, that's how much speed she had generated, and she withdrew her claws, scraping them along the ground for extra stability as she followed the ghost's directions. Grateful didn't really encapsulate how she was feeling about this vengeful accomplice as a guide. She'd studied a mock-up of Vankila enough times to know she could make her way back through the maze to where she had come from okay, but she was hunting living prey through this labyrinth. Having Broom help rush her towards the one alchemist on this floor whose work could release everyone that was left felt comforting. Pivoting down a right-hand corridor, she paused in front of an illuminated doorway where said male alchemist was frantically pressing the elevator button, desperate to get up and out of there. There was a prison guard in front of her, attempting to block her path to the person she needed. They dragged an enormous, studded hammer along the ground beside them.

'That seems dumb,' Tommi murmured, dropping down as he swung the huge object. It was intended to keep her at a distance. She grinned at him instead, taunting him as she leapt and ducked and weaved closer, inch by inch, until she sprung up between his legs and severed his femoral artery with her claws. There was no need to be over the top about it as she walked away, leaving him to bleed out in a matter of seconds at best, minutes at most. The alchemist was smashing the button even harder now as Tommi closed in.

'Don't you know?' she asked. 'In case of emergencies, *always* use the stairs.'

Chapter 11

Dreckly

Dreckly couldn't quite believe it. The tour bus she was on was slowing down as they drove through the centre of St Andrews. The first and only time she'd seen it had been during the evening, in an entirely different century, when she had run for her life, freezing and full of fear as she continued her escape from Vankila. Now, it was a pretty little university town directly across the River Tay from Dundee. A light rain had turned into a steady downpour and the streets were slick with water, which was perhaps the only thing about the place that felt familiar to her.

'You been here before?' Sorcha asked, the banshee pressed against her shoulder as they sat together on the bus.

'Mmm,' she replied. 'A long, long time ago.'

The Burke sister squeezed her hand, knowing how hard this was for her. The two were dressed like tourists, Sorcha rocking the 'I Love Nessie' T-shirt Dreckly had refused to wear. She already had a camera draped around her neck and the most unsexy pair of cargo pants she had ever seen in her life attached to her body. Dreckly figured she had suffered enough. The long, country road that led to Scotland's Secret Bunker was empty, the day too miserable for most tourists to make the trip outside of an organised tour group.

Built in 1951 to appease the fears of the British Government in the lead-up to the Cold War, the Treize were hiding their Alcatraz in plain sight. Passing by a decommissioned tank at the entrance, Dreckly gave Sorcha a loaded look. As the bus rumbled to a stop, they followed the line of other obedient tourists out and, under the protection of several umbrellas, they hurried towards the entrance. Dreckly frowned at the Crocs Sorcha was wearing as they splashed through the puddles, that too was crossing a line the sprite was reluctant to toe.

Everyone had been careful, arriving slowly and scattering around Scotland as the trap was gently laid. Sorcha had been there the longest, holed up in a little cottage near Perth that had been easy to access by river. It had been Dreckly's suggestion for them to pose as tourists. As part of a group, it meant that tickets were bought for them for various attractions in bulk. The fake IDs barely had to be good to get past the initial check at the start of the day and they weren't checked again. Dreckly and Sorcha – known as Miyah and Cassidy to their present company – filed into the building with their squad of fellow sightseers.

Shuffling past the ticket booth, they assembled in the aged reception area. Everything in this place was aged, that was kind of the point. It felt somewhat like stepping back in time when you crossed the threshold, everything frozen and stale. They were led towards the beginning of the bunker's downwards path, which would eventually dip some 150 metres below the surface. Dreckly only half listened to what their chubby tour guide Xandy was saying as she looked for cameras.

There weren't any here, only at the entrance, and she questioned if they were even working. This wasn't the security focal point and that's exactly why she had targeted it. Back in 1951, if everything had gone to shit and the world had been plunged into Judgement Day, the UK's leading politicians – the Prime Minister, Lords, even the Queen – would have ended up living in this concrete mole hole. Cheerfully, things hadn't turned out that way as they continued their slow descent through a long, grey hallway that seemed to slope downwards for ever.

Sorcha elbowed her, which meant 'take photos, you fake ass tourist', and she did so as they came to a stop at the first series of rooms in the bunker: a command centre and RAD operations base. A voice recording shared details of the specific layout, and Dreckly snapped pics, pretending to be interested in the coordinates that were displayed on a map. Their footsteps echoed through empty dorm rooms, with bunks that had never been slept in and beds that had never been unmade. There was a tiny chapel that looked as redundant as it felt, and she wondered if anyone had ever gotten married there. It felt like a horror-movie version of the last wedding she'd been to, which was beautiful and illuminated and outdoors and *free*.

There was a Polish couple engrossed in a video presentation in one of the command rooms and Dreckly slipped by them, Sorcha on her heels. Nearly walking past the door marked 'communications room', she halted and they ducked inside. It was a weird sight to behold: two women who looked exactly like them in body shape and height. They were even wearing the same outfits, from the camera down to the Crocs.

'It's *The Parent Trap* come to life,' Sorcha muttered, starring at their doppelgängers.

Dreckly smirked. 'The original was better than the remake.'

'Ya damn straight,' the banshee replied, leaning against the door as she listened for the tour group to pass by. 'You two ready?'

They nodded, waiting just a beat before they slipped through the door as Sorcha held it open and quickly shut it behind them. Mildred had hired the girls, out-of-work actresses, and Dreckly had no idea what they'd been told. They probably thought they were performing in some secret camera YouTube stunt, but they had been paid in advance and according to the demon, that's all unemployed thespians cared about. They would be taking the places of Miyah and Cassidy as they finished the tour of Scotland's Secret Bunker. Their tour guide would never know that two members of his party had disappeared somewhere in the concrete jungle of this place.

Now, they just had to wait. Like some true *Alice in Wonderland* shit, there was another door on the other side of the door they'd stepped through. Dreckly and Sorcha crept through it, both nervously eyeing the lone figure in the room: a dummy dressed head-to-toe in British military garb. This room had a lock and Dreckly clicked it in place behind them, turning off the light as they settled in.

'I do not like the idea of us chilling in the dark with a mannequin,' Sorcha whispered. 'What if it starts moving towards us through the dark, ready to slit our throats?'

'I'd feel it.'

'The knife on your throat? Oh yeah, you'd feel that.'

Dreckly elbowed her. 'I'd feel it through the air, trust me. We're not gonna get murdered by a mannequin.'

She wasn't one hundred per cent sure about that, but she wasn't about to tell Sorcha she was monitoring the air particles around the dummy just as closely as she was those outside the door. Staff members moved through the mock displays beyond both doors, switching off lights and double checking there was no one left behind. Then the doors were officially closed at the tourist attraction for the day. Dreckly was just about to move when she sensed something else moving through the dark. It was pressed against the outer door; Dreckly reached for the knife at her waist when she heard a playful *meow*.

'Oh my God, it's a cat,' she sighed, getting to her feet and switching on the light.

'What is? What's a cat?' Sorcha said, hopping up and shaking her limbs loose.

'Outside the door and yeesh, I kind of see what you mean. That is creepy.'

They both stared at the model that was propped next to a telephone, as if ready to answer at the very first ring or reach for any one of the fifty sets of keys hanging on the wall behind them. An ancient computer with an equally ancient keyboard sat unattended in the corner and Dreckly leaned over it, fingers hovering over the dusty keys. With a deep breath she typed the names Avona Humpalot and Alottav Agina, followed by the words 'approved visitation'. The second she hit enter, her senses kicked into overdrive, alerting her to the presence of someone else in this tiny box of a room as the air moved around them.

She spun, seeing nothing but the frozen mannequin, Sorcha, and every other piece of equipment exactly as it was. Her heart thudded under her chest and despite Dreckly's best intentions, she leapt when the previously inanimate model slowly began to move. Sorcha screamed as she darted back too, grabbing a prop vase from behind her like she was ready to beat the damn thing to death if she had to. It turned in a fluid motion to the two of them, Dreckly's knife out and poised as she prepared to get just as bloody as the banshee. After all, she couldn't suffocate something that didn't breathe and she was fairly certain this thing wasn't alive. It had no eyes, no facial features, yet somehow she knew it was looking and seeing her.

'Hello, Avona Humpalot and Alottav Agina,' came a voice she assumed was from the mannequin. It had no lips, but since she highly doubted it was the antique teapot communicating with her she kept her eyes trained on it. 'You are expected and granted entry to Vankila.'

There was a long pause as it waited for her reply.

'Thank . . . you?'

The mannequin moved in such a way that she understood it to be a nod before it grabbed a set of generic keys off the wall. It lifted back a metal sign that had the words 'RED WARNING: VENTILATION MODE' emblazoned across the front. Dreckly thought it had been firmly secured to the wall, yet the mannequin lifted it back with ease, entering and twisting a lock. The entire sign sank into the wall, further and further until it revealed a narrow passageway she and Sorcha would have to turn sideways to fit down. The department-store dummy of doom handed her two different sets of keys that were attached to a small pin.

'Please clip these to your person and remain wearing them at all times,' it instructed.

They did as ordered, Dreckly never once taking her eyes off the bizarre creature that could have easily been a robot but was something else entirely. The way it moved indicated free thought or at least more than cleverly hidden connecting wires.

'Very good,' it said. 'Now if you'll follow me, we can begin.'

'Uh, what's your name?'

It paused for a few beats too long, as if Dreckly had asked a most unusual question.

'I'm Rasputin,' it said, before gesturing for them to follow.

They followed Rasputin down the dark hallway, the door closing behind them as they walked, before entering what looked like a cleaning supplies closet. Unbuckling a different set of keys, Dreckly watched as the lock shifted. It was unlikely someone would get this far, but if they did when the closet was opened they would see your standard assortment of mops and whatnot. With the second lock, that all shifted and slid to the side as the props disappeared into the wall.

Soon they were staring at a metal staircase that spiralled down into the dark in a seemingly endless loop. It was a narrow space, so they had to go one after the other and Dreckly stared at the route with scepticism as red emergency lights flickered on, illuminating the path.

'There you go,' Rasputin said. 'Proceed down. Your guest liaison will meet you at the bottom. Have a lovely day.'

Dreckly took one step inside, her footstep clanging against the metallic surface of the stairs. She paused, leaning back as she and Sorcha stared after the *thing* which was making its way back down the hallway. It didn't walk like anything attempting to pass for human, its movements both jerky and fluid at the same time. It was like a nightmare plucked straight out of a *Puppet Master* movie.

'I feel like it being named Rasputin is a terrible omen,' Sorcha whispered.

'Our names are *Avona Humpalot* and *Alottav Agina*,' Dreckly replied. 'We can't read too much into it.'

'Except that Tommi's contact is an Austin Powers fan.'

'Now *that's* an omen,' Dreckly muttered, the pair beginning the slow and gradual descent down, down, down into the depths of Vankila. This wasn't the main entrance by any stretch of the imagination; it was one of four emergency exits that went largely unused for the most part due to their public access points. They were there as a back-up, which meant they were known by only a select few members of staff and forgotten by others. One of those members of staff was waiting for them, face illuminated by a tablet that had a grid of several Vankila security camera operations playing on it.

Dreckly was shocked to see that he was a boy in every sense of the word. He would have barely been in his twenties, not much older or younger than Amos, yet like the woman who had connected them there was a world-weariness in his expression. This kid had seen plenty in his time, regardless of how brief it was. He was dressed in a matching suit pants and jacket combo, yet with a T-shirt underneath that depicted an image from *The Goon* comic book with the title written in big, red font. He was wearing a pair of red and white Air Jordan 1s that matched, the outfit somewhat of a mix between corporate and casual, which made him look more like the baby-faced CEO of some tech start-up than their mole.

'Did I hear you bad mouthing Austin Powers?' he asked, smiling up at them. The gesture was genuine, but tense: they were all tense. 'I will have you know, we don't stand for Mike Myers slander in this house.'

'Given we're about to wreck the house, I guess it's okay then,' Dreckly replied, joining his level after what felt like the one thousandth step. 'Dreckly Jones, pleasure to meet you.'

He shook her outstretched hand, repeating the gesture with the banshee who introduced herself as well.

'Joss Jabour,' he said. 'Pleasure to meet you both. How'd you find Rasputin?'

'Weird,' Dreckly admitted.

'So fucking weird,' Sorcha agreed.

'Right?! And the whole time I keep thinking about how Rasputin was supposed to have a famously huge cock and, like, someone chose that mannequin's name. So does it have a dick? Or is smooth like a Ken doll down there?'

Dreckly laughed. 'You really are Tommi's best friend.'

'These are the things that occupy my mind at three in the morning when I try not to think about how we're all going to die,' he said, eyes wide. 'Which, speaking of, you'll need this.'

He handed them the tablet, quickly running Dreckly and Sorcha through the mechanics of the device, how to switch between views, and see what the security team would be viewing at any one moment.

'Now, I've got a change of clothes for you here and temporary tattoos that will give you the little Askari mark on your wrist,' he said. 'Sorcha, I have an immortal Custodian pendant for you; it's more believable that way but keep it tucked beneath your shirt. No one walks around with them flashing out like detective badges. It would be an immediate giveaway.'

'Got it.' The banshee nodded, crouching down and beginning to go through the items he'd brought them. There was more space down here at this level, but barely. They wouldn't be able to physically get changed until Joss was gone.

'So,' Joss huffed, an air of recital to his next words. 'Watch me on here as I navigate my way through to the security station. When I'm in there and chatting to them, that's when you move, because they'll be distracted. Knock on the door, I'll let you in, say Lorcan is looking for me or something and we'll swap.'

'Then it's over to me,' Sorcha smirked. 'Banshee thrall ahoy.'

'I need to leave here ASAP,' Joss said. 'The tips about Tommi will start coming in any moment and I need to be on the streets to clock her first before I alert Lorcan and the others. That will take a few key resources away from here and hopefully you'll have had enough time to locate what you're after.'

'When Ben is brought in, the labs will be offline,' Dreckly confirmed. 'The security guards being manipulated by Sorcha means they'll stay conscious and stay making their twice hourly check-ins. When Tommi starts taking the bottom level, we disable every alarm and alert possible to buy her minutes.'

Joss nodded. 'Once they get to the middle floors, where the labs are, you're not going to be able to contain the alerts. There're too many so just let it go through.'

'That's when the ground teams come in,' Dreckly said, taking a deep breath. 'They split up, use the four emergency exits, and I open the main one as a diversion.'

'It will be chaos in here then.' Joss nodded. 'The best you can hope for is creating enough mayhem that this administration level is distracted for a bit. The first place they will try and run to will be exactly where you are: security.'

'I'll kill the guards then,' Dreckly added, noting the way Joss flinched. 'I'm sorry, I know they're probably friends of yours—'

'We can knock them out,' Sorcha said, placing a hand on her arm. 'That's not a guarantee they'll live, of course, but it will take them out of the game for a bit and at least give them a chance.'

'Thank you.' Joss muttered. 'I appreciate that. I know it doesn't make sense – everyone here is an enemy to you – but there are good folks here just so deeply entrenched they can't see their way out.'

'How about you?' Dreckly asked. 'What's your exit route?'

'The most logical one,' he replied. 'Once they take Tommi and Ben, I'll stay in the field to clean up whatever mess there might be and interview any sources I can. Eventually I'll disappear. Right around the same time things get bad here, I will have been "abducted" off the streets.'

She could tell he didn't like this plan, probably feeling like it was a bit far away from the action. Yet it had been non-negotiable for Tommi: either he got to safety and away earlier or he wasn't allowed to be involved at all. Dreckly understood why: he wasn't a monster or wielder of any kind of mystical ability like them. He was just an immortal human who could die as easily as the mortal ones. Even the likelihood of him making it through all of this unscathed was slim.

'Aight, well,' he sighed, 'I'd say good luck but that seems a little redundant at this point and I'd feel like a dickhead. So . . . see you at security soon.'

They muttered their goodbyes, Joss leaving them with the tablet as Dreckly and Sorcha remained in the unnatural bask of the red emergency light. They tracked his path through the cameras onscreen, scrolling as he moved from one to the other.

'We're killing those guards,' Dreckly murmured.

'Oh, fuck yeah,' Sorcha agreed. 'Just didn't wanna upset the kid.'

In silence, they dressed. It was a relief to be out of the tourist couture but Askari administrative fashion wasn't much better, with Dreckly cringing against the sweater vest she found herself tucking a polo shirt into. She'd been given instructions about what kind of accessories they needed, that truly being her speciality, and as she adjusted the pair of horn-rimmed glasses on the bridge of her nose she knew they were perfect. People didn't *know her* in the same way they knew Casper or Heath, so the things she needed to blend were more subtle. Shifting her body type with extra layers and a stuffed bra or tweaking the shape of her face were all things that could be done easily and effectively.

'He's there,' Sorcha said, adjusting the newsboy cap on her head. 'Let's move.'

While Dreckly looked like a preppy pain in the ass, the banshee appeared as if she had fallen out of another time entirely with wide-legged pants and a matching waistcoat in the same shade of brown. It was clever, because many of the people who worked here had never really left behind the time period they loved the most. This point was made even clearer to her as they pushed out on to the floor, stepping through the door and into a practically abandoned part of the office.

Yet as they marched further in, passing desks that were occupied with Askari busily typing away on computers in some instances, typewriters in others, Dreckly was reminded of the organised bedlam of the old studio lots she and Mildred used to work on. There too you would find people dressed in completely different period attire, dashing across from one sound stage to another while a harried assistant chased after them with a stack of paper. When they reached the main floor, she had to urge herself not to panic as what looked like an M.C. Escher worthy maze of desks and cubicles and workstations stretched out endlessly. She glanced down at the tablet they were carrying to make sure Joss was still there, that everything was still going to plan, and to distract herself from the fear she thought was about to bubble out of her pores.

Some creatures could sense that, so she repeated a calming mantra to herself as Sorcha took the lead and weaved her way through the office labyrinth. The banshee had told her she could will people to look away, will them to pay no attention to the two women who were dressed just like any other Vankila workers and deep within their midst. She could tell the banshee was doing that now, feeling just the faintest ripple of power as they passed. Eyes stayed down at their station, heads didn't turn, and when Sorcha knocked on the security door with an annoyed sigh it all just seemed so normal, so natural. When Joss slipped out and they slipped inside in a seamless transition, Dreckly couldn't help but wonder if the banshee had accidentally dosed her a little bit as well.

'Fellas,' Sorcha beamed, hands wide and smile even wider as she inched forward. Her hips swayed in a subtle yet noticeable way, the movement drawing the eyes of the four men as she continued to croon. 'I'm going to need you all to wheel your chairs right over against the wall like *good* little boys.'

'Mmmkay,' one said with a grin, nodding in a manner that told Dreckly if Sorcha asked him the time, he'd build her an entire damn clock.

'Gooood,' she purred. 'Now I'm going to tell you a small story, okay? I want all eyes on me as I tell it and a nice, quiet, captive audience.'

Dreckly was already getting to work as the banshee did her job and she grabbed one of the empty office chairs to take a seat.

'The only time you're allowed to chat is when your friends call on the radio for the check-in every thirty minutes,' Sorcha continued. 'You tell them everything is green and you'll touch base again soon. Can I get a yes ma'am?'

A chorus of 'yes ma'am' echoed behind her, Dreckly only half listening as she glanced over her shoulder to see Sorcha moving from guard to guard, slowly disarming them one after the other as she spoke. Next would be the rope and the cuffs to secure them to those chairs. Sorcha would hold the handsets to their mouths so they could reply to their colleagues on schedule, telling them it was all ace and sunny. Cutting her gaze back to the screens in front of her, she flicked through until she found the laboratories.

The rage and anger that coursed through her veins when she saw the creatures held there made her want to commit an atrocity. Several, in fact. She knew how that felt, knew the fear and the horror and the hopelessness that came with imprisonment. She'd been born in this place, not knowing any better for years until she had her freedom and then . . . they'd tried to take it away from her again, putting her in that glass tube and expecting her to remain there like a piece of meat only good for lobotomising so they could maintain their power. That's what it was all about, of course: the Treize and their stupid fucking power.

'Not for long,' she whispered to herself, feeling the conviction of her words as she quickly checked and rechecked the floor plan. She disabled the security mechanisms that would have blocked her path, switching red lights green, and she raised the digital dial that would emit the gas used to knock out most of the supernaturals before they were rolled away on stretchers and taken to operating rooms for the worst of the experiments. Closing her eyes, Dreckly imagined herself moving through the bowels of Vankila like she was an air particle herself. She felt the support of the chair she was in, but she let that weight fade into the far reaches of her mind as she concentrated on the air itself and how it was flowing floors below her.

She channelled it, stretching her powers to the limits as she directed the gas from one valve into another. Her own strength waned as she pushed it to work fast, forcing the gas deep into the lungs of one scientist who was being particularly resistant. One by one, they all began to drop. As she opened her eyes to check whether that's what she was seeing on the monitor as well, Dreckly let out an exhausted sigh. With the slide of her index finger, she killed the gas. Feeling the sweat sticking to the fabric of her many-layered ensemble, she noted that she was puffing just a little bit as she watched the unconscious bodies of the scientists lying still. Two had been mid-procedure, their frames now draped over the being they had intended to slice apart.

'You okay back there?' Sorcha's voice cut into her mental fatigue.

'Yes,' she replied, noting the wariness there. 'I'm good to go. You?'

'See you on the other side, sprite.'

Tablet in hand, Dreckly flashed a smile that she hoped communicated what she felt as she left the relative safety of the security room. The whole mission was risky, but this part was the riskiest as the banshee and the sprite separated to go their different ways. That meant there was no other being to watch their back, no other being to divert the interested gaze of a curious worker if they glanced Dreckly's way. Yet Tommi and Ben's sighting had just come in, Dreckly watching as resources poured from her screen and through the office as they rushed to take the bait. Nobody was looking at her and that's why it was the perfect moment.

The security guards' passes could go anywhere and she used one to take her down to the fourth level, each floor being numbered in reverse just like the Sydney outpost. The fifth level was maximum security, the fourth level the laboratories, the third level medium security and interrogation suites, the second level minimum security and holding cells, and the first level – where she had just come from – administration. It seemed dubious that a place this significant would have only five levels, but each of them was *huge* and ran the space and width of several football fields. Not to mention all five were buried hundreds of metres underground – all facts she didn't want to think about as she stepped out of the elevator and turned right towards the labs.

She had insisted on this task. It was Tommi Grayson who had been given the vision by The Three of the beings locked up and restrained in this part of Vankila. Yet from the second it had been relayed to her, Dreckly knew that she was meant to perform this particular job. She had to. There was just one security officer stationed out the front of the labs, which made sense as you needed clearance to get to this level anyway and each door was supposed to be sealed with a discreet, red, flashing light. That signal was now flashing green behind him, but there had been no clue about the change so the guard didn't know that as he looked up at Dreckly's approach.

'Hi there.' He smiled. 'Are you here for Mead—'

His grin faltered, mouth opening and closing like a puffer fish as he fought for oxygen. Dreckly was pulling it from his lungs, finding it harder than she usually would have after what she'd pulled off only moments before with the gas, but not impossible, and eventually he landed with a heavy thud on his desk. He wasn't dead, just unconscious. That would do for now. She unclipped the set of keys dangling from his belt and pushed her way into the labs. If she was a bank robber, she'd be going straight for the vault. Instead of bills, though, her prize was cages. Dozens upon dozens of cages stacked together and on top of each other as supernaturals clawed through the bars, desperate to get out. They were stirring, working hard to do just that as if they sensed the change in energy in the hall-ways outside of the room when Dreckly entered.

The lights were activated by motion and they flicked on, one after the other, illuminating the horror before her. She felt dirty even just staring at this scene, every creature quiet as they assessed whether she was friend or foe. She wasn't in a lab coat and that would usually be the biggest indicator that she was an enemy. Frustrated, she ripped the stupid sweater vest from her body as she placed the tablet and other tools down, beginning to move from cage to cage as she spoke.

'My name is Dreckly and I'm here to free you, but the only way we can make that happen is if we all work together.'

Her sentence was punctuated with the metallic clang of a lock as she threw it back, releasing the first crammed cage of six werewolves. She had chosen them first, intending to copy Tommi's idea of releasing the most useful so they could help others while she moved on to more pressing tasks.

'Free everyone as fast as you can,' she ordered. 'There are others in the lab, then we assemble back here. All right?'

There was a chorus of murmured agreement as the creatures did as she asked; Dreckly had never doubted they would as she was the first person who had provided them with hope in a while. There was just one woman contained in the final cage and as Dreckly released her, she understood why she had been placed alone. She was an arachnia, her tall body and long limbs stretching out as she emerged from imprisonment. Standing at attention, this lady was easily seven foot tall, with cheekbones so sharp they looked like they would penetrate her skin. Dreckly could see the marks all over her body: the scars from wounds that had healed and the fresher incisions that were bleeding through the flimsy paper gown she had been dressed in.

'Vhat do you neeeed?' she said with a heavy Russian accent.

'Everyone free,' Dreckly replied. 'But no one can leave just yet; it's essential that's understood.'

The woman stared down at Dreckly with an intensity that told her she had been waiting a long time for this moment. With a single nod, she marched off towards the door that led to the other labs. The way she moved, it was like watching a daddy-long-legs in action, and the being clicked her fingers at four others as she passed them.

'Wiv me, quick.'

They followed her orders without question, Dreckly turning back to check all of the cages were now empty. She grabbed the tablet, swiping across the screen until she saw Sorcha staring back at her expectantly. The banshee threw her a thumbs-up and Dreckly returned it. Slipping out into the hallway, she was unsurprised to see a trail of blood as the Russian spider woman dragged the body of a scientist behind her with one hand. It was testament to Joss's naivety that he thought anyone here would be left alive: if they didn't die at the hands of Sorcha and Dreckly, they were going to die much worse at the hands of the beings they had tortured.

In one of the labs, a goblin was being helped off the operating table by a one-handed demon and a weathered werewolf, all three looking like they had seen better days. Dreckly stepped over the bodies of the scientists – also recently dispatched – and began going through every drawer she could find. She gathered what was useful – first-aid supplies in some cases and food in others – before stripping the dead scientists of their clothes. She tried to avoid the bloodied items, but she knew that wouldn't matter much to those who were receiving them. If the alternative between fighting for your life with your tits out was a bloodied tank top, you were wearing the tank top.

'Food,' she said, laying out what items she had when she returned to the main room. 'Fresh water and clothes here. Patch up what you can with the first-aid kits.'

The Russian was back, two werewolves behind her and carrying dead scientists. 'Anyvon who needs fresh meat, eat.'

Dreckly did her best not to rush back into the hallway, the wet tearing and ripping sounds difficult to listen to. She held no judgement towards what her people needed even if she avoided meat of any kind, human or not. There were others who felt the same way, coming with her as they raided every lab, every staff room, every storage cupboard, and brought the supplies back to the others. The Russian brought the guard from out the front too, strangling him while he was still unconscious. Dreckly made her third costume change, dressing in his attire and trying to make it look as reasonable as she could.

'An unattended guard station will look suspicious if anyone comes by,' she told the spider woman. 'I can discreetly disarm threats from a distance if needed, but hopefully just a presence will be enough until the time comes.'

'How long?' she asked.

'An hour, two at most.'

'I vill make sure everyone vaits.'

'Thank you . . .' Dreckly paused, realising she didn't know this creature's name.

'Silver,' the being supplied. 'You are a sprite, are you not?'

Dreckly stammered, truly shocked and surprised by the immediate recognition of *what* she was by a being who had no idea *who* she was.

'H-how . . .? People don't . . . I'm not used to being identified on sight.'

'Knew it ze zecond you arrived,' Silver replied. 'I hate your kind.'

Dreckly let out a weird laugh, never having been known widely enough to be hated. It was a bizarre kind of exhilaration but made sense now that she recalibrated the distance two arachnia had seemed to keep from her at the supernatural summit in Australia.

'Vut do I care? A sneaky sprite vants to break us out of here? If it was a shifter I vouldn't even care. You say you can get us out? Vine. Just get us out. Or we'll eat you.'

Dreckly nodded, her surprise still outweighing any fear she had for the threats just lobbed against her. Instead, her heart felt light and heavy both at the same time as she looked around the room, staring at the faces of these creatures who had been through so much. They were taking grateful sips of water from mugs held out to them; they were feeding each other and healing each other and caring for each other. The fact they had any empathy and compassion left made her hopeful. And terrified.

'All right,' she said, putting down the tablet once more as she checked the cameras. 'As I said, my name is Dreckly Jones. I was born here.'

'In Vankila?' someone asked.

'Yes,' she replied, ignoring the wave of whispers that spread through the group. 'It was many decades ago, but I escaped. I know they tell you it's impossible, but I did it – and I had help. I'm here to be that help for you tonight and I am not alone. Soon, Vankila will go into a state of emergency as it's attacked from above and below.'

'We're in the middle,' a witch noted.

'That's right.' Dreckly nodded. 'We need to stay here until that happens, that's when everyone will have the best chance to escape and you have a choice. If you head up to freedom, which I understand and fully relate to, all I ask is that if you see any Vankila staff members, you take them with you.'

'To freedom?' someone scoffed.

'To the grave,' Dreckly corrected. 'Even one dead soldier is one less living soldier we have to fight.'

'Vhat's ze other option?' Silver questioned.

'Every prisoner from down below is coming up,' Dreckly said, noting the impact her words had on the others as a hushed silence fell. 'I'm staying to help them along with everyone else on this level, both friends of mine and complete strangers. I don't expect anyone to stay after what you've been through, but I would never turn away the help.'

It didn't take long for the nearly sixty-two beings she counted to come to a collective decision. It started with one person barking out that they would 'rather fucking die than leave another soul down here'. That call received an overwhelmingly positive response that seemed to spread from creature to creature, regardless of what shape they were in.

'Ve vill all stay and help fight,' the Russian spider confirmed, summing up the attitude of seemingly everyone. Dreckly did her best not to become overwhelmed, biting the inside of her cheek to keep her emotions in check. She let out a shaky breath.

'You have no idea how much this means,' she said.

'Yah, ve do,' her seven-foot ally responded.

She left them to heal and rest and recover as much as they could in such a short space of time. That seemed like an impossible feat on paper, yet Dreckly knew how quickly one could improve when they'd been given so little for so long. In the security ensemble, she slipped through the labs and took the post of a man who was now most certainly being devoured by the creatures he had once guarded. Only one passing Askari came by, dropping off a nightly report which Dreckly signed without a word, before they left and she was alone again, watching on the security cameras as first Tommi and then Ben were brought in. They were both unconscious, neither one play acting, and her skin prickled as she forced herself to sit idly by and wait.

She knew Sorcha was watching the same thing, disabling the alarms for the third and fourth and fifth levels so that when all mayhem broke loose, it would be minutes rather than seconds before the rest of the building was alerted. Dreckly switched to the view of the bottom level, watching and waiting as she stared at a seemingly boring prison hallway. The second she saw an explosion of glass, she knew it was time. Getting to her feet, she wedged the desk chair in the laboratory doorway so there was no barrier to the exit.

Slipping her fingers between her lips, she let out a piercing whistle that echoed down the hallway. The response that bounced back was enough to have every guard in the entire prison shitting their pants.

Chapter 12

Casper

Berlin felt different.

Casper couldn't explain it, but from the second she touched down she could feel it. It was a strange sensation: this city was the place she had identified as home for so many years and then all of a sudden it just ... wasn't. She knew what had shifted: it was her. It was also the season. Berlin in summer could feel like an entirely new city, the days long and the parks full of people as the outdoors became everyone's personal lounge-room while they made the most of the glorious weather. Australia's climate had her better conditioned for this kind of season and she roamed the streets at night with a smile on her face. Of course, no one could see that expression, since it was covered by the burqa she was wearing in a lightweight blue fabric that meant her identity stayed hidden but her passage through the city was unlimited.

She passed Oslo Kaffebar, her old haunt and the venue that had once been the arcade bar 1984 run by a goblin known as Hogan and enforced by a rockabilly demon, Ginger. It was a gin joint now and it needled at her as she gazed inside, seeing all the humans occupying the space that had been one of their only true sanctuaries. There were still a few of those places left, even as the structures that had controlled their world for so long were disintegrating around them. Phases endured: the nightclub run by a pack of rogue werewolves known aptly as the Rogues stood as tall as it ever did. The neon sign flickered as she passed under it, as if winking at her with recognition, welcoming her to a place she and Barastin had danced in together in life. They'd frequented Phases just as much following his death, no one any the wiser to his presence by her side as she cut a lonely figure at the bar. The club felt somewhat muted as she entered it now, her eyes sweeping the place and seeing so few of the supernaturals she usually recognised.

'Humans,' a voice said from behind her, the tone reflecting her own disappointment. 'We're overrun with them, but it keeps the lights on.'

Casper grinned, turning around to see the face of her dear friend Yu as she leaned against the bar. With a toothpick dangling from her mouth and a uniform of tight, black leather pants and a white tank, she looked like the coolest person to ever cool as the medium embraced her in a hug. The former Praetorian Guard soldier hugged her in return, the gesture lingering longer than that of casual acquaintances. She and Yu went *way* back.

'Hell, it's wonderful to see you,' she said, grinning down at her friend.

'And you're married! What the fuck?! I hope you got a pre-nup.'

Casper laughed as the woman pulled her one hand towards her, inspecting the ring.

'I'm not joking,' Yu deadpanned.

'Divorce stats are the least of my worries right now.'

Her friend huffed with understanding, jerking her head towards the staff area. 'Shall we?'

Casper and Yu sliced through the crowd, who all seemed blissfully ignorant as they danced to a Doja Cat track spun from the decks of a DJ she didn't recognise. Usually one of the Rogues – Sanjay – was their in-house DJ but he was nowhere to be seen. Neither was Gus, the mass of meat that bounced rowdy patrons at the door, or Clay, the disco queen snapping pics of all the partygoers for Phases socials.

'Everyone's scared,' Yu said, as if reading Casper's mind. 'We've gone from eighty per cent supernatural capacity every night to, like, eight. The Treize know this is a preferred hangout. No one wants to be somewhere the Treize can find them right now.'

'It's that bad?' she asked, the pair stepping into a hallway that was still painted with a jungle theme from the previous owners. She slipped out of her disguise to reveal the satin summer dress she had been wearing underneath.

'Just because they haven't declared outright war on the entire monster population like they have down your way, doesn't mean things are sunny. It's not as overt as that, of course, but people are being *very* careful.'

Casper had expected them to turn into the staff room, but instead Yu led her downstairs and through the venue's freezer. There was a staircase there, which led to the cells the Rogues usually chained themselves up in during the nights of the full moon. Those original structures remained, yet the makeshift werewolf prison had undergone some expansions since the last time she saw it – significant ones. It looked like army barracks in a way, bunk beds and cots stretching out in every direction. Turned out the reason Casper hadn't seen much of Berlin's supernatural population since she landed was because they were all here. Heads turned as Yu and Casper passed, faces recognising her and whispers spreading as the former soldier and medium made for the raised level at the end.

All of this was directly under Phases, clearly making use of the existing structures and adding to them as well as it now connected with the apartment building next door. The loading dock looked like it had become their official meeting room, with the entirety of the Rogues gathered around a large table as she joined them.

'Well well well,' Clay beamed, jumping to his feet, 'if it isn't Casper the friendly ghostee with the mostee.'

He embraced her and she him, Clay being her third favourite among the group after Yu's long-time partner Dolly, who acknowledged her with a respectful tilt of the head. Dolly wasn't much of a hugger. Casper leaned back, examining the 'big ol' gay werewolf' Clay self-identified as.

'Are you wearing a beret?' she asked.

'Mami yes, we're going full revolution chíc. I thought you got the memo with this cute lil nineties supermodel number? You even got a new arm to match!'

'Not a new arm.' Casper smiled, holding up the bionic limb for him to inspect as she rotated her wrist and curled her fingers. 'Customisable LED lights, baby. I just choose what I want on the colour wheel.'

'Hey, that's good to know. If I survive this with any digits missing I can at least be cute.'

He gestured for her to sit and she did, noting that the table wasn't just occupied by the Rogues. She knew Ginger – the demon had been one of the key gatherers of intelligence for Heath for several years now. She hadn't expected to see Hogan there too, but it was a good sign: the more species the better. Their challenges were about as big as the goblin's afro if she was being truthful and she acknowledged the presence of two local witches as well. The remainder of the Rogues made up the rest: Zillia, Gus and Sanjay rounding out the numbers.

'Phases has become a refugee camp,' she said, looking around. 'How are you managing to hide all this?'

'Combined spells and charms of five different covens,' one of the witch's answered. 'Six if you count Journey, who's the sole survivor of hers.'

'And luck,' Yu answered truthfully. 'They think I'm the only one left and we've planted scattered sightings all over, making it seem like everyone else ran. They won't take me cos I have no magical properties, so I'm of little use to them.'

'We let the occasional Askari or Custodian break the protections, unknowingly of course,' Zillia added. 'They come in, look around, see only Yu and a club populated by humans now. There's nothing to say otherwise.'

'Plus, when Hogan's operation went underground a while back that started laying the groundwork for us,' Yu noted. 'But I fear our luck is about to run out. We're at capacity, people are sharing bunks, and it's only a matter of time before the Praetorian Guard start looking at what's under their feet.'

'Why not?' Sanjay snorted. 'They've looked everywhere else.'

Casper nodded, listening to their troubles intently. 'I may have a solution to that.'

Clay clapped his hands together with excitement. 'Praise Jojo Zaho, I knew you were here for a reason!'

Casper held up her bionic hand, trying to ease his elation. 'I didn't say it's a solution you're going to like, but it's one that will get you all up and out of here for a moment even if there's a cost.'

Dolly snorted. 'There's always a cost. No one wants to be hiding down here for ever. We want to be up there, fighting. We just need a good target and a battle we can win.'

'How about twelve?' Casper countered.

The offer was met with silence, the void at first loaded as she waited for someone to ask whether she was joking. They didn't. Instead, Ginger leaned forward with anticipation. The eagerness in her eyes was mirrored in the eyes of those around her, no one flinching or withdrawing or backing away from this fight. Clay twiddled his fingers together, spinning around in his chair like a Bond villain.

'Go oooooon,' he crooned.

'Barry,' Casper called, pulling him towards her in an instant. A chorus of yelps greeted his sudden appearance, the fear he sparked in others only making him stronger, and she saw her brother's unearthly glow brighten just a little with happiness. He wasted no time, however. There was too much happening, too much in motion, that he couldn't afford to be in one place for too long. Casper felt spoiled that she'd had him for the entire evening of the wedding, and she smiled at her sibling as she thought about everything he'd managed to pull off for her and Kala that night. He was pulling off even more now as he helped create a three-dimensional version of the paperwork Casper was laying out on the table.

'These are integral Treize sites across Europe, Asia and Africa,' she said, Barry creating versions of each that hovered there in the space above them. 'I'm proposing we attack all of them.'

'When?' Dolly asked.

'ASA-fucking-P,' Yu countered. 'I hope that's what you were about to say.'

Casper beamed. 'Actually, it was pretty damn close. We need you to all put the word out, now, via channels that you trust. We'll take whoever is willing to fight, we're not gonna be picky. The aim is to dismantle those locations and liberate whatever supernaturals are being detained inside.'

'Why so soon?' Hogan asked, only for Ginger to grip his arm at the question.

'Don't you get it?' The demon grinned, her teeth sharpening with anticipation. 'They're taking out Vankila, right? That's why you need the distraction?'

'It's more than that,' Barastin said, plucking the words right out of Casper's mouth. 'The Three have communicated that Vankila's fall is important, albeit impossible up until this point. So yes, there is a team moving on that target. But the question is then ... what's next? Say that's successful, how long until the Treize firm up every other site and location they have? How long until they execute all of your friends, family members, forgotten names that they've been experimenting on? How long until they get rid of the evidence and decide that they must strike back and strike back *hard*?'

Her brother was so good at this, his passion bleeding into his words and charging them with a life he no longer had. She could see the power in it as the meaning reached around the table, seizing the collective spirit of all present.

'We can't give them that chance,' Casper said, finishing for him. 'America, Antarctica, the Middle East, Russia, South America, every island off every coast off every continent is planning to do exactly the same thing we are. It's easy to defend one attack, but what about dozens? Hundreds? We can't win every battle, but starting enough of them might be our only opportunity to win the war.'

She knew more than just those around the table were listening to her and Casper glanced over her shoulder, scanning the faces of the many who had flocked to the Rogues for sanctuary. The fear was palpable, but it was amazing how useful that could be when directed at a common enemy.

'The Three are dying,' she continued. 'They cannot be saved no matter how many of us the Treize try to slice and dice. We may never get another opportunity like this and yes, some of us will die.'

'Some of us are already dead!' Barastin added, earning a hearty chuckle from those paying attention.

'Death before dishonour,' Clay said, gesturing towards one of his many tattoos. 'They dishonour us, again and again and again. Now we're forced to live like this, to hide underground like goblins – no offence.'

'Some taken,' Hogan murmured.

'I'm in like fucking sin, Casper and her dead, hot brother,' Clay finished. 'Just tell us how we're organising this, cos Lord knows I love strategic construction.'

If Casper could have cracked her knuckles, she would have. Instead, she dived right the hell in.

'We organise via power,' she said. 'We split everyone who is willing and able into teams, making sure there's a mix of skill sets in each group regardless of where they're being sent.'

'Goblins for brains, werewolves for brawn,' Yu murmured.

Casper grinned. 'Exactly! We need witches in every group, which is going to take some work as I know the covens like to stick to themselves.'

'We can convince them,' one of the witches said. 'We have to.'

'Good, because the basic security mechanism for each facility is a combination of tech and alchemy. We're going to need every skilled sorceress we can find, along with every agile arachnia and greedy goblin hacker if they're down for the cause.'

'Fuck it,' Yu shrugged, 'I even know humans who'd be down.'

Casper tilted her head as she listened to the murmurs of agreement spreading around the table, others nodding as they suggested names of humans they knew and who they thought could help as well. She glanced at her brother, Barastin's surprised gaze meeting her own. Neither of them had expected this, yet they couldn't turn down the help if it was offered. A mortal would just be canon fodder in most instances, yet Yu knew retired soldiers and special forces operatives – Clay, too. And in terms of helping with communications and transport and even temporary housing, the humans could be invaluable.

Once they had established their rule in secret, the Treize had never cared much for the human beings beneath them. They were occasionally useful for things like the witch hunts, where their hate and fear had been easy to ignite. It had forced the witches inward and the werewolves outward in the centuries that followed, yet Casper knew they had been disappointed by the lack of usefulness from humans ever since. Now they were cattle at best, their cities a playground for supernaturals, their petty politics and wars just something to be skirted around or avoided altogether. It was utilising them in the coming battle that would be so completely and utterly unexpected to their enemy. Judging by Barastin's grin, she knew her twin was thinking *exactly* what she was thinking.

'This whole thing's a bit queer, isn't it?'

Casper smirked at her brother's language, instantly knowing without knowing that he meant both them and the *whole* situation. She sipped her latte from the comfort of the café across the street while she stared at the Bierpinsel. It was absolutely the weirdest piece of architecture in a city full of weird architecture, the brush-like shape abruptly prodding up from the ground as if saying, 'Ha, look at me, damn it!' You could not *not* look at it, with the rainbow tower she and Barastin had once called home demanding the eye of any passing person. So many nights had been spent inside that place, there were so many memories with Collette and with her brother and with her old life, that she almost felt bad about what she was about to do.

'Now is not the time to get sentimental,' Barastin added, his mind always chugging down a path parallel to hers. He was visible only to her as his ghost form sat alongside Casper in the café, the pair watching as the peak-hour foot traffic started to dwindle. Once everyone was assigned their respective targets, Casper had been unsurprised to find hers was the

Bierpinsel. It had once been the most significant base for Treize operations in Germany, with Barastin and her maintaining a residence on the top floor. It had been dismantled once she left, the supernatural government's presence pulling out of the city while a cult of undead werewolves had run rampant.

Now it had been built back up. Or at least that's what the Treize were trying to do, as if they could sense the imminent threats coming. For once, they actually couldn't. With The Three's death looming and the sickly women refusing to offer any more of their predictive insight, the Treize were completely and utterly in the dark. *About time too*, she thought. All around the world, right at that very moment, every Treize site was about to be infiltrated. In some cases, they had been already: the guards just didn't know it yet. The Transylvanian headquarters was the only location left alone, it being relatively useless as a strategic target while all thirteen members of the Treize remained there and made it impenetrable. Even if getting inside to access The Three was a tempting prospect.

Yet like an octopus, their base of operations was only as useful as the tentacles they had to do their bidding. They wanted to sever those tentacles. More than that, they wanted to enrage the Treize enough that when they were forced to leave their sanctuary, they wouldn't have their usual resources to defend them. She thought of her friends watching and waiting the way she was as they counted down the minutes. Her wife was assembling the safeguards in Melbourne ahead of the big showdown there, the other one set to take place on the Gold Coast and deploy many of the human allies they now had thanks to selkies like Amos and shifters like Shazza. Here, in front of one of the biggest targets, her team seemed tiny. In fact, once Barastin left to spread himself as thin as he could helping all of the others, it would be just her and Yu as the only supernaturals involved. The other players were human, all folks that Yu trusted and had worked with in various capacities over the years.

'You should go,' Casper said, looking down at her coffee cup. 'The others need you more than I do.'

'You always need me,' he rebutted, but his form was already fading as he let himself disappear.

'Ain't that the truth?' she murmured, his eyes twinkling at the response just as Barastin evaporated entirely. She barely had to sit alone for more than a second before a woman in a pretty, yellow floral dress and floppy hat joined her. Casper nearly choked when she realised it was Yu, expecting her but *not expecting* such an effective disguise. She'd known her for close to a decade and never, ever seen her in anything close to resembling a skirt or dress.

'What?' Yu smirked, clearly enjoying Casper's reaction. 'Not all of us can pull off an emerald-green hijab quite so spectacularly.'

Casper blushed with the compliment. The disguise not only kept her hair hidden from view, but the draped maxi dress she had teamed it with hid many of her identifying physical features. She wouldn't need to hide them for much longer.

'Your brother here?' Yu asked. 'Oh my God, I didn't just sit on him, did I?'

'No,' Casper laughed. 'He's gone, just like we should be.'

'Aye aye, captain,' Yu saluted as they got to their feet, Casper leaving behind payment for her coffee. They walked away from the Bierpinsel, which seemed counterintuitive given that it was their desired target, but the steps they descended to the U-Bahn station below was just a brief detour. Few of the other targets were positioned in such wildly populated areas, which made theirs tricky because they wanted to minimise innocent casualties if they could. That meant waiting until the evening, the clock ticking closer to midnight as they navigated their way through the empty station platforms.

Pedestrians were practically non-existent and only light foot traffic remained around the Berlin landmark, which was key. Casper walked with purpose, Yu in step beside her, as a train pulled away from the platform and the rush of air sent their clothes billowing. They passed three homeless men sitting against a wall, the figures rising to their feet as they moved by and joining them as they pushed away the blanket of newspapers. Underneath had been weapons and tactical clothing, which became visible as they shed their disguises. Casper ripped her own away, feeling her hair flying out behind her as she marched. Yu grunted with relief as the hat was tossed and the summer frock stripped off, revealing a practical uniform of black bike pants and a singlet. It made Casper feel like there was a sense of normalcy to the world.

A street busker up ahead went to toss their saxophone as she saw them approach, before reconsidering and gently placing the instrument in wrapped cloth. The top hat and novelty glasses she had been wearing were properly hurled, however, as she tapped a businessman on the shoulder and a briefcase was discarded. The duo had already dispatched the barrier that led to a small set of stairs used by maintenance workers at the station. They disappeared into the dark, several small lights at ground level clicking on as they went and illuminating the path for others. Casper had used this route back when she had lived in the Bierpinsel and she had been desperate to find answers about the conspiracy behind her brother's murder. She had trodden down this very same train track as she'd snuck away to Latvia, completely unaware about where and what her search would lead her to.

This had been her gateway to freedom once and that journey had led her back here. Now, a woman in tactical gear – the same woman who had looped the station's security cameras just fifteen minutes earlier so nothing would be amiss – held open a deteriorating metal door for her. The others were already moving up the rusted stairs cautiously as they ascended right through the core of the Bierpinsel. Yu and the other woman were at Casper's rear, the pair just as silent as everyone quietly puffed their way to the top. This stairwell was never on the Bierpinsel's building plans, Barastin's death unearthing it as he became unrestricted to the conventions of physical walls. It opened up in the wardrobe of what had once been a spare bedroom Collette used for visitors.

The bodies ahead of them stilled, with four stiff head nods moving down the chain to communicate they had reached the top. Casper turned back to make sure the two women behind her got the message, Yu sliding a tactical headset down like a headband as she offered a thumbs-up. As a general rule, Casper tried to avoid guns if she could and the ones she had used in the past were handguns that could be hidden easily. What Yu and the other woman were carrying was overt and they adjusted the serious firepower in their hands. Casper's talents lay elsewhere.

She didn't need to close her eyes and slip away to the lobby to initiate contact. She didn't have to search for or hunt down these ghosts: she'd known them all her life. They were the friends she'd made while sitting in a Berlin cemetery – two ghosts and a spirit – when she had been too afraid to make acquaintances with the living. They were the souls of those who had once suffered in Bamberg, many of them she had come to know well as she had visited once a year, every year, since she was sixteen. They were the humans and the monsters and the many in-between who Casper had walked alongside when they had no one else to keep them company. They were the ghosts that only she could communicate with and control. She wouldn't be doing the latter today: they were in charge.

Casper pushed a part of herself outwards and into them as she imbued each of the rapidly appearing dead with some of her power. Many had been waiting for an opportunity like this for a while; others were just keen to have something physical to do. Either way, their ranks rapidly increased from what had been considered small – just a party of eight – to more than sixty as the stairwell shone bright with the glow of the eager dead.

'Marta,' Casper said, acknowledging the cemetery witches, 'Geneva, Beatrice, always a pleasure.'

'Tonight, it's all of our pleasures,' Beatrice said.

Casper was usually wary of dealing with spirits, but this one was so keen to volunteer it had been impossible to deny her or the power boost her involvement would bring them. With just Yu and herself as the only supernatural operatives on this mission, and the six well-trained humans, it was risky but Casper's abilities were significant. Keeping their own numbers low was a strategic choice, meaning that more bodies could be spared to pack out the other missions that were happening right this second. Casper consulted the watch on her wrist, just to make sure. Looking up at the lead soldier as he braced against the door, she felt the presence of the ghosts surge around her.

'Blow it,' she said.

A charge saw the door fly outwards, their party filing in one after the other and wasting no time. The ghosts didn't have to wait, of course, Casper feeling and hearing and sensing them as they poured through the floors simultaneously. The spare bedroom was now an office suite of some kind, containing just three workers who sprung back from their stations. The human soldiers moved on quickly, following their orders, as Casper pointed a long, pale finger at the trio who clustered together.

'Flee or perish, those are your options,' she said. 'Take nothing with you and know that no one else here can help you.'

Two had their shaking hands in the air, surrendering, but the third lunged for something under a nearby desk. He didn't make it far, Beatrice throwing his body back. The force broke the man's neck, his own ghost quickly wrapped up in the essence of the spirit as she dragged him where he needed to go. Casper examined the weapon he had been reaching for, a blade of some kind. *Aspirational,* she thought, given the tattoo on his wrist told her he was an Askari who would have been better off fighting her with a stapler.

'Evacuate and do it quickly,' she told the others, pointing to the darkened doorway she had just appeared through. 'That will take you down to the station.'

With little more than a whimpered '*danke*', they sprinted through it as Casper stormed towards the remainder of the commotion. She hit the fire alarm as she passed, hoping that the innocent would flee while Treize loyalists would stay and fight. It was a hollow gesture in a way, because she knew not everyone they killed was going to be a maniacal evil genius. She had to believe she was trying to spare someone. The idea of mercy quickly dissipated as she cleared the floor, feeling the absence of life there as she swept downwards, passing dozens of explosive charges they had laid on her way.

The main floor was an issue, as she had expected it to be, with the Praetorian Guard training quarters proving the most trouble. Glancing over her shoulder, Yu spotted Casper and laid down a supressing fire as she descended the staircase to the same level as everyone else. They had disabled the elevators, making sure there would be no nasty surprises coming up from the loading bay.

'Push them back towards the Custodians,' Casper ordered, Yu barking the command as the humans focused on the more manageable targets.

That left just Yu and Casper to handle the PG soldiers, of which there were surprisingly few. She'd expected at least thirty, yet once she quickly counted the dead bodies she realised there had only been a dozen or so all up.

'Flee or fight!' Marta the ghost yelled as she flew towards them, barely making physical contact but doing enough to disorient a soldier as they slashed at the air with short swords. The message was clear and so was their response, with the ones left vowing to fight as they took up defensive positions. Yu emptied her clip into a werewolf as he charged at Casper, recognising the greater threat, before tossing the weapon and grabbing a throwing axe off the wall. She tossed it with a grunt, the blade lodging in the head of a female fighter right in the medium's path. Casper couldn't focus on the other assailants around her; she had to trust that Yu would keep them busy. She needed to channel all of her focus into restraining the two women who were attempting to fight off the ghosts that were holding them in place.

Jakea and Jaira were identical twins and respected Praetorian Guard soldiers given they were relatively young compared to peers like Heath and Lorcan. They were deadly, having gone round for round with Tommi once in a failed attempt to recruit her. Casper had never heard them speak, but she hoped they would as she told them to surrender. They said nothing, just a determined furrow to their brows as they fought against the dead and Jakea's grip tightened on the whip in her hands.

'Do it!' Yu shouted from behind her. 'You have to do it!'

Casper steeled herself, knowing that she did: these two would never give up and never quit.

'I'm sorry,' she said, meaning it. 'It will be quick.'

She curled the fingers of her hand, turning the flesh into a fist as she brought Beatrice towards her. The spirit delighted in the opportunity, two souls this old rare in her experience. Casper flinched as the ghosts released them for just a moment, before covering them like locusts and snapping their bodies free of life. Their corpses fell to the ground and Casper had to risk slipping away for a second, finding the lobby crammed with the dead who had been unwilling to lay down their weapons. Jakea and Jaira were there, of course, Casper willing and urging and pushing from the core base of her power for all who were there to disappear until they eventually did.

A flash of pain dragged her back to the physical plane and her eyes opened to the sight of Yu tackling a soldier out of her path. Her friend took the knife blow to the shoulder that was meant for Casper, it having only skimmed her now instead. The assailant flipped on top of Yu, pinning her arms with their knees as she reached for a different weapon. Yu's legs were flailing, her back bucking, as the man raised a hand weight over his head. Casper snatched up a discarded baseball bat at her feet, swinging it with full force as the metal connected with the man's skull in a devastating *clink*.

His brain matter was exposed to the elements as Casper looked down at his motionless body. She delivered one more blow, double tapping to be safe rather than sorry. She helped her friend to her feet, Yu flinching as she inspected the knife embedded in her flesh. Casper braced the woman's shoulder as she met her pained gaze with a firm nod, yanking the blade out the way it had entered. Yu screamed, slapping a hand down over the wound, which was deep but not by any means close to being fatal. Casper tore a satchel open from Yu's waistband, dousing the bleeding hole with the powder that made her friend scream even louder before she quickly tied a bandage around it and pulled it tight.

'Now what?' Yu said, panting as she looked around at the carnage inside Bierpinsel. Among the bodies were the living too, the humans shouting and pointing at them to leave as the survivors rushed from the premises. The female soldier was smashing computers and starting spot fires in equal measure, the remaining ghosts copying her as they exerted the last of the physical presence Casper had loaned them. She felt it flowing back into her, yet not the same as it had been going out. She staggered just slightly as the weakness hit her. Yu was externally hurt and Casper was internally, the two women grabbing each other as they began limping towards their colleagues.

'Now,' Casper began, 'we get the fuck out of here and hope our friends did too.'

Chapter 13

Sadie

When Sadie had woken in a strange bed in a strange room, fear had been the first emotion that pulsed through her. The beat of her heart had seemed to pump right through her throat as she'd tried to orientate herself in the dark, still half asleep and not fully cognisant enough to remember why she'd been so afraid in the first place. Instinctively her hand had slid to her stomach, the sheer presence of her belly and the trio of humans cooking away inside enough to calm her. Then she'd remembered. The dead farmhand. His brother. The gun. Simon.

That's the bed she was in, she'd realised with a deep sigh of relief. It's where she had stayed for the past two days, sleeping so soundly and moving so little that every time she woke her baby brain had gone into overdrive. She'd pulled out one of the pillows she had wedged between her legs and under her stomach, throwing it above her as she'd carefully inched her way to the edge of the mattress. It was a delicate dance she had to perform every day, her body straining in ways it never had before as Sadie did her best not to aggravate it any further with physical or mental stress.

The latter had been unavoidable and for the first time the former had come into play as well, with every limb and muscle and tendon aching as she got out of the bed. She'd barely seen Simon since, the werewolf making sure the house had been packed with her sisters for the past two days regardless of whether she felt it was safe for them to be there or not. They'd all worn double headphones on his orders and Sadie understood the human cushioning: there had been two more nights of the full moon and the days were just as rough when he was left in a weakened state. So the cottage had been crammed with Burkes, even if she'd been unconscious for a bulk of the time so unable to enjoy their company.

From the sheer silence of the house as she tiptoed through it, she could tell her sisters weren't anywhere that was close. She took a long, hot bath and watched as the darkness outside the window started to lighten with the coming of dawn. Barely, mind you. Dressing in a clean pair of green, satin pyjamas Shannon had left folded in a chair next to Simon's bed, Sadie wasn't disappointed to find the day was grey as she pulled back the curtains. It was fitting for her mood, yet she was determined to change that.

Stripping the bed, she started a wash cycle so eventually when the werewolf did return he would have clean, fresh sheets that weren't covered in banshee. Their senses were much more sensitive than other creatures and living in a house with her was one thing, but to have her all over every surface in his room and her sisters crowding the limited physical space he had was another. Sadie smirked as she lit a sage stick, wondering exactly how badly she would get teased by the witch Kala Tully as she tried to purge them all from Simon's room.

Shivering as she opened a few windows around the cottage to get the air flowing, she paused to listen to a rhythmic *thwack thwack thwack* coming from the back of the house. It was loud enough that she heard it over the rumble of the kettle boiling, and she reached for the shotgun by the fireplace. Meri had shown her how to use it during her first week here, with Sorcha taking her out for target practice twice a week ever since. Sadie had never felt the need for it before, but she did now. The incident had left her rattled and whether she could summon her wail quickly or not, she wouldn't be stupid enough to get caught outside the cottage again without a weapon. Pulling three shells from the locked drawer on the mantelpiece, she loaded them and gently opened the back door just a crack to investigate.

What she saw couldn't have been closer to the opposite of what she was expecting. Simon Tianne stood there shirtless, barefoot, and clad only in a pair of dirty jeans as he swung an axe down and split a log in two. It was freezing out there, Sadie's breath forming steam clouds as she stared out the door. Yet he was drenched in sweat as he repeated the movements again and again and again. There was a growing mound of firewood at his feet and from the drag marks coming from the forest – not to mention the claw marks in some of the trunks – it didn't take much deduction to establish Simon had done a spot of light gardening while in werewolf form last night.

'You gonna shoot me with that thing or just gawk?' he asked, punctuating the sentence with the heave of an axe.

'Sorry,' she mumbled, lowering the shotgun.

'Don't apologise. There's not much good that can come from what happened, but if that's the lesson you take away from it then that's an important one to learn.'

Turned out Sadie wasn't the only person beating herself up, she realised as she watched him reposition another log and wipe sweat from his brow.

'Will you come inside?' she asked, noting that he hadn't bothered with headphones. This werewolf was taking the self-punishment thing too far if that equated with a death wish.

'We've got no firewood. There's a big snowstorm coming.'

'Correction: we had no firewood. Now you've become a one-man deforestation unit.'

He smirked but didn't stop – swinging, chopping, sweating and repositioning.

'Boys are so dramatic,' she said and sighed, rolling her eyes. 'Congratulations, you're a man mulching machine. Now if you insist on continued severe corporal mortification can you do it inside, please?'

The axe missed its mark this time, swinging through the air as he brought it to a stop to turn around and stare at her. No, not stare: blink rapidly as if she'd given birth right there at the back door.

'It's easier for me to berate you from the comfort of the couch,' Sadie added for good measure. It finally did the trick, with the werewolf huffing out a 'fine' as he started collecting the wood and piling it at the door. Content, Sadie went inside and finished cooking up the breakfast she had been making for herself, adding an additional portion for Simon. He said nothing as he marched inside, closing the doors and then the windows she had opened before starting the fire and throwing two thick logs inside. He disappeared for a shower and she was happier that way, selecting an Ann Peebles LP to play on the old record player nearby. She dropped the needle on the opening chords of '*I Can't Stand the Rain*' just as pitter-patters began to fall on the rooftop.

Sadie was already eating when the werewolf returned, looking slightly better but still comparatively worse for wear considering his usual physical presence. Dark bags hung under his eyes and he moved much in the same way she did: slowly and as if everything ached. He took the seat next to her at the counter, dropping his head into his hands with a groan. He stayed like that for some time, Sadie continuing to devour a werewolf-worthy portion of bacon, eggs, sausages, tomatoes, avocado and beans. Sniffing, Simon glanced up as if realising there was food there for the first time. His own heaped plate was right in front of him, but he pulled the steaming mug of coffee towards his mouth first.

'Mmmm,' was the only noise he made for a while, before picking up a knife and fork. She'd checked what he'd eaten the day before, when her sisters were here and he was trying to avoid them while battling his own physical pain, and was pleased to see all of the rabbits she had caught in the traps were gone. The stupid things had nearly cost her her life, so she was glad the fresh meat had been useful for something. Despite her head start, Simon still finished breakfast way ahead of her.

'That was the best meal I've ever had,' he said, letting out a satisfied exhale.

'Right,' she snorted. 'A fry-up was the best meal you've ever had?'

'Everything tastes better after the full moon.'

'Townspeople?'

'Lol, *please*.'

Now it was her turn to stare at him, blinking rapidly, as the fork hovered at the edge of her mouth.

'What?' he scoffed, amused by her response. 'Werewolves lol too.'

'Do they, though?'

He grinned, white teeth flashing. 'If you don't finish those chilli eggs, I'm going to have to eat them.'

'Only an animal would steal from a pregnant woman,' Sadie said, words muffled through the mouthful she'd rapidly shoved into her gob. 'There's more in the pan.'

The rain outside increased from a gentle sprinkle to a genuine downpour as Simon navigated his way around the kitchen to get a second serving.

'I thought you said snow was coming,' she murmured.

'It will,' he replied, pouring himself another coffee and filling hers too. 'You can smell it.'

She examined him over the top of her mug, trying to ignore the way he looked in a navy blue knitted sweater and clean, loose jeans. It wasn't even eight o'clock in the morning yet, she needed to pull herself together. Instead, she signed him a message.

'You should put your headphones back on,' she told him.

'No.'

She didn't need to reply with 'what?', Sadie was quite certain her expression said as much. She signed it anyway.

'You heard me: no,' he repeated, crossing his arms over his chest. He sipped his coffee slowly, as if gauging her reaction.

'You could die,' she whispered, not even angry just flabbergasted. 'I can't control it, Simon. I can't control if I cry out or how far that cry might travel. Plus, with werewolf hearing—'

'So wear a ball gag.'

'Are . . . are you fucking joking?'

He barked out a laugh, shaking his head. 'Of course I'm fucking joking. And yes, I know the risks but I'm here anyway.'

'When I go into labour . . .'

'That's a different story,' he said. 'Then yes, obviously. But I was stupid to listen to your sister.'

'Which one?'

'All of them.' He sighed. 'Sorcha, in particular. I'm a were-wolf, even when I'm not in beast mode my enhanced senses are the exact reason I was sent here to protect you. I can't block one of them off, I need them all and I need them all operating at one hundred per cent.'

He meant it, she knew he did, which is what made her all the more worried for him.

'You think you should've been able to hear him, that you should have heard him lurking about before you left,' she whispered.

'Yes. His scent was familiar here, too close to his brother's, so it wasn't immediately obvious to the Aunties. The bigger issue is we were so focused on threats from the outside, we didn't pay attention to those coming from the inside. That won't happen again.'

'What do you mean?' Sadie questioned.

'From now on, it's everyone else's job to think big picture and it's my job just to think about you.'

Sadie gulped.

'Only you,' he reiterated.

She was quiet for a few long moments, pushing her plate away as she sat. Suddenly she had lost her appetite. *Fuck,* she thought, feeling the heat in her cheeks that signalled only one thing. Tears.

'Hey,' Simon said, moving quickly around the kitchen so that he was suddenly beside her. 'I'm sorry, I didn't mean to—'

'It's not you,' she sniffed, 'it's me. I never wanted these fucking babies. I know that's such a horrible thing to say but I'm *twenty*! Just the weight of being a mum this young is enough, let alone the weight of the world on this womb.'

'I know,' Simon said, soothing Sadie as he held her to him. He didn't shush her or tell her it was going to be okay. They both knew there was no guarantee of that and the situation, frankly, sucked.

'But it's like this whole pregnancy, will it be worth it?' she sobbed, purging the darkest thoughts from the cycle of her mind and into the real world. 'Everyone who comes close to it dies. The father, Wally—'

'That's two people.'

'You! All of you in danger and risking your lives for kids you haven't even met yet, just because they fulfil a damn prophecy! What if the kids suck? What if they're three *Omen* babies?'

Sadie knew she'd gone full hysterical by that point, yet it didn't matter. Simon had already seen enough of her emotional, hormone-fuelled outbursts that there was no point holding back.

'Stop, that's enough now.' His voice was firm but still soothing. 'You *are* not an incubator, Sadie. I don't know how many times I have to tell you that. And yes, your babies are important. Your children bring the first real hope our kind has had in hundreds of years. But you're also forgetting one of the main reasons we're all here, willingly risking our lives.'

His thumb under her chin forced her to look up at him.

'You, Sadie,' Simon said. 'They're here for the woman who begged to spare the life of the man who was trying to kill her *and* her unborn babies.'

'I killed his brother first.'

'They're here for the woman who went out hunting rabbits while eight months' pregnant so the werewolf guarding her would have raw meat for the days between the full moon.'

'I would have put whatever you didn't want in a pie anyway.'

'They're here for the person thoughtful enough to open all the windows to make sure the cottage didn't smell like banshees when I got back.'

She didn't have a retort for that one and it was very hard to break away from his stare when his face was just inches from her own, those dark eyes penetrating her very soul. It was still too close to the other side of the full moon for most wolves, yet Sadie got the impression that the wolf she sensed lurking under the surface of Simon's stare never really went away ... no matter what time of the month it was. A high-pitched tune cut through the quiet of the cottage like a knife, Simon leaping around like he was ready to attack the washing machine. His claws slid out easily, like it cost him nothing at all as his finger-nails turned into deadly blades. She placed a hand over his, calming the murderous instincts.

'Please,' she said, 'don't murder the laundry.'

He looked confused, as if he'd never heard of such a concept. She smiled, wiping her face as she pushed past him and retrieved the warm linen from the dryer. He trailed behind her to the bedroom, as if not believing such a normal answer among all the abnormal of their lives.

'Laundry? Who's doing laundry at this hour?'

Sadie gestured to the bare mattress and folded-up doona in the corner of his bedroom without any further words necessary.

'*Oh*,' he said, understanding illuminating his features. 'Thanks.'

'Least I could do,' she said, throwing one corner of the fitted sheet towards him as she wrestled with the other. 'You gave up your bed during the days you needed it most.'

'I wasn't sleeping,' Simon grumbled, the guilt not entirely expunged from his system. They were quiet as they made the bed, this ritual torturous with just one person but made so much easier with two.

'What happened to him?' Sadie asked, not looking up as she smoothed out one of the wrinkles with her hand.

'Do you want to know?' Simon replied, the bedroom door swinging as he whipped the last pillow up off the wooden rocking chair that was placed there. 'Or could it be enough for you to trust that we did as you asked and didn't kill him?'

'It could be enough.' She nodded. 'But you didn't let him go.'

'We can't. He knows too much, saw too much. We're lucky he doesn't understand enough about this world outside of the farm, but even then Meri is tracing his contacts, double and triple checking that this vendetta was restricted to just him.'

'How did you know?' Sadie asked, frowning as she thought back to the scene in the woods. 'You weren't here when I killed his brother by accident. Besides the headphones and self-enforced isolation of it all, I can't imagine it came up a whole lot when you arrived.'

He looked hesitant, as if he didn't want to say at first. Yet she and Simon had reached some kind of point where there was no going back now: everything that had to be said *needed* to be said out in the open.

'A ghost,' he said. 'The ghost of my uncle, actually, which scared the shit out of me at first but wasn't entirely surprising.'

She laughed. 'I never knew my uncle, but if his ghost suddenly appeared I would be surprised, Simon.'

'Right, yeah, I was in a way but also . . . not. I've known that Wehi, our tribal elder, has been in communication with him for some time so I knew he was around. Yet they often don't make themselves visible to us unless they absolutely have to.'

'And he had to?'

'It's not an exact science by any stretch, but Casper and her brother and Tommi and Wehi have something worked out where key players are monitored by someone even if we can't see them. I was waiting at a motel for the snow to clear, got the message, shifted on the spot and ran the rest of the way.'

'You ran,' Sadie said, not a question but a statement as she flashed back to her vision. 'You ran through the snow in wolf form; I saw it. That's why I knew I had to keep him talking, because someone was coming but . . . I think I *knew* it was you.'

'That's interesting,' he said, frowning as he watched her sit on the edge of the bed.

'It doesn't usually work like that; my visions are primarily one scene and you watch it play out ahead of time like a movie,' Sadie murmured, rubbing her belly as she remained deep in thought. 'It can be minutes ahead of time, even hours and sometimes days. Yet this was closer to the actual event than I've ever experienced before.'

'Wait, you saw your own death?' Simon questioned.

'Yes. No, I'm not sure,' she huffed. 'It's like I was seeing through his eyes, seeing myself as he viewed me almost in real time, but then I was also seeing you. It was a sizzle reel of different places, different people and different times.'

Her hands skimming over the mound of her stomach had become an unavoidable habit over the past few months, like twisting the hair around your fingers or biting your nails. Yet Sadie suddenly stopped the gesture, the movement stilling as she looked down at herself. Her visions *didn't* usually work like that, but it wasn't her visions she had been shown.

'Babies start hearing sounds during the second trimester,' she said, wide-eyed, as she turned to Simon. 'Their cognitive abilities and brains are developing rapidly. By the time they get to the third trimester, they're reacting to sounds and external stimuli too.'

'It was the triplets?' he said. 'You think the visions you saw were theirs?'

'Why not? There's not exactly a go-to banshee baby book. There's no *Mamaste: How To Raise Your Baby Banshees to Upend the New World Order*. I've just been going off what we know about human babies and making a guess for supernatural ones that lands somewhere in-between.'

'What about your sisters? Did they get additional abilities when they were pregnant?'

She tilted her head at him, noting that was a good point. 'No, but … these aren't normal banshee babies. They're supposed to be more powerful and predictive and prophetic and all that. I just thought they would grow into it.'

Something caught her eye over Simon's head and she used his shoulder as a crutch to pull herself up, shutting the bedroom door properly as she stared at what had been pinned there. It was a map of the Dawson farm, with Post-it notes pinned to it and areas circled in various colours. It extended far beyond the property, however, with the acres surrounding it also meticulously annotated by handwriting she recognised as Simon's.

'What's this?' she asked, turning to face him. He was standing not far behind her and she felt comforted by his presence at her back.

'It was what I was looking at before I came here,' Simon said. 'Trying to get familiar with the property and the geographical strengths, weaknesses, all of that.'

Her eyes flicked back to the map, noting the trail of paths that felt familiar to her. 'How do you have my exact walking routes on here?'

'Uh,' he looked nervous, 'I had the Aunties track you, report back. I didn't want to leave anything to chance.'

'Will you stop me from walking everyday now?' she asked, because she would understand if that ended up being the case, yet she was poised for a fight anyway. She'd battle for that freedom.

'No, of course not,' Simon said, reaching out to rub the back of her neck. It was *so stiff* and *so tight* from not moving for two days in bed that she had to resist the urge to let her eyes flutter shut. 'I would never take that away from you. I know how good it is – not just for you, but for the babies, too – to move and get out there in the fresh air.'

'What's the footnote?' she murmured.

'How did you know there'd be a footnote?'

She jerked her head at the organisation behind her, the meticulous plans on top of plans on top of back-up plans mapped out in front of them.

'Right,' Simon smiled, the werewolf looking cute when he was bashful, 'I'm coming with you; that's it, that's the footnote. Not the Aunties, not your sisters, just me. Everyone can keep doing their daily visits, but here at the cottage where there's a clear structure to defend.'

She couldn't fight him on that, much as she itched to, so she didn't. Instead, Sadie pivoted her priorities over the next few days to things that really mattered. Like the birthing training she practised with Dr Kikuchi as an addition to their daily check-ups. Like the 'baby lessons' Shannon ran her through, Sadie grateful that she had years of helping raise her nieces and nephews under her belt so it didn't seem so daunting. Like detailing the specifics of as many different banshee predictive abilities as she could find in *The Collected Banshee Histories* and consuming every account of The Three she could put her hands on. Like getting updates on Sorcha and the others as often as she could from Barastin. Like her daily walks with Simon, which dropped down from three to just one due to the intensity of the weather as the South Island winter really set in. Like preparing for exactly where the babies would sleep.

'No,' Simon had said, watching her from the doorway of her room when she'd first attempted to get started. 'No way.'

'No way what?' Sadie had snapped.

'All three babies in the one room? With you? No. Way.'

'But—'

'You will *never* sleep and you being somewhat conscious is going to be important when it comes to feeding them, keeping them alive, getting th—'

'Okay okay, Super Nanny,' she'd huffed. 'Do I just stack 'em like Jenga blocks, then, or what?'

He'd laughed at her comparison, picking up the first of the three wahakura she had been gifted from Tiaki Ihi.

'There are three rooms in this house,' he'd said, moving through the cottage as she followed him. 'You've already got the change table in the spare bedroom so why not just make that whole space theirs?'

'Because your room is right next door,' she'd gestured, 'you'll hear every cry, every fart, every whimper—'

'I will anyway,' he'd replied, tapping his ears. 'Werewolf hearing. Besides, after we finish soundproofing the lounge I think we should soundproof here as well.'

'In case one of them has the wail.'

'In case all three do.'

'Shit,' Sadie had muttered, biting her lip. That was a terrifying possibility she hadn't entertained yet, but she didn't panic immediately. The Three functioned as a unit together, all three women's predictive abilities enhanced and influenced by the others. In everything she had read, there had never once been a mention of the wail. They had a million other different gifts, but not that.

Her pregnancy project shifted into creating the nursery with Simon and her sisters, Sadie conscious of the fact they all seemed to be working together to keep her mind occupied on physical tasks. She didn't begrudge them that. When she and Simon would walk each day, her hand in his as they negotiated the icy terrain, her sisters would descend on the cottage, splitting tasks between them. Catriona and Keavy worked with Dr Kikuchi to finish her conversion of the lounge into a fully functioning medical suite for the caesarean. It did deprive them of a place to hang out, so if Sadie wasn't in the kitchen, she was in her bed or Simon's, the additional space for her growing width much better than a couch as she read. Ina and Shannon were the mothers and took control of the nursery, making sure it was stocked with all the supplies and clothing a new mother times three would need . . . plus things they usually wouldn't, like noise-cancelling headphones for the babies.

The Aunties helped Simon finish the soundproofing of the space, with Meri repurposing the built-in wardrobe into a bed that folded up just like one you would find in a caravan, allowing for storage underneath. It meant that someone – whether it was Sadie or one of her sisters – could sleep in there with the children if they needed to, without the bulk of the old bed frame taking up most of the space.

When Sadie returned from her walk one afternoon, Simon carrying the fresh rabbits she'd managed to snare, she noted the smell of paint that teased her nostrils. She looked at the werewolf inquisitively, but he just smiled. She rushed to the nursery, finding her sister Nora working in a pair of paint-splattered overalls as she finished packing up with her fiancé Deepika.

Sadie was speechless. Nora's gift was her ability to sketch death scenes, her older sibling having a particular affinity for being able to interpret what Sadie or any of the other Burkes visioned. She was a skilled artist, but this . . . this was beyond anything that Sadie had seen her do. An entire wall had been turned into a mural, Sadie recognising one of the main images that was painted there as the scene from the prophetic pages about The Three. The women stood there together, hands linked, with long, white hair and eyes that cried blood as depicted in the original banshee myths.

The dark green of their gowns flowed into the blue water of the River Corrib, a significant landmark from their ancestral home in Galway. Yet that's where the comparisons ended, as the scene took on new life and it shifted to portray other women, seven of them: just like there were seven Burke sisters. Plus her cousins, her mother, her auntie, her nieces and nephews, and as it progressed . . . other beings. Nora had taken the traditional story of the *bean sí* – the banshee – and made it modern, replicating the style but telling a new story. It was a hopeful one. Sadie's hands slapped over her mouth. She looked at her sister, emotions bubbling up and out of her body as she tried to process how much this meant to her.

'I wanted them to know where they came from,' Nora said, tucking a loose strand of hair behind the arch of her headphones. 'I wanted them to know the power they've inherited and to never be afraid to use it, the way we were.'

Sadie pulled her sister to her by the straps of her overalls, awkwardly hugging her from the side because if she attempted it from the front Nora would be in Antarctica.

'I love it,' she signed when she released her, making sure both Nora and Deepika could see. 'I love you both so much.'

It wasn't until later that night that she noticed the other addition to the nursery. She was alone, rocking back and forth in the chair she'd stolen from Simon's room as she stared at the mural. The werewolf had warned her that if she stayed in there for ever, she'd get high off the paint fumes.

'Good!' Sadie had told him. 'Since that's the only high I'm allowed to have!'

She'd banished him from the room so she could be a creep and stare at Nora's work some more, the plastic sheets to protect the floor and stop any paint drips still there. In her stretchiest pair of maternity pants and the only lacy T-shirt bra that allowed for her ballooning bosom, she was rubbing kiwi-fruit-seed oil on her exposed belly when she paused. She used her toes to stop the rocking of the chair, her eyes fixating on three cots that sat in the room. They were positioned to the side so as to give Nora and Deepika the best access to the wall, but the craftsmanship was unmistakable.

She got to her feet, wiping the excess oil from her hands as she felt herself drawn to the woodwork. Gently, carefully, she kneeled down and examined the intricate shapes that had been carved into the deep, brown oak. The ridges and the bumps and the curves felt so familiar to her, Sadie recognising the wood from the trees that protected the cottage around them.

'Oh my God,' she mumbled, forgetting for just a moment that she lived in a house with a werewolf. A crash from the kitchen followed by stomping footsteps heralded Simon's arrival and he burst through the door.

'What is it?' he barked, looking for a threat. 'What's wrong?'

From her kneeled positioned on the floor, she looked up at him with awe as she realised what he'd done. Her few seconds of silence meant he decompressed, gaze shifting from her hands tracing the shapes of the cots to her face and back again.

'It was supposed to be a surprise,' he said, deflated.

'Simon, I'm *surprised*.'

He smiled, dropping down on to the floor next to her as he gently touched the surface of a cot. 'The wood's not properly treated yet, but there was nowhere else to keep them when it's this cold outside.'

'Simon,' she urged, certain that he wasn't properly understanding her reaction. 'They're perfect. You don't . . .'

She reached out to touch him, cupping his cheek in her hands as she felt like she was properly seeing all the many layers to this man for the first time. He glanced away, focusing on the cots instead which had the woven *wahakura* sitting comfortably inside.

'My father taught me,' he said, smiling at a memory she couldn't see. 'And when he died, my uncle made sure he kept teaching me. Jonah's work was incredible; this is nothing compared to what he could do.'

'It's everything,' she whispered, withdrawing her hand. Sadie suddenly felt shy as he looked back at her and she fidgeted with the cap of the oil bottle. He took it from her, examining the label with a grin.

'Kiwi oil, ha! This is from my mother, isn't it?'

Sadie nodded. 'It was part of the care package Tiaki made me, from all the Aunties. I'd like to say the chocolate fish lasted more than a few hours but—'

'No explanation needed, they're a delicacy,' he said, squirting out some of the oil and rubbing his hands together. 'Let me do this for you.'

'You don't—'

'Let me. I was wondering what it was that you rubbed into your skin every night. Now it all makes sense.'

'It's for the stretchmarks,' she said, trying to keep her breath regulated as he moved behind her. She leaned against him, watching as Simon's hands ran down the length of her pregnancy line at first and then in slow, circular motions.

'Keisha swears by this stuff,' he said, Sadie noting how his voice sounded as ragged as she felt. For the love of God, she hoped he didn't notice the way her nipples hardened beneath her bra as he continued to touch her. It had only been her touch for what felt like so long, her eyes fluttering shut as she sunk back further into him and his chin rested on her shoulder as he worked. His breath was hot against her ear, Sadie wondering if his matched the heat in her blood as his hands skimmed higher, slower, and brushed against the material of her bra. She let out the softest gasp, unable to help it, and he brushed again, purposefully as he applied pressure to her nipple.

It was agony and gratification all at the same time, Sadie arching against him now as both hands began to knead her breasts. She'd caught him glancing away from her cleavage a few times, leading her to believe that Simon was more of a boobs than a butt man, and she couldn't have been more grateful for that theory being proven right. His lips were open and brushing against her cheek, Sadie only having to turn her head slightly to kiss him. She knew her hormones were crazy, but it felt like she might come right there on the spot as his tongue caressed hers.

Sadie had biological reasons for being turned on, but she couldn't imagine what his were as she felt his own hardness pressed against her back. She didn't care, though, pulling his face to hers and holding Simon there tightly as she kissed him feverishly. With her free hand, she unclipped her bra and felt relief when he pulled the straps away in less than a microsecond, as if anything keeping her covered was the most annoying thing in the world.

When he dipped his head, Sadie swore out loud as his big, warm lips closed over her nipple. He moved from one breast to the other as he kissed them, teased probably being a better word. There was the gentle deployment of teeth involved and she heard his muffled laughter as she reacted. Her skin, her pores, her fucking blood cells felt like they might combust, and she worried she was pulling on his hair too tightly as her fingers sunk into his scalp, gripping and holding him to her. She kissed his bare shoulder, not sure when she had torn his jumper and shirt off but one hundred per cent certain it had been her doing. The bumps of his skin were raised and she felt them under her lips, kissing the tattoo there as she worshipped every inch of him.

Yet the smooth skin of Simon's back began to shift right before her eyes as she stared at it. The brown morphed to a textured white that she recognised as snow, before a squirt of red was splashed across it. A body fell into the cushion of soft ice, the dead, lifeless eyes of Dreckly Jones staring up at her as someone leapt over the corpse. It was then that she realised there wasn't just one body, but dozens, all littering the surface as a battle raged. The last thing she saw was the unmistakable arches of the white, glittering mountains that overlooked the Dawson farm as the brutal scene played out.

The sound she must have made was different to the others, Simon sensing something was wrong as he pulled back and slid her into the cradle of her arms. Her fingernails were digging into the surface of his skin, drawing blood as she held on to him like an anchor that would bring her back to the present. His fingers were stroking her face, his words whispered against her ears as he tried to comfort her, tried to pull her back to him, until she finally was. Her gaze refocused as she stared up at him, his hands stilling as he looked down at her with worry.

'What did you see?' he asked, knowing without her needing to utter a word that she had just been subjected to a vision.

'The battle,' Sadie whispered. 'The battle happens here.'

Chapter 14

Tommi

'They cut out their tongues.'

Tommi had seen a lot of horrible things in her time, but after she had dispatched the Praetorian Guard soldier cosplaying Bob the Builder with his hammer, she had time to see just one more. As she pressed the Alchemist for answers, she realised the gargling sound they were making wasn't out of fear or shock. That was definitely part of it, but the bigger part was their distinct lack of tongue.

'What the fuck do you mean?' she asked, looking up to face Broom the ghost while straddling the Alchemist.

'Look,' the ghost pointed, gesturing inside the being's mouth. 'What better way to safeguard against Alchemist's telling others how they sealed each cell than by cutting out their tongues.'

Tommi stared down at the person beneath her, annoyed. Their eyes were wide, the skin around their face marked with alchemist shapes and symbols that she knew held just as much power as the words spoken.

'That is the dumbest shit I've ever heard,' she huffed, yanking the Alchemist up and behind her with a grunt. She began to drag the man back through the halls of Vankila as he kicked and squirmed and attempted to resist.

'Now, thanks to a smart little Aussie witch,' Tommi started, 'I know that's only partially true: yes, your words spoken during a ritual are important but not as important as the process and the resolve of your intent, both of which can still be executed with or without a tongue. And might I just say –'

She tossed the man on to the floor, his body sliding along until it came to a stop in front of the first of the unopened cells.

' – why the fuck you'd *ever* want to help the people who cut out your tongue is beyond me.'

The cells behind the Alchemist were the work of Yixin and Quaid, the pair having now freed seemingly dozens of inmates as they continued to work their way to the very back with the assistance of those they had busted out. They had enough magical nipple pasties to get them there, so Tommi focused on the job that was in front of her.

'Start releasing the bindings on each of these cell doors right the fuck now and you have my protection,' she growled. 'If you don't, I won't touch you but . . . I can't speak for everyone else here.'

As if to punctuate her point, there was a deep growl from the cell closest to them as a female werewolf pushed up against the glass. The Alchemist was nodding, hands shaking as they got to their feet and worked on the first cell that Tommi pointed at. That growl hadn't belonged to just anyone: she recognised the face of Sushmita Kapoor from a photo she had been shown. The woman saw the recognition in Tommi's eyes, frowning at her as she tilted her head. Once the Alchemist was finished drawing shapes and making movements with his bare hands, the glass wall didn't explode like it did when Kala's charms were activated. It dissolved, like a popsicle melting away on a hot summer's day. Keeping his head down, the Alchemist moved to the next cell and began repeating the process as Sushmita stepped out and made a beeline for him.

Tommi jumped in front, blocking the werewolf's path. 'Can't, I'm afraid. Made a promise.'

Sushmita growled at her, letting Tommi see her incisors as they sharpened into fangs. It was a neat trick and Tommi could do it too, growling back as she showed the woman her own.

'I'm not here to have a howl-off with you,' she snarled. 'I'm here to free as many as I can and if you wanna kill that Alchemist, you better have a solution for how we do it without him.'

Sushmita's dark eyes cut into Tommi and she knew she couldn't risk showing even the slightest indicator of fear. In truth, she wasn't afraid: Sushmita had apparently been a force in her time, but Tommi was also a force in hers.

'You look like a whore,' the woman growled. 'And you smell like my brother.'

'Fair point on the first,' she said, having to concede. 'As for the second, that would be because Ben's here and fighting for you upstairs in about . . . oh, I'd say a few more minutes.'

'This is a breakout?' Sushmita questioned, pushing past her to look beyond Tommi and at the creatures beginning to emerge from their cells.

'Yes, hence all of the, uh, breaking out and stuff.'

Tommi wasn't quite sure how she was going to break it to Ben that his sister was a massive prick, but instead she shook her head free of the thought and vowed to make use of the former pack leader instead.

'Armoury,' Tommi called to her. 'Broom said it's just around the corner, near this level's main entry and exit at the guard station.'

'Who's Broom?' Sushmita questioned, eyes narrowed with suspicion.

'I'm *right* here, how rude!' the ghost huffed.

'She can't see you,' Tommi told him, before telling her: 'He's an undead ally but that's beside the point. You want to be useful and help me bust it open or just stand here and breathe down the Alchemist's neck?'

She thought the fellow werewolf was snarling again, but she realised with horror it was a smile. There really wasn't enough variation in the expressions for Tommi's liking.

'Lead the way,' Sushmita said, her voice dangerous and low.

'Nobody touch him,' Tommi called, pointing at specific supernaturals who looked ready to feast as she ran past the Alchemist. 'We need him to get out so if you snack, we're trapped.'

A few looked like they were backing away, but she gave Broom a knowing look as he stayed behind to monitor the situation. Tommi took the lead, Sushmita half running, half limping beside her, while Quaid Ihi rounded out their trio on the other side. She was surprised to see him there, barefoot and nimble as they raced in the direction of the armoury.

'Yixin said I should come,' he whispered, throwing a not-so-subtle look in Sushmita's direction. *To watch your back* was, said without being verbalised.

'Aye, appreciate the help.' She nodded, truly grateful, as they screeched to a stop. The weapons were protected behind a steel grate, the long structure spanning out in front of them with what looked like an immovable steel door meeting in the middle. Tommi knew that nothing was impenetrable: you just had to put your mind to it. She watched Quaid extract his werewolf claws, his fingernails shifting from human to beast so quickly there could never be any mistaking that he was an Ihi. She knew Ben could do close to the same, not as fast and not as precise, but good enough as his pack's bloodline was rumoured to be the second most powerful behind the New Zealand werewolves. Yet Sushmita didn't seem to have that gift, or if she'd had it once she had lost it now, the years locked in a cell claiming more than just time as she twitched her fingers with frustration.

'Don't,' Tommi said, reaching out to grab Quaid's wrist as he started towards the armoury. 'You're gonna break your hand and tear out every claw you have trying to get through there successfully.'

'What better opportunity could I be waiting for?' he questioned, not mad, just genuinely baffled about why she had stopped him.

'There's a better way,' she said, pivoting back to face the growing crowd of freed prisoners down the cell hallway. Broom had been able to give her intel on who was detained there and where, Tommi committing as much of it to memory as she could. She pointed at one of those recollections now, her own clawed finger singling out a bald man with dwarfism as he stumbled out of his cell. There was a muzzle around his mouth and he was yanking at it, trying and failing to release it.

'Oy, you!' she called, the fella jerking around with the command. 'Fire elemental, right?'

He nodded, looking shocked that she knew who he was as he began slowly walking towards them. 'We could use some fire elements right about now.'

She jerked her head at the armoury behind her and he increased his speed, jogging until he was right up against the streel and examining it with his fingers.

'You mind?' she asked, gesturing around her mouth. He paused, as if suspicious for a moment, before giving her a single, stiff nod. It was instant now, the pain and time it had once taken her to illicit traits of the wolf feeling like a distant memory as her own razor-sharp claws sprung to the surface. With a grimace, she shifted her entire hand into a werewolf claw and slashed it in a downward motion along the fire elemental's neck. She sliced through the muzzle easily, severing the leather there before carefully pulling away the additional straps with her human hand so as not to cut him.

He took a deep, jagged breath as she pulled it away from his lips and he inhaled with relief. A grin twitched along his face as he repeated the gesture, offering her a big, cheesy smile before he promptly made himself throw up. She hadn't spent time with a fire elemental before, so Tommi didn't have any expectations going into their encounter. That said, she hadn't expected to watch a man who looked like a micro Jason Statham regurgitate molten lava right before her eyes. The neon orange liquid made a hissing sound when it connected with the steel grate, Tommi leaping back as the creature contin-ued to spew wherever he deemed essential.

'Well, that's . . . neat,' she remarked, Quaid snorting with amusement beside her. Sushmita was stalking away from them, back turned as she lost interest in the armoury's bounty.

'Where are you going?' Quaid asked her, just as she dropped down to all fours. It looked more natural somehow, like that was her preferred state.

'Guards,' she growled, lopping away. 'There are usually guards here . . .'

Their station had been unattended when they arrived and Tommi counted it as a blessing, mentally marking it down as a problem to worry about later. When the contents of the fire elemental's very uneasy stomach had made a hole big enough to fit through, Quaid and Tommi ducked inside and wasted no time. Their vomiting accomplice didn't stop, however; he seemed to gain momentum as he moved to nearby cell doors. It was messier than the Alchemist, but just as effective.

'Ho-ly shit,' Quaid breathed, Tommi pivoting around to see what he was so impressed by and understanding immediately. 'This is sick as!'

Between the Rogues training room and what her supernatural hit squad had carried on the road to hunt the Laignach Faelad, she had seen some extensive and impressive arsenals in her time. This made all of that look like a cute hobbyist's collection as her eyes poured over every kind of gun, sword, spear, knife, axe, mallet, whip and mace imaginable. Quaid had let out a whistle, summoning others to the armoury to grab what they could as quickly as possible. As supernaturals spilled into the space, Tommi made a beeline for the rack of tactical wear. She'd think about arming herself in a moment, yet the most important thing right then was seizing the opportunity to get herself out of that scraggy outfit and into something that gave her better protection, coverage and freedom of movement. The closest she could come to her size was a touch tight, moulding to her almost like a second skin of thick material as she wiggled her ass into it.

'Allow me,' a deep voice boomed.

Before she had chance to see who it was, the zipper was pulled up the length of her back and the Velcro latches stuck into place. Turning around, Tommi was surprised that her wardrobe assistant had been one of the scariest motherfuckers she'd ever met: Yixin.

'Dinnae ken you were such a gentleman,' she said.

When he smiled in response, staring into his mouth was the epitome of looking into the void and the void looking back. It took something truly significant to draw her eye and she couldn't help but pull away from him as an object glistened over her shoulder. Unlike the other weapons, this was one of four that was in a glass case as if it was special. It was for display, not for use, but by God Tommi wanted to use it as she approached the case. It looked kind of like an axe, kind of like a short sword, but with a hand grip that allowed for optimum control as you swung or slashed this death eater wherever you wanted.

Without pausing to think about it for a second, she smashed her werewolf claw through the glass, yanking the weapon from the display and assessing the weight in her hands. Adjusting her grip, Tommi moved on to an open drawer full of knives which she slid into holders that wrapped around her waist and arms. There was a built-in holster at her thigh, which she filled with a loaded Glock before stashing a supply of ammunition in a pouch at her hip. She was reaching for a set of knuckledusters – not out of practicality, just because they looked cool – when she heard a horrible rasping cry from outside the armoury. She ran towards it, preparing to lose her shit if anyone had started trying to eat the Alchemist, but it wasn't any of the monsters. The man was dead all right, an arrow piercing right through his throat. Her head whipped in the direction of the source, following the flightpath until she settled on the missing guards Sushmita had gone in search of.

She'd sure found them. There were two armouries on this level and while she had run towards the main one, it was clear they'd run towards the other. Sushmita was there, face bloodied as she struggled in the grip of a PG soldier who had what looked like a tactical Bowie knife pressed to the flesh at her throat. She was still alive and that's all that mattered Tommi said to herself as her eyes scanned the numbers.

'They're blocking the elevator upwards,' Quaid growled.

'Like we weren't gonna kill them anyway,' Yixin countered.

'There's more than one way to ascend,' Tommi said, gaze moving from the prick who had killed the Alchemist and was lowering his crossbow. Broom was shuffling behind them, illuminating the alternate exit routes.

'Let's make sure we can do that, then.' The demon grinned, hurling an axe from behind his shoulder *so hard* it sliced through one Praetorian Guard's soldier and sent another one flying with the impact. Tommi never heard the sound as their bodies hit the floor, leaping into the fray with a swarm of support behind her as the two opposing forces met head-on. There were bullets and blood and metal clanging together as the prisoners took on the people who had oppressed them for so long. Tommi was more than a little in love with her shiny new toy as she sank it through the bottom of one man's jaw until the pointy end cracked his skull like a human skewer. She yanked it back, copping a blow to the face with the butt of someone's rifle. It knocked her to the floor, blood pouring into her mouth from a reopened cut at her lip. She spat out a mouthful of fluid and a loose tooth as she rolled swiftly to the side, narrowly avoiding the spray of bullets that were fired her way before an arachnia sprung on to the attacker's shoulder, all eight legs wrapping around and *through* him as they sunk their teeth into his flesh.

The fella screamed and Tommi dashed to the next objective, which was locating Sushmita and hoping that she was still breathing. The PG soldier who had tried to slit her throat was in for a messy fight, Ben's sister having managed to push herself backwards and utilise gravity to headbutt him. Twisting out of his grip, she smashed his head against the concrete floor repeatedly as he continued to fall until what remained looked less like a skull and more like a dropped meat pie. Tommi grabbed her arm as she sprinted past, yanking her away from the scene.

'What are you doing?' she hissed. 'Let me back in the fight!'

'I am!' Tommi snapped, swinging her weapon to dislodge the barely visible lock on a door that had been disguised to look like part of the wall. 'But your fight needs to be up there.'

She pointed into the stairwell where red emergency lights were beginning to flicker on. A horrendously loud siren split through the air, causing Sushmita and Tommi to flinch as it pierced through their sensitive werewolf hearing. It was way too late, yet the alarm was officially raised.

'Please,' she yelled over the thrumming in her skull. 'Your brother needs you to fight up there with *him*.'

Sushmita looked ready to argue, but Tommi had used the magic 'b' word. The werewolf nodded, eyes wide as she wiped away the blood from various cuts and wounds on her face.

'Up?' Sushmita questioned.

'Up,' Tommi affirmed. 'Take as many with you as you can, prioritise the weak.'

'What about the rest of you?'

Her eyes had flicked over Tommi's shoulder and she spun around to see the elevator doors open, revealing another wave of Praetorian Guard soldiers. Broom was gesturing to her right, Tommi listening to what he was telling her.

'I have a ghost suggesting a very terrible idea to me right now,' she said, turning back to Ben's sister. 'So I'm gonna work on that and you work on getting us many people up and out as you can. If I'm not there when you need to go, don't wait for me.'

Sushmita didn't have to be told twice and there was slight relief to the knowledge that if it came down to it, she would prioritise the others rather than waiting around for Tommi. They split apart, Tommi hearing Sushmita yelling and pulling the prisoners through the doorway and up the stairwell after her. She had to flip to the side, launching herself through the air as she snapped an arrow from its path which had been aimed at her. She nearly broke it in her hands, before realising it was beeping. There was a red light emitting from the tip and she hurled it back in a panic, it thankfully landing in the middle of a PG throng. It gave her an idea, though, and she yanked the corpse of the woman who had tried to fire it at her free from the carnage post-explosion.

She was loaded up and Tommi grabbed as much as she could, Broom urging her to hurry as she worked. Back moving, she rushed around the battle, using two throwing knives to dispense with a duo of soldiers who had the fire elemental pinned. He shouted out a thanks to her as he leapt on their injured bodies, stabbing them with a flurry of movements. She'd looked away before the inevitable vomfest came, but she heard the sound as lava spewed from his mouth. Her destination was the far end of the floor, where what looked like a series of commercial fridge doors were built into the wall. She had listened closely to the accounts about the creature they'd encountered at the Sydney lab. 'Made not born,' that's what Dreckly had said, and they had suspected that if there was something like that anywhere else, it would be at Vankila.

Yet Broom hadn't been able to pry that far into the building before they arrived, his ghost form too weak without their physical action to fuel his manifestation. Now that they were there and chaos was properly reigning, he had been able to see. Whatever the Treize had made, it was behind these walls.

'It's how they get rid of the bodies,' a voice said, Tommi so caught up in placing the explosives she hadn't sensed the presence behind her. Weapon in hand, she spun to face the ghost of someone who didn't look much older than a child. Dreckly had been a child in here, she reminded herself. Appearance was not indicative of age in this world.

'Is that right?' she asked, sensitive about how she phrased the question. 'Is that what they did to you?'

The girl nodded, her two plaits flopping down around her face with the movement. 'Once they're done with us, we're fed to them. We're usually dead, but not always.'

Tommi couldn't help the rumble that shook its way free of her ribcage, the growl seemingly delighting the dead girl whose eyes illuminated with excitement.

'I'm so sorry that happened to you,' she said, meaning it. 'I'm so sorry that happened to all of you.'

She kept working; there was no time to waste as she affixed the explosives to the door and checked the timer on each. This wasn't her area of expertise, but Yu had shown her enough over the years that she felt sufficiently confident to set each of them for two minutes.

'This will let them out,' Tommi told the ghost. 'I won't lie to you about that. Yet it will also mean they feast on the people who put you here.'

Hopefully, she added in her mind. The ghost looked confused for a moment, Broom floating over to join her.

'It's all right,' he said. 'I will stay here with her. Can you take physical form?'

'A little bit,' the kid whispered. 'Sometimes.'

'Good, well, when you need it the most you will be able to and if I stay with you, we can help each other.'

'Help each other how?'

'Make sure no one else leaves this level.'

The ghost girl looked delighted by that, Broom turning to Tommi with a nod. This was goodbye, permanently, with whatever happened down here in the coming minutes enough to see both of them released from the current plain they had been trapped on for so long. It would give them closure.

'Thank you,' Tommi whispered.

'No,' Broom countered, 'thank *you.*'

She ran. That's all that was left to do as she sprinted away from the ghosts, away from what she'd made the call to unleash, and towards the bigger battle as the clock continued to tick away. She swooped down just once, sweeping up a belt of grenades from the corpse of a PG soldier, but that being the only seconds she could afford to lose. The explosion was loud enough it cancelled out the tedious warning siren for a few solid seconds, but Tommi did not slow for a beat even as the fight paused up ahead. Everyone – from the PG to the prisoners – froze in combat as they looked towards the sound. She had no idea what was behind her and she didn't risk looking, feeling like Tom Cruise as she karate chopped the air with the pace she set.

'GO!' she screamed, her people knowing she meant it. They didn't work here, they didn't need to contain shit, and as she streaked past them Tommi was joined by Yixin, the fire elemental and several of the survivors, all doing their best to keep pace with her. She moved past the first emergency door, running further down to the second, which was unlocked and left half open for her by Sushmita whose scent was all over it. She sent a prayer of thanks up to the prickly werewolf, swivelling around as she ushered others through.

'Go, go, go!' she shouted as they dashed inside, their steps echoing through the stairwell as they pounded upwards. The Praetorian Guard soldiers were torn, some bracing to face what looked like a bubbling wave of goo if it weren't for the blinking eyeballs everywhere. Others were racing towards the elevator, discarding their honour as they comprehended where those creatures had come from. They weren't going to be fast enough, however, as tendrils snaked out of the darkness.

Tommi was the last through, ripping all of the grenade pins loose as she hurled the belt of bombs with a grunt. It would still be seconds before they went off, but she closed the door behind her on the screams. She fucked off up the stairs, shifting both of her hands as she leapt from rail to rail like the werewolf she was, rushing to get upwards as fast as possible. When she heard the grenades going off one after the other, she sped up even more and dived through the door Yixin had propped open for her.

The demon slammed it shut, with the fire elemental wedging himself between the creature and the structure as his skin glowed orange. He was absorbing the flames, she realised, watching as the wee man looked like a heated stove top shifting to searing red. The irony of those down there being destroyed by their own creation wasn't lost on her as she groaned, crawling over to examine the next obstacle. She didn't have to pull herself to her own feet, however, Yixin's thick arm looping under her torso as she was lifted upwards and dragged to the next fight.

'Can't rest yet,' the demon said, Tommi's feet skimming along the floor as he pulled her along. 'If Topper can eat an explosion, you can keep going.'

'I hate you,' she mumbled, as her feet started to slowly make contact with the ground and her steps gained momentum. By the time he released her, she was marching into the madness.

Chapter 15

Dreckly

Dreckly was certain she was about to die as she was thrown backwards and landed with teeth-chattering impact. She blinked, the image of the Praetorian Guard soldier who had tossed her still coming into focus as they ran at her, knife drawn. She tried to rouse her wits quickly enough to suck the air from his lungs, but she was so, so tired and so, so much of her energy had been spent. She clearly heard herself think, This is how I die. Yet at the last second, a streak of black and blonde flew out of nowhere. Knees drawn to their chest as they remained airborne, they hit the man so hard the concrete wall he made impact with cracked dramatically. He was dead on impact, yet the figure who looked like they were wearing a skin-tight wetsuit made certain with a quick snap of their neck. It was disorientating at first to recognise the face as they looked up at her from underneath the thick bangs and shoddy bleached mullet that had been cut into their hair as a disguise.

'Tommi?' Dreckly croaked.

The werewolf's grin was missing a tooth and her face was smeared with blood. Her own or someone else's? Dreckly couldn't be sure as Tommi leapt upwards.

'Fuck yeah, bitch, we getting out of here or napping?'

Tommi reached down, tugging Dreckly to her feet as she let out an anguished scream. At first she couldn't tell what was wrong, there was just *so much* pain, yet as Tommi held her up against the wall the agony became more localised. Grimacing, she squeezed her eyes shut for a second as she took deep breaths.

'Open your eyes, sprite, it's not fatal.' The words seemed harsh but the way Tommi said them was soft, fingers gently prodding the injury. 'Your arm is broken, just above the elbow.'

'How do you know?' Dreckly grunted.

'The wee bone protruding is a dead giveaway.'

Dreckly's eyes flew open as she stared down, only to see Tommi had been lying to her.

'Made ya look. But seriously, it's broken.'

Releasing Dreckly for a minute, the werewolf grabbed the strap of a nearby discarded machine gun and slashed it free of the weapon. Fastening it around her neck, she constructed a makeshift sling for Dreckly before tugging her by the hip. Tommi took the lead, positioned in front of the sprite as they moved along the physical and human debris of the hallway.

'Have you got everything you need here?' the werewolf asked. 'Cos if it's cool with you, I'd suggest we don't linger.'

'Ben's free,' Dreckly told her, the sprite truthfully having very little to do with it once the emergency sirens went off. She'd made it to where he was being held only to witness the aftermath, Ben embracing with a smaller and meaner looking woman who she realised must have been Sushmita, his sister. Their reunion was brief, however, as they moved on and up to begin sweeping through as many cells as they could. Medium security meant no alchemy wards, which was a plus, but just as many guards, which was a minus.

The confined spaces made the fighting impossible to avoid and as they navigated their way through, Tommi dropped to one knee to let off a series of shots and protect Dreckly's route. Part of a wall started to crumble around them and Dreckly strained to hold it back, funnelling the air to halt it while they rushed through. She was about to release her hold just as she ducked a crumbling piece of plaster when she saw the unmistakable limbs of the Russian arachnia Silver scuttling along behind her.

'I don't know if you'll get a bigger shoe to squash a bigger spider than that wall right now,' Tommi murmured, the sprite hearing the fear in her voice.

'She's friend, not foe,' Dreckly said. 'I think.'

Sighing as she started to release the wall, it collapsed behind the creature just as she made it clear. Pulling herself up to her full height, the arachnia dusted a piece of debris off her shoulder like it was insignificant to her.

'Vank you,' she muttered.

The three of them moved, following the stream of others as they were being ushered away from the crumbling carnage and towards any one of the upward exit points. Ghosts had began appearing during the struggle, Dreckly knowing they were mad and growing in power given that she was able to see them. She watched as they skipped from one person to attack another, seeming to know exactly who they needed to condemn and who they should let pass as Vankila fell around them. Ben looked like he was among the last of the living who waited, Yixin smashing two Praetorian Guard soldiers together like he was trying to make them kiss in spite of the several arrows that protruded from his back. Dreckly nearly stopped dead in her tracks as she saw him, but the werewolf and arachnia had a firm grasp and they kept yanking her forward.

'Yixin!' she cried, *literally* crying as his glowing eyes flashed towards her. He looked confused for a moment, not as if he didn't recognise her but as if he was trying to put the pieces together as he connected the child he had once known with the woman that was before him now. He released the corpses, cradling Dreckly to him as she pushed herself into his chest, careful to avoid her broken arm.

'Hello, little sprite,' he said.

'This life,' Dreckly sniffed, looking up at him. 'Not the next.'

Surprise danced across his expression as she repeated the words he'd once said to her when Yixin lifted her into the roof and the tunnel that would eventually have her crawling to freedom. His thick, clawed hands stroked through her hair in a gesture that reminded her of what her father used to do to soothe her to sleep. Dreckly pulled away, stepping towards the stairwell Ben was ushering them towards. Then she paused. The air up there was rapidly moving, friction whipping backwards and forwards as bodies moved forward and trotted down the stairs in a swift but orderly fashion. *Soldiers,* she thought, recognising the stiffness of movement. Specifically, Praetorian Guard soldiers.

'Shut the door!' she shouted, kicking it out of the werewolf's hands and slamming her back against it. He looked at her like she was mad. 'Praetorian Guard!'

'Fuck!' Ben exclaimed. 'That was the last exit we had. How many reinforcements, Dreckly? Can we take them?'

'No,' she said honestly. 'There's eight of us and *more* than eight of them.'

'We have seconds before they hit this door,' Ben huffed. 'We're gonna need some kind of plan.'

'Let them come,' Silver said, shaking out her limbs while Tommi stared up at her like she was in love with the arachnia. There was a yell behind them, followed by a gargled cry, and they spun round to see the main elevators open and several bodies thrown out. Dreckly had told them they needed to avoid that route because it was too tightly monitored and guarded by the people they were trying to avoid if they could, it being the preferred mode of transport up and down the Vankila levels. That was all past tense, she realised, as she watched Heath and Mildred poke their heads out with scepticism.

'Oy!' the Scot shouted. 'We commandeered the lift!'

No further words were needed as they all began sprinting towards it, Dreckly guessing they must have been monitoring them on the cameras. It was a risk wasting time and resources to take the elevator, but Heath and Mildred had been willing to take it once they saw the others were trapped. They had to leap over the piles of bodies at the entrance, Heath's muscular arms straining against the sliding doors as he fought to hold them open. Yixin went first, helping to lift in Dreckly and Topper the fire elemental. Ben, Sushmita and Silver needed little help, Tommi bringing up the rear as she and Quaid hurled circular objects towards the stairwell. They landed at the exact moment the door was kicked open, those on the other side shouting with surprise as the smoke bombs went off and clouded their view.

The siblings spun around, Heath letting go of the elevator doors as they sprinted for them. Quaid dived through and Tommi launched herself into his arms. He caught her perfectly, the sliding barrier feeling like it was taking forever as Dreckly watched the smoke obscure who was on the other side. A figure dashed through the clouds of grey and sprinted towards her, a sword in his hands. *Lorcan,* because it couldn't be anyone else. Instinctively, Dreckly took a step forwards but found her momentum stopped by Tommi tugging back against her good arm.

'Don't,' the werewolf urged, her lips so close to Dreckly's ear that she felt the breath against her neck. 'You won't survive it now.'

The pull was still very real, the tug like a magnet, and Dreckly wanted to give in and run towards her revenge. But the werewolf's grip was tighter than she realised, both of her arms taut around Dreckly's torso. She couldn't flee from the elevator as the doors slowly closed on the face of the man she so desperately wanted to annihilate. His brow was furrowed and his gaze intense as he raced, yet she saw the shock of recognition as he saw those assembled inside.

Heath, his old friend and enemy, an array of prisoners he had either locked up or whose detainment he had enforced, and at the centre of it a woman he had once claimed to love restraining a being who had escaped from him not once, not twice, but now three times as the elevator sealed itself off from his entry. Dreckly sagged with relief as the motorised motion pulled them upwards. It wasn't a smooth ride, the metallic cube not exactly feeling secure as the floor shook around them. Yixin braced himself against the wall of the elevator, his shoulders hunched over and his horns still scraping the roof as he struggled to hide his discomfort. Tommi released Dreckly, curling up inside the arms of the old Pictish warrior as he attempted to wipe the blood from her face.

'What did you get up to down there?' he asked, clearly so proud of the havoc she had managed to wreak in such a short amount of time. Dreckly couldn't hear what the werewolf muttered up at him in response, but she didn't miss the way Ben was watching the two of them with interest as Sushmita sagged against him. Mildred wasn't embracing Yixin, instead the two demons were doing something Dreckly didn't quite have a word for. They had moved closer to each other, staring intensely as their eyes glowed and the edges of their fingertips touched. She hadn't seen demons interact like this before, yet she knew instinctively it was something profound. Not romantic, not friendly, something . . . more.

'What floor are we coming out on?' Quaid asked, breaking up all of the different reunions with his question but looking like he was ready for anything.

'Right up to reception,' Mildred replied, breaking her gaze with Yixin as she calmly wiped blood from two long, arched blades against the linen of her pant leg.

Heath struck out, plunging a screwdriver into the controls and ripping out tuffs of wiring and sparking cords in the process. The light in the elevator cut out, only to come back on a moment later with that horrible red emergency glow she hated so much.

'Make that ground,' he beamed, looking like a cat that had just delivered a dead bird from its mouth to the inconvenience of your slippers.

'Good.' Tommi sighed, Dreckly realising that she looked and sounded as tired as she felt. 'I'm tired of fighting my way up.'

'What about everyone else?' Yixin asked.

'We have people guiding them,' Dreckly told the demon. 'Whoever's left, that is.'

'We've done all we can now,' Heath added. 'The facility is compromised, we've saved who we can and that was the mission. Now it's time to save ourselves.'

The elevator jerked to a halt, a mechanical screech sending the whole structure into a rocking motion as the light cut out in earnest this time.

'You just had to say it,' Tommi huffed.

'This isn't my fault!' Heath countered.

Dreckly was quiet, feeling the air particles around her as she sorted the stale from the fresh.

'We're close to the surface,' she murmured. 'Inches.'

'Let's close 'em,' Tommi said, the werewolves able to see in the dark when the others could not. 'Quaid, give me a leg up?'

She could hear not see them as they moved through the black, the friction of fabric audible just before there was a grunt and thud. Then another thud, three of them all up, and then a slither of grey light appeared through the ceiling and she saw Tommi's legs kicking it wider. She went feet first, like she was doing an upside-down chin-up, but slowly as she inched her body upwards and Quaid supported the weight of her back. The elevator jerked downwards and back up, Tommi letting out a squawk of discomfort while Dreckly closed her eyes to avoid panicking. Heath was not of the same disposition, and he screamed out Tommi's name, half stumbling, half falling towards the manhole she'd climbed through.

'I'm all right, I'm all right!' she called back, tension in her voice. 'I'm working fast.'

'We need to distribute our weight,' Dreckly said. 'And we need to do it slowly, gradually.'

They did so, shuffling and inching about. She tried to ignore the metallic strain she heard, tried to block out the idea that they could very likely plummet to their deaths. *I really don't want to die like this,* Dreckly thought. *I really don't want to die like this, I really don't want to die like this, I really don't want t—*

'Dreckly!'

She jumped, her eyes flying open to find Mildred's face in front of her own. They were practically nose to nose, the demon placing her cool hands on Dreckly's cheeks.

'Dreckly, it's okay, breathe.'

Her eyes scanned the elevator behind her, finding there was more light than before and that Heath, Quaid, the small man they were with and Sushmita were gone. Ben was assisting Yixin through the hole they all must have left through, Dreckly's own panic having blocked out their actions. As the larger demon disappeared, Ben turned back to Silver, who eschewed his help to scuttle through the gap herself. The werewolf had to supress a shudder as he faced Dreckly.

'Come on,' he urged, voice gentle. 'You're next.'

She stared at his outstretched hand, frozen.

'You go first,' Mildred told Ben. 'Reach back, help her up.'

He leapt through quickly, listening to her orders, and Dreckly followed him. She squinted, staring into the sunlight.

It blinded her at first, the sprite unable to see anything through the white until Ben's hand reached back through. She gripped his forearm, hesitating for just a moment.

'What about you?' she asked, turning to Mildred who was standing right behind her. The demon smiled, pushing her forward.

'Right after you.'

Dreckly groaned with pain as Ben tugged her upwards, Mildred helping so her legs had a grip and she didn't bump her broken arm. It was unavoidable, however, Ben bracing her waist with both hands as he helped lift her up. Yixin grabbed her under the armpits and suddenly she was on the ground, *real ground,* and she could feel grass beneath her body. She let out a relieved sigh, the simple act turning into a sob followed by a series of them. The tension and fear she'd felt towards the end finally released, Dreckly realised with horror that she had never expected to make it. She'd gone into Vankila thinking she would never come back out. The fresh air that she sucked into her lungs as she lay there on her back felt even better than the first time she had been in this exact same position over a hundred years ago.

With a shuddered breath, she sat up just as Ben appeared out of what had once been disguised as a sewer grate. She crawled over to him and he held her, planting a kiss on her forehead as she breathed in their sweat-drenched scents. They separated, Ben reaching back down to grab Mildred as she climbed on to the roof of the elevator. The demon extended her hand just a second too late, the structure jerking as the ground beneath them shuddered. The cry wasn't Mildred's but rather Dreckly's as she nearly threw herself through the hole, only stopped by Ben as he held her back. Their fingers nearly brushed, Mildred bracing her legs as she went to jump. As she kneeled, the cables snapped and the elevator plummeted away. The demon didn't make a sound as she fell back, her hand still outstretched and reaching towards Dreckly's as she disappeared into the darkness.

'MILDRED!' she screamed, fighting against Ben as he pulled her backwards. She was kicking and crying, certain that if she just got free of him Mildred would be okay and waiting for the right exact second to climb to safety like they all had. Instead, she saw the fabric of the demon's shirt fluttering with the rush of gravity as she fell to her death, the only speck of white amongst the encroaching black. Forever Alice spiralling down the rabbit hole, only this time there was no way out.

'Knock her the fuck out if you have to!' his sister was yelling.

'She just saw her friend die, Sushmita! Have some compassion!'

'What good is compassion if we're all dead too!'

She didn't understand the argument, didn't understand his sister's rage and why the woman couldn't just let her *grieve for a fucking moment* until the ground started to buck beneath them. She watched fissures spreading out from the hole she'd climbed through, growing wider and wider as they cracked even bigger. Ben had been slowly dragging her and she tried to find her footing, running uneasily alongside him as they sprinted. It reminded her of being at sea, Dreckly swinging wildly from side to side on her old boat the *Titanic II* in rougher conditions. It sounded like an eruption behind them and she looked back to see the grassy hill all but disappearing as the ground gave away.

'RUN!' Sushmita was shouting, diving into the bed of a truck that was already moving. Ben stayed by her side, pulling her along with him as they tried to keep upright.

'I'm so sorry for this,' he puffed.

'So sorry for— ARGH!'

He threw her – actually *threw her* – at his sister, and Dreckly passed out with the pain as her broken limb collided with the werewolf. It must have only been a few seconds, as when she came to she was still bouncing along in the truck, wedged between Ben's legs as he tried to still how much she was being tossed around. It was all but impossible, Dreckly understanding why as she half sat up and saw the truck they were in was racing alongside another on uneven surface. She turned to survey the scene, Sushmita open-mouthed as she stared at the Scottish countryside disappearing into a massive sinkhole. Theirs weren't the only vehicles, Aruhe having done a good enough job that battered cars of almost every type were dotting the countryside. Creatures were packed into them, some clinging to the roofs and the doors and the bumpers as they sped away. Some weren't fast enough; Dreckly slapped a hand over her mouth as she watched a mini-van get eaten by a crater that opened up in front of it. There were others on foot, some she could recognise as Praetorian Guard soldiers, others supernaturals who were sprinting for their lives. Many wouldn't make it.

She winced as she turned around, Tommi shouting to the ginger-haired driver she recognised as Joss from earlier, their Austin Powers-loving insider. The werewolf was screaming at him to 'fang it', but she could already hear from the rev of the engine that they were going as fast as they could go. St Andrews was up ahead, but it was still too far away and there was no indication the cavity would stop any time soon. Yixin and the others were in the companion vehicle, Silver poised on the roof like she was ready to leap through the air the second one of the tyres gave out. Aruhe was driving that one with Sorcha riding shotgun, the suspension going through a hell of a time as they bounced over the rapidly dissolving land. They had been the last to make it out, so they were at the very back of the group with this convoy having waited. She couldn't let it cost them their lives. Half crawling, half guided by Ben, she stuck her head in through the back window of the cabin.

'Make for the River Tay!' she yelled.

'What?' Tommi shouted back, looking at her like she was correctly losing it.

'We're never going to outrun this thing, make for the water!'

Atlanta, Avary, Amos and a handful of other selkies were nearby – a back-up plan in case anything went wrong. Anything was well and truly going wrong and what good were back-up plans if you didn't use them.

'Joss?' Tommi asked, looking uncertainly at the driver.

'Fooooook it,' he replied, swerving so hard that if it wasn't for Sushmita's grip on her shirt Dreckly would have been thrown out of the tray.

'Who's gonna tell them?' she shouted, watching as Aruhe continued on her path.

'Argh, she'll get the idea soon enough,' Joss called back, tooting his horn repeatedly to get their attention. She did, swerving off not long after him as they cut a route towards the water. Dreckly gestured for Aruhe to keep tooting, the werewolf not understanding the message but Sorcha picking it up as she took over honking duties. The duo of vehicles flew towards the water, the River Tay looking about as uninviting as Dreckly remembered her father telling her it was. They finally hit a road, but the smooth surface was short lived as it started to crack and buckle underneath them. The honking was working, however, Dreckly seeing the first of several selkie heads emerge from under the surface.

'Joss, you're gonna have to hit the water at speed,' Heath told him. 'If you stop for people to get out, we're earthworms.'

'What the fuck do you mean *hit it with speed*, you lunatic? We don't have enough seat belts in here, if I hit it—'

'DO IT!' Dreckly screamed, having just pulled her horrified gaze away from the abyss that was only metres from catching up with them. There was nothing further to accelerate, the cars maxing out the odometer and the rapid descent giving them added speed as the sheer drop off into the River Tay raced closer.

'Sushmita, handle Heath,' Ben ordered. 'I've got Dreckly.'

She looked to the other vehicle, seeing that everyone there was bracing to do the same. As they hit the final clip of land, there were just a few seconds of suspension as the cars travelled out, out, and over the edge before gravity took control. By that point they were already flying away, Dreckly watching Tommi dive from the car with Joss in her arms as Ben did the same to her and Sushmita with Heath. She didn't see any of them hit the water, but she sure as hell felt it as both the impact and the cold felt like it was cutting through her skin. Her scream was lost among the bubbles, Ben kicking upwards as they both punched through the surface with noisy gasps for air.

'I'm all right,' she said, seeing that he was struggling as she pushed away from him.

'But—'

'Don't try to help me, help yourself. I'm half selkie, Ben. This is more my element than yours.'

It was true; even with one arm she was doing better than anyone else, with the exception of the selkies and Sorcha. The banshee was counting heads, which was difficult as the current was rough and they were all being swept out to sea. Yixin was having the most trouble, Dreckly pointing him out to Avary who made a beeline for him. She and Atlanta were the strongest and most capable, yet there were more of them than there were selkies and they had to use their resources sparingly. Amos came for her and she shook him off, directing him towards Ben and Sushmita first as he helped keep them afloat.

She didn't need the assist; the water was always *home* to her in some way – even if it was a freezing Scottish river with a notorious undertow. She stayed buoyant, just the one arm fanned out to keep her stable as she remained captivated by the sight in front of her. The sinkhole was still expanding, the world opening up and swallowing everything in its path, as if the only way to purge Vankila was to consume it entirely. It didn't move past the waterline, though, the collapse running only as far as the bed of the River Tay.

'I swear I didn't do that.'

Dreckly turned to find Tommi floating beside her, the minimal hand movements needed to stay afloat telling the sprite that the werewolf was confident in the water. She hadn't panicked like some of the others and she'd turned selkies away when they'd tried to help her too, redirecting them to those whose need was more pressing. Heath was buoyant too, having kicked off some of his clothing so he wouldn't be weighed down. Together, the three of them stared at the chasm that had once been St Andrews.

'It's not you,' Heath puffed. 'Explosives can't do that, sweetheart. Look at the way it stopped when it got to the town.'

'Your friend Gaea?' Tommi questioned. 'How many earth demons are there in this part of the world?'

'Not many,' he replied. 'And none that can do that.'

'It's balance,' Dreckly answered, gaze still transfixed. 'Doesn't have to be a who or a what. Think of all the years of evil and suffering and pain that happened in that place. The Three's death will bring balance in its own way; this was nature doing the same.'

She felt a brush against her shoulder, turning to see Tommi right there with her. 'Mildred?'

Dreckly couldn't even verbalise the loss, she just shook her head as she felt the salt of her own tears streaking down her face to mix with the salt of the river.

'I'm so sorry,' the werewolf murmured, looking like she wanted to hug her but both physically unable to amongst the torrent.

'She knew,' Dreckly croaked, realising it in the moment but not fully processing what that meant until now. 'She made me climb out first because she knew it was going to fall, she knew she was going to die.'

'Speaking of death . . .' Heath started, copping a frustrated splash from Tommi who screamed at him for being so insensitive. 'I'm sorry but Mildred wouldn't want us to get eaten by

Nessie while we're all bleeding our way out into the open ocean, commiserating about her sacrifice.'

'Nessie is not the problem,' Atlanta said, swimming towards them. Dreckly didn't even need to see Sorcha wrapped around the selkie's back to know that was where the banshee would be. 'The problem is what we saw before you arrived.'

'Praetorian Guard reinforcements,' Amos answered as he supported Ben and Sushmita with his weight. 'They came in by boat, speeding up the river from Kingoodie.'

'That's good for our friends who escaped by land,' Tommi said. 'Their access to them is cut off now. How long is it until they work out there's a bunch of sitting ducks south-west of them?'

'So we're fleeing by sea?' Joss said, Aruhe and he clinging to each other on the back of another selkie. 'Is that what we're doing? Cos Bell Rock Lighthouse—'

'We're not going to Bell Rock cunting Lighthouse!' Tommi shouted. 'Lorcan took me there during one of my first trans-formations; it's a site *they* use. Soon as they establish we're alive, that's one of the first places they'll look.'

'I know somewhere we can go,' Atlanta spoke up. Sorcha gave her a concerned glance, one that Dreckly shared.

'Are you sure?' Sorcha asked.

'We went to them for a reason,' the selkie answered. 'In case something exactly like this happened and now it has. There's nowhere safer.'

'We can't gamble with our lives on a myth,' Dreckly said.

'What myth?' Silver shouted, the arachnia doing her best to kept as much of her body out of the water as she could. Two of her eight legs were perched on the shoulders of a selkie as they skimmed the surface helping Topper, the rest were curled up close to her body.

'When the Treize dragged banshees from their homeland in the seventeen hundreds, they loaded them on to ships and set course for Australia,' Dreckly told them. 'They left Ireland with just over two thousand banshees, but only fifteen hundred made it.'

'What happened to the rest?' Tommi questioned, Heath filling in the blanks of the story that had been written in their history books.

'Selkies sunk the ships, taking down Treize ships as well,' he said. 'Everyone drowned at sea.'

Tommi's eyes lit up with excitement, pointing between Sorcha and Atlanta. 'Like you! Like you were supposed to drown!'

'Banshees tend to do very well at sea when selkies are around,' Dreckly said. 'The myth is there's an island where the women that were saved were taken, a utopia free of the tyranny of the Treize where banshees and selkies lived together in harmony.'

'What is this, Wonder Woman?' Joss quipped. 'That story was never proven *real*.'

'It's not a myth,' Atlanta growled. 'And it might be the only way we survive.'

Chapter 16

Casper

Out of the back window of the car, speeding away from the city, Casper watched the Bierpinsel blow up. She supposed it would have been more impressive during the day, but even at night it took her breath away as the orange flash came first and then the black sky ignited. Her old home disintegrated into a cloud of flames and concrete ash, the figures of people running away from the scene backlit like little ants.

'There goes the neighbourhood,' Yu huffed, Casper turning to see her friend's sweat-drenched face watching the same sight.

The humans driving their getaway car were demons behind the wheel, swerving and accelerating as they floored it out of Berlin. Phases had emptied when everyone had gone on their separate missions; only those who were unable to participate or too weak to be moved stayed in the city. The goblins had taken them underground, deep, where even the Treize couldn't find them once they attempted to retaliate because they were certain that's what would happen. Phases had been a stronghold and a sanctuary. When their enemies wanted to inflict the most harm on them as quickly as possible after this, that's where they would go.

So everyone had to scatter to the wind, just like the Australians had done after the Sydney attack. The Rogues had more than happily stolen that idea because it worked, with their party heading to a sleepy town in Hungary called Szarvas. It was every part of a ten-hour drive and once dawn broke, they were able to take their first break at the five-hour mark. Pulling over on a back road just outside of Prague, Casper was keen to get Yu out of the car and cleaned up now that they'd reached their first assembly point. She'd done the best job she could with her wounds, but it was nothing compared to what a Paranormal Practitioner would be able to accomplish.

The woman waiting for them was a sweet-looking demon. There was so little interaction with the outside world on this country property that she had let her tusks grow out in earnest. They curled around her face in beautiful shapes as her sturdy hands took the limping Yu from Casper, ushering her inside. The humans hovered near the car, uncertain whether they should proceed or not, and Casper made herself the bridge between them, leading their party to a cottage at the back where they were told everyone could rest, shower and change. There was food waiting there too, Casper grabbing a sandwich before she marched back outside to see who else had made it back.

She froze when she saw the bodies, Hogan crouched near three of them with a bowed head. They were covered in bloodied sheets, Casper steadying herself for a second before she too crouched down to inspect the faces. Zillia was the first, the petite werewolf only identifiable by the layers of gold jewellery she wore draped around her neck. Her face had suffered too much trauma to be recognisable, the medium also noting a gunshot to her torso that looked just as fatal. She sent not quite a prayer exactly, but more of what Kala would have called a loving incantation filled with the memory of the werewolf as she had lived rather than how she had died. The next face she didn't know by name, recognising her only as one of the witches who had been at the table when they planned their attacks at Phases. She was reaching for the sheet of the third when Hogan stopped her, hand gripping Casper's.

'It's Ginger,' he said.

His grip implored her not to look and she respected that wish, leaving the sheet as it was.

'She died saving me,' the goblin said, wiping tears from his face. 'And for what?'

'For the next Ginger,' came a voice behind them, and Casper looked up to see the hard, unflinching face of Duo. The pilot had once been described to her as someone who could fly *anything* anywhere. She'd proven that more than once, including getting the medium from Uzbekistan to Cornwall at the drop of a hat and flying Heath and Dreckly to Scotland for the Vankila raid while everyone else had taken different routes. A scar that ran diagonally across her face meant she wore what looked like a permanent snarl, but even if it hadn't been there Casper got the impression that would have been her resting expression. Like most of Heath's network of associates, she was a seriously efficient and seriously scary person. She also had a point.

'Casper.' Duo nodded, addressing her curtly.

Casper returned the gesture, getting to her feet and her question being answered by the pilot before she even had a chance to ask it. 'The others are inside. I flew them back a few hours ago.'

'Were you successful?'

The pilot looked down at the dead, as if considering the bodies in front of her before answering that question.

'Yes,' she replied eventually. Casper gripped Hogan's shoulder, giving him a comforting squeeze as she moved by to see who was left.

Dolly was leaning against the outside doorway, smoking, and she startled when Casper made her way towards her. Not because the werewolf was particularly a big fan of hers, but the medium knew that her appearance meant news on the fate of Yu, and Dolly looked like it had been the only thing occupying her mind as she waited.

'I didn't realise you were back,' the werewolf said, stamping out her cigarette. 'Is she—'

'Hurt but nothing fatal,' Casper replied. 'She's with the Paranormal Practitioners in the front room.'

Dolly was gone in a flash, not staying for a second longer when she could have been with Yu, and it made Casper's heart ache for Kala. She would check in with her soon, she was itching to, but first she needed to assess the carnage here. There were fewer people inside than she had expected, which was not a good sign. It meant folks had died at the scene but, unlike Zillia and Ginger, their bodies had not been retrieved. The beings that were being worked on were injured seriously, but most of them would survive their wounds in the same way Yu would. Many she knew by name, passing through their ranks and asking how they were, gripping their hands, sharing information she had heard. She paused when she came across Clay and Sanjay, both patched up and seemingly okay, but the body they were crowded around was not. It was Gus, the hulking block of muscle and key member of the Rogues. Sanjay was on one side, Clay on the other, both gripping the hands of their long-time friend as he let out quick, panting breaths. They were shallow, growing shallower, and Clay's enormous biceps flexed as he gripped Gus's hand even tighter, as if willing him stay.

Sanjay was praying; Casper did not recognise the words but the tone was unmistakable as Sanjay sat there with his eyes closed. There was nothing to be done. One of the werewolf's legs was missing above the knee and that combined with a deep stab wound meant that he was bleeding out. As she watched, he died right before her very eyes, the small puffs of air from his lips disappearing altogether as it went quiet. Sanjay's eyes flew open, as if he didn't quite believe it. It required barely a second of her as she closed her own, slipping away to try to find Gus in the lobby. Yet the werewolf was already gone. He had been ready.

When she returned to the room, stumbling slightly against the table Gus had been spread out on, Clay was sobbing. She had no idea how to comfort him, how to comfort any of these people, as they drowned in their grief. The only thing she could do was leave, walking out of the house and towards a beautiful old tree at the side of the property. There was a wooden swing there and she sat in it, feeling the weight of the world on her shoulders. When her brother arrived, Casper didn't bother to wipe away the tears that were gently rolling down her cheeks. He didn't address them either, letting her sit there and silently cry. She felt the cold compression of his ghostly hand in hers and she gripped it.

'Kala?' she said, knowing other updates would be coming but needing that one first.

'Alive and safe,' Barastin started. 'Thanks to Sprinkle.'

She turned to gawk at her twin.

'I got there just as things were getting bad but then our favourite wee witch disobeyed her curfew and set an entire squadron on fire.'

'Shut. Up.'

'From my dead eyes to your living ears, I swear it. She was wearing a Supergirl shirt and everything.'

Casper laughed, slapping a hand over her mouth to soften the sound. She would have given anything to have been by their sides, watching those soldiers perish before the pyro powers of a tween witch.

'There were losses,' Barastin said, bringing an abrupt halt to her temporary elation.

'Who?'

'You're thinking in terms of people rather than places.'

'Oh God, we . . . lost a city?'

'A state,' he corrected. 'The Treize had better defences than we were anticipating on the Gold Coast.'

'It was just supposed to be an outpost!'

'That's what we thought, too, but Tasmanian devil shifters had four water demons they were torturing on site and the situation was more volatile than any of us expected.'

'Multiple water demons,' she murmured, scrunching her eyes shut with frustration as she thought of the human allies they had there. 'Was it a flood?'

'A tsunami.'

'Fuck.'

'The devastation is considerable. The whole state of Queensland is gone and a good chunk of New South Wales, too. Selkies tried to save whatever survivors they could, but there weren't many.'

She dropped her head into her hands, trying to breathe.

'Borders are redrawn after every war, dear sister.'

'I know.' She exhaled, leaning back. 'Have you told Amos? Dreckly?'

'No, not yet. They've got other things to worry about right now and I need to manage the time.'

'Are you stretching yourself too thin, dear brother?'

He smiled as she looked across at him, the fatigue visible like tiny cracks that covered his entire visage.

'What other choice do we have? Tell me, how's the Bierpinsel?'

'Ash,' she began, recounting the events of their own incursion as concisely as she could. From the deaths of Jakea and Jaira, to Yu's injuries, she realised they had fared better than almost every other team. Queensland had taken the biggest hit, but there were other major losses as well: Alaska and Argentina mainly, making the trifecta of geographies hit badly all 'A' countries. Yet overall their many, many missions had been successful collectively: they hadn't won them all, but they had won enough to destabilise the Treize and make the most significant inroads in the history of their kind. One of the biggest among them, Vankila, had also been effectively eviscerated, with a bulk of those freed being able to flee via land while a smaller party, significant to her, had fled via sea.

'There's more,' Barastin said. Casper threw him a look like 'don't you fucking dare'. But he had to. 'Sadie had a vision.'

'That's rarely a good thing.'

'No, it's not. And she's getting them in concentrated doses through the foetuses, so it's visions to the power of three, *Charmed* style.'

'Don't bring your favourite show into this,' she huffed. 'What did she see?'

'The Treize, in person, on site at the Dawson farm.'

To kill her, she thought. It was the only logical reason all thirteen of them would leave the stronghold in Transylvania. She listened as Barastin dictated the vision to her, Dreckly's death, and the assembly of everyone who was left to fight. So many people had lost *so much,* she understood why it felt like a smaller fight than what they had been through already. People needed to start picking up the pieces, rebuilding what they could now while there was still time, and chase down any who might have escaped and would pose issues later. They didn't know about Sadie, that had been intentional, so the task of defending and protecting the babies was down to them and just them.

'Wait,' she said. 'Wait . . .'

'On what? You to collect your thoughts?'

'Yes, you rude asshole! I had an id—'

'What?'

She rubbed her eyes, which were dry and sore from fatigue, as she tried to think it through and think it through *quickly*. 'You sure it was all thirteen of them in New Zealand?'

'Yes. Simon has scouts monitoring the passage in, but Sadie thinks it will be nine days until the whole Treize arrive with whatever Askari, Custodians and Praetorian Guard soldiers they have left.'

'The Askari have jumped ship.'

Casper and Barastin both looked up to see Clay coming to join them, the usual epitome of joy and elation looking like he might never feel either one of those things again.

'They abandoned the Treize?' she asked.

'Like rats from a sinking barge,' the werewolf replied, flopping down on to the grass in front of the swing. 'Custodians, too, although that seems to be less uniform and more case by case.'

'So who is left there to defend The Three?' Casper asked. 'No one, because they think that if they kill Sadie and her children before they're born then . . . what, crisis averted? Everything goes back to normal?'

'The Three are dying regardless, they're forcing this shift,' Barastin replied. 'Nothing will ever go back to normal after this.'

'Let's make sure it never does,' Casper said, looking between the two of them.

'*Kill The Three?*' her brother practically spat. 'I have to strongly advise against murdering the women who have helped us this far when they have absolutely no other reason to.'

'Not kill them,' she huffed, rolling her eyes with annoyance. 'Remember the prophecy: nothing can save The Three when they choose to return to the river after they've seen enough.'

'What river?' Clay asked.

She batted a hand. 'A metaphorical river, that's not the point. When they choose to leave this plain, they will regardless. I don't think it's a physical thing so much as a conscious thing they choose, with the birth of the triplets restoring the void they would leave behind. I'm proposing we help them with their final transition.'

A warm breeze ran over her skin, picking up just enough so that it rustled the tree above them. She watched the green leaves as they danced from the branch, several falling with the warm gust so that they sprinkled around Clay like confetti. The werewolf focused on their motion, as if such a simple thing could bring him relief. She hoped that it would, but Casper knew the reality. Clay had lost more than one of his friends today and that was the kind of grief you didn't get over. It stayed with you, it changed you, and you had to learn to live with it. Barastin's silence meant that he didn't think her suggestion was a terrible idea.

'I think you should do it,' he said quietly. 'We owe it to them.'

'I agree,' she replied.

'But just because the Treize won't physically be there, that doesn't mean it won't be dangerous; someone will stay to guard them. And whoever's not on the trek to New Zealand will be looking for any of us they can find. You can't go alone.'

'So she won't,' Clay said. 'I'll go with Casper.'

'No disrespect—' Barastin started.

'I feel like disrespect is coming,' Clay muttered.

'But a strung-out werewolf is not a fitting guard for my sister.'

'You know, I liked you so much better when you were alive.'

'And I liked *you* so much better when—'

'Stop it!' Casper snapped. 'Stop. It. This is not helping. How long is the drive to Romania?'

'The Transylvanian region is at least twelve hours from here,' the werewolf said. 'If I'm flooring it, that is. Pee breaks, rest breaks ... Actually, Officer Dick is here, he would be a good person to bring.'

'Is Officer Dick your *booooyfriend*?' Barastin teased.

Clay barked a laugh. 'You fucking wish, ghost. Officer *Dick* Creuzinger, he's a cop, he's here, he was on the road with me. If we hit any major human roadblocks, he's our best bet to push through them and he can share the drive so Casper can rest.'

Barastin puffed out his cheeks, looking for an objection but unable to find one.

'Speaking of,' the werewolf said, getting to his feet. 'Everyone else is patched up. It's your turn, Casper.'

She looked down at where he was gesturing: the cut on her arm that Yu had taken the brunt of looked worse than she remembered. All of the other types of pain she had experienced had numbed it. Blood caked there now as she let Clay take her to one of the Paranormal Practitioners. The werewolf had his arm on her elbow, guiding her back towards the house when she paused and turned to face Barry.

'I know you have places to go, people to see, things to watch,' she started, 'but you can spare a second to tell Kala I'm all right?'

'Already have.' Her brother smiled.

'Thank you,' she replied, meaning it deeply. 'And one other thing: when I help them move on, will you be there?'

Barastin nodded. 'Nowhere else I'd rather be.'

He vanished, disappearing from the tree swing as the structure rocked in the wind, like he was never there. She fell in step beside Clay, taking his hand as they walked, the wolf gripping hers tightly regardless of the dirt and blood dried between their fingers.

'When should we leave?' Casper asked, feeling like it should be soon but wanting it to be years from now.

'Tomorrow night,' Clay said. She knew he'd been in the Marines – Yu and he had bonded over the time they'd served together during a boozy night at Phases she had spent with them. As far as people to escort her on this task, a former soldier and a cop felt like pretty damn accomplished assistants.

'Everyone else is moving soon,' the werewolf continued. 'The more distance between us and them the better. We'll take different roads just in case.'

'Why take roads at all?' she questioned. Clay followed her gaze to the light aircraft that had been covered with camouflage netting.

'A plane trip to Transylvania seems excessive,' he said, quirking an eyebrow.

'Not for us,' Casper corrected. 'For them. For anyone else who's willing to defend Sadie and the others.'

Clay looked hesitant as they walked and she guessed what he was thinking.

'They've been through a lot,' Clay said, verbalising it. 'I guarantee you that every single one of them would be willing to go through a lot more if they think it would help. They want to finish it.'

'They're not the only ones,' Casper murmured. She fell silent, resting her mouth but not her mind as she was led to a small bathroom in the house by one of the Paranormal Practitioners and asked to shower. She did so, washing away the grime and dirt and blood and mess until she was clean. She had a small bag of clothes with her, changing slowly as she discovered and rediscovered more wounds. The cut required stitches, not many, and there was a small laceration on the back of her neck that needed a dressing, but not much else.

Clay was correct, everyone had been through so much and the bodies weren't even buried yet. The exhaustion as she asked them to give even more was profound, but he was right about that too. As they gathered outside – everyone needing the fresh air and sunlight – Casper broached the subject, and no one said no. Yu stepped in to divert the humans, asking them to stay and protect the safehouses they already had planned for use. There were still supernaturals fleeing to those locations and who were vulnerable just like the Paranormal Practitioners where they were currently. They agreed, but no one looked more enthusiastic about the prospect of invading the foreign air space of multiple countries than Duo. It was like Casper had told her they were going to an air show, her eyes illuminated with glee.

'I'll need a bigger plane,' she said, before correcting herself. 'No, I *want* a bigger plane. The one I've got is fast and agile, but it won't take the weight of the people and the weapons we need to transfer.'

'I know somewhere,' Yu said. 'Private airfield one hour from here. It's rich-people shit, though, nothing tactical.'

'I can fly annnnnything,' Duo sneered. 'Give me a G5 and I'll make it move like a Boeing F/A 18F Super Hornet.'

'All of those are just numbers and words to me,' Casper remarked, Hogan whipping out a laptop as his fingers began flying over the keyboard.

'I can hack the airfield manifest,' Hogan said. 'See what's coming in over the next forty-eight hours and you can take your pick of what you like on the menu.'

'Whoever needs rest, get it now,' Casper said. 'Protecting that banshee and those babies is the priority. To do that, I want you all in New Zealand as soon as possible, so that might mean some long hours and longer days ahead. Humans, I can't thank you enough for everything you've done for us so far. You know what you're doing, so stick to your own schedule and move when you feel like you need to.'

'What about you?' Dolly asked.

Clay started singing a dramatic rendition of a banger from *The Rocky Horror Picture Show*, Casper waiting patiently until he hit the last vocal lift on 'from Transylvannnnn-Iiiii-ah'.

'Transylvania,' the medium said, trying to cover the smirk she felt fight for dominance on her face. 'Clay, Officer Creuzinger and myself will leave tomorrow night to make sure things are tied up at this end.'

She wouldn't say any more about the specifics, not because she didn't trust their company but because she didn't trust the means their enemies would go to in a quest to get answers. There was little else to do, everyone splitting to go their separate ways and Casper doing all she could not to collapse on to one of the recently vacated cots that had been made up for them. She checked the time as she sunk down, switching the time zone on her wristwatch to Australia's. Closing her eyes but not to sleep, she entered the lobby, hoping that Kala or Sprinkle might be dreaming right at that moment. She searched, pulling through the lives and memories and consciousness of others, and her body relaxed just a little bit as it connected with a familiar thread.

Casper pulled on it, chasing it to its sources like she was running but without the proper sense of a physical body. Kala was waiting for her in the dark, spinning around as she looked for the imminent arrival of the medium. Sprinkle was there too, hugging her aunt's side. She called out to them, her heart feeling like it would expand right through her chest and out of her body with the looks they gave her. Casper pulled them tight to her, gripping Kala's face as she kissed her and Sprinkle hugging them both at hip level. So much had been lost, but she still had this: she still had her family.

The Romanian countryside looked fake. It just did, there was no other way to explain it as Casper stretched out in the back seat after waking from a long nap. She stared out of the window; between the green hills and fields of flowers, it seemed as if they had driven on to the set of *The Sound of Music*. It was rapidly approaching early evening, the sun still a few hours away from setting just yet, but the warm, yellow light added to the hyperreal effect that Casper was having trouble processing.

'I know,' Clay said from up front. 'It's like we're in Smurfville.'

'It's called Smurf Village,' Officer Creuzinger countered, not looking away from the road as he adjusted his grip on the steering wheel.

'Does it matter?' Clay huffed.

'I'm just saying, if you're going to make an analogy make sure it's—'

'There!' Casper said, pointing. The peak of a small but not inconsequential mountain came into view. It wasn't as if you could quickly look up 'Treize HQ' on Google Maps or anything. There was no Uber Rideshare that would take you right to the castle doorstep. So getting there was one thing, but the specifics of where *there* was was something else entirely. They knew the rough region – Transylvania – and Clay knew a specific landmark thanks to sneaking a peak from under his blindfold when he had been brought before the Treize for a special assignment, which meant they knew there was road access. That's as much as they knew, meaning the rest was up to Casper.

The benefit of being the only one left alive with her *Taken-*esque very particular set of skills meant it was impossible to defend against her. The Treize didn't have another medium like her once she hopped off their payroll, so they couldn't have known the Romanian countryside was littered with ghosts all leading the way.

'Right here,' she said, indicating the turn-off that could have easily been missed among the shelter of the forest trees surrounding it. 'Then your second left.'

The Three, of course, knew she was coming and she wondered how long they had known. The dead knew as well, wanting the same release those three women were craving after what she had to guess were centuries upon centuries of servitude that slowly morphed from a willing sacrifice to a shackle. A weathered letter box was supposed to signal that their next turn was nothing more than a dirt road leading to a residential address, yet the ghosts were insistent. The face of an old woman ghost with wrinkles so deep they looked like they were cut right into her skeleton nodded with confirmation as the car crept past. They began a steady incline, the path wrapping up around the base of the mountain. Officer Creuzinger kept a sharp focus on the road ahead, eyes scanning the path for potential threats, while Clay prepped a series of weapons.

Casper had her own resting on her lap, something that she hadn't seen in a long time and had deemed unnecessary to use at the Bierpinsel when she needed to go under the radar for the first half of their mission. There wasn't a better opportunity to use it than now, however, and she slowly unclipped her bionic limb and gently placed it in its travel case for later. Clay wound down the car window, the fresh air streaming in and slapping all of their faces with its cool texture after more than a day stuck inside a stuffy car. He looked like a dog with his head out the window, tongue lolling about, but she knew he was hunting for scents on the wind.

'Pull over here,' the werewolf said. 'We'll need to go the rest of the way on foot.'

Officer Creuzinger did as he was told, the three of them getting out and stretching almost immediately. Casper's limbs were stiff, but as she rolled her shoulders and affixed the weapon Heath had made for her based off a comment from Sprinkle when they'd fought The Oct, she felt better. She felt ready.

'What do you want me to do?' Officer Creuzinger asked.

'Stay here,' Clay said. 'Lock the doors, sleep while you can. If we make it out, we'll need wheels.'

He nodded, looking down at the gun that was in a holster at his hip and checking to see if it was fully loaded. It was and just the knowledge that he was armed made her feel a little better as she and Clay marched into the forest.

'Lock the doors?' she said, once they were out of earshot.

'What was I supposed to say?' the werewolf smirked. '*Hey, if anything in these woods wants to kill you and feast on your body while you writhe in pain, the locked doors on a metal box ain't gonna do shit?*'

'When you put it like that . . .'

The ghosts of two teenagers illuminated the path for her, Casper aware that Clay couldn't see them but trusted they were on the correct route as they bent over to half crawl up the steep forest floor. Her arm was designed for battle, specifically with impure abominations given the silver, serrated blade that sat at the end of the carbon-fibre structure. Yet it also made a great walking stick and she used it to gain traction, stabbing it into the soil and pulling herself up while Clay utilised his claws. They were both puffing and sweating when they reached the top, pausing inside the border of the forest as they stared out at a castle. That term was generous, but Very Large Stone Mansion had less impact to it as they watched and waited till nightfall.

The place looked abandoned, neither one of them seeing another being as they inched around to a side entrance. Looking up at one of the four towers that marked each corner of the building, Casper knew that The Three were kept in the northern one just like she knew there were things in that forest very much alive and very much waiting to see how this would play out. The air felt like it had a tangible, electric presence as the sun set and Casper stepped out of the trees. The sound of a gun cocked at her side, Casper registering some kind of rifle in Clay's arms as they marched towards the door and into the dark bowels of the building.

Chapter 17

Sadie

It hadn't happened yet, that's all Sadie could be sure of. The battle would inevitably come to the Dawson farm. Many would fight and die here. But it hadn't happened yet. The specifics of when was up in the air, even as she had Nora sketch out the vision she'd seen and even as she examined those drawings over and over again. One thing was certain: Dreckly was definitely the dead woman.

'You don't see fate, though, right?' Simon said, pacing in front of the fire the night she'd had the vision. She was finding it difficult to look at him; even with the both of them now fully dressed, Sadie still felt exposed. The way he looked at her made Sadie feel like Simon felt just as naked.

'No,' she replied, signing as she glanced around the cottage at all who were there: the Aunties and her sisters mostly, all with their headphones firmly on or she wouldn't let them indoors. Simon still refused to wear his. 'There's no such thing as fate per se or even the future. My visions are a glimpse of how things are tracking if they stay on a particular path, but that's why the Treize had The Covenant enforced: so banshees wouldn't have the opportunity to change it.'

'It's the same for me.' Shannon nodded. 'I see a future that's likely, but it's not concrete. Things can change and we can change them, just like when Sadie saved Texas.'

'The state?' Meri asked.

'The father,' Nora answered.

'The dead father,' Sadie added hastily, her answer being both truthful and treasonous. She'd had another man's hands on her just an hour earlier, his mouth, and she hadn't spared a thought about it at the time. Now she was thinking of Tex, how she had cried and screamed and grieved for him, all the while certain she'd never let anyone touch her again. And now . . .

'So this isn't set, Dreckly isn't dead yet, and we can change this,' Simon said, desperately looking for a solution to the problem.

'Yes and no,' Barastin replied, moving forward to inspect the drawing Nora had sketched as he pointed out key details. 'That, that, that *and* that right there are members of the Treize. That means something. As successful as we've been with Vankila, with the Bierpinsel, with everything else, something sends them here. We've been effective at depleting their numbers and shrinking their resources, we've thrown their world into chaos, and flipped their power base.'

'Yet they still come here?' Shannon questioned. 'With the very last of their power? That doesn't make sense.'

'Yes it does,' Sadie signed. 'They're coming to kill me.'

There was silence for a beat, the impact of her words rolling around the room in a wave. Simon was the first to break, the wolf spinning with a growl as he smashed the mantelpiece with frustration.

'It was always going to come down to this,' she signed. 'We tried our best, we did everything we possibly could, and maybe that changes *something* down the line. But the reality is the second those babies are born The Three die and the Treize's power base is finished. Our best defence was that they didn't know about me before, but something indicates that they do now ... They're coming here to kill the children before they take their first breaths.'

'Over my fucking dead body,' Simon growled.

'Over *all* of our dead bodies,' Barastin snorted. 'Literally, in my case. No one is going to allow them to waltz in here and let that happen. That's what you've seen: Dreckly and every-one who's left standing coming here for a final showdown and to head off the Treize.'

'Tell them not to come!' Catriona suggested. 'If nobody else comes, then—'

'We'll be under-defended,' Meri snapped. 'We can't allow that. And we might not be diverting anything, just throwing the bridge down and allowing them over the moat.'

'If Dreckly comes here, does that mean she'll die?' Simon questioned.

'Probably,' Barastin admitted. 'But I guarantee if you tell her that, she'll be just as determined to come.'

'Forget Dreckly for a moment,' Sadie said. 'How do the Treize get *here*? We know they have planes; is it just a matter of watching the airfields public and private? Can we intercept them in transit?'

Meri made a satisfied sound as she nodded. 'Now that's an idea.'

It was the morsel of one, but that was all it took for a plan to be born that night. Barastin had to disappear, like he always seemed to be doing these days, muttering something about needing to speak to Wehi immediately. The discussions didn't stop once he was gone, Simon breaking off to call Tiaki and Keisha as the Ihi pack decided to relocate to the Dawson farm as well. In fact, they weren't the only ones. As news trickled in about the other attacks on Treize bases all around the world, from all types of supernaturals, it became clear that anyone who was left wanted to help.

If the Treize were coming here to kill Sadie and destroy their last chance for hope, then they were going to have fierce opposition because everyone else was coming as well. The rest of the night was dedicated to the specifics, Sadie both hungry and tired as she watched the grey light of morning make itself known outside the cottage. Yet still Shannon wanted to go over everything she could remember in her vision. What was the weather like? How deep was the snow? Was it melting?

'That's enough,' a voice said from behind Sadie, her heavy eyelids flying open as she examined the face of the speaker.

'Simon, this is crucial,' Shannon countered. 'Any little detail can help us pinpoint exactly when this is going to—'

'Her health is crucial,' the werewolf replied, seemingly calm for the first time in hours. 'Look at her: she's exhausted.'

In truth, everyone was. This wasn't a Sadie-specific situation, which was why her fatigue had slipped under the radar.

'She should go to bed,' Dr Kikuchi agreed, reaching over and feeling the pulse at her wrist. 'We can skip the morning checks for today; it's better if you sleep.'

'And it's better if you all leave,' Simon said, beginning to collect the glasses and mugs that were scattered around the kitchen and lounge. He saw the protest on Shannon's lips, but had a better rebuttal of his own. 'We're watching both the air and the seaports. We have scouts from the Solomon Islands to Motu Ihupuku waiting for the nearest sign. When they're coming, we'll know.'

Sadie had been sitting in a specialised maternity beanbag that Dr Kikuchi had sourced from Narnia for all she knew and Simon's muscles flexed through his T-shirt as he slowly helped her up. She was grateful for the assist and grateful for the ushering out of the party gathered, even if it meant that she would have to be alone with him and a discussion was . . . unavoidable.

'What do you want to eat?' he whispered quietly, as the Aunties and banshees and everyone else began moving out around them.

'Whatever.' She shrugged. 'Just a sandwich or something to shut the greedy fuckers up so I can be unconscious again.'

He squeezed her shoulder, moving away to begin making the snack when Sadie turned to face her sisters. She shivered as the morning chill poured into the house, Keavy holding the door open for the others.

'Days,' Sadie said, frowning as she said it. She wasn't sure where the information was coming from, but she was certain she was right. 'Nine days, that's how long we have until the vision plays out.'

If her sisters wanted to know how she knew, they were gracious enough not to ask in the moment. Or maybe they just trusted her weirdness at this point. Both reasons were valid.

Simon pushed a plate into her hands: three of her favourite banana sandwiches sliced diagonally, exactly how she liked it. She went to thank him, but he held up a hand to stop her.

'Not a word, just eat,' he said, returning to the kitchen as he began working his way through the dishes left behind. The cottage didn't have a dishwasher, so everything needed to be done by hand and that was usually a process she enjoyed. Tonight, the thought made her want to pass out, so she ate her sandwiches quietly, drank the tea he made her, and didn't object when he took both of the empty dishes out of her hands to be washed when she was done. She went to turn away, her slippers shuffling along the floor as she moved down the hall, when Simon caught her hand. There was need in his eyes and something else she saw too, something that surprised her: fear. Simon Tianne, big, scary-ass werewolf, was afraid.

'Sadie,' he said, voice soft, 'can I sleep with you tonight?'

She knew what he meant. Not sex – hell, that wouldn't even be possible in her present condition, regardless of what they'd been doing before – but comfort. He was seeking her companionship, and right then in that moment, there was nothing in the world she wanted more than to offer it to him.

'It's day,' she replied, noting the flash of disappointment in his eyes. 'But of course.'

The light was back almost instantly as she let go of him.

'Except we're sleeping in your bed,' she called behind her. 'It's darker.'

It took her three times as long to get in and under the covers as it did him, Sadie just positioning her head on the pillow when she heard Simon come in. She was manoeuvring an additional pillow around her belly when the light switched off, it testament to her sheer and utter exhaustion that her pulse didn't race when she heard the swish of his clothes. Was he a boxers or a briefs man? She likely wouldn't find out for a while as the mattress shifted with his weight, Simon climbing in beside her as he pulled the covers over them both. Sadie had her back to him and she felt the warmth of his body, then his touch as he snaked an arm around her.

It was tentative, cautious, as if waiting to see how she would respond. She greedily grabbed his hand, pulling it around herself as her fingers laced with his. She had probably never been in more danger in her life, yet she had also never felt safer, as the werewolf's massive body wrapped around her and they made a perfect shape. Simon breathed her in, inhaling her scent deeply as he nuzzled against her hair and the back of her neck. Her eyes were nearly closed when she felt the subtlest of kicks, the kind of tiny 'hiyah!' that would have caused her to flinch months ago but now barely registered. Simon stiffened beside her and she realised that he'd felt it too, their clasped hands resting atop her abdomen.

'Was that . . .?'

'Mmmhmmm,' she murmured, as another kick answered it. He felt that too.

'Same baby?'

'No, that's Maurice. First kick was Robin, she sits lower down.'

She had been wearing a downright tent of a bed shirt, the words 'MILF TO BE' scrawled across it – a horrendous gift from Sorcha but one she had ended up loving as it was the comfiest thing to sleep in. Pulling the hem up high so her belly was exposed under the covers, she ran Simon's hand over the bare skin there like a radar scanning for kicks. The third came quickly after the first two, as it always did, desperate to keep up with its siblings and pushing up right under his hands.

'Oh my God, I feel it!' he exclaimed. 'Who was that?'

'That's Barry, Barry is always last.'

His laughter tickled her skin as Simon's body rumbled against hers, hands still running over her stomach as she guided him.

'Maurice, Robin and Barry,' he chuckled. 'You named them after the Bee Gees?'

'What am I if not trying to stay alive?' Sadie said, defending her choice and resisting the urge to add an 'uh uh uh' after the fact. 'And it's not their real names, obviously. I just needed something to call them that wasn't "the little bitches" all the time.'

He laughed even harder, teeth pressing into her shoulder in a way that left her smiling in the dark.

'That was Sorcha's name for them, might I add.'

'I guessed as much,' Simon breathed, his hands no longer skimming for kicks and the babies mercifully back to being still in there. He planted a kiss on her shoulder as they resettled, yet there was only silence for a little while longer. She felt like he wanted to get something off his chest and she was right.

'Can I ask you a question?'

'Scary Spice was always my favourite,' she murmured.

'What?'

'Spice Girl. It was always Mel B.'

He chuckled, the sound like audible honey in her ears. 'I wouldn't have picked that. She was my favourite too.'

'What was your real question?' Sadie pushed.

He hesitated, as if he'd lost the nerve from a few seconds earlier. 'What happened before, between us . . . was that just because of what you said?'

'Remind me of what I said, epic case of baby brain right here and I talk a lot of shit.'

'You don't,' he corrected. 'And, uh, what you said about pregnancy making you horn—'

'Oh my God, no!'

She had to brace her knees to roll over, but it was important that he saw her expression. Sadie could barely make him out, yet she knew he could see her clearly in the dark, thanks to his werewolf vision.

'That had *nothing* to do with me wanting to kiss you and nothing to do with wanting you to kiss me,' she began. 'Okay, well, not nothing but . . .'

She tried to find the words, using her fingers to run over the grooves of his face and feel where he was even if she couldn't see him.

'I don't have the answers,' she admitted. 'I wanted you and I want you still. I didn't stop to think about it.'

'I did,' Simon replied. 'I've been thinking about it a lot.'

'As if,' she scoffed. 'No way you've been writing sonnets at the thought of the banshee blimp waddling through the cottage.'

'They're more haikus, really.'

Sadie laughed, her fingernails dragging along his jawline in a way that made him growl low and deep.

'You have no idea how you look to me,' he said, voice quiet but sincere. 'You emit a light that moves with you wherever you go, basking anyone lucky enough to be near in it. You radiate, Sadie. You radiate kindness and sweetness and compassion and bravery all at once. I have no idea how you do it.'

The air stilled around her with his words. Or at least that's what it seemed like to her. Sadie had always felt as though she moved through life like a ghost, present but not really participating. It was around her sisters that she came alive, her family really the only ones who saw the special in her until Texas Contos had come along. Although they'd known each other their whole lives, they hadn't really *known* each other until they were running for their lives. That experience, those events, had changed her. She'd found her power and she'd found herself in the process. She sparked. When he died, she thought perhaps that spark had gone out, not because he was the source of it, but because it was hard for anything to stay illuminated in such all-consuming blackness. Yet now, things were blacker than ever. And still, Simon saw it. He saw her.

'You don't have to say anything,' he began.

'I want to, so badly but . . . you could die. I know that's horribly selfish of me, but with everything that's coming how can I let myself love you just to lose you? I don't know if I can survive that a second time, Simon.'

'And what about you, huh? Like you're not in peril. And I don't just mean from them, I mean from your body. You're delivering triplets in a home birth. I know the stats.'

'How do you know the stats?' she asked, surprised.

'I read your books.'

'You what?'

'Of course I read them. I've caught feelings for a pregnant chick; I wanted to try to understand what you were going through.'

There were a few small things that started to click into place now, things she'd put down to him being observant, that were really things he'd learned from consuming her reading material. Things like how he always had a snack ready, even when she never asked. Things like how he noticed when she was tired, even if she'd never said anything. Things like how he would just hand her a heat pack, even when she hadn't verbalised how much her lower back was killing her. Damn it, he was good. Even now, his hand was on her belly, resting on top of her own, like he was ready to protect her at all costs.

'Say we survive,' Sadie pushed, 'what then? Look at you, for fuck's sake! You strutted on to this farm looking like *The Māori Bachelor*. Any werewolf with eyeballs would take a bite out of you, and I'm going to be the soft, saggy Sadie: a twenty-year-old *mother of three* and the babies aren't even yours. Is that something you want to be involved in, Simon?'

'Yes,' he said, the second she gave him an opportunity. 'Undoubtedly. And I can see that face you're making at me even in the dark.'

'You're also secret rich.'

'It's not a secret. The Tianne and Ihi family are some of the biggest developers in the country.'

'See, I grew up poor. You'd buy me a Birkin bag for an anniversary present and I'd get you a tin of baked beans.'

Simon half laughed, half choked as he sat up. 'I'm not fucking Drake, Sadie. And now you're picking at dumb shit.'

He's right, she thought. *He's so right.*

'You're wrong,' Sadie told him.

'Fine.' He sighed, agitated but clearly amused. 'We don't have to have this conversation now or ever again, really. But I just want you to know all the reasons you've outlined have to do with why *I* shouldn't feel anything for *you*.'

'You're a werewolf and I'm a banshee.'

'You just keep avoiding the topic of how *you* feel altogether.'

'You could eat me if I put a moon lamp next to your bed. I could kill you with an ill-timed hiccup.'

He settled back down next to her, Sadie swearing that she could feel him smiling in the dark. She thought the silence was a brief reprieve until he picked up again, but she realised with disappointment that he intended to stay quiet.

'So that's it?' she asked, feeling petulant as hell.

'You don't want to talk about it and that's okay,' Simon whispered, zero hurt in his voice. 'I will say one last thing, Sadie, and then I swear I'll drop this until you're ready. The ghost of my dead uncle could have gone to anyone. In fact, there were a dozen people on the farm when Wally's brother showed up that day who could have gotten to you quicker. But he came to me. He warned *me*.'

'Why?' she asked.

'Because I think he knew that I would do anything to protect you and not just because the fate of our world hinges on it.'

Despite her fatigue, Sadie was suddenly wide awake with his words. She rolled over to face him, although to be fair there was a significant barrier keeping them apart. His thumb ran down her nose, smoothed over her lips, and along her jaw as she tried to remember how to breathe. *Go to sleep,* the gesture said, his fingers brushing her hair back off her face in repetitive motions that made her scalp tingle.

'I won't let anybody hurt you,' he whispered, pressing a kiss to the tip of her nose as her eyes slowly closed.

'I know,' she murmured, letting his words wrap around her like a weighted blanket as she fell asleep.

It was like watching the army roll into town. And in some cases, they actually rolled.

'You can't bring a tank here, Philandro!' Simon shouted at a guy who very much disagreed about the matter.

'Heath said I could bring my tank!'

'Heath said *you were* a tank, that's why they needed you,' Philandro's identical twin brother Kilandro responded.

'*Oh.*'

'Keep the tank,' Simon snapped, exasperated, as he waved the two siblings along. 'Just make sure you're somewhere it can actually be useful, all right? South side is weakest.'

'Tank you very much,' Philandro muttered, the machinery tearing up snow and dirt as it crunched in the direction Simon had ordered.

Sadie was rugged up in the tray of his truck, cushions stacked around her along with blankets and snacks as she watched the procession of supernaturals that started that morning and didn't seem to stop over the coming days. Simon caught her smiling at his agitation as he pulled his beanie down tighter on his head, frustrated. He pointed a finger at her in warning.

'Don't,' he said, a shadow of a smile playing on his features as he walked off.

She said nothing, just smiled and took a noisy sip as she sucked the green juice she'd made for herself that morning. Sadie had wanted to be there, wanted to see it all, wanted to see those who were there to save themselves as much as they were to save her. She had what could only be described as a

Bane mask at the ready, the sinister-looking contraption – a muzzle for all intents and purposes. It had two small filters on either side of the mouthpiece so she could breathe, but in case of wail emergence she could yank it up from the cord where it dangled around her neck and suppress the sound until she was back in the confines of the cottage.

They'd tested the soundproofing – not with her wail, of course, but with every single one of her sisters, Dr Kikuchi and Simon all screaming from inside while she listened from the woods. She'd heard nothing, but Meri had as she stood with her. That was an issue, given the number of werewolves on the Dawson farm was large and growing larger by the second. Sadie fingered her mask with unease, hoping its addition would be enough as she watched a caravan driven by Tiaki Ihi and Keisha Tianne roll up slowly alongside her.

'Look at you,' Tiaki beamed. 'Perched in there like the Queen of fucking Sheba.'

'Simon and Dr Kikuchi have united against me,' she replied, happy to see the women in person after months of virtual visits. 'Said I'm not allowed to move until the triplets vacate the premises.'

'So, what?' Keisha asked, jumping out of the passenger side and stomping through the snow. 'My son has you being driven around like a Thanksgiving Float? Where is that boy?'

'This was the concession,' Sadie said, jumping to his defence. 'They took away my daily walks, but this means I can still get fresh air.'

Keisha leaned over the side of the tray, looking sceptical about the situation but unable to fight Sadie's wishes. The werewolf was staring down at her belly like she could see through the puffer jacket and blankets that were covering it. In a way, the banshee realised, she could: their hearing was so sensitive, Keisha was actually listening to the heartbeats. Her tough exterior cracked as she looked up at Sadie, a mushy smile on her face that could only belong to a mother.

'They sound healthy,' she mused.

'And big,' Tiaki added, joining them. 'You thought about names yet?'

'Pekapeka,' Keisha suggested.

'She's not naming her children after a bat,' Simon said, breaking away from the group of shifters he'd been talking to and embracing his mother. '*Kia ora, māmā.*'

'*Morena tama,*' Keisha replied, holding him tightly as he bent down to hug her. 'And that's the name for one child, there's two more!'

'Why Pekapeka?' Sadie asked, watching as Simon embraced Tiaki next.

'When our people first came ashore in their waka, they had never seen bats like the ones here,' Tiaki explained. 'They were blind, so it was believed they were guided by the spirit world, passing between the living and the dead, the seen and the unseen.'

'One of The Three is blind,' Sadie mumbled, understanding the seemingly random name choice a bit better now. In a way, that's what all banshees did: existed in the world between the living and the dead, not unlike mediums.

'See!' Keisha beamed. 'She gets it! It's a great name.'

'She's already naming them after the Bee Gees, Ma, let it go,' Simon said, slipping by them to meet the rumbling mound of earth some fifty metres away.

'What?' his mother looked horrified, following after him as the eruption of dirt turned out to actually be a creature of some kind. A creature with a distinct interest in Simon, she noted as it pawed affectionately at the werewolf. Sadie tried not to notice how Tiaki's gaze watched her own and she hoped the Ihi matriarch didn't read the jealousy that was definitely curdling in her throat. If she did, she said nothing of it as she offered to drive Sadie back to the cottage. Her nose was ice cold and numb, so she was more than happy to accept. It also gave her an expansive view of what everyone had been up to, with the Dawson farm being converted into a playing field that would give their team the advantage.

Her sisters were alongside the Aunties, getting their hands dirty as they dug trenches. A plane had landed a few hours back, a terrifying pilot giving way to a terrifying mix of goblins, witches, werewolves, arachnia and more from Lord knows where. Kala and her niece Sprinkle had arrived overnight, joining her for tea in the morning and catching her up on everything that had been happening elsewhere. Barastin had made sure to give her Sorcha updates constantly since her sister left, so she knew that her sister was alive and had been successful in her mission with the others to cause as much trouble at Vankila as possible. Yet the relief she felt when Kala told her they were travelling back as fast as they could and that they would be there, soon, was substantial.

Seeing what she saw as Tiaki drove her around the property, viewing it all through her eyes, it was hard not to feel hopeful. Many of those currently setting traps and offloading weapons wouldn't survive, but she couldn't despair. She was having almost constant visions now, not like she usually would where they were long and continuous. These were bite-sized flashes, scenarios constantly changing and evolving as the path to get there constantly changed and evolved too. She was seeing Dreckly alive as often as she was dead now, Tommi too, yet the person's face she kept searching for wasn't there. Sadie never saw Simon, regardless of how desperate she was to have any clue about what was coming for him.

Dr Kikuchi was waiting for her at the cottage, Tiaki joining them as they ran through their daily checks and revised the series of labour exercises she would need to remember. The triplets had moved into position some time ago, Sadie being the most prepared person unprepared for whatever their birth would bring. She was straddling a stool in the kitchen while making nachos when Simon returned in the evening, worn out and weary. He shouted something about the 'amazing smell' as the scent of slow-cooked beef wafted through the cottage and she heard the sound of the shower starting. She didn't even hear him approach from behind, his wet hair brushing her neck as he nuzzled against her. She smiled as he rested his head on her shoulder, hands snaking around until they sat on her belly.

'I've been wanting to do this all day,' he mumbled, Sadie unable to manage much more than a contented 'mmm' as he kissed her neck.

'If you keep doing that,' she sighed, aware of how heavy her voice sounded, 'I'm never going to finish this pico de gallo.'

'So don't finish it.'

He cupped her face in his hands, the brush of his lips starting soft. It remained that way, sweet and luxurious, but he kissed her for so long she felt like her lips might be swollen afterwards. This werewolf, stupid as he was for getting involved with her, was the source of her optimism. She was about to tell him as much when he pulled away, his expression cold as he stiffened. Sadie couldn't quite place the look, interpreting it as a threat response at first until Simon spun around and faced someone she hadn't even known was standing there. It was another werewolf, another Ihi if she had to guess, and she didn't have to do that for long as the man stood there blinking in shock.

'You fucking idiot,' he said.

'Cuz,' Simon responded, 'listen—'

The man looked around the same age as Simon, although smaller and less bulky. It wasn't until he stormed down the hall and towards the front door that she realised who he reminded her of: Tommi. And Aruhe, now that she thought about it. *Cuz,* she repeated, discounting it as just a term of endearment between friends before she realised the man was Simon's actual cousin, James Ihi. And his best friend, he had told her. In fact the wolf's arrival at the farm was something he had been desperately looking forward to among the headache of everything else. Now Simon was in pursuit of him, trying to explain to his cousin when the two men paused in the doorway of the nursery. She didn't have to guess what had caught James' eye as he stepped inside, followed by Simon. Their voices travelled easily enough to where she remained sitting in the kitchen.

'You carved these?!'

There was silence in response.

'Simon, your work looks exactly like his does. I know this is yours.'

'Of course it's mine.'

'And the *wahakura*—'

'Are from *your* mother, so check yourself.'

'Check *your*self! What the hell are you doing, playing house with the banshee on the eve of battle like she's your woman? Like those are your babies?'

'What the fuck is your problem?' Simon snapped, and Sadie could hear the anger rumble through his voice. 'The Ihi pack have been protecting her for months, before she was even pregnant! The Aunties—'

'She's not one of us, brother!'

'What, she's not a werewolf? Or she's pakeha? Because either comment is about as offensive as the next, cousin.'

'You're not in a Whitney Houston movie, Simon! Guard her! Guard the children! Keep them all alive! Save the day and then we go back to our lives.'

'Back to what? You think anything is going to be the same after this? Isn't a different world exactly what we're fighting for?'

'One where a banshee can be with a werewolf?' James scoffed.

'Why not?'

'You are delusional, my guy. We do not mess with Otherworld Women.'

'All right, now it's time to get the fuck out,' Simon hissed.

It wasn't exactly eavesdropping if the eaves were inside your house, so Sadie inched off the stool as she made her way down the hall to intervene. James was his favourite person in the world, Simon had told her that one night in bed. Tensions were higher than kites because of everything that was looming

Maria Lewis

down on them. She would not allow the bond these two shared to be severed by words thrown around in the heat of the moment that neither of them could take back.

'If you don't leave,' Simon was telling James, 'I will drag you by the scruff of your neck and kick you out the door; I swear to God I will do it. I can't have you bringing this hostility under our roof.'

'*Our roof?!* You have your whole life ahead of you, why would you ever burden yourself with—'

'A pregnant wailing woman?' Sadie interjected, her considerable girth blocking the doorway to the nursery as she joined them.

'Sadie,' Simon said, face immediately softening as he turned away from James and towards her. 'Whatever you heard, he didn't mean those things. He didn't understand what he was saying.'

'Oh, I think he did,' she murmured, eyeing James with scrutiny as he crossed his hands over his chest. 'If you think I don't know all the names we've been called, believe me, I've heard 'em: bean chaointe, weeping woman, bean si, keening woman, banshee bitches. Heard. Them. All.'

'Then hear this,' James said, stepping forward only for his path to be blocked by Simon. 'This isn't personal. I'm sure you're a nice teen mum –'

'I'm twenty, you asshole.'

'– or whatever, but one day Simon will lead our pack. Most of the supernatural world already thinks he does. But when Tiaki or Keisha eventually pass – hopefully years from now rather than days – it will be him. They need to look towards a leader and a werewolf who can strengthen our people, not weaken them. They need a leader whose loyalties and time won't be divided between someone who's not even a werewolf.'

'That's a very outdated way of thinking,' Sadie said, attempting a measured response as she felt a piercing anger in her gut.

'It's how we've survived.' James shrugged. 'I'm sorry, but it's true.'

'In the past,' Simon countered. 'Our future is looking different every day and in it, she's not my demise, James, she's my salvation.'

'How can you be so sure?' his cousin questioned, tone soft as he pleaded with him.

'Because it's what Jonah said to me.'

'What?' James and Sadie squawked together.

'His ghost, when he came to warn me . . . I wasn't entirely telling the truth when I said that was all that happened. He said to run to her, because she was our salvation, and she was mine, too.'

Sadie braced herself against the door frame for support, her breath shallow as Simon turned back to James.

'Besides, I'm not meant to lead our pack,' he continued. 'What did Keisha tell Tommi? The strength in this family has always come from the women.'

James barked out a laugh. 'Tommi Grayson is not our future pack leader.'

'No, you dickhead: Aruhe. She's our future. Why do you think I fought so hard to get her back? The Aunties knew it. I do too.'

Whatever was happening between them, Sadie wasn't watching but the silence was loaded with resolution. Her gaze was focused elsewhere, namely at her bare feet and the fluid that was pooling around them.

'Now,' Simon began, turning to her for a moment before switching his attention back to James, 'I need you to apologise to Sadie.'

'I don't need his apology, Simon,' she said, voice steady as both men turned to her. 'What I need is for him to get Dr Kikuchi.'

She saw the triumph falter on Simon's face as he looked confused for just a moment, before his eyes widened as he glanced downwards.

'My water just broke.'

Chapter 18

Tommi

The chattering of her teeth stopped as they swam through the mist, the previously loud roar of the ocean raging around them quiet as they pushed through unexpectedly calm waters. Tommi couldn't see much more than a foot in front of her and her instincts told her to stick close to the selkies. Their small party had been joined by others, Avary abandoning them briefly to swim for back-up and return later with an entire Scottish pondant. There had been more than sixty swimming with them by the time they found the warm current in the North Sea.

She didn't see land for most of this process, Tommi just firmly affixed to the back of a selkie who told her their name was something that sounded like Groagge. It was clear they had little interest in conversing with her and that was fine: speeding through the sea and avoiding any ship sightings near the surface really sucked all of the energy for usual quips out of her. They went around the top of Scotland, since going near the bottom of London would bring them too close to Treize strongholds in the United Kingdom they'd rather avoid. She hoped those strongholds were actually now theirs, but there wasn't an appropriate time on the journey for a quick check-in on their attempted coup.

There seemed to be a noticeable shift in demeanour once they passed the uninhabited island of Stroma, the coast of mainland Scotland visible as they crossed in the middle of the night. They were being pursued, she realised, being too tired and too afraid to pick up on the signs until they had passed. The intention was to go wide around Scotland and cut back to Ireland as they headed towards the mystical island, but it had been Atlanta's idea to change course. They hugged the coast instead, using the natural, scattered islands of Scotland's geography to their advantage as they attempted to lose an enemy Tommi never saw. When Heath swam up beside her, clinging to Avary's back, his finger brushed along her cheek as she rested her head on Groagge's shoulders.

'Tommi, you awake?'

'No one has slept for the past forty-eight hours, Heath, and I can't feel my toes,' she mumbled. 'Of course I'm awake.'

'Look up for a minute then, will you?'

Her head felt heavier than a bag of bricks, but she did so, following where he pointed as dawn broke, the yellow and pink light reflecting on the surface of the water. They had wrapped around the Isle of Skye, mountain peaks visible in the background as she stared at the ruins that sat upon a rocky hilltop.

'Dunscaith Castle,' he told her, 'where I trained.'

'With Scáthach?' she asked him. He nodded, watching the landmark as they passed it. The ancient warrior woman was there now, Tommi not having to squint in order to see the bluish-grey figure of her ghost standing proudly next to the ruins of what had once been her domain. It was the last calm they had for a while, with the seas growing rougher and the conditions worse as they moved past Northern Ireland and closer to their destination. The eventual eerie mist was almost comforting after that, Tommi happy to take a break from what felt like being personally slapped by the sea at regular intervals. She knew the selkies didn't like it either, however, as Groagge muttered something about being annoyed by their inability to breathe underwater. It would have meant this whole pesky surface swimming thing could have been avoided altogether.

The point was moot, Tommi watching with worry as Dreckly slid from the shoulders of Amos after hours of being glued to that exact position. She didn't necessarily swim through the water so much as glide through it, looking very much like she belonged there to Tommi's untrained eye. Sorcha wanted to do the same, yet Atlanta wouldn't let her and she soon found out why. Bubbles popped up alongside them, just a few at first then a steady stream as heads started to slowly break the surface. The numbers of their own party were not insignificant and their presence wasn't unexpected, Avary having made sure the island's occupants were aware of their imminent arrival.

It still didn't make it any less terrifying as they pushed through the mist, which extended right to the shoreline where even more people waited for them. The descendants of the banshees long thought to have died at sea were waiting, many with blankets and food in their hands as they inched forward cautiously. Tommi wanted to assume there hadn't been visitors here in a long time, yet she wasn't sure that was true: they just might not have been visitors of the non-scaled variety. She was half slid, half shoved off Groagge's back and into the water, her head dipping below for just a moment as she felt sand brush against her toes. Her limbs were like lead as she pushed forward, giving up entirely once she got close enough and crawling up the sand.

She collapsed on her back, staying there amongst the pristine white granules as she stared up at the grey sky. Water lapped around her body and she patted the sand, feeling around for Heath until she felt the firmness of his thigh. Tommi squeezed it, turning her head to smile at him through her cracked lips. If he looked more like a drowned rat than the usual blond hunk, she didn't even want to imagine how she appeared to him as he dragged her over to his side with just a tug of the wrist. Salty hair plastered to her face, he pushed it back as he looked at her, the exhaustion in his eyes mirroring her own.

'Strip off your clothes please.'

'What the fuck?!' Tommi barked, jerking around to meet the patient gaze of four banshees hovering nearby.

'Your clothes,' the woman repeated. 'Both of you need to be undressed and bathed in the hot springs immediately.'

She looked down at Heath, who shrugged, and she rolled off him. Tommi graciously took the bowl that was handed to her as she struggled to walk up the sloping sand, sipping slowly as the cool liquid touched her lips. At first she thought it was just fresh water, but there was an unusual, almost citrus-like aftertaste to it that made her think it was loaded with more than just H^2O. *Please be drugs,* she thought, wincing as she pulled her arms free of the tactical suit she'd been wearing as several banshees helped her. *Please just be so many drugs that I pass the fuck out and don't wake up until nothing hurts any more.*

Somebody out there must have been listening, because she didn't remember a whole lot once her toe hit the steaming water of a hot spring. She knew she said something, murmured something, but there wasn't another clear, cognitive thought until she was stirring inside a hammock many hours later. She didn't know that's what she was in at first, the werewolf slowly coming to as she pushed and pulled and wriggled against layers of animal fur that she had been wrapped in. Tommi let out a shriek as she started to get momentum, flipping herself out of the hammock and on to the floor in a heap of limbs. Lifting herself up, she examined the setting with scrutiny.

Tommi had never been to the Maldives, yet she'd studied enough celebrity vacay shots to recognise how the architecture of the bungalow she was standing in felt similar. Not identical, however, as there was nothing tropical about it and the architecture was more solid, with heavy woods and layered materials. It was like this building had been built into the trees around them, with branches used as shelves and support materials to hang several hammocks from, including the one she had just fallen out of. There was a small plate of food nearby and more water, which she drank greedily and was disappointed to learn was free of drugs this time. Her gums stung where she had lost a tooth, maybe more than one as her tongue gently touched the space there and she winced. The food was a plate of what looked like varying types of sashimi, with fresh fruit and nuts at the side.

Tommi downed it all, eating around the injuries. She noted the other hammocks were empty, so if this was left here then the whole plate had been intended for her. That's what she told herself, because if she was meant to have shared this with anyone all they were going to get was the circular wooden surface the food had been presented on. Glancing down at her body, her fingers ran over the fur outfit that hung like a dress and was fastened at alternate sides of her hip and shoulder. She felt like an extra from the Destiny's Child '*Survivor*' video as she tiptoed deeper into this unusual house, a look she didn't exactly hate. The merging of indoors and outdoors was intentional, she realised, with wooden platforms leading between each of the different circular buildings where she found more hammocks, more living quarters, more food (that she ate) and more heat, pausing to warm her fingers by an open fireplace for just a moment.

When she heard whispered voices, she followed them towards the next building and a hammock that was as overflowing with furs as hers had been. It was rocking slightly and the whispers turned to giggles for a moment before Tommi ripped back the first layer expecting to find a mischievous banshee playing hide-and-seek with her or something. Instead, she screamed – outright *screamed* – as she covered her eyes and spun around. She was ready to sprint from the building when she collided with Heath's bare chest as he was running in, Tommi refusing to remove her hands from her eyes as she kept shouting '*WHAT THE FUCK?*' over and over again.

'Tommi, what is it?' he said, pulling her hands free only for her to bury her head against his chest and try to block out the image. 'Are you okay? What's going on?'

She pushed against him, backing him out the building and on to an exterior platform, away from the impact of what she'd just seen. She heard the thud of footsteps pounding along the wooden floor as she spun to see Joss emerging from the doorway, fur haphazardly wrapped around his torso as he tried to hold it in place.

'Let me explain!' her best friend said, his face about the same colour as his hair.

'Oh,' Heath murmured, stifling a laugh. 'Oh *no*.'

'You're fucking my SISTER!' Tommi screamed, Heath having to hold her back as she pointed a condemning finger at Joss. Aruhe choosing just that moment to appear behind him, hair tousled in a way that implied extremely recent shagging.

'You're fucking my BEST FRIEND!' Tommi shouted, her finger shifting to the other culprit.

'I thought you knew!' Aruhe countered, eyes wide as she tightened the fur wrap around her exposed shoulders.

'I thought Heath was joking!'

The Scot's laughter was like a volcanic eruption behind them, his chest rumbling against her as he wrapped two arms around her waist and picked her up. He carried her backwards in earnest as she kicked, yelling at him to let her go. Aruhe looked thoughtful as she watched the scene play out, tilting her head with fascination.

'Honestly, she's taking it better than I thought she would,' the werewolf mused.

'This is what you call well?!' Heath cackled, continuing to yank her backwards.

Joss's expression had shifted from embarrassed to forlorn. He looked like he'd just signed his own death warrant.

'She's going to kill me,' he muttered, running a hand through his ginger stubble. 'Soon as she has calmed down, she's gonna pretend everything is fine and then wait for the right moment, when I'll never see it coming, and kill me.'

'OH, YOU'LL SEE ME COMING, MOTHERFUCKER!' she yelled in response.

'I'd worry less about Tommi trying to kill you and more about Quaid,' Aruhe was muttering, and Joss looked even more horrified if that was possible.

The last thing Tommi saw as she was pulled around the corner was Aruhe snuggling up to Joss as she tried to comfort him, and she groaned like the sight caused her physical pain. She didn't get a good glimpse at much else as she was dragged out of the cluster of houses and into the greenery surrounding them, Heath not letting go for her a second even as she eventually eased up on the kicking and, slowly, the swearing. He sat down on a log, taking her with him so that she was held in his lap as he tried to give her more time to calm down. He nestled against her neck, resting his chin there while he waited.

'Are we done?' he asked, tone sweet as she simmered down.

Letting out a long, deep sigh, she closed her eyes. 'Aye.'

'And you're gonna promise not to kill Joss?'

'Aye,' she repeated. 'Especially cos I'm pretty sure Aruhe seduced him rather than the other way around.'

'Given your horrified reaction, I'd say there was enthusiastic complicity from both parties, mmm?'

She sighed again. 'Aye, fine. You're right, I was a beamer. I'll apologise to them later.'

'No, don't apologise, that was the best laugh I've had in . . . months.'

Tommi turned to face him, feeling just the slightest drop in her gut as she stared at him. 'I need to tell you something.'

'I don't need to know.'

'Yes, you do.'

'No, Tommi, I don't. Whatever happened between you and Ben in Dundee stays in Dundee. I trust you, I love you, but I'm not an eejit: I know how easily pretending to fool around can go too far when your adrenalin is high.'

'It didn't go too far it ju—'

'Stop,' he said, yanking her to him. Heath kissed her and it felt like a baptism, washing away all her sins as she wrapped her arms around him. She wanted to attach herself like a barnacle to his bones – that was how deep the feeling was as she pivoted to straddle him. When Tommi pulled away from his lips, she didn't let go as she stayed holding on to him tightly. His hands ran up and down her spine, as if calming the beast that co-existed with the woman inside of her. Their hands clasped around each other, Heath led her to the beach where the mist had shifted and the ocean was somewhat visible beneath the endless, glittering night sky.

'They drugged us,' she said.

'Yes, smart too. Best way to control an unprecedented situation full of potentially dangerous visitors arriving among your community.'

'Try to sound like you respect that choice just a little less, will ya?'

'Nah.' Heath smiled. 'Too long at sea, too many injuries for all of us, too long without fresh food and water . . . Our bodies would have gone into shock, so knocking us out to take care of everything and wake up healed? Who wouldn't want that?'

Tommi still hurt, so she wouldn't say 'healed' exactly, but it was clear balms and agents had been applied to her worst injuries. The surface of her skin was still sticky to the touch in some of those areas. Heath led her up a stone path, towards a meeting place where it seemed everyone on the island was gathered. Aruhe and Joss were already there, huddled together on the other side of a firepit. Tommi had to look away, she was that embarrassed by her earlier reaction. Or overreaction, rather. She couldn't help but note that it looked as if they were all at some kind of dress-up party, everyone who had escaped with them wearing the same furs for warmth while they recovered over the course of what she had to guess were a few days.

The selkies and the locals were dressed differently, in outfits that much more closely resembled their individual personalities. They looked like a combination of found and made pieces, with some clearly bearing the markings of modern textiles while others had been made by hand. She was surprised to see Barastin there, the ghost gesturing to Amos and talking as rapidly as he could before the selkie yelled at him. It took her aback, Tommi not having seen flashes of anger from the creature. She'd only known him for a little while, but she reassessed her judgement when he sprinted past her. It was grief, she realised, watching as his temporary human legs looked uneasy and Amos rushed to the water. Dreckly was hot on his heels, the sprite's arm still in a sling as she threw Tommi an anguished look and raced to catch up with Amos.

It didn't take long to learn why: the young selkie had lost the 'human lassie' Heath had said he cared about so much in one of the Australian attacks. It wasn't the only loss, naturally, and Tommi had to sit down with the weight of it all as Barastin brought everyone up to speed. On any other day, Sadie's prophecy of Dreckly's death would have been enough to shake them to their very core, let alone the death of so many they cared about. There were victories too, but that didn't soften the sting of the loss or the greater dilemma of the Treize going to New Zealand.

'But how would they know?' Sorcha was asking, as dismayed by this news as anyone given it was her sister – her nieces – that were the target of the next wave. 'Everyone was so careful, the Ihi pack were so careful!'

'My only thought,' Barastin began, 'is that it has nothing to do with something that we fucked up and everything to do with a shift in power. The attacks have weakened them considerably and in the same way there are beings that can sense dead bodies or magnetic forces or ghosts, there are those that can feel a wane in power and a rise in it.'

'It was inevitable,' Joss muttered. 'Given what we did, eventually their eye would be drawn to the shiniest fucking thing like magpies. I'm just mad we didn't realise this sooner.'

'We have to get back there,' Tommi said. 'As soon as possible.'

'Damn right,' Quaid murmured in response.

Her eyes flashed to meet his and she knew that itch he felt to be back home, back on his own soil, and back fighting with his family. There was something else there too, something in his gaze as it lingered on their surroundings. Okay, yes, he had been imprisoned for a few years so anything besides a cell would look spectacular. Yet of all the people who were floored and enamoured and enchanted by this mythical island, she hadn't expected it to be Quaid Ihi. Sitting there, though, drinking in every detail around him like it was a banquet, she understood the reluctance to leave a place that was meant to be legend and an alliance that should have been historic rather than hidden.

'Forget what we missed or didn't,' Tommi continued. 'That's great what you said about Casper and Clay, great about Duo, and great about everyone else en route to fight the Treize at the farm. But we need to be there as well and we need to be there *yesterday*.'

'We will take you,' Atlanta said, Avary and many of the other selkies nodding in agreement. 'We will take all of you, and those of us that want to join will.'

Silver raised her long, spindly hand. 'Not to be ungrateful, but I don't know if I can travel like that again.'

'It will be different,' Atlanta countered. 'We weren't prepared then, we are now. There's equipment here to make the journey easier. I guarantee you we can get all of you to the South Island quicker and safer than any other means of travel right now.'

'I have to agree,' Tommi said, much as the thought of getting wet again made her want to attempt burying herself under the nearest rock. 'We're not freshly injured and running from a PG pursuit. My only question is how soon can we leave?'

'In the morning,' Dreckly said, her body wet as she returned from the ocean. She was alone, the solitary figure of Amos behind her as he sat on the shore, head in his hands. Tommi had a lot of respect for this woman, someone who had faced the physical manifestation of her fears and come out the other side, even when those close to her had not. Yet in that moment her respect levels were God tier.

'You can't,' Aruhe begged. 'If you go back, you'll die, Dreckly! Sadie saw it.'

'Maybe,' the sprite shrugged, 'maybe not. As I'm sure the banshees here can tell you, their powers undiluted by the punishment the rest of their kind experienced, the outcome of a vision is relative.'

'You putting yourself in the same place it occurs is not,' Heath said. 'Stay here, start rebuilding, stay safe.'

'No,' Dreckly replied, zero wiggle room in her tone whatsoever. 'If I go to my death, then so be it. But I will die fighting at the place where it's needed most.'

'Bad fucking ass,' Tommi muttered, the sprite's eyes shifting in her direction.

'Where can you make land?' Barastin asked, turning to Atlanta.

'The Bluff,' she replied. 'It's a seaport just outside of Invercargill.'

Aruhe nodded. 'It's protected and from there it's a straight shot by land to Arrowtown.'

They kept talking, working through specifics as Tommi focused on Barastin. There was something wrong with him and she was quite certain she was the only one who could see it. It was like his reception was patchy, the ghost weakening and strengthening before them as she stared at his uneven image. When they split, Tommi shouted at him in her head. She didn't mean to shout, but she only knew how to get his attention at one volume as she silently sent her will his way. The ghost noticed, looking tired as he glanced over at her with a distinctly 'ugh, do I have to?' expression. *Yes, you have to,* she thought back at him, quite certain that message too arrived in vocal ALL CAPS.

'I'll catch up with you,' Tommi told Heath, the pair shifting apart as she headed deeper into the trees and Heath went to inspect the 'equipment' Atlanta had alluded to. Barastin joined her shortly after, his light dimmer than usual as the surrounds around them brightened with a dull glow.

'You know I can't say long,' he said. 'I have to—'

'Be elsewhere, join a different ghost Zoom, live stream with some spirits somewhere, I get it,' she said, cutting him off. 'What aren't you telling me?'

He froze, the immediate response of a guilty party.

'You have absolutely no poker face, do you?'

'I hate poker,' he mumbled, clearly still startled she had asked him outright. 'What do you mean?'

'Only I can see it and for the life of me, I can't work out why but you're . . . weak.'

'Rude bitch.'

'Tell me I'm wrong! You look like an echo of your former self.'

'I'm doing a lot, Tommi. There's no one else like me, no one else who can cross between the plains and liaise as fast as I can.'

'At what cost?' she pushed, seeing the flash of truth in his raised eyebrows. 'Oh my God, Barry. *At what cost?*'

'One I already paid a long time ago,' he said, like it was a weight off his shoulders. 'This is not natural, you know? I'm being loaned power from more than one source, Wehi too.'

'Snitch now or I swear I'll call the *Ghostbusters*,' Tommi huffed, crossing her arms over her chest.

'When this is done,' Barastin began, 'my loan needs to be repaid.'

She felt her mouth pop open as she realised precisely what he meant. 'You'll ... you'll die.'

'I'm already dead, Tommi.'

'But finally. Permanently.'

'Yes.'

Her knees felt weak as she processed the magnitude of that confirmation, her thoughts immediately turning to her friend. 'Does Casper know?'

The ghost laughed, as if she'd asked the dumbest question in the world. 'Of course not.'

'You have to tell her.'

'I do not. And you won't either. We wouldn't have gotten this far if Wehi and I hadn't done what we did, and Casper's head needs to be firmly in the game. She'll learn soon enough.'

'Oh Barry,' she said, wanting to reach out and touch him as her fingers outstretched.

'It's a relief, Tommi,' he replied. 'Please never tell my sister that, but after so many years helping others move on and dragging those who won't ... you begin to envy it. Eventually it starts to feel like you're the last person left at the party, everyone else has gone home.'

'And you're cleaning up all the cigarette butts and empty bottles,' she murmured, the ghost nodding.

'I have been happily tethered to my sister and she to me for so long, but Corvossier is not alone any more. She has a life. It's about time that I let go of mine.'

Tommi didn't like the little croak that escaped her lips, wanting desperately to hug him, to hold him, to tell him to make a different choice. But that was how *she* felt and it would be completely disregarding everything Barastin had just said to her about how *he* felt and what *he* wanted.

'I need to go,' he reiterated, a dual meaning in his words. She nodded, reluctant to let him leave yet also conscious of the fact this might be the last time she would ever see him.

'Don't,' Barastin said, holding up a hand as if he couldn't take it.

'Don't what?' she sniffed.

'You look like you're about to start singing *"Candle in the Wind"*. Just let me go, Tommi.'

She sighed, nodding. 'Goodbye, Norma Jean.'

He cracked a smile as he disappeared. She felt grateful she'd had a chance to say goodbye at all as she made her way back, thinking of all the others who had come to know and love him once Barry had let them into his weird little world. Tommi tracked the scent of everyone else to a building that looked like a Finders Keepers market on steroids. It was a collection of everything that had been lost and found over the years, an invaluable treasure trove of objects that spanned history. Among it all was the equipment Atlanta had obviously been talking about: wetsuits and oxygen tanks and mouthpieces and weight belts and an endless array of implements that would be useful to them. Heath looked up at her arrival, several diamond necklaces looped around his neck and a pirate hat tilted on his head.

'I'm, uh, more of a . . . treasure protector,' he said in his best Nicolas Cage impression.

She laughed, unable to help it as she leaned into his shoulder and listened to whatever Avary was talking them through. Heath had known both Barry and Casper since they were children. The loss she felt would be nothing compared to what he would feel. Was it better to know what was coming, she wondered? Or was it better to plunge towards the unknown with hope and optimism? Her gaze shifted to Dreckly, who knew what was coming for her and had remained unflinching regardless. She had promised not to tell Casper and she would keep that promise for Barastin, but when the time was right Tommi decided that she would tell Heath. She had to.

Tommi stared up at the sign above her as she climbed the endless spread of black rocks. It was that school-bus yellow, with dozens of street tags pointing in various angles as they directed the viewer towards the locations listed. Tokyo was 9,567 kilometres away, the equator over 5,000, and none of that information was useful for her to know as she made land at New Zealand's southern tip, but it was comforting none the less. It meant she didn't have to spend another second in the water and she tossed the oxygen tank over the barrier as she climbed it, Keisha Tianne grabbing her with a grunt as she launched herself over it.

'You look like a soggy lot,' the older werewolf said with a grin, seeming not to mind that the freezing water from Tommi's soaking wetsuit was now covering her. It was this that kept Tommi's tongue in check as she turned back to pull Quaid over the barrier. With the exception of the selkies, the sprite and Sorcha, he was the only one of them who didn't look like he was deteriorating from the inside out. He was ecstatic and she paused for a moment, thinking of everything that had happened since she had busted him out of that cell. It was exhausting and terrifying and traumatic, but after any amount of time in Vankila it must have been exhilarating. And now, after all of it, he was home.

She smiled as she watched him embrace his pack, Wehi and Keisha just two members of the many more that would flock to their youngest pup as he returned to where he belonged. And *who* he belonged with. Wehi caught her staring at him, just the shimmer of acknowledgement there as he frowned slightly. *Yes, old man, I know your secret,* she thought. Just like Barastin, she pledged to keep his sacrifice exactly that: secret. If he could tell that she knew, he didn't say anything but he did jerk his head behind him. There were dozens of werewolves there, many from the Ihi pack but many more from packs she didn't recognise. They were there to offer them more than just a ride to the Dawson farm, they were there to provide them with protection as they headed to the location of what Tommi was determined would be their final battle.

Yet behind them, she saw other faces. Not just one, but *hundreds* that she recognised from the night of her coming-of-age ritual. They had been the faces of her direct ancestors and the faces of werewolves she bore no blood link to, their connection being merely the burden of carrying this same lycanthropic curse. Chester Rangi was among them, the shifting creature once referred to as a mischief demon not exactly holding the form of a ghost but not exactly holding the form of a human either. He was other and more, as she had come to know. She let out the smallest gasp as she recognised a face only seen on paper and in a recollected memory from Wehi that she had been projected into during *ahi hikoi*. She had never known him, and yet she would know him anywhere. It was her father, Jonah Ihi. His smile was barely visible, the gesture more of recognition as he raised his chin ever so slightly.

'What are you looking at?' Aruhe asked, pulling down the zipper of her wetsuit.

'Yeah,' Quaid echoed, following her gaze. 'I don't see anything.'

With her half-siblings standing on either side of her, Tommi smiled in a way that reached down into her soul.

'Aye,' she whispered, 'but you can feel it.'

Chapter 19

Dreckly

Death was everywhere. That's what it seemed like to Dreckly even as they'd managed to duck it and dip it and dive it, it was still surrounding them like smoke wherever she looked. She had survived when Mildred had fallen. Amos had survived when Kaia and all her friends had drowned. Casper had survived when so many Rogues had been lost. She had visited a mythical island that represented all of the hope there could be between the union of different species . . . and yet her heart still felt heavy with despair.

Her mother's people had felt it when they joined her out at sea, so many swimming with them as they raced against time to make it to Aotearoa. She couldn't feel any form of elation, not as she watched selkies emerge from the safety of the depths all over the world and make their presence known in what could very well be one last stand. The only glimmer of relief came on their last afternoon at sea, when she felt the air pulse around them as a killer whale broke the surface.

There was never just one, of course, with the rest of the pod making themselves known as they breached alongside them.

She watched as Sushmita reached out, laughing alongside Ben as the werewolves' fingers ran along the slick blackness of the whales' backs. If she died, like Sadie had seen, she would take this ocean vision with her to the grave. In fact, even once they made landfall it still fuelled her. Dreckly was never a huge fan of the cold, and the South Island of New Zealand at this time of year was *freezing*. She thought they were almost through winter, yet the season seemed particularly stubborn when it came to relinquishing its frosty fingers as they drove through Arrowtown.

It was easy to understand why Tiaki and the Aunties had chosen this place to hide Sadie. There was really only one main street, the quaint shopfronts and general stores looking like they were made out of gingerbread as snow dusted them like frosting. There was nobody about, the whole town like a dessert with the black trees dipped in white chocolate and the street signs displaying a font that was last in fashion when Dreckly was fighting in the Second World War. It was a place out of time, and had been perfect for their purposes. Yet it wouldn't stay that way for long.

When they reached the Dawson farm at dusk, it was clear the future was coming for Arrowtown and coming for them all. Slipping out of a car and stepping away from the convoy that had retrieved them for the road trip up from Invercargill, she huddled deeper into the full-length thermal coat she had been given. She went to inspect a tank that was being positioned on the property, her gloved fingers running along the cold metal. Dreckly pulled back to a different time, a different battle, and a different war.

'You like our baby?' a man asked, his head popping out the top like an inquisitive meerkat.

'Panzer I,' she muttered, more to herself than the beings who were watching her.

'Lady knows her tanks,' he replied.

'Lady incapacitated more than her fair share of Nazi Germany machinery.'

A second head appeared next to the first, the two men clearly twins; they both looked like they had about a thousand more questions for her when Tommi called her name.

'Gotta go, boys,' she said, marching away from them. 'Don't let any honey near that fuel nozzle.'

She heard them muttering behind her and she smiled, even though the idea of the Treize showing up with jars of molasses to disable the fuel function the way she had once done seemed ridiculous. They were not the ones who had been relying on guerrilla tactics up until this point, after all. Tommi looked panicked as Dreckly jogged up to her, face illuminated solely by the headlights of the parked cars.

'She's gone into labour!' the werewolf blurted, no question about who the 'she' was in this scenario.

'Holy shit,' Dreckly murmured, thinking about the young woman she had once made fake identity documents for on her boat.

'I mean, her water broke so . . . that means going into labour, right?'

'Why are you asking me? I've never had kids.'

'But you're old!' Tommi insisted. 'All one hundredy and stuff, I assumed you know shit.'

'I've worked very hard to avoid knowing anything about childbirth personally.'

'Respect.' The werewolf nodded, her eyes scanning the

crowd over Dreckly's shoulder as she looked for the person she was after. 'Sorcha's just pulling up now. I'm going to take her straight to the cottage. Will you come with me?'

'Sure.' She looked on as Tommi practically hauled the banshee out of a moving vehicle.

It was hard going, the three women jogging through the night towards the edge of the forest where the cottage sat protected among the trees. Heath was up ahead of them, holding a flashlight so they had a beacon to move towards. All of the Aunties were clustered around the structure, like a wall protecting the vulnerable inside. Dreckly didn't know most of these women but Tommi did, positioning herself in the middle of their trio as they moved forward.

'Sorcha's here,' she said. 'Let us through.'

And they did, but they blocked Heath from moving past their line of defence. Tommi threw a look back at him, but he shrugged and waved her on. Dreckly felt relief when she saw the face of someone she did know, Tiaki Ihi, who was waiting for them at the doorway as they stepped inside.

'No men,' she said by way of explanation. They shook off their coats and ditched their snow-covered boots as Tiaki led them through the house. Dreckly didn't need to know Sadie's other sisters by name to recognise them on sight, clustered half-in the nursery, half-in the hallway, each one as fair skinned as the last with hair in varying shades from bright red to strawberry blonde. In contrast, Sorcha's blonde pixie cut stood out among them as she embraced her siblings.

'Shannon, how's she doing?' Sorcha asked, addressing the eldest of the sisters.

'She's in early labour, which is good.'

'Why?' Tommi asked, vocalising what Dreckly wanted to know as well.

'With a multiple birth you can go into labour basically any time after thirty-five weeks, way before a regular baby would be full term,' Shannon said. 'For triplets, you want them to cook in there as long as possible so they have the best chance outside the womb. Sadie will be at thirty-eight weeks tomorrow, which is great, and her going into labour naturally rather than Dr Kikuchi having to induce her is even better.'

There was a plastic curtain blocking their view of the living room and the kitchen, but Dreckly could see through just enough of it. Since they couldn't physically go to a regular hospital's maternity ward for security and banshee wailing issues, it looked like the Paranormal Practitioner had done her best to bring a maternity ward to them. She had converted the living area into a fully functioning operating room, with Dr Kikuchi and her wife both dressed head to toe in scrubs while they prepped the equipment. Sadie, meanwhile, looked way calmer than Dreckly was expecting as she sat on an enormous exercise ball and breathed oxygen through an elaborate mask-type contraption. Tiaki's 'no men' policy clearly excluded one man, and she watched with interest as Sadie gripped the hands of Simon Tianne, whose legs were braced around her. He was whispering into her ear and from reading his lips, Dreckly realised he was counting her through the contractions. It felt too intimate, observing them like that, and her gaze travelled to the enormous mound swelling from Sadie's stomach.

'You have got to get those things out of her,' she said, turning to the group and interrupting whatever Nora had been saying.

Shannon laughed, a look of understanding on her features. 'Dr Kikuchi wants to give it just a little bit longer, then she'll perform the caesarean.'

'She's not going to push them out?' Dreckly wondered.

Tommi gave her a horrified expression. 'And what, give her vagina a Glasgow smile in the process? Get the fook outta here.'

'I'm trying to work out how long we have,' Dreckly explained. 'If they're here to kill the babies, kill Sadie, then the Treize must be close.'

'They can't know *when* the birth is happening,' Tiaki countered, 'only that it's imminent but yeah . . . I'd expect they're close by.'

'We need to move, then.' Tommi nodded. 'This right here is out of our control and firmly in Sadie and Dr Kikuchi's. All we can control is what happens out there, so let's go and leave them to it.'

'Shannon, you stay,' Sorcha said. 'Let me just see her quickly, then I'll join you guys.'

'You're her favourite,' her sibling countered. 'You should—'

'You're a mother; you and Ina have been through this. I'm no use to her if I stay, but I'm useful out there.'

Sorcha slipped away, Shannon fastening headphones to her head as she waited for her sister to return and they would switch positions. The banshee was gone for just a few minutes, returning with steely conviction as she joined the others and they left the house.

'You're not staying?' Dreckly asked of the other Burke siblings.

'Sorcha's right,' one of them said. 'We're all more use out there than in here. Plus, it's dangerous. The cottage is soundproofed within an inch of its life, but if one of the babies wails or Sadie does . . .' She trailed off, her silence implying the horror of what could happen to a person physically if that was the case.

Sorcha nodded as she shrugged into her coat and they sealed the door behind them. 'Shannon, Simon, Dr Kikuchi and her missus are the only ones that stay behind and they've got headphones *on top* of headphones that will hopefully avert a cranium-exploding crisis.'

'Simon?' Tommi frowned, snow sticking to her cheeks as she turned around to examine Sorcha's face. 'Did I hear you right?'

'He won't leave her side,' Tiaki said, dragging the werewolf forward by the elbow as they headed back to the main farmhouse. 'Let's not get into it.'

Dreckly didn't miss the sideways glance that Tommi threw Heath, the pair of troublemakers looking like they wanted to dive *so far* into it. Glancing back at the cottage over her shoulder before it faded from view, the last thing she saw was an army of Aunties standing guard around it. Their faces were firm and unflinching despite the weather, acting like a neon sign that communicated their willingness to die rather than let you pass them into that house.

'Sadie's vision had the battle taking place during the day,' Heath puffed, holding a Burke sibling up on either side of him as they struggled through the terrain. 'So how long have we got until first light?'

'Not long enough,' Tiaki said, inhaling deeply but never slowing for a second. 'I can already smell them on the wind.'

'Fuck,' Sorcha cursed.

'It's going to have to be enough time,' Tommi snarled, voice determined. 'We have no other choice. We have to hold them off until those babies are born.'

Dreckly had thought it was as simple as Tiaki scenting them and the Treize knocking on the door the next minute, but the reality was closer to hours. And they were agonising, each one feeling like a decade rather than a full sixty minutes as basically every supernatural she had ever met rushed around to mobilise like their lives depended on it. Because they did.

Heath was handing out weapons like candy, clearly knowing the best people to divvy them up amongst, while Tommi moved through the ranks of the foreign werewolves, embracing those she knew, like Sanjay from Berlin, and incorporating others into teams with Aruhe. They were the best and bloodiest ground fighters, with so much hinging on them, but she always observed the softer side too. She watched as a tearful Tiaki embraced her son, Quaid, after years of forced separation. His brother James was there too and an older man who looked like his tattoos were inked on leather rather than the surface of his skin.

Dreckly belonged among the island of misfit toys, which felt right to her. She assembled her own team consisting of Yixin, Silver and Topper: all fellow Vankila escapees. If she could have, she would have had Amos by her side. The selkie had been justifiably devastated by the news out of Australia, and she felt like the two of them were bound together in their grief when they had retreated to find privacy on the island. She had lost enough people in her lifetime to be able to console him through the process, steering Amos away from the questions of if Kaia had suffered and the specifics of how they died. They had drowned, like what was estimated to be millions of others, as Queensland and half of New South Wales had been completely wiped off the grid.

'I have no one now,' Amos had said, once the tears had stopped and reflection had set in. Losing loved ones was hard, yet somehow losing them to a crusade they had willingly volunteered themselves for wasn't any easier. She had always thought that it should be, that the knowledge of Harvey and everyone else dying for a cause they believed in should be some comfort. It never was. Gone was gone and it was difficult to feel anything but the void left in its place.

'That's not true,' Dreckly had told him, taking his hand in hers. 'You have me. You have Atlanta. You have Avary. You have a whole world of support that you never had before. That won't feel like much right now, but it will eventually.'

What she didn't say – but what she had been thinking – was that the death of the humans would liberate Amos in some way. Unlike her, he wasn't meant to exist as part of two worlds. Yet he had tried to, bound by the love of not just Kaia Craig but of Cabby and Storm as well. Now he was free to be who he was meant to become, which meant swimming alongside an aquatic army with Atlanta, Avary and so many others right in that moment.

There was a howl that split through the night as it shifted into early morning: they were nearly there, the Treize on the property and marching towards them. As Dreckly sprinted towards the towering figures of Yixin and Silver, she processed the scene around her with a kind of hyperreal detachment. Aruhe was screaming at Joss to stay inside, that this battle was no place for him. Kala was ordering Sprinkle to guard the children, the young witch solemnly accepting her duty as she ferried the Burkes' banshee offspring to a safe place. Wehi was humming, eyes closed but body open as ghosts manifested around him. Tommi was embracing Heath, the pair's arms locked around each other as they passionately kissed in the snow. If these were to be everyone's last moments, this was how they spent them. And then there was Ben, the crowd parting so that she saw the werewolf standing there with his sister. Sushmita couldn't stop shivering and Dreckly knew it had nothing to do with the cold.

'We heard you need some back-up singers,' he said, Ben Kapoor looking like a beautiful idiot to her as he and his sibling stood alongside a demon, a fire elemental and an arachnia.

'Ben,' she began, voice soft, 'you should join the other werewolves. This is not the place for you.'

'Oh, but Sushmita can stay?' he teased.

'Yes,' Dreckly replied, knowing that her response surprised him. She saw the flash of recognition in his sister's eyes, her respect. 'She survived Vankila like the rest of us. Everyone here has survived that place as a prisoner. Your family fought beside the Ihi pack once, you should fight with them again.'

'Because none of you plan to survive, right?' His question didn't warrant an answer, it was that obvious. She gave him one anyway.

'This is the Fuck Shit Up Crew,' Dreckly said, earning an appreciative snort from Yixin. 'We're here to do as much damage as quickly as we can.'

He stepped towards her, taking her hand in his as he stared down at her. She expected the heat to flush through her like it usually did, but all she felt was numb as Ben's eyes penetrated.

'Let's fuck shit up, then,' he replied.

She nodded, not willing to fight him on this and not having the energy either. With a jerk of her head, they split from the main party and jogged for the perimeter. It wasn't close enough to daylight for Sadie's vision to play out the way Barastin had described it to them and she was surprised by the relief she felt at that knowledge. It meant they were in new territory, an unseen future, and that comforted her as they dug into their position at the side. The idea was simple: their group looked big and threatening, but they were small. The enemy would want to take them out quickly, drawing away some of the biggest threats so everyone else could take on the rest.

'Here they come,' Sushmita growled. Yixin and Silver made murmuring noises, yet it was still a few more moments until Dreckly saw the Treize emerge from the shadows. They weren't alone, but their numbers surprised her. She had expected more soldiers, more of the Praetorian Guard lined up against them, just like Sadie's vision had dictated. Yet the bodies in front of them felt depleted and as she looked closer, she realised many of them appeared battle worn already. There weren't even the full thirteen members of the Treize remaining.

'The selkies,' she whispered, hope flaring in her chest as she realised the Treize's plan to storm the farm had been completely and utterly flipped on its head. As she watched a panting Praetorian Guard soldier dragging an axe through the snow, arms scarred with deep bite marks, Dreckly saw that she had been thinking of their side as the last-ditch effort before anni-hilation. When really, it was them.

She watched as they came to that same realisation, the enemy taking in the sheer numbers they were facing and the diversity of beings that were determined to make sure they never left this property. Dreckly didn't have a werewolf's sense of smell, but she had to guess they could scent the fear thick on the breeze. It excited the wolves like blood in the water and without warning, without any fanfare or ceremony, suddenly it was *on*.

Dreckly hadn't seen the Praetorian Guard soldiers that emerged from the trees, but clearly the werewolves had. She watched as Tommi and Tiaki led the charge, the women stripping free of their clothing as they sprinted into the onslaught. They morphed on the fly, leaping into the air as humans and landing on the ground as wolves. The ranks behind them did the same, Dreckly suddenly understanding why the Ihi pack was so feared among their kind. She had *never* seen that much control or that much swiftness before, let alone the ferocity as teeth clashed with swords. Those that couldn't fully change shifted what they could, using wolf arms and wolf jaws and wolf agility as they ran at the army.

Heath's yell led the humanoids forward after the first wave, demons and goblins and shifters descending into the fray while witches hung on the outskirts, hands and lips moving fast as they fought with unseen forces. The ground rumbled beneath their feet and she was sent back to the terrifying moments of fleeing from Vankila, only for soil to be shot skyward. An earth demon folded a member of the Treize amongst the bosom of their soil, the pair fighting before they sank back into the ground. More than enough Praetorian Guard soldiers had taken the bait as their attention was drawn to them, Dreckly's breath catching as she viewed who was leading that incursion.

'Lorcan,' she whispered. She had assumed he had been killed at Vankila, swallowed by the hole that seemed to destroy everything else. Yet of course it would be this way, their party exploding against his as she watched Yixin roll into himself like a giant bowling ball and smash a path forward. Towards Lorcan, she realised. At first it was panic, Dreckly worried that the demon would snatch his defeat from her grasp. Yet when he made a wide berth of the man and held off the blows of those around him, she understood that he was keeping him back for her. Lorcan hadn't seemed to realise that, however, and he looked ragged as he expertly spun a long sword through the air and stormed towards her. The time for theatrics was through; Dreckly was sick of this vendetta and sick of the man who motivated it.

Her arm was still broken, now encased in a plaster cast, but it didn't matter. She needed neither if it came down to it and it did, the fingers of her free hand curling as she wrapped the air currents around her. She created a barrier for herself, arrows aimed her way deflected off the strength of the particles as she twisted and contorted and spun them to her will. Lorcan slashed at her with little effect, Dreckly watching with interest before she cursed herself for toying with her food.

'I don't want to kill you, Dreckly,' Lorcan huffed. 'But I'll do it if I have to!'

'Liar!' she spat, his words making her blood flame with anger. 'You didn't want to lock up a child while their mother died in prison, but you said it was right. You didn't want to detain me for a live lobotomy, but you said it was the only way. Now you're here with an army saying you don't want to kill me when if you'd had the chance, you would have done it back in Vankila. I saw it in your eyes and I see it in your lies.'

She ducked as he lunged at her again, pivoting out of the way until they reformed in almost exactly the same positions they had been before, just on opposite sides. Always.

'Have some agency right now; take responsibility for your choices and decades' worth of terrible ones,' Dreckly growled, not sure why that was so important to her in the moment. 'How can you ever put all of those actions together and say it was the right thing, you fucking monster?'

'Because I have to!' he shouted back. 'Leading isn't easy, it requires tough choices and those brave enough to make them. It's not just about power for the Treize –'

She snorted audibly at that.

'– it's about keeping things the way they were. Everything and everyone has their place and supernaturals have theirs; humans, too.'

'Listen to your words,' she hissed, shaking her head. 'Wanting beings to stay in their rightful place . . . according to whom? The Treize, whose place is above everybody else at all costs?'

'It's the way things have always been, Dreckly; it has worked.'

'No, it has worked for you. It has worked for those in charge. But look around you: this isn't an uprising, this is a revolution and we're fighting for what has to be a better way.'

Thrusting her arm forward, she sent all of her power towards him at once. The years and the suffering and the deaths and the misery created a tornado of air force that knocked him off his feet and sent him flying. She ran after his flailing body, knowing she would get only one chance at this as he landed in the snow with a spray of blood.

Leaping on his chest, Dreckly grabbed his face in her hands as he coughed up a mouthful of fluid, green eyes wide as he realised the extent of the damage. It was like being hit with an invisible car driving at full speed, such was the magnitude of the impact she had channelled right at his chest. It had caused unseen internal damage and a growing amount of external. If you could recover from something like this, she didn't want to know as she dug her fingernails into the skin of his cheek and blocked out the chaos around her.

'This is for my father,' Dreckly said, mentally chasing the particles of air that were being sucked into his lungs. 'This is for Mildred, for Yixin, for Silver, for Topper, for Sushmita, for Amos, for every prisoner and every ward and every cause you believed you were helping with your ignorance.'

He was being suffocated from the inside out, yet it was testament to his strength that he managed to choke out a few words as she drained him of air.

'I . . . only ever . . . wanted to do . . . what was right,' Lorcan strangled. The tragedy of it was she could see in his eyes that he really believed that, still.

'Die right,' she spat, holding his gaze until there was no life left in it whatsoever. She had waited more than one hundred years for revenge on behalf of those she loved and herself. To achieve that was something else and she staggered back from his corpse, unable to help the sting in her eyes as she thought of the avenged. There was little time to reflect on it, however, as she saw Ben and Sushmita flung through the air by a demon on a side that was distinctly not theirs. He had what looked like a scythe in his hands, ready to swing down upon them when she shoved his body sideways with a gust of air that should have sent him tumbling.

Somehow he stayed standing, swinging his weapon wildly as he looked for a physical opponent rather than the small woman with her arm in a sling standing across the field. It was the distraction they needed, Sushmita's smaller and meaner form able to spring up as she sunk her teeth in his neck and threw her head wildly about in an attempt to decapitate him. His flesh was green and thick, and Ben had to leap up and attempt the same task from the front before they were able to bring the monster down.

The rhythmic firing of the tank acted as a backing track as Dreckly funnelled additional air into the flailing form of an ally, putting out the flames that licked their body as they dived into the snow and rolled about to extinguish the fire. She stepped over Lorcan's corpse, moving on to the next task, the next mission, the next assault that required her help as she spent everything she had on what she promised would be their final battle.

Chapter 20

Casper

It was empty inside, yet so full, as Casper made her way through the darkness. Like the forest outside the castle doors, she knew they were being watched and Clay let out a warning growl as they moved deeper. She could see where they were going because of the ghosts, each one like a candle illuminating the path upwards. He could see where they were going because he was a predator, but the werewolf wasn't the only one.

'Sprint,' he told her, words firm. 'I'll find you if I can.'

She wanted to object, but right at that moment something lunged from the dark. Casper twisted on the spot, spinning as Clay ducked and she swung her arm wide, bracing against the impact as it connected with a ghoul. She was surprised; that kind of cretin was the last thing she expected to find running rampant inside the Treize's headquarters. Yet she also knew there were dungeons in this place, deep and dark and deserted: the ideal sanctuary for smelly, slimy ghouls.

And this, it appeared, was a trap. She and Clay watched as the severed torso fell in two at their feet, landing with a wet *thwack.* The werewolf looked up, eyes glowing yellow with intensity. He was shifting into more beast than man, and even though Casper knew he couldn't shift fully without the assist of the full moon like Tommi, this was dangerous enough.

'Go,' he growled. She nodded, touching his face gently before she spun away from him and sprinted. She pumped her arm for momentum, taking the stairs two at a time as she ignored the sounds of the fight breaking out down below. Casper had her own problems to worry about, more ghouls waiting at each level as she thrust forward with her weapon and sent one shrieking down the stairs behind her. She stabbed and slashed and struck out with her bladed arm like she was fencing, their hot blood spraying her across her face as an invisible ghost army cheered her on. She couldn't risk lending them her strength and imbuing them with power when she didn't know what was to come and what she would need when she got to The Three. Thankfully, she didn't require them as a whitish blue line burst in front of her so bright she had to shield her eyes.

'STAY AWAY FROM MY SISTER, YOU GROSS WET GOBLIN BOYS!'

She smiled, pulling her hand away to see the figure of Barastin looking like a righteous, glowing warrior as he fought them off for her. They didn't need to speak; they'd always known how to work together as a team. As he moved she ran alongside him, slaying whatever he missed. It felt like it took for ever, yet suddenly they arrived in a wide hallway and the door was *right* there. Tommi had described it to her in the purgatory dream she'd somehow lived through, The Three and her dead friend Mari taking her there. It was that recollection that helped her recognise it, along with Barry, who of course had been there more than once. He kicked back a ghoul as he held the door open for her.

'Hurry!' he cried. 'They won't come through here!'

He was right, Casper dashing inside and turning back with interest as the ghouls stopped at the threshold. Whatever it was about these women, they proceeded no further. This was not their domain.

Finally, she comes.

At last.

Took long enough.

The voices echoed through her being, something she felt rather than heard out loud. Barastin shut the door, locking it for good measure as she turned to face The Three. They lay there together, thin and sprawled out on one enormous bed. IVs hung from their wrists, connected to medical equipment that was useless for what had ailed them. Like so much of this place, the machines had been abandoned and left to beep there dormant. The remnants of what else had been tried lay around the room, and Casper gently touched the charm that hung at her own neck. It had once been made for her by Kala as they faced their first battle together. She had created other protective trinkets for her since then, which she also wore, as well as the wedding ring that wrapped all of their love up in it. Yet that very first spell was special to her and Casper needed its strength as she looked at the failed alchemist rites painted on the wall. There was a portable lab that had been set up nearby with a series of vials containing the blood and essence and magic of countless creatures who had been cut apart by the Treize over the past few years.

Do not focus on the past.
Nothing can be changed there.
No, it can't.

She turned back to face them, her gaze moving past her brother as she re-examined the three women lying there before her. They were borderline skeletal, as if life had slowly sucked them dry and, in a way, she guess it had. In white, silk robes, their bones poking through, their hands clung to one another, their legs interwoven and limbs all connected as if they were one. Their long grey hair had curled and grown into each other so that it was impossible to tell where one started and the other began. Casper was furious, she couldn't help it, and she wiped away angry tears as she bent down to slowly remove the needles from their arms one by one.

'I'm sorry,' she said. 'I'm so, so sorry.'

You did not do this.
Neither did they, in a way.
We chose this.
Yes, yes, we wanted our end.
Not at first, mind you.
Quite right, no. We were worried.
It was the only way, though, we realised.
We needed to return to the river so they could emerge.
Oh, they'll be so beautiful.

Casper brushed a hand along each of their faces, trying to comfort them, wondering if they were in pain as their end crept nearer. They each let out a small gasp of relief, as if human contact from a place of kindness was a salve to their souls.

We are not in pain any more, dear sister.

You must not cry for us.
Do not focus on the present.
Nothing can be changed there.
No, it can't.

Casper jumped like she'd received an electric shock, her fingers glued to the skin of the final woman as she was thrown forward into a view that was not her own. It was not a vision, she realised, but what The Three were viewing as it happened. New Zealand, the final battle, and she floated among it, unseen but seeing all just as they did. She watched as Tiaki Ihi whimpered, the wolf's dark form hunched over the body of a young man . . . her son, James Ihi. He was dead, Casper could feel it even though it was obvious just from the way his naked body lay there, blood melting the snow around him. The werewolf threw her head back, howling in anguish. The sound morphed into a roar, one that became a chorus as she launched herself at a series of armed men with two other wolves growling by her side. Casper knew it was Aruhe and Quaid Ihi, just as she knew the first wolf had been Tiaki. There was no logical way she could truly know that information, yet there it was, presenting itself to her like fact.

She was in the ocean now, plunged among it as selkies rose up out of the depths. They had driven a ship to wreck, the hull smashing against rocks they had cloaked and Praetorian Guard soldiers jumping from it as it sank. Shore wasn't far and some had managed to make it there, tattered and beaten, but most had not as the selkies climbed up the side of the ship like ants devouring a corpse. They pulled the soldiers under, their serrated teeth biting into their skin in some cases, others just yanking them deeper and deeper down until they drowned.

Suddenly her hands were bloodied, shaking and pulling back from the wounded figure of Heath as Tommi screamed for help. There was something protruding from him, some kind of metal object, and his eyes were wide open. He wasn't dead, however, and again that was just something she knew. He was blinking and breathing just as slowly, his arm clutching Tommi's as she desperately packed snow around the wound. A Paranormal Practitioner slid to their side, examining the blow and telling her that if she didn't remove the object he would die but if she did remove it, it was likely he would never walk again. She saw the anguish on her friend's face, her dark brown eyes darting from side to side as they morphed from the wolf's to the woman's. Tommi stared down at Heath, as if looking for an answer there, yet even though his lips moved he couldn't speak. She told the Paranormal Practitioner to do it, do it, for the love of God, and just save him.

A body floated amongst what had once been a city, the blonde hair now white as the figure looked like it was levitating past a crumpled car wreck. Their eyes were open and a white film covered them, shielding the dead from what they shouldn't see any more. Grey selkie hands touched the small bullet hole above Kaia Craig's heart, the puncture from an enemy's gun killing her before the wave even arrived. Amos cupped her face with his hands, the pain so raw as he looked like he wanted to scream her name under the water. She was not the only dead down there. So many would be left behind, reabsorbed by the earth and the ocean, but she was who he had been looking for as his powerful tail flicked and he pushed upwards, his hands gripping under her armpits.

As he broke the surface, Kaia's corpse tucked protectively next to him, she watched the pain on Jarna 'Cabby' Cabin's face as the woman hung over the side of a battered dinghy. They had been looking for the body of a brother as well, a father, but the only miracle they would have that day was the one of Cabby somehow managing to survive when so few had.

In the entrance hall of the very building she had stormed, she stared into the eyes of Clay as they looked up at her, through her, and into the ceiling as he lay sprawled out on the floor. It seemed like he was trying to make a concrete angel, blood not flowing from him slowly but fast as a swarm of ghouls descended until he disappeared beneath them entirely and they feasted on his flesh.

Feet stumbled along the uneven surface of rocks that came in every colour and size, each one wet with the spray of a river that ripped relentlessly by them. Blood mixed among the water as it fell like rain droplets at first, then heavier as Dreckly carried Sorcha to the edge of the water as best she could. The compress around her neck and the bandages at her stomach couldn't stop the blood flowing from the banshee as the sprite gently lowered her on to the riverbed of rocks. Atlanta was waiting, the selkie's own body baring the marks of battle as she half crawled, half pulled herself up out of the water until she was cradling Sorcha in her arms. The banshee smiled up at her, stroking the face of the being that was tattooed on her shoulder as they looked deep into each other's eyes and whispered the things only they knew about each other.

Casper felt gentle breath against her skin as Simon carried the baby forwards, the screeching cry of new birth having dulled to just a whimper. The bloodied child was pressed into Sadie's arms, the young banshee's eyelids heavy as she fought to stay conscious and hold the first of her children. Its fat little fingers clutched at her skin as she lay on the operating table, Dr Kikuchi handing the next baby to her sister Shannon and the third to her wife. Hot tears splashed down Sadie's face, the werewolf from a world completely different to hers kissing them away as they fell. Shannon's nose brushed against that of her niece, this baby wide awake but quiet as it watched her through tiny eyeballs set inside a swollen face. She saw all three of the children born before her very eyes, Dr Kikuchi working fast to sew Sadie shut as she told them all that she was going to be fine, it was all going to be okay.

White hair floated along the surface of the water and at first, she thought it was her own. But there was too much of it and it was too long, the strands belonging to young women with skin just as pale as their hair. They were watching the birth as well, but from the depths of a river. The water was rapidly rising, but none of them bothered to move as their dark green gowns grew heavier and heavier until their heads disappeared underneath.

Casper stumbled back as she readjusted to the view that was now her own once again. The Three lay in front of her, their last breaths taken just seconds earlier, the original trio of banshees frozen in their dying embrace around each other. Blinking, she tried to readjust to everything she had seen, knowing that it was the present and knowing that it was real. Yet she had come here for a reason and that was to make sure these old, ancient beings didn't have to die alone. Steeling herself, she closed her eyes and let her entire self be pulled towards the lobby more easily than it ever had been in her life. Barastin was waiting there for her, smiling at the three hunched ladies as they looked around the vast expanse before them. She could feel their trepidation, she could see their fear as they clung to each other, she could sense their worry as they stood in the unknown for the first time in thousands of years.

'It's all right,' Casper said, infusing her voice with as much warmth as she could. 'I'm here with you all; Barry, too. You're not alone.'

'There's nothing to be afraid of,' her brother added, the twins bookending them as they began a slow stroll. The lobby, usually empty until she willed it otherwise, was full. There were so many there with them, showing The Three rather than telling them how very *not* alone they were. It hurt Casper to see the faces of her friends among them, knowing that this too meant they were dead and leaving her as well.

It's the inevitable conclusion of the journey.

Even here, in her world, The Three's voices rippled through her in an unspoken way that was entirely unique.

Their sacrifices are worth it.

For those who hereafter come.

A better world awaits them now.

A messy one, yes.

All futures are messy.

You must focus on that.

Things can be changed there.

Yes, it can.

She let go of the hand she had been holding, feeling the pull in the sister as it began to take her onwards. They looked ready to go and they felt it too, but they hesitated as they looked back. Casper couldn't help but wonder what they were waiting for, yet The Three weren't staring at her. They were looking at Barastin. Her head snapped to her brother as he gave her a pained smile.

'Somehow I thought this would be easier,' he said, voice soft.

'No, Barry. What do you . . .? Don't, you can't!'

'I can and you can,' her twin replied, Casper knowing what he was doing in an instant like it had been her very own thought. She hated herself in that moment, hated all the things she had noticed but failed to pay attention to as she had been swept up in her problems and her life and her love and her conflicts. She knew he was stretching himself too thin, knew he was working with more power than he should have had, even for him. He had made a deal with the spirits, she realised. Never make deals with spirits, they knew better, because every deal came at a cost. Over Barastin's shoulder, she saw the face of Wehi Ihi emerging from the crowd. A medium in his own right, Casper understood that her brother wasn't the only one who had made that deal. The two had worked together, with the price having to be paid once the mission was done.

'Brother,' she sobbed, watching as Wehi's hand rested on her twin's shoulder. 'Please don't leave me. Please, I'll do anything.'

'Will you stop me from finding my happiness?' he asked.

Her cries cut short, Casper knew that she would never prevent that. She would never ask that of him. She saw it in Barastin von Klitzing's eyes, the eyes she had looked into her whole life as a perfect mirror of her own. He was tired, drained and completely sapped of the energy that had always made him sparkle like he was covered in glitter. The thousands, millions, endless crowd of ghosts that now spanned around them weren't just there for The Three. They were there to accompany two old, beloved mediums the way Barastin and Wehi had accompanied them once.

'It's my time, beloved sister.'

She knew it. She felt it. She hated it.

'I will love you always, you know that,' she whimpered.

'Always,' he replied. 'And I you. You know you're never alone.'

She snapped her hand over her mouth, unable to stop the sobs as they racked her body. He took the extended hand of one of The Three, Wehi and Barastin adding their considerable weight to the influence as it flowed endlessly onwards.

'Casper and Creeper signing off for one last time.' Barry smiled, giving her a wink.

Just like that, he was gone. They were all gone. Only Casper was left and she sank down, the cold stone floor unforgiving as she fell to her knees. They had done it, they had changed the world, they had saved it. But it had cost them everything.

Chapter 21

Sadie

The reception wasn't great at the cottage. Sadie had never been much of a tech genius while Simon – it turned out – had another gift to add to the one thousand he'd already obtained. The babies were mercifully quiet and settled as she grabbed the handheld monitor from its charging station, rushing down the hallway to where he had managed to get the smart TV up and actively working on the wall. Light bulbs flashed in front of an empty podium while a news scroll rolled across the bottom of the screen, Sadie hoping desperately that she hadn't missed anything. Simon pulled her on to his lap; there was plenty of room on the couch but the two of them preferred to be close together, always, if they could be. The fact that he could wrap his arms around her waist now didn't hurt either. He held Sadie to him and they both stared transfixed at the television as faces they knew – and some that they didn't – assembled in front of the waiting media scrum.

Aruhe Ihi was front and centre, with Dreckly Jones and Shannon Burke positioned on either side of her. Further behind them were only a few others Sadie recognised: Yolindi the old

Australian witch, Avary the selkie, and Joss, a human but an enduring one at that. She could feel the tension in Simon's body as he watched his cousin place her paperwork in front of the microphone, lowering it just a touch with a self-conscious smile. Sadie used her fingers to rub the back of his neck, loosening the muscles there with one hand, and he made an appreciative murmur as they watched.

'Morena,' Aruhe began, it being close to midnight where Sadie and Simon were in New Zealand but the complete opposite end of the day in London. 'My name is Aruhe Ihi and I'm a werewolf.'

There was a whirring of cameras as they clicked, and the flashing of bulbs only increased as the other two women stepped forward.

'Hello, my name is Shannon Burke and I'm a banshee.'

'Good morning, my name is Dreckly Jones and I'm a sprite.'

Aruhe returned to the mic. 'The three of us have been selected to speak on behalf of the supernatural community today, with those gathered behind us representing witches, immortals, arachnia, goblins, selkies, shifters, demons, alchemists, mediums and more. The past few months have been historic, with many humans learning for the first time that they are not the sole occupants of this planet. Of course, we have always been with you in your mythology and folklore and religion. However, the time has come for us to step out of the shadows and back into the light, where we can co-exist alongside you like we once did hundreds of years ago. This process has not been a peaceful one and many of your kind and ours have been lost as we fought for the transparency this transition required. We understand there are going to be many challenges involved as we move forward, facing our fears and our prejudices as we work together towards a new world, a better world, a world where we can all survive and thrive *together*.'

'Survive and thrive,' Simon muttered, looking away from the television as he turned to stare at Sadie. 'One hundred per cent Joss wrote that line.'

Sadie smiled, looking at their Scottish speech writer, who was nodding along with Dreckly's words as she took over the mic. With his ginger hair and pale skin, he looked like one of her relatives rather than an immortal twenty-something who was handling the roll-out of their supernatural revelations behind the scenes. He had a great political mind and it was one that had convinced Shannon to become a public face of their movement alongside Aruhe and Dreckly.

'We need a mum,' he'd said simply. 'Someone who presents as soft and sweet and non-threatening.'

There had been no one more perfect for that job than Shannon, and Sadie watched her sister charm them through the screen, unable to help the pang she felt when she thought about how Sorcha would have been even better at that task. She would have had the whole world eating out of the palm of her hand up there. But Sorcha Burke was dead, her ashes sprinkled among the sands of Martins Bay so Atlanta could visit her anytime she wanted. Sadie wasn't sure when she would visit again, the memory so devastating to her as she looked at that beautiful, relentless landscape and wanted to burn it the fuck down. After all, what was the point of that place if Sorcha wasn't there to see it?

The small baby that had stirred against her chest had reminded her exactly what the point was. She had looked over her shoulder, to Shannon and Ina standing with their own children as they silently cried. Nora and Deepika had been further back, a baby in each arm, while Catriona and Keavy had clung to each other. Her cousins and her auntie had had to hold her mother up, Máire Burke not much longer for this earth. Of the family members they had watched flutter into the wind in clouds of grey ash, Sorcha's death had hurt the most. Partly because they believed they'd already lost her once, only to lose her again so soon afterwards.

It was a cruelty, Sadie thought, that her sister had sacrificed her own life for the three fat, healthy babies she would never meet. Yet there had been so much cruelty in the immediate aftermath of the battle. She knew she should have saved some sympathy for every single member of the Treize that was executed on the Dawson farm and the soldiers who had foolishly followed them into the fight. Instead, she could only think of everything they had done to her, her people, and the endless others. Sorcha would have sung a line from *Chicago* at her theatrically: *They had it coming*. And they did. So Sadie saved all her sympathy for herself and her friends as the devastating toll began to be calculated. She saved it for Simon, who sprinted into the forest and shifted on the spot when he learned of James' death.

The agony was too much for him to handle in human form, Keisha had told her, staying with Sadie and helping her with the children while she remained on bed rest. Her sisters had needed the space to grieve too and she needed to give it to them as the mass disposal of bodies took place outside the cottage. No one had even broken through the Aunties' wall to get close to the house while Sadie had been giving birth inside, they were that much of an immovable force. Their number had remained solid, but there were so many others who had been lost. Wehi, their tribal elder, was enough to devastate the pack and many of the local werewolves left immediately to begin preparations for the traditional funeral rites on Ihi land. Tiaki, Aruhe, Quaid and Tommi were among them – Meri too, although the older woman split duties with Keisha for as long as she could. Simon left with them as well, not returning to the cottage.

She knew it wasn't because of her, but it stung none the less. It was bizarre, to have so much hurt and pain, but to also have so much love, as she stared down at the faces of her beautiful daughters. The Three were dead and they were here in their place, the power of the original banshee women who could see no evil, hear no evil, speak no evil passing on to them. Yet when she stared at them, watching them sleep in the separate cots Simon had carved for them, curled up in their *wahakura*, she couldn't imagine that they could see anything, they seemed so peaceful. Right up until they weren't, of course, Keisha and Meri having such great instincts when it came to anticipating the cries and what they needed.

'Sometimes a baby's just gonna want to have a bitch fit,' Keisha told her, juggling a crying babe in one arm and a sleeping babe in the other. The third was painfully sucking on Sadie's breast, Dr Kikuchi providing the commentary as she ran through her weekly checks.

'Yes, I know when to switch tits,' she snapped, not meaning for the words to come out as harshly as they did but fatigue and grief doing that to her. It was testament to the Paranormal Practitioner's strength of character that she shrugged it off.

'Now you're sounding like a real mum,' Dr Kikuchi smiled, looked delighted at the banshee's prickliness.

It was a small thing, but she was starting to feel like it too. Her stitches were healing, her stomach was soft but no longer swelling, and with the exception of her extremely huge and extremely sore boobs, her body was starting to feel like hers for the first time in *months*. Her daughters looked more like their father than they did her, Texas's Greek genes dominant over her Irish ones with his tan skin passing on to their children. It made for an unusual combination with the dark, rusty shade of their hair, which was much closer to her mother's than Sadie's lighter ginger ever had been. She asked when Keisha and Meri would leave her, assuming they would join the pack to mourn like everyone else had. She'd heard them crying, she knew they hurt just like she did, but what Keisha Tianne said to her surprised Sadie more than she expected.

'You're family,' the werewolf told her.

She didn't understand what she meant right then, but she did later. With the baby monitor positioned against the outside door so she could see if they stirred, Sadie made the most of her time alone no matter how brief it would be by chopping wood. She'd watched Simon do it enough times that when she felt strong enough, she'd tried. And she'd sucked. So she tried again, Meri finding her a shorter axe that was easier to wield. Chopping her own firewood made her feel strong, and the sweat she worked up despite the cold evening air made her feel alive. She nearly didn't hear the twigs snap behind her that night, but she did just in time as she spun around with her weapon raised. Sadie let out a small gasp when she saw who it was, the axe slipping from her hand as Simon emerged from the woods.

He was naked, his chest rising and falling as he puffed, which told her that he had run all the way there in his wolf form. The snow had long since melted and the falling leaves crunched under his feet as he marched towards her, not slowing down for a second and her not wanting him to as she rushed to meet him. His picked her up in one smooth gesture, lifting Sadie off her feet as he kissed her. It didn't matter how many days had passed, how many weeks, months, it could have been years for all she cared as she wrapped her legs tightly around him. When he kissed her, she felt *everything* and she wanted to make sure he felt everything too as she used her mouth to communicate exactly how much she'd missed him. When he pulled pack, he was smiling with surprise, like this wasn't the reaction he had expected.

'Hey there, Little Red Riding Hood,' he whispered, fingers gently brushing the hair off her face.

'In that story, she didn't exactly welcome the wolf from the woods.'

'Are you going to swing that axe, then?'

She pressed her lips to his, kissing first the top lip and then the bottom. She kissed his cheeks, his eyelids, his nose and his chin. Slowly, he set her back down on the ground as he looked Sadie up and down.

'You look different,' he murmured, fingers resting on her neck.

'I am different,' she replied. 'I'm a mother.'

'I . . . I wasn't sure if you'd be happy to see me.'

'Of course I'm happy to see you. I understood why you I left I was just—'

'Mad?'

'Sad,' she countered. 'Which was confusing, because I was so happy because of them but also so destroyed because of Sorcha and—'

She couldn't finish her sentence, her voice breaking over her sister's name, and she bit her lip to stop it quivering. Simon pulled her to him like he could feel her pain, Sadie's fingers digging into the flesh of his back.

'I'm sorry, I'm so sorry,' he whispered. 'I came as soon as I heard about Sorcha. I didn't know, Sadie. I would never have left you if—'

'Are you back?'

'What?'

'Are you *back* back? Or is this just a drop-in to say goodbye properly? Because I can take it either way, but I need to know.'

He blinked, his amber eyes staring at her but not flinching away from the abrupt questions. Simon's answer was just as direct.

'I'm back,' he said. 'For good and for as long as you'll have me.'

'Right.' She nodded, stepping away from him as she retrieved her axe and the baby monitor. 'You better get inside then, cos I'm freezing and you're naked.'

His eyes crinkled with a smile that warmed her more than the heat from the fire once they got into the cottage. Sadie was about to go and wake his mother when he stopped her. There was a pile of his clothes folded neatly on the kitchen bench, waiting for him.

'She's gone,' he said. 'Meri, too.'

'What? When?' She didn't want to panic, but they had become a big part of her life over the past month.

'I'd have to guess from the second they smelled me. They have grieving rites to attend to, things they missed for me.'

'Because they knew you'd be back,' Sadie said, processing Keisha's earlier statement while Simon dressed. There was a flare of joy within her heart as she realised that part of her life wouldn't be going away either. Keisha would stay. Meri would stay. Tiaki would stay. And most importantly, so would Simon.

'And they knew they were the only people I would trust to protect you if I wasn't here.'

Sadie smiled, looking at the matching tracksuit set Simon was now dressed in. It was light green and she didn't think any shade had ever looked better against his skin.

'Can I see them?' he asked cautiously, as though not sure what she would say.

'Of course,' Sadie huffed, taking his hand as she led him to the nursery. 'But wake any of them and I'm tossing you out.'

A warm chuckle rumbled from his lips as they crept into the darkened room, the soft lights of a star mobile on the ground casting delicate shapes on to the ceiling in a soothing motion. At the centre of the nursery were her three daughters, their cots having to be pressed as closely together as possible otherwise they would cry. They needed to sleep separately for their own safety, Dr Kikuchi said, but even then their fat little arms had reached out over the edge of each cot to cling to each other.

'My God,' Simon whispered, the awe in his voice reflecting the awe in her heart. 'They've gotten so big so fast.'

His finger gently brushed against the closed fist of one of the babies, which was ten times the size now to what it had been when they were first born and Simon had held them.

'That's Sorcha Máire Burke,' she said. 'Always angry, always fiery, always with the little fist that tries to beat my boob while I feed her.'

'She was the first one out,' Simon murmured, looking down at her like she was already his favourite, even though you weren't supposed to have favourites. 'She was the one I held.'

'How could you possibly know that?' Even Sadie struggled to tell them apart at times visually, it was their personalities that made them possible to differentiate.

'Scent,' he replied, nodding at the baby on the far left. 'She was second, chasing fast after Sorcha.'

'That's Bari Hobart Burke.' Naturally, she was Casper's favourite given the baby was named after her twin brother.

Since so much of Queensland and New South Wales had been destroyed in Australia, supernatural and human refugees had flooded the rest of the country. Many of them headed for higher ground, the trauma of the waves of destruction still too fresh for them to exist easily on lower plains. It was because of that Kala had donated her Blue Mountains property to her coven; there was enough space and sanctuary there that they could rebuild their lives in an already overcrowded area. The survivors of the Petersham family of wombat shifters, including Shazza, had relocated there too and were living alongside the witches like it was the most natural thing in the world and neither species had been forced apart by centuries of insidious Treize behaviour.

Because of that, Kala had relocated to the Dawson farm permanently along with Sadie's sisters. It shouldn't have been surprising to her watching how close the witches and the banshees were, all of them working together to begin construction on separate houses that would dot the land like a supernatural commune. The Dawson pack were more than happy to sell off plots of land to whoever wanted to stay, practically giving them away by only accepting prices that were at least fifty per cent under their value. Yet there was no greed here, just bonds and community that had been forged amongst so much adversity. It was like how Sprinkle had gone from protecting the children and the elderly at the farmhouse during the day of the battle to now basically commanding an army of Sadie's banshee nieces. They moved together in a pack, all of the little girls so close and *so* loud.

Then there was Casper, who had returned to her wife and her life only in part. The loss of her brother affected her deeply, many of the werewolves thinking that she too had become a ghost. She was only ever seen at night, her pale hair and pale skin highlighting her against the dark surrounds as she wandered the property alone, grieving. She would visit most nights, her visits weirdly always coinciding with whenever the babies would stir for an evening or early morning feed. She would watch as Sadie fed one child after the other, taking them from her arms and gently rocking them until they were burped and put back to sleep. They had a good system going, like a conveyor belt of operations between the different supernatural women – some mothers, some not – who lent her their support and their wisdom and, most importantly, their company.

Yet it was always Bari Casper gravitated back towards, Sadie having given Casper her own set of keys so the medium could come and go as she pleased. She knew she had been there when The Three had died, guiding them and her brother and Wehi as they had travelled to where they needed to go. Yet the journey to healing for her would be a longer road than for most of them, Sadie knew, and Kala had told her that she thought the bond she had with Bari was helping immeasurably with that.

'And who's our third Bee Gee?' Simon asked, straightening the blanket that the middle baby had kicked off in their sleep.

'TJ with the powerful thunder thighs,' she whispered, watching as the little croissants for legs were covered. 'Tex James Burke.'

Simon stiffened, turning to Sadie as if he had misheard for a moment. She ran her hand up his arm, reassuring him with her touch that he hadn't.

'TJ,' he repeated. 'Tex James.'

'Her name came from two men: one who was important to me, one who was important to you.'

Simon pulled her to him, crushing Sadie in a hug so all-encompassing that it was minutes before she realised he was crying. She clung to him, trying to offer as much support as she could through her considerable lack of height compared to his. Sadie singing '*More Than a Woman*' to her babies might have been the only thing that soothed them to sleep in that first week – and throughout much of her pregnancy, in fact – but she never had any intention of naming her trio of girls after the Gibb brothers (even though one of them did accidentally share a name now). She had never been able to settle on a name – let alone three – and she had never been able to make up her mind when trying to approach that process. She wanted to get to know them, and over the first week of their life, as she dealt with the losses of her family and friends, she had. One day she'd woken up and the names were just there, all three them, fully and perfectly formed.

'I love you,' Simon whispered, the words pulling her from the recollection. She loved him too, but she had never dared say it when there was so much up in the air. As she leaned back, arching her neck to look at him, she realised how lucky she was to hear those words. Luckiest of all was the fact that she got to *feel* those words again when she thought she never ever would.

'I love you too,' she replied, smoothing away the tears of this big, scary werewolf who felt safe enough with her to be vulnerable. 'Come on.'

She led him from the nursery and to her bedroom, which actually *felt* like her bedroom now rather than just a temporary site she was existing in until she either lived or died. Sadie had made it her space, with Dreckly having helped her source native plants that could grow indoors and recreate the greenery effect she loved so much back in their Sydney terrace. There were all the usual suspects, with Devil's Ivy taking particularly well to the conditions and creeping around her room like the lacy trim on a dress.

'There should be no baby shit in this room,' Dreckly had said, yeeting a packet of dummies out the door and into the hallway. 'You need to have a space that's *just* for you. They've got the nursery and they'll take over the whole house eventually.'

Sadie had to lunge forward to retrieve the breast pump Dreckly was about to toss out. 'Not that! I pump while I'm reading in bed.'

'Ew.'

'You're here for plant advice, not life advice,' she huffed, snatching the device safely away from her.

'Good, because I would be absolutely crap at the latter.'

Sadie sensed a sadness in her and she couldn't help but pry, wanting to be there for her in the same way Dreckly had been there for Texas and her once.

'It's Ben, isn't it?' she asked, noting the surprise in the sprite's expression as she looked up from the bouquet she was arranging in a beautiful old vase. 'I may have spent the past few months in isolation, but I notice stuff. I noticed you two.'

'There is no "you two",' Dreckly said, a gentle smile on her lips that felt bitter-sweet. 'Not any more.'

'You seem . . . oddly okay with that. Him too.'

Sadie had known Ben since she was a child and had only gotten to know Dreckly more recently, so she couldn't help her curiosity when she'd seen them on the farm together. They weren't handsy like Tommi and Heath, sneaky like Aruhe and Joss, or even wifed up like Casper and Kala: instead, they were like two planets orbiting each other, neither one quite ready to give in to the gravitational pull.

'I had to make a choice and so did he,' Dreckly said and sighed. 'His sister needs him. Sushmita's someone who has only known war and he's just starting to realise how difficult it's going to be to reacclimatise someone to peacetime. He doesn't have room in his life for another woman and I can't do the things that I need to with him as an anchor.'

'You mean the paranormal press conference?' Sadie questioned.

The sprite nodded, the flash of her blade punctuating the gesture as she dethorned a stem. 'Mildred was always the one who ran towards every battle, ran towards every cause, regardless of what it cost her. I was always the one running away, and she let me for the most part. Now that she's gone, there's just *so much* mess left and *so much* work that needs to be done to fix it. She gave up her life for mine; who would I be if I didn't step up and become the woman she expected?'

On paper Dreckly was in her forties, but as a sprite her lifespan was wildly different to that of a regular human. She had decades' worth of knowledge and wisdom and experience that her friend Mildred had once put to use to help others. Sadie couldn't help but think she'd left behind a rather beautiful legacy if it had inspired Dreckly to do the same.

'Just because it's not your time right now,' Sadie started, 'that doesn't mean it won't be down the track. For you and Ben, I mean.'

'Maybe.' The sprite had smiled, stepping away as she examined the bouquet.

Those flowers were on the other side of blooming now as Sadie closed the door behind her, Simon sitting on the bed with a look of wonder as he stared at the space she had made distinctly hers. It didn't take long for his attention to return to Sadie, however, as she lifted the sweater dress she'd been wearing over her head in one smooth movement. The miracle of maternity bras was that most men couldn't tell the difference and she knew Simon definitely couldn't as she climbed on to his lap. He looked at her like she hung the moon. As he wrapped his hands around her, Sadie knew it wouldn't have mattered if she was wearing a burlap sack: Simon could only see her and she could only see him.

She let out a giggle of surprise as he hoisted her up, getting a firm grip on her considerable ass and pulling her as tight to him as she could fit. His hands unclasped her bra, fingers moving slow as he slid the straps down her arms while never once breaking eye contact. Sadie had him naked without remembering how, her greed tugging the clothes free until they were both wrapped around each other, hands and fingers and mouths touching as she bound him to her with her body.

'Wait,' Simon said, breathless as he hovered above her for a moment. 'Can you do this? Is it too soon?'

'You can have sex six weeks postpartum.'

He looked like none of those words meant anything to him.

'It's week eight,' Sadie stated, ripping the foil packet between her teeth as she discarded the condom wrapper. That *did* mean something to Simon and he grinned, full pearly whites, and she laughed.

The sound quickly turned into gasps as they wasted no time bridging the only barrier that was left between them. It felt like elation, like levitation, like *elevation* as they both used each other to transcend the pain of their pasts.

Later, when they had gone back for seconds and thirds, Sadie lay in Simon's arms totally spent. Even her bones felt drained, every last morsel of adrenalin having been excised in the process of *showing* him exactly how she felt. He too seemed just as exhausted, yet neither of them could sleep as they stared at each other in the low light flickering from a candle near Sadie's bedside. They were fools in love and she knew at her core this was just the first of many nights together as he brushed the damp hair off her neck.

'Can they see?' he asked her.

'I don't know,' Sadie admitted. 'At least, I have no way to tell yet, but I haven't had a vision since they were born, which is …'

'A long time.'

'The longest I've ever gone without one,' she agreed. 'I think my first memories were visions. I have no way to grasp what they see and how, let alone whether it's a shared perception like The Three or individual.'

'And no wail?'

'No.' She smiled. 'That's just mine. And without babies trying to spin themselves around my spinal cord like mini strippers, I'm in control of that again.'

'That's what you think,' Simon murmured, reaching down between them and making her cry out.

Sadie's life had never been easy, so this one with him as they lived and loved in that cottage together felt like more than she had ever risked dreaming about. He was still part of the Ihi pack and would be for ever, leaving once a month to fly home and run with his family on the North Island, but he was also part of her pack. He belonged with Sadie and the girls; she was so sure of it as she watched the way their chins wobbled with laughter when he blew raspberries against the dome of their bellies. It was in the way they were docile and calm as he strapped one to his front and one to his back, working on his laptop like it was completely normal while he bounced the third in her rocker with his foot. It was in the way they clung to him like they clung to her, his black hair gripped in their fists like they instinctively knew he would protect them no matter what. It was in the way that when one of the babies grizzled during the press conference, he disappeared and returned in a flash, Sorcha nuzzled against his neck as they kept watching.

'Look, those are your aunties up there,' he said, using the soft tone that Sadie now recognised as strictly for the girls.

With the threat of the Treize gone, communications were open to them again and it was like reconnecting with the modern world once she was able to text and Zoom and doom scroll with the touch of a button. Her phone buzzed on the table, vibrating with a message alert that she saw was from Tommi as she lifted it up. Sadie laughed, showing Simon the werewolf's message on her screen.

'I told Aruhe not to wear white,' Simon read out loud. 'It makes her look like a virginal bride.'

He smirked, shrugging. 'She probably is a virgin.'

Sadie looked down her nose at him, not even needing to see the keyboard as she hastily typed a reply to Tommi.

'What are you saying to her?' he asked suspiciously.

'I'm telling Tommi that you're a sweet idiot who thinks Aruhe still has her V plates.'

'What did she say?'

'Well, the first message is just "AHAHAHAHAHAHAHA" in all caps, but the second says she can never unsee how incorrect Simon is on that matter.'

He looked back at the screen, eyes narrowed, and she knew what he was doing as his gaze darted from Joss to Aruhe and back again.

'Here,' Sadie smiled, reaching out for Sorcha, 'let me take her. I'm going to call Tommi. You finish watching this, tell me what I miss.'

With her wireless headphones firmly in her ears, Sadie listened to the dial tone as she started the first of what would be many laps up and down the hall. There was something about the motion that Sorcha loved above all the others. There was no hello, just the bark of a harsh Scottish accent down the line as Tommi answered.

'How did he take the news that his teenage prodigy has thirty-four plus thirty-fived?'

'You know very well I didn't phrase it like that.' Sadie grinned, biting her cheek to avert the burst of laughter she could feel desperate to explode.

'Have a crack, see what he says. Just put me on speaker.'

'I absolutely *will not*,' she chuckled, not even wanting to imagine the reaction Tommi was so keen to stoke. 'How are you? How's Heath?'

When the werewolf smiled, Sadie didn't just hear it, she saw it. The vision of her cosy hallway disappeared completely, being replaced with the face of Tommi Grayson as she stood on the edge of a clifftop overlooking the sea. The terrible blonde mullet she'd once worn was gone, the bangs growing out to full length as they hung shorter around her eyes in the vibrant shade of neon blue she so preferred. Strands fluttered in the gentle breeze, the warm morning sun beaming down on her as she held the phone to her ear. She pulled her gaze away from the islands she could see dotting the horizon, the sea as blue and glistening as her locks. Behind her, she looked back at the remnants of Dunscaith Castle which were slowly being built back up in the Isle of Skye in Scotland, where she was now living. With his blond hair pulled up into a bun on top of his head, Heath wheeled around the structure as he shouted instructions to the young werewolves working on it. The ghost of a fiery-haired woman stood behind him with her arms crossed, nodding with approval as Sadie's view moved from being of Tommi to *through* Tommi, seeing what the werewolf saw every day, their world and the spirit world intermingled.

'He's good,' Tommi said, and Sadie felt the warmth spread through her own chest like she was looking at Simon. She saw the memory flash in the werewolf's mind, unable to help herself as she was pulled from someone else's present into someone else's past. Heath looked like death, that was testament to how close he'd come as he lay there on a bed in the farmhouse. He was clean and bandaged, a stark juxtaposition to Tommi, who was dirty and bloodied as she gripped his hand, head bowed beside him. When the steady rise and fall of his chest skipped a beat, the werewolf's reaction was instant as her head jerked up. Heath's eyelids looked like they were fighting to open as Tommi held her breath, the man's gaze taking a moment to readjust as he looked around the room. His lips moved, like he was trying to speak, and Tommi brought a bottle of water to his mouth as he slowly took a tiny sip. As soon as his eyes locked on her, it was like a laser beam focus and they never left, watching as she pulled his fingers to her lips and kissed them, her mouth wet from the tears that had streamed down her cheeks.

'Why are you crying, baby girl?' he croaked.

'Because of you, ya bastard.'

Her response clearly delighted him as she laid a kiss on his lips, on his neck, on his head, on his shoulders, all over him, like she was trying to love away the dark.

'Why did you take that blow for me, huh?' she asked, voice breaking. 'It was meant to be me in your position right now.'

'Aye, it could never be you,' he replied. 'I could never let it be you.'

'I had to choose, Heath. Your life or this, and I pray you don't hate me for the choice.'

He frowned, as if properly reading her disposition for the first time. 'I have no legs, do I?'

'You have 'em, you just might not be able to feel or use them . . . ever again.'

Heath closed his eyes, processing the information slowly, his expression calm as Tommi anguished beside him.

'It's a lower spinal injury, so Dr Kikuchi thinks you'll be confined to a wheelchair for—'

'What about my knob?'

'W-what?'

'My knob, will it work?'

'Heath, I'm telling you you're gonna be a paraplegic and all you care about is "will my knob work"?'

'It's not *all* I care about, but it's definitely a consideration.'

'Tell him his knob will work!' Dr Kikuchi shouted, passing the door in a flash, her arms loaded up with bandages.

'Yesssss.' Heath grinned, holding up a hand for Tommi. 'High five?'

She slapped his hand down, a look of disbelief on her face. 'Fucking men!'

Tommi went to get up in a burst of frustration when Heath's other hand shot forward, pulling her down by the torn hem of her shirt until she was practically lying by his side.

'Now calm down, ye stereotypical werewolf,' he mused. 'Aye, I care if my knob works and I think you should too.'

'I care if *you* work,' she snapped.

'And I do, I'm alive, sans legs but they had a solid run – literally – a few thousand years or so. I could do with a good sit.'

Tommi laughed, her face breaking from angry to relieved with the gesture as he planted a kiss on her forehead, comforting her as the laughing turned to crying.

'I'm sorry to scare ya,' he whispered. 'But I'm here; I woke up with you by my side, that's all that matters to me now.'

The memory disappeared in a kiss, their embrace in the bed dissipating as Tommi looked at Heath now as he cracked his knuckles through a pair of fingerless gloves that gave him better grip in the wheelchair. He was mortal, Sadie knew it in the same way Tommi had lived through it, the pair having found an Alchemist to reverse the ritual that had once been performed on him when he entered the Praetorian Guard. He gave up his immortality for her in the same way Yu had for Dolly, neither of the former soldiers considering it much of a sacrifice when it meant they got to live out the rest of their days in sync with the person they loved. He looked up from the work he was watching, catching Tommi observing him as he flashed a big smile at her. She threw him the finger and he let out a sharp laugh as they both turned to meet the new arrivals.

Walking across the newly erected bridge to the castle and the training grounds was Ben Kapoor, Sushmita following closely behind him along with several other werewolves who looked barely a day over fifteen. Tommi embraced Ben, knowing better than to hug his sister in that same way as their party formed a small circle.

'Everyone say g'day, this is Tommi Grayson,' Ben ordered as they mumbled their responses. 'She's going to be helping you over the next few months as you learn how to be rogue wolves and live on your own. You're gonna do everything she says or—'

'Or I'll tear ye throats out,' she finished, smiling with a flash of sharpened teeth.

The fear among the young wolves was palpable. They had heard of her. They knew she could do it.

'This over here is Heath, our master at arms,' Tommi continued, jerking her head over her shoulders as the rest of the team assembled. 'That's Dolly and Yu, your combat instructors, and Sanjay here is going to teach you how to manage the beastie within.'

'We're gonna learn control?' a young werewolf asked, a girl.

'Nah,' Tommi shrugged, throwing her a wink, 'control is just another word for suppression and we're not about that here. It's gonna be tough, but when you're ready to leave you'll be able to live alongside your wolf rather than fighting with it all the time. I know some of you have no packs to go back to, and others would rather die than return to the packs they do have, and that's okay too. Whatever you decide, your time here is going to help you survive with that choice.'

'Who are theeeeey?' someone asked, up on their toes and staring down at the water's edge as several selkies emerged. They were guided by Atlanta and Amos, the duo holding out their hands as the younger creatures struggled with the rocky terrain.

'Those are selkies, they'll be training here too, along with some arachnia when they arrive later this eve with our goblin instructor Hogan.'

'Is he gonna teach us *goblin* things?' a werewolf asked.

'What, like lurking under a bridge?' Tommi snorted. 'No, ya wee bampot, Hogan's gonna be teaching you life skills, tech skills, shite that you need out there in the real world just as much as you need to know how to wield a crossbow.'

'Aight, enough with the questions,' Heath shouted. 'Come on, I'll show you to where you'll be sleeping.'

It baffled Tommi, but the kids always loved Heath in a way that was just instant while she felt like she had to work for it. Sushmita followed after them, a bag hitched over her shoulder. Tommi turned to Ben with a question in her eyes.

'She didn't want to make a big deal of it,' he said, 'but she needs this. She needs the help. There's just . . . so much rage there.'

Tommi nodded, her face solemn. 'I know exactly how that feels.'

'I knew you would.'

Ben excused himself, expertly negotiating the terrain as he hopped down the rocks to greet the selkies and embrace Amos in a bone-crushing hug. Sadie saw it all, a flash of the future as it played out on the island, the generations of not just lost werewolves but all kinds of supernatural creatures struggling and in pain as they came there to learn. They came there to form the family bonds they hadn't found through blood, the very mantra of the Rogues living on even though Zillia, Gus and Clay no longer did.

'Sadie?'

She blinked, Simon's voice grounding her in a time and a place when she had been spinning through both. She was staring down at Sorcha, the baby looking up at her with wide, intelligent eyes. Her little, fat fingers were gripped into fists as they curled around Sadie's pinkie.

'Baby, what is it?' Simon asked, moving towards her as she stood frozen at the other end of the hallway.

'I just saw the future,' she said, looking up at him with wonder. 'All of our futures.'

His mouth fell open and he glanced between her and the baby she was cradling, making the same connection she had.

'How ... how was it?' he whispered. Worry and fear were etched into his expression in a way that she understood so well after everything they'd been through.

Sadie's eyes were full of tears as she tried to form the words.

'It was *wonderful*.'

Glossary

Alchemist Those who have the ability to infuse and convert materials with magical properties through a combination of symbols, science and ceremony. Alchemists were instrumental in the founding of the Treize, particularly the Askari themselves. Obsessed with immortality, it's rumoured their formula is responsible for the prolonged lives of Praetorian Guard soldiers and Custodians.

Arachnia Traditionally considered a nightmarish vision from Japanese folklore, arachnia emerged from the shadows relatively late compared to other supernatural species and were discovered to have existed worldwide. Their natural state is comparable to a large, spider-like creature, with traits similar to the arthropod.

Askari Foot soldiers and collectors of ground truth. The first point of call in the supernatural community, they simultaneously liaise and gather information. Mortal, yet members often work their way up into the Custodian ranks. Identified by a wrist tattoo, which is the alchemist symbol for wood to signify a strong foundation.

The Aunties A pack within the Ihi pack, this fearsome all-women group are responsible for voting on and enforcing pack law.

Banshee Thought to be extinct by the wider supernatural community before remerging in Australia, a banshee is a supernatural being cursed with the ability to sense death or impending doom in its various forms. Exclusively female.

Bierpinsel A large, colourful tower in the centre of Berlin: the Bierpinsel is the base of Treize operations for Germany and much of Europe.

Blood pack The family unit a werewolf is born into by direct descent, usually operating on a specific piece of geographical territory.

Coming of age A ritual all werewolves must complete before they're considered mature members of their blood pack. A wolf can only choose to go 'rogue' once they have survived the coming of age.

Coven A grouping of witches within a particular area, covens can include members of the same biological family as well as women of no biological relation. No two members of a coven have the same magical ability, with similar powers spread out over other covens as an evolutionary defence mechanism. Members of a coven can draw on each other's powers, giving them strength and safety in their sisterhood.

The Covenant The series of rules established for banshees to follow once they were deported en masse from Ireland, Scotland and Wales in the seventeen hundreds. If The Covenant is broken, the penalty can range from imprisonment in Vankila to death.

Custodians The counsellors or emotional guardians of beings without other help, assistance or species grouping. Immortality is a choice made by individual Custodians, with those choosing it identified by a necklace with an Egyptian ankh.

Demon One of the oldest forms of supernatural beings, pureblood demons are known for being reclusive and rarely interact with those outside of the paranormal world. Certain species of demon have a fondness for the flesh, leading to half-blood demon hybrids usually identifiable via physical traits like horns or tusks (often filed down so it's easier to blend in to society).

Elemental Originally thought to be those who could control the elements – earth, air, fire and water – elementals are paranormal beings descended directly from nature. Able to physically become the elements if they so desire, they share a strong allegiance with shifters, werewolves and selkies.

Ghost Translucent and bluish grey in colour, ghosts are the physical manifestation of one's soul after death. Their presence in the realm of the living can be for several reasons, ranging from an unjust demise to a connection with a person or place. The strength of any particular ghost varies case-to-case.

Ghoul Usually found in underground sewer systems and living in nest formations, ghouls are considered a lower class of paranormal creature due to their lack of intelligence or individual personality traits. With razor-sharp claws and serrated teeth, they can be deadly in numbers.

Goblin Highly intelligent and supernaturally agile, goblins are known for their speed and lethal nature if provoked. Although not immortal, they have exceedingly long lives and prefer living in urban environments such as cities or large towns. They are one of several paranormal species impacted by the lunar cycle.

Medium A being that can communicate with and control the dead, including spirits and ghosts. Extremely rare, the full range of their abilities is unknown and largely undocumented.

Outskirt Packs The collective description for werewolf packs from the Asia-Pacific region who fought against the Treize – unsuccessfully – for the right to self-govern and expose their true nature to the human world. Formed in 1993 and disbanded upon defeat in 1998, key leaders included Jonah Ihi, Sushmita Kapoor and John Tianne. This conflict was known as the Outskirt Wars.

Paranormal Practitioner The healers and medical experts of the unnatural world. Usually gifted individuals themselves, they wield methods outside of conventional medicine.

Praetorian Guard A squadron of elite warriors that quell violence and evil within the supernatural community. They're gifted with immortality for their service. Founded by a member of the original Roman Praetorian Guard.

Rogue A werewolf who chooses to live and operate outside of their blood pack.

The Rogues Comprised of rogue werewolves who have decided to leave their blood packs, this group functions from within the nightclub Phases in Berlin and includes global members who have come of age.

Selkie The source of mermaid and merman folklore, selkies are aquatic humanoids that inhabit any large body of water. Despite some human features, tribes of selkie from certain parts of the world have been known to take the form of marine animals like seals, dolphins and sharks.

Shifter Found globally, shifters have the ability to transform into one specific creature depending on their lineage. Often confused with werewolves due to their capacity to take animal shape, shifters can transform outside of the full moon both fully and in-part.

Spirit Incorrectly compared to ghosts, spirits are their more powerful counterparts. A term used to describe the dead who can travel between pre-existing plains and occasionally take some physical form, they usually preoccupy themselves with the business of their direct ancestors.

Sprite Said to be the result of a union between selkies and earth elementals, sprites are highly secretive and rarely identify themselves to other supernatural creatures. They struggle being around members of their own kind and prefer to live close to nature.

The Three A trio of semi-psychic women who guide the Treize with regards to past, present and future events. The subject of the phrase 'hear no evil, see no evil, speak no evil'. Origin and age unknown.

Treize The governing body of the supernatural world, comprising of thirteen members of different ages, races, nationalities, abilities, species and genders. Given their name by four French founders, they oversee the Praetorian Guard, Custodians, Askari and Paranormal Practitioners.

Vampire Rodent-like creature who lives off the blood of animals or people (whatever they can get). Endangered in the supernatural community due to widespread disease.

Vankila The Treize's supernatural prison, located in St Andrews, Scotland, and built hundreds of metres below a Cold War bunker.

Werewolf Considered one of the most volatile and ferocious paranormal species, werewolves are humans that shift into enormous wolf-hybrids during the nights of the full moon. Outside of the lunar cycle they retain heightened abilities, such as strength and healing, with the most powerful of their kind able to transform at will and retain human consciousness. Often found living in blood packs, they are resistant towards most forms of paranormal government.

Witch A woman naturally gifted with paranormal abilities that can be heightened with study and practice. Although the witch gene is passed down through the female line, skills vary from woman to woman regardless of blood. Witches believe their power is loaned to them temporarily by a higher being who redistributes it to another witch after their death. Highly suspicious and distrustful of the Treize due to centuries of persecution, they are closed off from the rest of the supernatural community.

Acknowledgements

Originally this was supposed to read 'I'd like to acknowledge myself, that's it' but as good as that joke is, it reads way too wanky and since this is the last book in the Supernatural Sisters series, it would be my final chance to thank anybody properly. So. Pivot.

First up, my editor Anna Boatman – the only person, besides myself, who has been there from the beginning, right until the end. The first person who fought for Tommi Grayson in the battle arena known as acquisitions and, if not for her, the rest of the world wouldn't have gotten to meet Casper and Dreckly and Sadie and Kaia and Amos and Aruhe and Joss and Shazza and the Ihi Pack and the whole universe.

Thank you to the entire Little, Brown team, namely the ever-patient Sarah Murphy, Christopher Sturtivant for putting up with my various bullshit, Nazia Khatun, and anyone else I'm most likely (definitely) leaving off, not intentionally but because I delayed writing these acknowledgements so long knowing I'd inevitably do this. Cheers to the Hachette Australia homies, namely Bella Lloyd and Meg Kennedy, and my agent Ed Wilson who has survived COVID scares, pandemic shutdowns and newborn babies like a legend.

There have been so many cover artists over this series, so thank you to everyone who reinterpreted this story beautifully and visually with their own signature. Huge thank you to every scientist, historian, Elder and expert that answered my questions over the years and helped make the IRL parts of this world so authentic and lived-in and empowered with your knowledge and, in many cases, mātauranga specifically.

Mai rānō, all the real ones from way back. You know who you are, I've thanked you in the past eight books, but chiefly Blake and Sam Howard, Ramona Sen Gupta, Jean-Anne Kidd, Rae Johnston, Anna Gough, Amunda Wilkinson, The Jabours, Keegan Buzza, James Stein, Nicola Scott, Andrew Constant, Mandy Spettigue, Caris Bizzaca, The Sultanas, Leah Fineran, Laura Murphy-Oates, Jodi McAlister, Keri Arthur, Amy Remeikis, Ron Cobb and Robin Love, Angela Slatter, Amanda Bridgeman, Kodie Bedford, Sam Chen, Jessie Hohaia, Sose Fuamoli, Michelle Grace Hunder, Michel 'The Bloody Samoan' Mulipola, Hanelle Harris, Corey Te Wharau and all of Film Club.

Finally, as always, the readers and booksellers get the final place of thanks because without them I wouldn't have been able to take this dream I had as a teen and turn it into something that has taken me around the world over the past eight years. No biracial werewolves, bionic mediums, Indigenous witches, Auslan banshees, time-travelling sprites or 50-something bodybuilding wombat shifters get to exist if no one gives a shit. So thank you, endlessly, for giving a shit then and for giving a shit now.

The Supernatural Sisters series might be done on the page, but it lives on as long as youse all keep giving your shits.

M xx

Everyone is talking about Maria Lewis . . .

<u>Praise for *The Rose Daughter*</u>

'Boasting a compelling lead, an exciting plot, and an outrageously sexy werewolf, *The Rose Daughter* is **an absolute joy to read**. Come for the story, stay for the *Josie & The Pussycats* jokes'

The AU Review (5 stars)

'An imaginative world that is both **compelling and addictive**'
Newtown Review of Books

'One of those books where I'm torn between wanting to stay up reading for 10 hours straight but also wanting to **savour each page**'

Bookish Bron

<u>*Praise for Who's Afraid Too?*</u> (Nominee – Best Horror Novel, Aurealis Awards)

'**Feminist werewolf antics [and] good old fashioned sex**. More books please!'

Natalia Tena (*Harry Potter, Game Of Thrones*)

'**Being curled up in a werewolf fantasy is a respite and a haven!**'
Teri Hatcher (*Lois & Clark, Desperate Housewives*)

'Maria Lewis is definitely one to watch'

NY Times best-selling author Darynda Jones

'A fresh, funny, sexy & downright sassy take on the werewolf genre'

Geek Bomb

Praise for The Witch Who Courted Death (Winner – Best Fantasy Novel, Aurealis Awards)

'[Takes] a fresh look at the things that make us scream'

The West Australian

'An unashamedly feminist story about a woman out for revenge'

Readings

Praise for The Wailing Woman (Nominee – Best Fantasy Novel, Aurealis Awards)

'World-building at its finest'

The Nerd Daily

'An absolute master of the genre'

Bookish Bron

'An excellent urban fantasy novel . . . magic, intrigue and romance'

Canberra Weekly